Praise for Minerva Spencer's Outcasts series:

"Minerva Spencer's writing is sophisticated and wickedly witty. Dangerous is a delight from start to finish with swashbuckling action, scorching love scenes, and a coolly arrogant hero to die for. Spencer is my new auto-buy!"
-NYT Bestselling Author Elizabeth Hoyt

"[**SCANDALOUS** is] A standout...Spencer's brilliant and original tale of the high seas bursts with wonderfully real protagonists, plenty of action, and passionate romance."
★Publishers Weekly STARRED REVIEW

"Fans of Amanda Quick's early historicals will find much to savor."
★Booklist STARRED REVIEW

"Sexy, witty, and fiercely entertaining."
★Kirkus STARRED REVIEW

"A remarkably resourceful heroine who can more than hold her own against any character invented by best-selling Bertrice Small, a suavely sophisticated hero with sex appeal to spare, and a cascade of lushly detailed love scenes give Spencer's dazzling debut its deliciously fun retro flavor."
★Booklist STARRED REVIEW

"Readers will love this lusty and unusual marriage of convenience story."
-NYT Bestselling Author MADELINE HUNTER

"Smart, witty, graceful, sensual, elegant and gritty all at once. It has all of the meticulous attention to detail I love in Georgette Heyer, BUT WITH SEX!"
RITA-Award Winning Author JEFFE KENNEDY

More books by S.M. LaViolette & Minerva Spencer:

THE ACADEMY OF LOVE SERIES

The Music of Love
A Figure of Love
A Portrait of Love*

THE OUTCASTS SERIES

Dangerous
Barbarous
Scandalous
Notorious*

THE MASQUERADERS
The Footman
The Postilion*
The Bastard*

THE SEDUCERS
Melissa and The Vicar
Joss and The Countess*
Hugo and The Maiden*

VICTORIAN DECADENCE
His Harlot
His Valet
His Countess*

ANTHOLOGIES:

BACHELORS OF BOND STREET
THE ARRANGEMENT
*upcoming books

MELISSA
And The
VICAR

The Seducers Book 1

S.M. LAVIOLETTE

Crooked
Sixpence
CS
P
Press

CROOKED SIXPENCE BOOKS are published by

CROOKED SIXPENCE PRESS
2 State Road 230
El Prado, NM 87529

Copyright © 2020 Shantal M. LaViolette

All rights reserved. No part of this publication may be reproduced, distributed, or transmitted in any form or by any means, including photocopying, recording, or other electronic or mechanical methods, without the prior written permission of the publisher, except in the case of brief quotations embodied in critical reviews and certain other noncommercial uses permitted by copyright law. For permission requests, write to the publisher, addressed "Attention: Permissions Coordinator," at the address above.

To the extent that the image or images on the cover of this book depict a person or persons, such person or persons are merely models, and are not intended to portray any character or characters featured in the book.

If you purchased this book without a cover you should be aware that this book is stolen property. It was reported as "unsold and destroyed" to the Publisher and neither the Author nor the Publisher has received any payment for this "stripped book."

First printing May 2020

10 9 8 7 6 5 4 3 2 1

Any references to historical events, real people, or real places are used fictitiously. Names, characters, and places are products of the author's imagination.

Photo stock by Period Images
Printed in the United States of America.

Chapter One

New Bickford, England

Melissa Griffin stared into red eyes that burned with malevolence.

Her breath froze in her chest but her heart made up for her lungs' mutiny by thundering in her ears. She took a minute step back, but her tormentor strode inexorably closer. She shuffled to the side, but he followed her sideways, too.

"What do you want from me?" She forced the words through gritted teeth.

The foul, evil beast said nothing, stalking ever closer.

There were only two choices: she could run or she could fight—and there was no chance she would vanquish such an implacable foe.

Mel silently counted to three, grabbed two fistfuls of her skirts, and broke into a run while screaming, "*Heeeeelp!*"

She flew past a tiny daub and wattle cottage that looked like it should have housed angels instead of this nasty brute. Something struck the back of one leg and Mel risked a glimpse at her pursuer: he was right behind her, dogged and menacing and—

"Ooof!" Melissa slammed into a wall that was hard and warm and . . . human.

The human wall grunted. "Here, then, don't be afraid," a deep voice soothed.

Mel was blind to everything except the red eyes and razor-sharp claws behind her and plowed through the thicket of limbs, climbing the stranger's body as if he were a tree.

Strong arms slid around her, lifted her, and spun her around before depositing her on the ground, his body a shield—a substantial one, at that—between Melissa and that *fiend*.

"Hector!" Her protector's deep voice was overlaid with a tone of command that demanded to be obeyed.

When only silence met his order, Mel stood on her toes and peeked over broad, black-clad shoulders, pale blond hair tickling her nose.

Her jaw dropped at what she saw: the demon had screeched to a halt and was ambling away in the opposite direction, behaving as if butter wouldn't melt in his mouth, er, beak.

"Why that—that—"

"Rooster?" the same deep voice said, this time laced with amusement rather than command.

Mel realized she'd pasted the front of her body to the back of his and took a hasty step back. He turned and she blinked; it might have been the conceit of a city dweller, but she'd not expected to see a man as lovely as her savior in the middle of a country lane. In fact, Melissa could not recall seeing a man as beautiful—yes, beautiful—as this one *ever*. And he was wearing a clerical collar.

"I've been rescued from that—that *hellion* by a vicar?"

Rather than be insulted by her disbelieving tone he smiled, a warm, charming, gorgeous smile that should not have belonged to a man of the cloth. Not that she knew anything whatsoever about vicars and what type of smiles they should or did have. Men of the cloth tended to be thin on the ground in her line of business. For all she knew, *all* clergymen were this attractive. Perhaps it was a prerequisite of the job? Was that how they filled their pews on Sunday?

"I'm afraid I don't have the honor of being a vicar—yet. So things are even worse, you see: you've actually been rescued by a mere curate." He executed a graceful bow. "Mister Stanwyck at your service, Miss. . ."

Melissa pulled her gaze away from his mouth, which definitely was wasted on a vicar, and said, "Er, Griffin."

"A pleasure, Miss Griffin."

His eyes were the clear, guileless blue of the sky and they met her own rather than roaming her body. Mel's inner critic—as vociferous and relentless as a Greek choir—pointed out that not every man in Great Britain wished to lay themselves out at her feet. Even if it *had* seemed that way since she'd been fourteen.

"I know everyone in New Bickford so you must be a visitor, Miss Griffin."

"Yes. I—I've come to the country to convalesce."

Melissa and The Vicar

His brow furrowed and his expression shifted to one of genuine sympathy. "I am sorry to hear you've been ill." He wasn't just mouthing a platitude; he actually *sounded* sorry.

"I am on the mend now, just—"

"Mister Stanwyck! Yoohoo!" The voice floated toward them from the direction of the quaint little cottage which the vile Hector apparently called home. Right now said villain was placidly scratching among his hen harem, pausing a moment here and there to execute what must have been some type of hen-attracting side-step shuffle, his chest puffed out.

Melissa glared at him; how *dare* he look so harmless?

The curate greeted the approaching woman. "Hello, Miss Philpot. And how are you this afternoon?"

The woman in question was a tall, gangly female easily twice the curate's age who was sporting a coquettish smile and the eyelash batting airs of a schoolroom miss.

"Oh, Mr. Stanwyck, Gloria will be so relieved you are here." Her bulbous green orbs swiveled toward Melissa and her steel gray eyebrows dropped like twin guillotines. "And you've brought. . .your sister?" The last word was spoken in such a hopeful tone that Melissa had to bite her lip to keep from laughing.

The curate pressed his too-beautiful lips together in a mild smile that was belied by the twinkle in his eyes. "I'm afraid my parents did not see fit to bless me with any sisters, ma'am, only brothers."

Miss Philpot was nothing if not adaptable. She turned from Mel, her expression softening as she gazed at the curate. "Well that is certainly the lord's work if they are all as handsome and sweet-natured as *you*, Mr. Stanwyck."

The curate accepted the compliment with a smile and gestured to Melissa. "This is Miss Griffin. I'm afraid she just had a—well, I don't suppose you would call it a run-*in* so much as a run-*away*, with Hector."

Mel narrowed her eyes at his witticism and was rewarded by one of his stunning smiles.

Miss Philpot wagged an admonishing finger at the vicious animal. "Oh, Hector! Have you been over-vigilant?" She spoke in a tolerant, cooing tone that sent Hector into another of his sideways step-slides. Miss Philpot tittered appreciatively at the maneuver. It seemed the bird's debatable charms worked on more than just his hens; maybe Hector was smarter than he looked.

Miss Philpot turned to Mel. "I *do* apologize for Hector's enthusiasm, Miss, er, Griffin." The affection in her eyes—a residual product of Hector's charm—slid away to reveal a zealous gleam that would have done a Spanish Inquisitor proud. "Are you just visiting our village on your way to . . . somewhere else?"

Miss Philpot wasn't the only one waiting for her response with interest. The cerulean blue eyes of the curate were also turned her way.

Something about his clear gaze made Mel shy and fidgety, a feeling she'd not had since selling oranges on street corners when she was a girl. She brushed off the skirt of her walking costume, as though Hector might have been pelting her with rotted fruits and vegetables rather than just his—she paused to eye the rooster, and was forced to admit, *very* scrawny—body.

"I am staying in a house down the way." She gestured with the hand that wasn't clutching her reticule and then realized she'd motioned in the direction of the ocean. Both members of her small audience wore slight frowns of confusion. Melissa bestowed her most winning smile on Miss Philpot, curious to see if it had any effect on the woman. It did not.

"I'm sorry, I'm afraid I'm a bit turned around." She pointed toward the path she'd just sprinted down a few moments earlier. "I am staying at Halliburton Manor."

Miss Philpot's eyes widened. "Halliburton Manor?"

"Yes, that is correct." Why was the woman looking at her that way?

"Ah . . . I see. How unusual that we heard nothing about it."

Mel wondered if she was supposed to place an announcement in the local newspaper or contact the town crier. "I expect that is because I dealt with an agent in London and brought all my own servants."

"Ah. And you are staying there, er, alone?"

Melissa suppressed a twinge of annoyance at the prying questions; this was the sort of curiosity she should have expected when coming to such a small village. "I—"

"Mister Stanwyck!" a voice trilled from the direction of the cottage. "How delightful to see you. But Agnes, why are you keeping the reverend standing out—oh," the newcomer said when she noticed Melissa. "I'm so sorry. I didn't see you there."

Melissa and The Vicar

"Gloria, this is the new tenant in Halliburton Manor—Miss Griffin. Miss Griffin, my sister, Miss Gloria Philpot."

Mel would have known without being told this was Miss Philpot's sister since the two women were mirror images of each other.

"Halliburton Manor?" Miss Gloria aimed a curious expression Melissa's way. Just what was it about her choice of residence that was so interesting?

Miss Gloria opened her mouth, no doubt to take over the inquisition, but the curate took charge of the conversation. "You must be walking to town, Miss Griffin? Perhaps I might show you the way?"

Mel thought he looked . . . hopeful.

The Misses Philpot, on the other hand, looked forlorn.

"But, Mr. Stanwyck, didn't you just come *from* town? Won't you come in for some tea?" The elder Miss Philpot stared accusingly at Melissa while she spoke, as if Mel were some sort of siren leading the curate toward jagged rocks.

"And I thought you were going to look at our wisteria trellis, the bit that needs mending," Miss Gloria added when the curate didn't jump on the offer of tea.

Mel couldn't help herself. "Yes, Mister Stanwyck. I should *hate* to deprive you of tea. And the trellis."

A muscle at the corner of his shapely mouth twitched. "I'll just walk Miss Griffin into the village—and show her the church along the way—and be back in half a jiffy. Not to worry, I shall see to the trellis before the day is out." His hand was at her elbow and he'd managed to turn them both and start down the path without Mel even realizing it.

"Goodbye, ladies. It was a pleasure to meet you," she tossed over her shoulder at the frowning women. She turned to the reverend, who was walking briskly, as if to put some distance between himself and the two disappointed members of his flock. "A *half* a jiffy, Mr. Stanwyck? I don't believe I've heard that particular expression before."

He chuckled, his hand falling away from her arm. "Why do I feel that you enjoy a bit of mischief-making, Miss Griffin?"

"I certainly don't *run away* from mischief—not like I run from nasty little feathered, beaked goblins."

He made a *tsking* sound. "I can see you're going to hold that slip of the tongue against me, aren't you?"

"Perhaps."

He cut her a look of mock severity. "To err is human but to forgive is divine, Miss Griffin."

"I'm afraid I'm far more familiar with erring, Mr. Stanwyck." He had no idea just how true that was.

"Hmm, I *see*. Well, I must warn you that Hector is something of a favorite in these parts. It would cast a shadow over your reputation to be heard bandying about such opprobrium regarding his character or, er, stature."

Mel laughed. "Well, I wouldn't want to have a shadowy reputation."

"Indeed." He grinned down at her, looking like the least probable example of a clergyman in all of Britain. "Now, I'm afraid we departed before Miss Philpot could winkle out all your pertinent details."

"Winkle away, Reverend."

"When did you arrive at Halliburton Manor, Miss Griffin?"

"Just yesterday."

"Ah, that explains why neither of the Misses Philpot knew of your arrival. They are early to bed—with the chickens, as it were."

Mel cast him a sideways look and then wished she hadn't. With his striking white-blond hair, huge blue eyes—fringed with dark, rather than blond, lashes of course—and classical features, he really was a gorgeous specimen of manhood and that *was* an area which she could claim expertise. Although he resembled an angel, he was as solidly muscled as a bull beneath his loose-fitting suit—she knew that from having his arms tight around her.

The fact that he was dressed in the sober attire of a clergyman somehow made his fair good looks even more appealing. Or perhaps that was just the novelty of him?

While Melissa was more knowledgeable about men than she cared to be, she'd rarely associated with the wholesome type and she'd *never* spoken to a member of the clergy—at least not that she was aware of. Something about walking beside him made her feel. . . anxious. Most likely it was just that he did not fit neatly into any of her categories of men. Or perhaps it was because she thought God might strike her down at any moment for having the audacity to associate with one of his Chosen Ones.

"Have a care, Miss Griffin." A strong, steadying hand reappeared at her elbow and he steered her around a prominent tree root in the path.

Melissa and The Vicar

"Thank you." She'd do better to pay more attention to where she was going and less to inventorying the man beside her.

"Do you have an appointment in town or can you take a moment to come and see our fine church windows?" he asked after they'd walked a moment in silence.

She had nothing *but* time. But did she really want to go inside a church? After all, it hadn't been her intention to actually attend services or even interact with any of the villagers. That had been the point of leasing a house *outside* of town.

"Our windows are considered some of the finest in this part of England," he added, the humor in his voice making her risk another glance. Lord! His eyes were *sparkling* at her. Were curates supposed to sparkle? Surely not.

"Well, I can't say no to that, can I?" Mel asked, her tone tarter than she'd intended. "But I cannot stay long because I'm to meet up with my aunt."

"I'll show you only the high points and that way deliver you to your aunt in good time."

"Oh, you needn't deliver me to her, I'll be—"

"I can introduce you to the vicar, Mr. Heeley, if he is about."

"No, really, you needn't go out of your way." Lord, the last thing she needed was to meet more clergy. It would be a miracle if she didn't turn to a pillar of salt, or smoke, or stone, or suffer some sort of divine punishment, not that she'd ever actually *read* any of the Bible or had any idea of what type of punishment was meted out between its covers.

"It would be my pleasure," he said, interrupting her muddled thoughts, but not before she realized that she *wanted* to see his windows and be delivered to the village by him. When was the last time a man had cared enough about her safety to deliver her anywhere? Well, a man other than her dear friend Joss, of course. Perhaps it might be nice to receive such care? That realization only served to annoy her; she had most certainly *not* come to the country to engage in casual flirtation—especially not with a bloody vicar.

"Is giving every visitor to New Bickford a personal tour part of your strenuous curate's duties?"

"Oh yes. I'm responsible for any number of things: taking tea with parishioners, mending trellises, showing off church windows, rescuing damsels in distress from feathered predators—Ah, here we are, to the left if you would, Miss Griffin." He gestured toward an ornate gate set in an old stone wall. "This is the back way into the churchyard now, but it used to be the original lychgate." He lifted the heavy horseshoe-shaped latch and pushed open the gate. "It is a rare example of the Gothic style." He waited until she'd gone through and closed it behind her. "Back in those days they called this a *resurrection gate*."

Melissa noticed they'd stepped into a graveyard filled with worn, tilted headstones. "Why is this gate no longer used?" She frowned, "Actually, just what is a lychgate *for*?"

He gestured to the heavy beams topping the gate. "It was a place to shelter the coffin before burial, hence the gate's unusual substance. The path we just came down is what people used to call a *corpse road*."

Mel shivered.

"Are you chilled, Miss Griffin?" He wore a look of concern but she saw the humor lurking in his eyes.

"No, that was merely a case of the shivers, which is exactly what you expected after telling me such a gruesome piece of information." She raised an eyebrow at him. "Confess it, Mister Stanwyck—you *wanted* to give me the shivers."

He laughed, his even white teeth adding to his list of perfections. "You'll have to forgive me; I have so few amusements."

Somehow Mel doubted that.

"It is at this point in my tour where I point out our magnificent spire." He leaned low and close, as if to view something from her height and perspective, and then held out his arm and pointed. "Can you see just the tip of it above that big chestnut tree?"

Melissa was conscious of the heat of his body and his clean, masculine scent. She ignored her body's unwanted twinge of interest and followed the direction of his pointing finger, to where a foot of gray stone was visible above the tree canopy.

"The church and the gate were built together?" she asked, aware of the pulse beating at the base of her throat and glad when he stood and put some distance between their bodies.

"You have an excellent eye for architecture, Miss Griffin."

"Now you are guilty of flattery, Mr. Stanwyck."

He gave the same warm chuckle as before and Melissa decided eliciting such a velvety laugh could prove an enjoyable pastime. Before she could give that alarming thought the scrutiny it deserved, another man dressed in the clothing of a clergyman came toward them.

"Ah, Mr. Stanwyck. Good morning."

Melissa and The Vicar

"I was hoping our paths would cross, Vicar. Mr. Heeley, may I introduce Miss Griffin? She is new to our area and has just taken up residence at Halliburton Manor."

The vicar, a bone-thin man who looked to be in his late sixties or early seventies, stiffened at something his curate said, his reaction not dissimilar to the Philpots'. But he recovered quickly and turned his deep-set gray eyes on her. His mouth curved into a warm smile. "Welcome to New Bickford, Miss Griffin. I am very glad to hear that Halliburton Manor has a tenant again."

"Thank you, Mr. Heeley."

"I encountered Miss Griffin not far from the Philpot cottage. She was, er, finding it difficult to pass."

The vicar chuckled. "Ah, Hector, was it?" He nodded at his own question, not appearing to need an answer. "He is a fierce protector who is cast in the mold of the ancients. A most excellent rooster."

The curate gave her a look that said, *See, I told you so.*

Mel's lips parted.

"Indeed, you speak the truth, Vicar," Mister Stanwyck interjected when Melissa couldn't quite find the words she was looking for to express her thoughts on Hector. He cut her a sideways glance and rocked back on his heels. "Hector is one of the Titans."

"And how long will you stay with us, Miss Griffin?" the vicar asked, pulling her away from the narrow-eyed look she was giving the teasing curate.

It was time to share the story she'd concocted. "Until the end of the summer." She cleared her throat. "I was ill last winter and have come to the country with my aunt to partake of the country air."

"Ah, I see. You are from the city?"

"Yes, we are both from London."

"Well," the vicar said, his tone brisk as he rubbed his hands together, as if he'd just completed a task and was brushing away the remnants. "I know I'm biased, but I believe there is no town in Great Britain better than ours for peace and healing. We are a close community but also one which respects the privacy of our members."

Melissa hoped he was correct. Because anyone who pried too deeply into her story would find something they wouldn't care to discover.

"Well, I shall leave you and Mr. Stanwyck to continue your tour. It was a pleasure, Miss Griffin, and I shall see you on Sunday."

Melissa made some non-committal sound, waiting until the vicar was out of earshot before turning to the curate.

"I can't help but think people are surprised to hear I'm staying at Halliburton Manor?"

His cheekbones—high, sharp, and beautiful—looked even more appealing with a faint red stain. "I'm afraid the last inhabitant, er, well, she met a rather tragic end."

Mel dipped her chin when he stopped. "Yes?"

"She was a widow. Her husband was—" he grimaced. "Well, he was killed in a military engagement in India. Mrs. Symes took her own life."

It was a sad story, of course, but she still didn't see—

"Mrs. Symes had not seen her husband for eleven months." He hesitated and said, "She was with child when she died."

Ahh, now she understood the odd looks. And the reason for them made her fume.

"I see—a tragedy *and* a scandal." She cut him an arch look that was not playful. "Or do the good and proper villagers even see it as a tragedy?"

He blinked in surprise. "Death is always a tragedy, Miss Griffin." It was an answer, but not one to the question she had asked. He leaned toward her, his blue eyes shadowed with concern. "You look flushed. I believe I've tired you out dragging you about."

She swallowed her irritation at the story he'd told. She'd known something was going on when the two older women, the Philpots, had assumed that faint, virtuous air. Melissa had been the recipient of that look more times than she could count.

Take hold of yourself, Mel!

Yes, she'd better. After all, she'd known a small community often meant small mindedness, but she'd come here, anyway.

You came here to rest and make some important decisions, not to battle rural prejudice.

She forced herself to smile. "Thank you for your concern, but I'm fine. I am, however going to be late so perhaps I'd better be on my way. Maybe you can show me the church some other day." Though not if she had any say about it.

No, the story he'd just told her made it painfully clear she didn't need to make friends here—in fact, that was a terrible idea. And making friends with a man of the cloth—especially this handsome, kind, and curious curate? Well, that was the worst thing she could do. For both of them.

Chapter Two

Magnus's clerical collar felt oddly stiff and scratched his neck as he watched Miss Griffin walk away down New Bickford's narrow main street—its only street, really—with her aunt, Mrs. Daisy Trent.

Mrs. Trent had been waiting for her niece at New Bickford's tiny inn, the Sleeping Ferret, enjoying a pot of tea in their private parlor.

And what an aunt Mrs. Trent was. Certainly nothing like any of Magnus's numerous aunts, none of whom were tall, buxom, and bold eyed. He also suspected Mrs. Trent was wearing cosmetics, although he wasn't familiar enough with such things to be certain.

The two women looked nothing alike. Miss Griffin was a delicate, pale, almost ethereally beautiful auburn-haired goddess who appeared too fragile for this world. Her aunt, on the other hand, epitomized earthiness. Not just her lush body, but her full smiling lips and the knowing glint in her eyes. Magnus had felt as if she were inspecting his person and stripping away his clothing in the process. It was a strange feeling and he'd no doubt imagined it.

After the women had taken their leave from Magnus they'd disappeared into Cooper's Mercantile together. It hadn't been his plan linger outside the shop and spy on the two newest members of New Bickford through the diamond-paned windows, but neither was he in a hurry to get away.

Magnus was re-living his brief conversation with the delectable Miss Griffin when a voice behind him pulled him out of his pleasant musing.

"Mr. Stanwyck—a word, please."

He turned to find Mrs. Pilkington and her three daughters approaching him and bit back a groan.

"Ah, good afternoon, ma'am."

If you asked anyone who knew Magnus even a little bit whether he was arrogant, proud, or conceited, they would have thrown back their head and laughed. It was true: he wasn't proud about his physical appearance, which he viewed as a product of two attractive parents, rather than any efforts on his part.

Melissa and The Vicar

He'd never aspired to be a pink of the *ton* and his clothing—even before he'd entered the clergy—had always been functional and comfortable rather than stylish. His only real contribution to his outward appearance was to keep his body healthy and fit, which happily was an unexpected byproduct of being an active country curate.

Just because Magnus wasn't conceited about his looks didn't mean he was insensible to their effect on the feminine sex. It hadn't taken him long to realize that excessive interest in his person was an inconvenience for a curate who was not in a position to marry.

It wasn't his ability to resist all the lures that were tossed his way that worried him. Rather, it was the sheer exhaustion he experienced from having to fight so many silent, relentless skirmishes.

Like Mrs. Pilkington and her three daughters, for example.

"Mister Stanwyck," Mrs. Pilkington said in her strident voice while her daughters spread out around him. The eldest Miss Pilkington moved into position on his left flank, her middle sister on his right, and the youngest drifted somewhere behind him—a maneuver they must have learned from studying a tactical map of Hannibal's movements at the Battle of Cannae.

Magnus took pride in meeting his opponent head on and without flinching. "Good afternoon, Mrs. Pilkington." He turned slightly and nodded to the girls. "Ladies."

"I have not received your response to our Summer Soiree invitation yet, Mr. Stanwyck."

Ah, yes, the blasted soiree.

Magnus had begun to suspect that *soiree* was another word for "curate auction."

"I apologize for my tardiness in responding, Mrs. Pilkington. I haven't forgotten. I'm afraid I'm not yet sure of the date of my brother's wedding and I couldn't miss that."

Mrs. Pilkington's pale, reptilian eyes widened. "Would that be your brother the Earl of Sydell?"

Magnus ground his teeth; his family connections had only served to increase his appeal as a matrimonial object. "No, ma'am. It would be my eldest brother but one."

"Lord Michael?"

The fact that she knew his brother's name sent a frisson of terror up his spine. Clearly she'd acquired a copy of the peerage.

The only reason she wasn't "Lord Magnusing" him all over the county was because of the vicar's comment early on in Magnus's curacy: that the title of a man of God superseded those given by men, even the King.

"Yes, it is my brother Michael who will be—" A movement across the street captured his attention. It was Miss Griffin and her unusual aunt leaving the mercantile, each carrying paper-wrapped parcels.

"Who is that?"

He turned to find Mrs. Pilkington's tiercel gaze fastened on the two women.

"That is Miss Griffin and her aunt, Mrs. Trent."

"Oh, the new tenants at Halliburton Manor."

"You know of them?" he asked in some surprise.

She gave Magnus an annoyingly smug smile. "Mr. Pilkington was instrumental in the preparation of the house."

Mr. Pilkington was in the building trade, so that was her grand way of saying her husband had done some repairs on the long-vacant cottage.

"She's come from London to partake of our healthy air," Magnus said.

Just then, Mrs. Trent threw her head back and laughed rather raucously, drawing the attention of more than one passerby.

Mrs. Pilkington frowned at this open display of revelry. "I do hope she is not a hurly-burly sort."

Her youngest daughter, Emily—the only one who didn't have a militant gleam in her eyes—squirmed at her parent's harsh statement. "*Oh, Mama.*"

Mrs. Pilkington's head whipped around, her eyes narrowing and her long nose twitching, the expression causing her to bear a striking resemblance to the ferret on the sign she had the misfortune to be standing beneath. She fixed her daughter with a freezing look. "Yes, Emily?"

The girl stared; her eyes held like a rabbit before a hawk.

Magnus stepped in. "I hope you'll excuse me, Mrs. Pilkington, but I'm afraid I'm late for Mrs. Tisdale."

An unchristian snort escaped from her mouth. "Oh, her again, is it? A creaking door hangs longest."

Magnus suppressed the flash of irritation he felt at her unkind comment and swallowed his retort—that Mrs. Tisdale was not a creaking door, but a sick, lonely old lady. Instead he smiled, bowed, and headed off down the street. Conveniently in the same direction as Miss Griffin and her aunt, not that he had any plans to catch up with them.

The path to Mrs. Tisdale's tiny cottage pulled him off Miss Griffin's trail not far out of town, but it did not pull her out of his mind.

Magnus told himself that his interest in her was a normal reaction for any man. After all, he couldn't recall ever meeting a woman as beautiful as Miss Griffin. In addition to her striking auburn hair, creamy complexion, and remarkably voluptuous figure that her walking costume had only served to accentuate, she also possessed a kittenish upper lip that made her plush lower lip appear positively sinful. And, if all *that* wasn't enough, her tilted green eyes had sparkled with a weary humor that had shot right to his chest.

Well, to be honest, it had shot a few other places in his body, as well. Just because he was a man of the Church did not mean he was immune to beauty and feminine charms.

Magnus adjusted the strap on the battered leather satchel he always carried, the jars and bottles inside making it heavier than usual. The vicar's wife had loaded him down with calf's foot jelly and a poultice that she'd promised to one of the parishioners he planned to call on today. Magnus didn't have the heart to tell Mrs. Heeley that her jelly most often got passed from household to household until it finally ended up in a pig trough on an outlying farm.

Mrs. Heeley was widely known to be the worst cook in the county—perhaps all of Britain. But she was so good-natured that nobody wanted to hurt her feelings. And so she continued to preserve her bodyweight in dreadful jams and jellies every year, much to the chagrin of her parishioners.

"I don't know how you can bear it—all those people," Magnus's oldest brother Cecil had said the last time Magnus had gone home to visit.

Although Cecil and he were the oldest and youngest of the six brothers they were still the closest. Magnus found their mutual affection both amusing and odd because they had nothing at all in common. Cecil had no time for people—indeed, he actively avoided them—and Magnus rarely met a person he didn't like.

"What *people* do you mean, Ceec?" Magnus had asked his brother.

"I mean those malingering sick people, lonely old pensioners, and desperate on-the-shelf spinsters—all clambering for your attention and clinging to you like so many limpets."

Magnus smiled now as he recalled Cecil's horror. His brother liked hunting, hounds, and horses. Other than that, Cecil seemed uninterested in the world around him, not the best characteristic for a man who would one day inherit the marquisate and its extensive properties and people.

Their parents had long despaired of him ever pulling his attention away from the sporting life long enough to marry and produce children. It wasn't that Cecil was a carouser—he didn't enjoy drinking or gambling—it was just that he had no interest in flirting, dancing, or attending house parties.

When Magnus hadn't been quick enough to refute Cecil's words his brother had continued in the same vein. "I don't understand you, Mag. You've got Briar House and a good chunk of land. With some damned fine trails," he'd added, because there was nothing more important than fox hunting. "You don't *have* to do this curate bobbery."

Magnus had been having this discussion with members of his family ever since he'd decided, at the age of fifteen, to join the clergy. By the time he was twenty he'd given up trying to explain his call to the Church. He was the first, and perhaps only, member of his family as far back as anyone knew to have shown an interest in a career usually taken—unwillingly in most instances—by second sons.

While Magnus had stopped trying to explain his calling to others, he still had to justify moving so far from home to pursue it.

"You don't need to go all the way down *South* to be a mere curate." Cecil said the word *south* as if it were a vulgar epithet. Which it was to most Yorkshiremen.

"I know that, Ceec, but I *like* New Bickford and I *like* Reverend Heeley. And, as difficult as it is for you to believe, I *like* being a curate and I *like* tending to old people, on-the-shelf spinsters, and—who else was it you said?"

Cecil had ignored his jest. "How the devil a man can engage in so much blasted praying and live like a monk, I'll never know."

The comment about living like a monk had surprised Magnus; after all, Cecil had been the most loyal man alive to his mistress, Alice Thompkins, an older widow who lived in one of the cottage on their

Melissa and The Vicar

father's estate. Magnus guessed his brother would have married Mrs. Tompkins long ago if he thought his parents would permit it.

Now, Magnus's other brothers—Michael, Henry, James, and Philip—on the other hand, were a completely different story from Cecil. Tales of the earl's wild younger sons were told in every taproom in West Riding.

Lord how those four had teased Magnus when he'd turned sixteen and was still a virgin. It was a testament to his incredibly stubborn nature—which his doting mother claimed was his *only* sin—that he'd not allowed them to drag him to a brothel. But he'd stood firm. And he'd remained chaste even when other men at his seminary visited brothels or kept mistresses. Such activity wasn't encouraged, but it was tolerated as long as it was kept discrete. After all, more than one of his fellows had observed, becoming a vicar was not like becoming a Catholic priest.

No, they weren't taking a vow of celibacy, but Magnus couldn't conscience paying women to slake his physical needs. Instead, he managed his needs himself, no matter how unfulfilling that might be, and looked forward to discovering the joys of the matrimonial bed with his wife. Until that day arrived, he tried to avoid thinking too much about the sexual act if he could help it. Today, he was finding he couldn't help it.

Something about Miss Griffin had brought thoughts of a carnal nature to mind.

Magnus climbed the steps to Mrs. Tisdale's tiny house, his face burning at the images running loose in his head. It wasn't Miss Griffin's fault that she emanated a seductive sensuality that wrapped around him like the tendrils of ivy.

An unwanted surge of lust rolled through him at the thought of her tilted eyes and that long upper lip. Magnus grimaced; the innocent young woman was probably unaware of the effect her face and figure had on men.

He pushed away the lustful thoughts and rapped on the front door.

Nobody answered, so he opened it a crack and stuck his head inside. The old lady was hard of hearing and her maid-of-all-work only came in the mornings. "Mrs. Tisdale?"

There was no answer so Magnus stepped inside and lowered his satchel to the hall floor. That was when he heard a faint tapping and soft cry overhead.

S.M. LaViolette

Magnus bolted for the narrow stairs. He'd never been anywhere on the second floor before but assumed it was where her bedchamber was.

"Mrs. Tisdale?" he called when he reached the landing, which held three doors. The first was a box room and the second a spare bedroom. He opened the third door more slowly. "Mrs. Tisdale?"

"Mister Stanwyck." The voice, breathy and hoarse, came from the far side of the bed, which was unmade but empty.

Magnus found the old lady on the hardwood floor, her leg bent at an odd angle beneath her. He dropped down beside her and gently shifted her so her weight was not on her leg. She screamed.

"I'm terribly sorry, Mrs. Tisdale," he soothed, covering her blue-veined, painfully thin legs with her flannel nightgown before turning to look at her face. Her eyes had closed and he was wondering if she'd lost consciousness when her papery lids fluttered open.

"Cold," she said, even though the house was almost unbearably warm and humid

Magnus did not think that could be good. "I'm going to lift you onto the bed where you can get warm and be more comfortable."

She grimaced but nodded.

As careful as he was picking her up, she still gave a blood curdling scream that tore at his heart. Not until he'd laid her down and covered her with the heavy quilt did he risk looking at her face.

She was staring at him, her eyes tight with pain.

"I need to go for the doctor."

Her hand shot out far faster than he'd believed she could move. "No! Not yet."

"But—"

"Just. . . don't leave me alone. Stay a moment." She was breathing too fast and bright spots of color had settled over her knife-sharp cheekbones. Her hand tightened on his, her bony fingers like the claws of a bird. "Please."

It was the first time he'd heard her speak that particular word. "Of course I'll stay." He hooked a foot around a nearby chair and pulled it toward the bed without letting go of her hand.

"Scared." Her breathing had slowed but was still jerky.

Magnus looked up from their joined hands at the word. Her blue eyes, usually so sharp and pitiless, were watery and vague.

"I'm here now, Mrs. Tisdale. Nothing to be afraid of."

She nodded, her gaze still fixed upon him, her grip unbreakable.

Melissa and The Vicar

Mrs. Tisdale was the village outcast. Magnus supposed there was somebody like her in every town in Britain. He had no idea what she'd done to earn the status and he doubted her neighbors remembered, either. She'd simply occupied the role for so many decades it was like an old coat that fit too comfortably to shed.

He knew better than to ask a woman's age, but he'd seen a book she'd left open once and the flyleaf had contained the words: *"To my darling Eunice, for those times we can't be together. James"* The date below the inscription had been 1751. Even if she'd only been twenty it meant she was now somewhere in her eighties. The elegant bones of her face and her huge, deep-set eyes proclaimed she must have been a beautiful young woman.

Magnus realized her grip had loosened and her lips were parted. Her breathing was stertorous, but even and deep: she was sleeping at last.

He carefully disentangled their fingers, tip-toed from the room, and then ran with undignified haste to fetch the doctor.

***

Melissa poured herself another cup of tea—which she'd found was far easier on her stomach than coffee—and broke the seal on Joss Gormley's most recent letter. Joss wasn't only her best friend; he was also managing the brothel in Melissa's absence.

Dear Mel:

I hope this letter finds you hale, hearty, and relaxing in the village of New Bickford. Business continues as usual. Laura asks that I pass along her regards and also wanted me to remind you about the expansion she proposed just before you left on your trip.

Melissa sighed. She'd been avoiding thinking about the proposal that Laura Maitland, one of her other business partners, had made. To be honest, her heart simply hadn't been in her business since she'd coughed up blood and almost died that day last fall. A brush with mortality made one reevaluate what was important in one's life.

She frowned at the unpleasant memory of that day, took another piece of toast, and turned back to the letter.

Please don't get angry.

Mel shook her head. "Oh, Joss. What in the world is it now?"

Laura did not stop at her reminder; she approached the owner of number nine and made an independent offer for the property, which he is currently considering.

Mel dropped her toast. "What?"

I know you wanted to wait until you, Laura, and Hugo had a chance to discuss the matter and agree on an offer for the property, but . . .

Melissa growled. She *had* wanted to wait. Now the seller, a hideously sly man, would know they wanted the building and would double the price. She ground her teeth. Laura was clearly running amok without Melissa there to curb her. While she could never love owning a brothel, The White House was her future. If she could sell it for a profit—like the woman she'd bought it from—then she could retire in the next few years. But that wouldn't happen if she paid a fortune for her next expansion.

"Bloody hell," she muttered.

I know how her behavior will have annoyed you, but it is nothing to Hugo's annoyance.

A laugh broke out of her as Joss's wry observation. "I'll wager you're correct, Joss," she said, smiling at the thought of her most prickly business partner's reaction to Laura's rash behavior.

I didn't think Hugo had it in him to feel anger—or anything other than self-love, really.

Joss despised Hugo—Melissa's most popular employee with both women and men—and made no secret of it. Of course, a lot of that dislike was due to a rather wicked trick Melissa had played on Joss a few months ago, when she'd used Hugo to get between Joss and the woman Joss had stubbornly refused to admit he loved.

It had been a foolishly dangerous plan, but it had worked.

She knew she should be grateful that the two men hadn't killed each other that night. Melissa's view was that all's well that ends well. Unfortunately, Joss hadn't seen it that way. While his anger at Melissa had abated, his loathing for Hugo had doubled. And, after he'd blackened Hugo's eye, the feeling was mutual.

Melissa and The Vicar

Mel made a *tsking* sound at the memory and turned back to her letter.

The result of Laura's precipitate action is that Hugo and Laura hate each other more than ever. I think there will be trouble between those two before too long. I'm glad I sold my interest in the business to you. At least I don't have to worry about the two of them badgering me night and day to sell to them.

No, but Melissa would when she returned.
If I return.
Mel paused, the letter crackling between her clenched fingers. Now where had that thought come from? Of course, she was going back—where else would she go?

Her mouth tightened. Nowhere: there was nowhere else to go. At least not anywhere she wouldn't have to hide her past and who she *was*. Even staying here temporarily brought a certain amount of anxiety. Men from all over Britain knew her and there was always a possibility—nay, an *inevitability*—that she would encounter one even in a place as bucolic as New Bickford.

Well, no point dwelling on that right now. This was only her third day here and nobody had recognized her yet. The handsome curate floated into her mind. She snorted. He was one more thing she could never have and should put out of her mind. The two of them were so different they might as well be separate species.

She straightened out the crumpled sheets of paper and turned back to the letter, the rest of which was largely to do with business, some repairs, two other new employees, and a young lord whom Joss had barred from the men's side of the business for excessive debt. It wasn't until the end that he said something about himself.

My father passed quietly in his sleep last week.

She laid a hand on her throat. "Oh, Joss."

As you know, it was a happy release. He'd become little more than a vegetable these past months and my sister was working herself to the bone.
Although she will go to Joseph, her betrothed, soon, I wish to spend a week with her before she marries. I have convinced her to take a brief holiday at the seaside. Please let me know if you would feel uncomfortable if I left Laura and Hugo in charge while I was gone for ten days.

Uncomfortable? No, that wasn't the word she'd use. *Terrified* was more like it; terrified that there might not be anything to go back to. But that was hardly Joss's fault. He'd only offered to help manage the business so that Melissa would agree to this stay in the country. He had his own life and expecting him to sacrifice it for the health of the brothel wasn't fair. Especially not when she *had* two managers who were supposed to operate the business.

She sighed and glanced down at the bottom of the page.

I miss you and hope you are well. Say hello to that spitfire Daisy from me and tell her that more than a few men are mourning her absence.
Your friend,
Joss

She folded up the letter, her mind on Joss's comment about leaving Laura and Hugo in charge: tantamount to leaving the inmates in charge of the asylum. The two whores were the worst possible combination: Laura was willful and rarely stopped to take other people into consideration.

And as for Hugo?

Just thinking his name made her head pound. Hugo was a force of nature. He was, quite frankly, the most sexually attractive man she'd ever met. It was boggling how much fascination he held for both genders—especially considering he wasn't good looking at all. His whipcord lean body, coal black eyes, and thin, cruel lips should have made him downright ugly. But there was something about him that drew and held the eye; a person would always notice Hugo in a crowded room.

He was the only employee who'd never refused a customer's request. When it came to sex, Hugo would do anything.

Leaving him in charge of her business would be putting the proverbial fox in charge of the henhouse. A fox who might ransack the building, sell all the valuables, and then set the whole thing on fire just to watch it burn.

"Melissa?"

She looked up to find Daisy standing in the doorway. "Yes?"

"Where were you? I called your name three times."

"Just thinking and relaxing—what I came here to do."

"Well, the time for relaxation is over—you've got visitors."

"At this time of day?"

"It's past noon, luv."

Mel looked at the clock on the bedside table. So it was. "Who is it?"

Daisy's full lips curved into a wicked look that had made her a lot of money over the years. "I'd hate to spoil the surprise."

Chapter Three

"Would you like another scone, Mrs. Pilkington?" Daisy had changed into a dress Mel had never seen before— a demure, high-necked pale blue gown with long sleeves. It should have made her look more "aunt-like" but it didn't.

"No, thank you, Mrs. *Trent*."

Mel hid a smile at the Pilkington woman's pointed tone and stare. She was like a bloodhound that could scent something but couldn't quite get the trail. Daisy's act wasn't fooling her for a second. They would all need to be careful around Mrs. Pilkington.

"The Summer Fête is in just three weeks," Mrs. Heeley said, blissfully unaware of any undercurrents in the room and accepting another scone, her fourth, Mel noted.

In addition to the vicar's wife there was Mrs. Pilkington and her three downtrodden daughters; Miss Agnes Philpot; her improbably named sister, Gloria; and two other women whose names Mel could not recall at the moment. An entire church committee, apparently. It seemed like an odd way to call on a complete stranger, but what did Mel know about such things?

She realized everyone was looking at her and waiting for a response. What the devil had they all been yammering about?

She looked at Daisy, who mouthed the words *summer* and *fête*.

"Ah, a fête." Mel cleared her throat. "I'm afraid I've never attended such a thing." They continued to stare. "At least not at our church in London."

Mrs. Pilkington's eyebrows shot up. "Is that so? And to what parish do you belong?"

Mel opened her mouth but couldn't make anything come out of it.

A knock on the door saved her.

"Yes, Jenny?" she said, wanting to kiss the curvy young maid who appeared as guileless as a cherub but in reality, had whipped a sizeable portion of the *ton* with a riding crop.

"You've a visitor, Miss Griffin." The girl's eyes met Mel's in a way that most maids probably wouldn't and she hesitated as if she were

Melissa and The Vicar

about to deliver a wicked surprise. Melissa would have to talk to Jenny about her acting later. The girl wanted to be on the stage, so she'd better learn to embrace her role. "He says he's a *curate*." She said the word the way another person—one who hadn't worked in a brothel until a few weeks ago—might say "mermaid" or "unicorn."

"Please show him in, Jenny."

Every eye in the room swiveled toward the doorway.

"Ah, good afternoon, Miss Griffin." Reverend Stanwyck's blue eyes widened as he took in the number of people in the room. "I see I'm interrupting something—"

"You are more than welcome." Mel said a silent prayer of gratitude for the curate's distracting presence. She motioned to Daisy, "You remember my aunt, Mrs. Trent?"

"Naturally. Good afternoon, ma'am." He gave Daisy an elegant bow that brought out her carnivorous smile and Mel wanted to groan. Could the woman behave any more like a tart if she tried?

The arrival of the handsome curate threw the dynamic of the room completely off-kilter.

Mel leaned close to Daisy. "Quick, what church do I attend in London?" she whispered as the reverend bowed and greeted the cluster of women.

"Don't ask me—the only church I know of is St. Paul's."

"Good Lord. Do they even have services there?"

Daisy snorted. "Why are you asking *me* these questions?" She gestured with her chin toward the curate, who was sitting in the middle of the flock of women looking far more comfortable than any man had a right to be. "There's your local expert."

Mel gave her a filthy look.

"Two sugars and milk, please," Mister Stanwyck said to the elder Miss Philpot, who'd somehow won the competition among the women to serve him his tea when Melissa did not immediately spring to her feet.

He took the cup and saucer, thanked her, and turned to his rapt audience. "Please, I was serious about not wishing to interrupt."

"We were just talking about Saint Botolph's Summer Fête," Melissa said, before Mrs. Pilkington could unsheathe her claws again and reintroduce the subject of London churches.

"Yes, we were speaking of the bazaar and what we had assembled thus far." Miss Gloria Philpot was staring worshipfully at the curate and had scooted all the way to the edge of her chair, until only the tiniest sliver of rump was keeping her from falling on the floor.

"I'm not sure I understand what a bazaar *is*," Daisy said, as if she were genuinely interested.

"It is the same as a fair or market, just with a more varied selection of items rather than vegetables and such. We set up booths in the park and people sell different things. At the end of the day all the money is counted and the booth that earns the most gets a surprise gift. All the money goes toward the church windows," Mister Stanwyck said.

Ah, the church windows again. Mel really must see them.

"Mister Stanwyck has a booth where he does the loveliest portraits," one of Mrs. Pilkington's daughters piped up—the oldest, Melissa thought.

All eyes were on the man in question, who was eating his biscuit, the elegant angles of his face darkening slightly. So, this was something that embarrassed him.

Melissa couldn't resist teasing him. "Ah, you are an artist, Mr. Stanwyck."

He took a sip of tea and set down his cup and saucer before shaking his head, his lips curved in a half-smile. "No, *artist* is far too strong. I am a. . . dabbler."

The women broke into a chorus of "no's" and "you're too humble's."

But Mr. Stanwyck was determined to change the subject. "Tell me, Miss Griffin, do you have a special talent that might earn money for the windows?"

Daisy choked and spewed tea into her lap. Mr. Stanwyck was immediately on his feet, hovering over her with an expression of concern on his beautiful face. "I say, are you quite alright, Mrs. Trent?"

Mel leaned close to Daisy and smacked her on the back. Hard.

"I'm fine," Daisy wheezed, lurching to her feet. "Please, excuse me." She clamped both hands over her mouth and fled the room. Mel imagined her collapsing with laughter in the kitchen and entertaining the others with the curate's innocent question.

"Would you like to go after her and—" Mr. Stanwyck began, his brow furrowed with concern. "Help her?" he finished lamely.

Mel gave him a grim smile. "I daresay she'll be fine. Tell me," she said, adopting a softer tone, "what do some of the other booths sell?"

Melissa and The Vicar

"Mrs. Heeley sells some of the jams and jellies she makes during the year." A pregnant silence followed this declaration.

"One year Farmer Sinclair brought ice and we had raspberry ices—in the middle of *summer*!" This was Emily Pilkington, the youngest of the three girls and by far the least like her mother.

"My sister and I sell wool stockings." This from one of the women whose name Mel didn't know.

Mrs. Pilkington made a derisive sound. "My daughters and I will be selling various needlework projects, such as antimacassars." Her expression was virtuous—as if God preferred chair covers to wool stockings.

"Lady Barclay donates cut flowers from her hot-houses," Miss Philpot added, not to be outdone by Mrs. Pilkington, a woman she clearly viewed as her nemesis.

Mel wondered where Lady Barclay was today and why she hadn't converged on her with all the others.

"Sir Thomas and Lady Barclay have not yet returned from London," Mrs. Heeley said, as if Mel had spoken out loud.

"They go every year for the Season." Mrs. Pilkington bristled with pride, basking in the reflected glow of her august neighbors.

"Last year Agnes and I sold potted herbs." This from Miss Gloria Philpot, whose pronouncement earned her a repressive look from Mrs. Pilkington. A tense silence settled over the room.

Mr. Stanwyck cleared his throat. "Ah, distribution from each unto every man according to his—or her—need, as it were," the curate interjected when the two formidable women engaged in a staring match.

Miss Philpot and Mrs. Pilkington turned to Mr. Stanwyck but Mel couldn't help noticing that neither woman looked entirely convinced by his aphorism.

"Is that from the Bible?" Mel asked, amused by his attempts to restore peace.

Once again, she caught a glimpse of unholy humor in his heavenly blue eyes. "Yes—from Acts."

Mrs. Heeley gave the young curate a possessive, motherly smile. "The vicar always says he's never had a curate with such extensive knowledge of scripture as Mr. Stanwyck."

The other women clucked with approval—even the two combatants settled their feathers—while the man in question squirmed.

"How very commendable, Mr. Stanwyck." Mel had to bite her lip to keep from laughing when he gave her a narrow-eyed look.

The rest of the visit passed quickly, with each of the women vying to out-extoll the curate's virtues.

Daisy resurfaced just as the visitors were taking their leave, dexterously thwarting Mrs. Pilkington's efforts to time her departure with the curate's.

As a result, Mel and Mr. Stanwyck were the last two in the entry hall while Daisy strong-armed the Pilkington brood into the back garden under the laughable pretext of needing advice about local flora. The closest Daisy ever came to nature was the silk flowers in her monstrous hats.

Mr. Stanwyck held his hat in his hands as he looked down at her, smiling. "You were wicked to have challenged my biblical knowledge while I attempted to smooth the waters earlier, Miss Griffin."

"Oh? I don't know what you mean, sir." Mel knew she could do innocence as well as a vestal virgin—whatever those might be. Perhaps it was in the Old Testament and Mr. Stanwyck might spend some time instructing her . . .

"You don't fool me for an instant."

Mel chuckled. "I'm sorry, that *was* wicked of me. But you have to admit you deserved it. All that petting and stroking can't be good for you—you'll end up with an insufferably big head. Look what so much praise has done to Hector?"

"Did you just compare me to a rooster, Miss Griffin?"

"I would never do such a thing. But if I *had*, I would've thought you'd treasure such a comparison given Hector's *titan* status in the community."

"Touché." He gave her a smile that did something odd to her chest. Melissa was trying to figure out exactly what it was when he asked, "By the by, you did an excellent job of dodging the question of what you might do at our fête."

"Are you calling me dodgy, Mr. Stanwyck?" she asked, her tone a perfect echo of his.

"I would never say such a thing," he mocked, not to be outdone.

Mel laughed.

He clapped his hat on his head and bowed. "I'm afraid I must be getting on, Miss Griffin. Please give my regards to your aunt and tell her I'm sorry I could not wait to say goodbye." He paused at the

Melissa and The Vicar

bottom of the steps and smiled. "You've got less than three weeks to come up with something for the fête."

Mel admired his tall, broad-shouldered physique as he strode down the walk, suddenly wishing he would stop, come back, and . . . *what?*

Just as he reached the end of the walk she called out. "What happens if I don't come up with anything? Will I end up in the public stocks?"

Rich laughter filled the emptiness between them. "Nothing quite like the prospect of a public shaming to motivate a person!" he called over his shoulder.

And then he disappeared around the hedge.

***

Although Magnus couldn't have said *why,* he was more than a little surprised when Sunday arrived and Miss Griffin and her aunt appeared in church. She'd not said she was *not* coming, but neither had she appeared enthusiastic when the vicar had mentioned it.

They arrived a few moments late and took seats in the very back pew, the one closest to the door, as if they were already planning for their escape.

It was not his week to deliver the sermon, a fact for which he found himself inexplicably grateful. He'd never felt shy about speaking in church before. In fact, he enjoyed both contemplating and drafting his sermons. So why was he grateful he wasn't delivering one today? Was it because he could imagine the mocking expression she'd wear while listening to any sermon of his?

And just why did he imagine she would look that way? She'd given no indication of . . . well, of *impiety.* So why would he think such a thing?

The truth was that she'd done nothing to engender such suspicions. No, it was more the way she looked. Magnus felt ashamed just thinking such a horrid thought—as if the way his body responded to her beauty was somehow evidence of *her* wicked nature, rather than his own lustful imaginings.

He gave a slight shake of his head; his thoughts when it came to Miss Griffin were very Old Testament in nature and he should devote serious consideration as to why he viewed her in such a light.

It also bothered Magnus more than he liked to admit that the thought of potential mockery from her—or from *anyone,* for that matter—would discountenance him when it came to his faith or his calling. Yes, he would get to the heart of the matter when he next meditated.

But for now, he tried to concentrate on worthier matters—like Mrs. Tisdale. He liked the cantankerous old woman and knew that being bedbound with a broken leg would likely drive her—and Dori, the poor girl he'd engaged to look after her—to distraction. Even though he knew Mrs. Tisdale would be in a *mood*, he was still looking forward to visiting her after church today.

Mr. Heeley gave a sermon on turning the other cheek, a barely veiled reference to Mr. Dawkins and his neighbors, the Misses Philpot, who'd resumed the same battle they fought every year: Mr. Dawkins's garden versus the sisters' ever-increasing flock, led by their beloved Hector.

Magnus's gaze wandered along with his attention, settling in the same place no matter how many times he wrenched it away. Miss Griffin had been here barely a week and already he believed she appeared healthier. She was still fragile-looking and lovely, but no longer as pale.

She looked up and caught him staring.

His chest froze even though the rest of him burned. He wanted to look away; indeed, it was the polite thing to do. But he couldn't. She held him captive, her green eyes as shrouded in secrets as a medieval forest. In that instant, Magnus felt sure that she saw the images his fertile imagination created when he was alone in his tiny curate's cottage at night. In his bed.

The corners of her mesmerizing lips turned up so slightly he wasn't sure he hadn't imagined it. And then she looked away.

It was as if a large fist released him and he snorted air through his nose, just like a drowning man gasping for air.

***

Getting Daisy out of bed, in a respectable dress, and on the footpath toward the church had taken every bit of energy Melissa possessed.

"I though you came out all the way to the back of beyond to rest and sleep and get better," the older woman groused, her carefully cultivated accent dropping away in her anger. "If I'd known you'd planned on gettin' up before the cock's crow and gettin' all churchy on me I never would have come."

They'd been passing the Philpot cottage at the time and Daisy had lowered her voice to a hiss, neither of them interested in catching Hector's attention.

Melissa and The Vicar

"I'm paying you to behave like a respectable guardian," Mel reminded her after they'd scurried past unscathed. "Why else did you think I wanted you here? For a quick frig and a ride on that dirty mouth of yours?"

Daisy muttered something under her breath.

Mel stopped and grabbed her arm, pulling her to a halt. "What did you say?"

Daisy yanked herself away. "I *said* maybe that is exactly what you need. When's the last time you've had anyone between your legs, man *or* woman? If you ask me, what you really need is a proper fuck to sort you out and get you out o' this black mood you been in for months."

"Well, I *didn't* ask you."

Daisy crossed her arms. "No, you didn't. You don't ask nobody nothin'—you're too much smarter than the rest of us, aren't you? But let me tell *you* somethin', Madam Melissa Bloody Griffin, you ain't fooling me. You're miserable and heartsick and no amount o' church or dressin' prissy or movin' to the country will help you get away from yerself."

Melissa worked her jaw from side to side, willing herself to calm down. She refused to do this—to argue with an employee. Because that's what Daisy was: her employee. They'd been friends and equals once, long ago, but that changed the day Melissa purchased the brothel. Now, Melissa employed eighty-one people; that was *eighty-one* livelihoods she held in her hands—eighty-one futures that relied on her making the right decisions.

And all the while she was making sure people got fed, paid, and housed, there were *other* people—men, mostly—who'd like nothing better than to take away what was hers. And there were other men—*moral* men—who just wanted to shut her business down. And then there were those in authority who wanted a piece of the pie to keep their mouths shut. And then there were her own qualms that woke her in the middle of the night—yes, in her *empty* bed—about making her money off the backs of others.

The old arguments she'd always used—that at least she gave whores a safer, healthier, and more prosperous place to do the job they did—well, those arguments were as frayed around the edges as a ragged blanket that no longer offered comfort.

But, at the end of the day, all of that was just so much philosophical dithering that she couldn't afford. A woman like her had two options: either being alone at the top or being used and abused at the bottom. Melissa knew she would take the first of those options every single time.

She looked up at Daisy, who stood a good five inches taller than her. "If you don't want to play the part I'm paying you to play then say so and you can go back to London and I'll send for some other *aunt*. And don't think I haven't noticed you twistin' Jenny and Sarah's tails and makin' them behave badly, too." Jenny and Sarah were two of the younger whores Mel had brought along to act as domestics in this farce. They were good girls, but this was the first time they'd been out of London and they were both eagerly, and easily, led into mischief. "I know it's been you encouragin' them to sneak out at night, Daisy."

Just like Daisy, Mel let her own St. Giles accent slip into her words when she became excited or annoyed; all those years of careful practice gone in a heartbeat.

Mel shook her head in disgust; Christ, give her anything but a whiney whore first thing in the morning.

"You do what you want, Daisy. I'm going to church." Mel set off without looking back. Only when she heard a scuffing sound behind her did she know Daisy had followed.

They trudged for a while in silence, Mel slowing a bit, until they were walking side by side again.

Daisy was the first to speak, just as they'd both known she would be. It wasn't because Mel employed her; no, Daisy spoke first because Mel's ability to carry a grudge was legendary. It wasn't something she was proud of, but she had to admit that she'd die of thirst rather than open her mouth to ask for a glass of water if she was angry enough.

"I'm sorry for getting the other girls riled up."

Mel grunted.

"And I'm sorry about the way I've been riding you. I'll do better about being . . . aunt-ish."

"Good."

After that Daisy filled the walk with chatter, knowing better than to expect too much in response. Another thing Mel wasn't proud of was how long it took her to shift her mood back once she'd gotten angry. But by the time they arrived at the small church—late, by the look of it—she'd calmed down enough to ask Daisy how she looked.

Daisy tweaked a hair into place, adjusted her hat a fraction, and smiled. "You look bloomin'."

Mel smiled up at her. "So do you."

Melissa and The Vicar

And then Melissa entered a church for the first time in her life.

***

Ten minutes felt like ten hours. The bench was hard and unforgiving, Reverend Heeley's voice droned on and on, his sermon was achingly boring, and the other parishioners far too interested in Melissa for her comfort. In fact, the only good thing about the entire ordeal was Mister Stanwyck sitting right up front like a prized ornament on a mantelpiece. Her brain hadn't exaggerated his handsome, angelic looks; he *deserved* to be sitting up front and visible.

Mel entertained herself by wondering what he was thinking. His handsome features were fixed in an expression of thoughtful attentiveness, as if every word that fell from the vicar's lips—and there were a lot of them—was of the utmost importance.

But his eyes betrayed him. They found Mel again and again and again.

At first, she pretended she didn't feel the weight of his stare. But just once, she let their eyes meet and lock. Daisy had finally needed to nudge her in the ribs.

"Oye," she hissed. "You've stop breathing."

She had. But so had he—she'd seen it on his face. She'd also heard him suck in air from all the way in the back of the church.

He avoided meeting her gaze again and the rest of the service was a misery.

When it seemed like things might be over Daisy whispered, "Are we staying to do the pretty? Or do you want to leave now?"

Mel wanted to see him—to talk to him—but she knew what it would be like once the doors opened: a cloud of females as thick as summer flies would descend on him.

So, they'd left early, drawing several scandalized looks from those in the immediate vicinity. Well, that was too bad.

"I'm going home and crawling back into bed," Daisy said with a huge yawn as they let themselves out the back lychgate.

Mel was too edgy to rest, and if she went home, she'd just fret about what was going on in London, what Hugo and Laura were up to, and a hundred other things that she'd promised herself she'd leave behind.

She reminded herself that she'd made the effort to come all this way to get healthy; she might as well give it a fair try.

What had Joss said to her when he'd seen her off that last day? "Go for long walks, Mel. Even if you don't think you want to, you'll be glad you did."

So Mel said, "I'm going for a walk."

Daisy stared. "Walking back home *is* a walk."

Mel ignored her and turned toward town. If she recalled correctly, there had been other paths; maybe one of them led down to the water. New Bickford wasn't directly on the water but she knew it wasn't too far off. She'd been here almost a week and still not dipped her toes in the ocean—another thing Joss had suggested. Mel should have asked somebody the best way to get to the water—some of the surrounding cliffs were far too steep to use—but one had to get to water if one just kept walking, didn't one?

She followed the path, taking the first left she came to. Almost immediately she found herself in a surprisingly dense stand of trees. Mel hesitated, wondering if she'd wandered onto somebody's private footpath.

Well, if they wanted her off it, they could tell her so.

The wooded area ended abruptly and she came out of the trees into a little clearing. Not far ahead the path ran beside a cottage. Mel paused and looked around. There were no out buildings, no garden to speak of, nothing, just a little house that looked to have sprung from the ground itself. Yet it appeared well-tended, so somebody must live in it.

Mel was about to resume her journey when the front door flew open and a whirlwind in skirts came flying out.

"You—you *evil* old witch!" the whirlwind yelled into the house, which looked dark beyond the doorway.

Faint laughter drifted from inside the house. The girl slammed the door—which sprang back open and hit the wall instead of closing—and spun around, shrieking when she saw Melissa.

Mel raised her hands in a gesture meant to be calming, but the woman flinched away.

"Are you here for *her*?" she demanded. But then she turned and spat on the ground, not waiting for an answer. "If you know what's good for you, you'll leave without stepping foot into her web." And with that she stormed past close enough that her skirts brushed against Mel's.

The little clearing was once again quiet, the only sound that of the door as it softly tapped against the wall.

Melissa and The Vicar

What had all *that* been about?

Mel squinted through the doorway into the house; she could see nothing.

Tap, tap, tap.

Mel yelped and spun around. What in the—

Tap, tap, tap.

The noise came from overhead and she looked up to find an old woman peering down from a closed window. She pointed at Mel and made a beckoning motion: come in.

Mel stared and the woman beckoned again.

She dropped her eyes to the doorway the deranged woman had just stormed out of, a picture forming in her mind. The woman upstairs was obviously bedridden and the girl who'd stormed off had been her caretaker. She chewed her lip, wondering what kind of woman could make another woman *that* angry.

Tap, tap, tap.

Well, it seemed like she was about to find out.

She sighed, picked up her skirts, and climbed the steps.

Chapter Four

Magnus told himself he was glad Miss Griffin and her aunt left before the service was over. He'd already spent too much time thinking about her. Not to mention making a fool of himself staring at her.

He was helping Mr. Heeley collect the prayer books when Dori Booker stomped into the church.

She saw Magnus and jabbed her forefinger at him. "*There* you are!"

Magnus knew what she was going to say before she said it.

He opened his mouth to plead with her to reconsider, but she shook her head. "Don't waste your breath, Mister Stanwyck. You can keep your money! I wouldn't spend another second in that—that—*harpy's* nest taking her orders, putting up with her—" whatever had been fueling her rage suddenly ran out and she burst into tears, launching herself into his arms.

Magnus gently patted her back. "There, there, Dori." He met the vicar's stunned gaze over her shoulder as he tried to stem the flow. "I'm sorry she was unki—"

"Unkind?" she wailed only inches from his ear. "She's a b-b-beast!" She began sobbing all over again.

By the time Magnus calmed her, assured her he did not hate her for quitting, sent her on her way with a few coins for the time she'd spent caring for Mrs. Tisdale, and then explained the situation to the vicar, he was about ready to burst into tears himself.

"Sit with me a moment, Magnus." Mr. Heeley sat down in the last pew.

The same place as Miss Griffin, part of Magnus's mind pointed out. He gritted his teeth against the fatuous mental observation.

"Magnus."

He looked up at the vicar. "Yes, sir?"

"You know I am excessively pleased by the way you've tended to our parishioners."

Magnus sensed a 'but' coming.

Melissa and The Vicar

"But sometimes being one of the Lord's shepherds means knowing when a sheep might need a more, er," he paused and scratched his chin. "Or perhaps I should say a *different*, er, pasture. Or perhaps a different shepherd?" Mr. Heeley scratched his head.

Magnus bit back a smile at the mangled metaphor, one of the reasons he enjoyed working with Mr. Heeley so much. Indeed, not a day passed that the vicar didn't come out with something worth writing down.

"That is to say," the vicar continued, looking pained at his own inarticulateness. "I believe it may be time to turn Mrs. Tisdale over to another shepherd entirely—one not in this particular flock, if you know what I mean."

"I *do* know what you mean, Mr. Heeley, but unfortunately I know of no other," he grimaced, "er, shepherds. It seems she is alone in the world, without family or friends." Without anyone but Magnus.

The vicar made a thoughtful humming sound but otherwise remained quiet.

Magnus stood. "I must go and make sure nothing is amiss, sir. I'll give her a stern talking-to and make her understand that this kind of behavior can't go on."

"Erm, yes, Mr. Stanwyck. Quite right. Take things in hand." He gave Magnus a vague wave and wandered in the direction of the vicarage, clearly putting the matter of sheep and shepherds out of his mind.

Magnus removed his surplice, fetched his coat and hat, and headed out at a half-trot, his mind running even faster. He had no idea why he liked the old girl. She was beastly to everyone and had earned her isolation. She was even beastly to Magnus when the urge struck her. He needed to find her a caretaker as iron-willed, stubborn, and impervious as she was. Where in the hell would he find such a being?

***

The spoon hit the edge of the bowl, bounced out, and scattered sticky porridge all over the tray. "I *despise* porridge."

Mel laughed at the venom in the old woman's tone. Good God, if she wasted that much hatred on a bowl of harmless oats what must she be like as an enemy? Because there was no doubt in Mel's mind the old woman on the bed must have racked up plenty of enemies in her long life.

In a way, Mel felt like she was looking at herself in fifty years' time. Or sixty.

"How dare you laugh at me, girl?"

"Did laughing become a crime and nobody told me about it?"

The old woman's lips puckered up like they'd been drawn tight by a string.

"If you don't like porridge, what do you like?" Mel asked.

But she just narrowed her eyes and tightened her lips even more, which Mel hadn't thought possible.

Mel shrugged. "Suit yourself. It's nothing to me if you don't get what you like to eat." She turned to leave.

"You can't just leave me here."

"Have a lovely afternoon," Mel tossed over her shoulder.

"Wait!"

Mel paused at the top of stairs. "Yes?"

Nothing but silence. She was just about to resume her journey when, "Come back," floated out the open doorway.

Mel knew she'd have to wait until hell froze over before the old woman appended a "please" to her command so she turned and marched back into the room.

"Yes?"

The old lady looked like she was chewing nails.

"Out with it or I'm leaving."

Her ancient face seemed to crumple. "You're so. . . *cruel.*"

Mel crossed her arms.

"All right, all right," the woman said, her expression shifting so quickly from pitiful to hateful Mel knew she'd been acting. Perhaps she should have hired this old woman to be her aunt?

"I like an egg, soft coddled in a little cream. And maybe a piece of toast." She shot the bowl of porridge a filthy look. "Not this pabulum. That gel only made this because she's a lazy slut."

"Oye!"

The old woman's head whipped up so fast Mel heard the bones of her neck crack. She pushed down any remorse she might have felt about startling her and made eye contact with the abrasive old bird.

"You talk about *any* woman like that again in my presence and I'll leave. And this time I won't come back. Do you understand me?"

The old lady's jaw dropped, but she nodded.

"Good. Now sit tight and I'll go and see what there is in your larder."

***

Melissa and The Vicar

Mel located an apron behind the kitchen door and removed her spencer. Next, she found the coal scuttle—half-full—and fed more fuel into the tiny cook-stove.

She'd just located an egg and small bottle of milk when a familiar voice startled her.

"Mrs. Tisdale!" There was the sound of a door slamming then booted feet loud on the bare wood floors. "I am *extremely* vexed with you, Mrs. Tisdale." Feet pounded up the stairs. "You have been naughty again and driven poor Dori Booker to tears. I'm not sure—" His voice continued to murmur but Mel could no longer hear the actual words.

She smiled to herself and opened a brown paper package that contained a fresh loaf of bread: Mrs. Tisdale was fortunate her angry caretaker hadn't taken the bread with her.

She set about preparing the meal while listening to the hum of voices emanating from upstairs. Perhaps five minutes after he arrived everything went quiet and then booted feet thundered down the stairs and the door to the kitchen flew open.

Mel didn't bother to turn around.

"Miss Griffin?"

"I hope you're not looking to be fed because I've only got one egg." Mel slid the pan filled with water and the small ramekin into the oven and turned to face him. "What is the time?"

Mr. Stanwyck's beautiful brow furrowed. "The time?"

"Yes, what time is it?"

He pulled out his watch. "Ten past one. Why?"

"Thank you."

He stared.

"I daresay you are wondering what I'm doing here," she offered when he said nothing.

"No. I can see you are making an egg." He peered at the cookstove and his eyebrows raised with obvious interest. "A coddled egg?"

Mel smiled at his hopeful tone. "Yes."

"I'm fond of a coddled egg." She laughed at his wheedling tone and he grinned. "Don't worry, I heard you: just one egg." He motioned to the small table with two chairs. "Please, Miss Griffin, won't you sit for a moment?"

Melissa sat.

"I understand you encountered poor Miss Booker on her way out?"

"Was that the caretaker?"

"The ex-caretaker now."

"Perhaps she can be convinced to come back."

He gave a rough bark of laughter and ran his hand through his hair, the tanned skin of his fingers a sharp contrast to his white-blond locks; he resembled a frustrated angel.

"No, I'm afraid that won't be possible—Miss Booker was quite adamant."

Mel gave him a moment to collect himself. She knew better than most what it was like to have employees leave on the spur of the moment.

He looked up from his troubles. "I'm sorry you've been dragooned into this."

"It's not your fault. Besides, I don't mind a bit of cookery."

He cocked his head. "What were you doing that you saw Miss Booker leaving?"

"I was looking for a way to the water."

"*This* way?"

Mel smiled at his astonishment. "I take it this isn't the right way?"

"Not unless you're a bird."

"I can hear the waves from here."

"That's because they are crashing against the rocks a hundred feet below."

Mel stood, picked up the thick cloth, and opened the small hatch of the oven. She turned to look at him and caught him gazing at her bottom. So, he was not immune to her body, after all. She cleared her throat and enjoyed the spots of color that appeared over his far-too-lovely cheekbones.

"Erm, yes?" His expression was as innocent as a newborn babe.

"The time?"

He fumbled for his watch. "It's been only a few minutes."

Mel gave the heavy pan a shake and nodded to herself when the egg and milk mixture shimmered.

He leaned over her shoulder to get a closer to look. "I like them a bit harder myself."

Mel turned away to hide her smirk. "As do I, Mr. Stanwkye. But Mrs. Tisdale gave specific orders—soft coddled."

Melissa and The Vicar

She put the small ceramic pot on a plate and added two pieces of toast to the toasting rack.

He leaned against the edge of the table and crossed his arms. "You move with an efficiency that says you've done this before."

"I've done my share of cooking." She realized, too late, that a member of the gentry—or at least somebody who could afford to rent a house like Halliburton Manor—would probably have servants for such things. She turned to meet his questioning look, which said he was thinking exactly that. "After one of our cooks walked out my mother believed it was imperative that I learn how to cook." That was true, in part—although it hadn't been a cook at mother's house, but at Melissa's business. And the person who'd decided she didn't want to be at the mercy of anyone else had been Mel herself.

She took a knife to the small knob of butter she'd found in cool water in the larder and gave both pieces of toast a liberal smear.

When she reached for the tray, he was there before her.

"Please, allow me, Miss Griffin."

Melissa turned and began placing the dirty utensils in the basin.

"Won't you come up with me?"

"Do you think she'll want me up there?" Mel asked, wiping her hands on the apron.

He grinned. "I know she won't—she's the most jealous old cat I've ever met. But I've told her she needs to learn to control herself or I shall have to find a new shepherd."

Mel frowned. "Shepherd?"

But he just said, "Come with me. Perhaps you can help her behave more nicely."

Mel snorted but reached behind her waist to untie the apron strings. She hung it over the door and turned to find him, once again, studying her intently with his warm blue eyes.

"Why do I feel like she won't thank me for helping her with that particular lesson?" Mel asked.

***

Magnus followed Miss Griffin down the stairs with the empty tray. The meeting between the two strong-willed women had been something of an anti-climax. Mrs. Tisdale had fallen asleep almost immediately after consuming the contents of her tray. Apparently terrorizing and driving away her domestic had taken a lot out of her.

In the kitchen, Miss Griffin began cleaning up the dirty crockery with the same brisk efficiency she seemed to do everything.

"What can I help you with?" he asked.

She'd given him the look he was starting to expect: a look that crackled with heat and electricity, like the air before a storm. There was always more in her eyes—teasing, challenging—than she gave away. "You could get me some water so I can heat it on the stove."

Magnus did that.

"What else?" he asked after he put the large pot on the cook-stove.

"Sit and entertain me while I tidy up."

He was ridiculously pleased that she wanted his company.

He brought one of the wooden chairs closer and sat. "What kind of entertainment do you desire?"

She smiled down at him. "Is this your first posting as a curate?"

"Yes."

"Did you choose New Bickford or are curates, er, deployed to their positions?"

He laughed. "It is not so rigid as that, but you must have connections to learn about many of the positions."

"And what connections do you possess that got you this plum position?"

He shrugged, uncomfortable with bringing up his family. If nobody had told her yet, he would rather not. "One can make many friends and connections at seminary, of course. People talk and word gets around when something opens up."

"How long will you stay?"

"As long as the vicar will have me."

"You don't have a burning desire for a congregation of your own?"

Magnus leaned back in his chair, stretched out his legs, and crossed his arms, smiling up at her. "Nobody ever asks me these questions."

She paused in the act of cleaning a very dusty salt cellar, a slight flush covering her cheeks. "I'm sorry, I didn't mean to pry—"

"No, no—you're not prying. I only meant that people don't seem to think about those things. My family treats my calling like a hobby or a distempered freak I will eventually grow out of. And the parishioners at New Bickford assume I will be here forever—people do not like change, you know—and eventually marry into the community and settle down." Magnus shrugged. "But what about you, Miss Griffin? I hope you won't think I'm being bold, but you already look healthier after only a brief time here."

"Thank you, I feel better."

Melissa and The Vicar

"Do you miss London?"

An odd expression flickered across her face. "Not very much. At least not yet. I am still discovering the country." The water was warm enough by then and Magnus stood and poured it into her basin.

He picked up a clean cloth that she'd taken from a small cupboard. "Shall I dry?"

That made her laugh, which made her ten times more beautiful, something Magnus wouldn't have believed possible.

"You are a paragon among men, Mr. Stanwyck."

"No," he said, drying the teacup she handed him. "Merely a bachelor. We men *do* know how to boil water, make tea, toast cheese—"

"Ah, toasted cheese! You are a chef, then."

"People have praised my toasted cheese in the past." He grinned and took a plate she was holding out. "Does it count if they were all starving young men?"

"Oh, Mr. Stanwyck. Are you about to embark on a sad tale of your childhood? Because you are far too sunny and pleasant and happy to make me believe you've ever been around starving people of any sort."

He gave her an affronted look that was only partly feigned. "Why does that description sound like it could be just as easily applied to a butterfly or a kitten, Miss Griffin? Are you trying to say I appear *shallow?*"

Her expression was suddenly serious. "I am trying to say that you have a rare character, Mr. Stanwyck, in that you bring joy with you and leave happiness in your wake."

Magnus was so stunned the plate slipped. They both fumbled to catch it, and it was Miss Griffin who caught it just before it struck the floor. She handed it to him without speaking.

"Thank you for saving the plate—and probably both our lives in the process," he quipped, his mind stuck on the way she'd looked when she described him.

"Does Mrs. Tisdale have no family?"

Magnus was torn between relief and disappointment that she changed the subject away from themselves to something safer.

"None that she will admit to."

"This is a nice house and her furniture is of good quality. I think she must not be poor."

"No," Magnus agreed. "She does seem to have enough money to be comfortable."

Miss Griffin took away the towel and Magnus saw there were no dishes left. He took the dishwater and emptied it outside. When he returned, she was removing her apron.

It wasn't until she put on her spencer and reached for her hat that he spoke.

"Thank you."

She turned to him, tying the primrose-colored ribbon beneath her right ear. "Who will take care of her now?" she asked, ignoring his thanks.

"I don't know. I will have to go and ask Mrs. Heeley's charwoman if she can come back and tend to her while I find somebody. She's the only woman Mrs. Tisdale hasn't made cry." He cut her a quick smile. "Well, and you, of course."

Her fascinating mouth—a mouth he realized was usually set in fairly stern lines—curved into a smile that was like a punch in the stomach. Lord. He needed to get his emotions in hand.

"I'll come back later and bring one of my maids with me. Sarah can stay overnight in the guestroom."

Magnus stared, arrested. "Why. . . that's *very* generous of you, Miss Griffin."

"The way you're looking at me is not exactly flattering, Mr. Stanwyck."

"Good Lord!" he expostulated, "How is that?"

Her smile turned into a grin. "I didn't think a curate was supposed to take the lord's name in vain." She laughed at whatever she saw on his face. "What I meant is that you looked at me as if you didn't expect I'd be capable of such kindness."

His face heated immediately; was that true? Was that what his surprise had meant? But no, he slowly shook his head, he hadn't thought that. Why *had* he been so surprised?

"I hope that is not true," he said when he saw that she was waiting. "If I looked startled it was only because I was pleased that you would be so generous to a stranger." He looked away from her gaze, which seemed to read his thoughts. Magnus knew that was impossible, but there was something knowing in her gaze more often than not. If pressed to describe her, he would say her eyes were world-weary, as if life held no more secrets, even though she must be near Magnus' own age.

And then there was her person.

Hers was a vivid beauty he found difficult to look at head on. That, coupled with her fire, made her a formidable woman. Yes, that's why it surprised him she'd take to Mrs. Tisdale—not that she was unkind, but that the sickroom was not a setting he expected her to have any patience with.

She reached out and laid a hand on his forearm. Even gloved and through the fabric of his coat and shirt he could feel her heat. Or at least he thought he could.

She gave him a firm squeeze. "I'm teasing you, Mr. Stanwyck."

She was doing more than that to him, but her coolly amused expression told him that touching him did nothing to her—at least not what it was doing to him.

He struggled to school his expression into something less fatuous. "Thank you, Miss Griffin, you can't know how much this will help—just until I can find somebody. I'm sure Mrs. Tisdale will be grateful when I tell her."

Miss Griffin picked up her reticule and gave an unladylike snort, the sound breaking the odd tension that had built up in the room.

"I daresay she'll be furious." She cut Magnus a glance from beneath lashes *made* for such sultry looks. "You know she wants you all to herself, don't you, Mr. Stanwyck?" Her lips quivered ever so slightly, her lids heavy over green eyes that suddenly looked darker. "She adores you—just like each and every female in your flock from nine to ninety."

If possible, his face became even hotter.

She turned away and was halfway toward the front door by the time Magnus worked up the nerve to ask, "And what about you, Miss Griffin? Do you count yourself part of my *flock* as well?"

Her low, seductive laughter echoed in the empty house long after she'd gone.

Chapter Five

*D*earest Joss:
   Thank you so much for your gossipy letter. Yes, that is sarcasm, just in case I might have been too subtle.
   First to business: Please tell Laura I am displeased by her overture to purchase the adjoining property from Mr. Taylor and request that she turn him away should he respond to her offer. I will address the issue when I return.
   I think you know what I have to say about Hugo and his recent antics. He has always required firm handling. I imagine he responds differently to male authority, but you certainly have my leave to use any means necessary—short of actually strangling him—to make him obey your direction. I would ask that you not discharge him, as much as you might wish to. He is an asset to the business and I have something of a weakness for him (don't ask).
   I was saddened to hear about the death of your father. However, I understand that your sister has worked herself to exhaustion and agree with the beneficial effects of country air. It is a shame I am a whore and bringing her to stay with me would destroy her reputation.
   I agree that you should go with her and spend as much time as you need. Laura and Hugo can manage for at least that long and I know it would do Belle untold good to have you with her.
   I wish I could have you with me, my dearest friend. Instead I must make do with Daisy, who complains endlessly about the lack of entertainment and early mornings and leads Jenny, Sarah, Ben, Thomas, and even Mrs. Bunch to misbehave. If I thought I could live without her cooking I would send Mrs. Bunch back to London along with the rest of my fractious household and hire new servants from the local populace.
   Ah, the local populace. Now there is a subject for contemplation. What they think of our odd household I could not say. I've seen confusion on more than one face when confronted with Daisy or Sarah or Jenny for more than a cursory interaction. I know there is a general, unarticulated suspicion about us all, so I have decided it is upon me to do what I can to convince the good villagers that we are actually what we claim to be: honest, moral, God-fearing women.

Melissa and The Vicar

I had a most amusing experience after church this past Sunday. I can hear you laughing from here, my dear Joss. Yes, I entered a church and the hand of God did not reach down and smite me.

After the service, I sent Daisy home to bed and took your advice and went for a long walk to nowhere in particular. I was hoping to see the water and follow yet another of your directives—to dip my toes in it—when I encountered one of the domestic dramas that must play out in thousands of households everyday unobserved. But this time, my darling boy, I not only observed, I also intervened!

The disturbance in question was a ninety-one-year-old lady who'd just driven her domestic to the point of homicide.

Yours truly came to the rescue and provided succor in the form of coddled eggs and toast. The local curate—yes, there is one here, along with a vicar—seems to have made a pet project of the old dear and arrived on the scene just in time to see me delivering sustenance.

All jesting aside, the curate seems to have sprung fully formed from the imagination of some writer who excels in extolling the benefits of virtuous, selfless living. Not only is he kind, caring, and clever, he has also been graced with enough physical beauty to have the local female population in a veritable frenzy.

I, too, must have been blinded by his charms because I was somehow talked around to helping with his obstreperous charge until he could engage yet another nurse-cum-housekeeper for her.

Melissa smiled down at the page as she sanded and then turned it. She could see Joss's face as he read this letter. Although he was as big as a house, as tough as an old boot, and had a battered visage that would have looked at home on a London dockworker, he had the beautiful, poetry-loving soul of a romantic. It was a characteristic that had led to his current state of lovelorn misery. No doubt he was reading all kinds of romantic situations in between the lines of her letter.

Mel dipped her quill and continued:

If you are concerned that I might imperil my pristine reputation in the village of New Bickford by cavorting unattended with the delicious Mr. Stanwyck (our curate), please comfort yourself with the knowledge I have paid young Sarah double her wages to stay with the Old Dear until a new sacrificial offering can be located.

Now, here is the amusing part. (You are probably thinking this already sounds amusing, aren't you? Naughty boy.)

S.M. LaViolette

Mrs. Tisdale was once a fallen woman. Or would she still be a fallen woman? Once fallen, always fallen? There is a philosophical question for you to ponder, dearest Joss. If a whore is no longer whoring, is she still a whore?

No, she did not confess the shocking truth to me, I found it myself while snooping through her possessions.

Now you are justly shocked.

I know it was bad of me, but I felt I deserved some compensation (other than the gratitude of the inestimable Mr. Stanwyck) for sacrificing myself on the pyre of Mrs. Tisdale's . . . well, I appear to have lost track of where I was going with that. Suffice it to say that I felt like snooping and did so. Yes, I took advantage of an old lady while she was asleep. Yet another black mark on my soul.

She was a member of the muslin crowd during the reign of the last monarch. You read that correctly: the SECOND George. Perusing her diaries and letters was like a trip through a historical novel—you would have loved it, dear Joss. It seems Mrs. Tisdale was once close with the Gunning sisters, especially the unfortunate Maria, who is thought to have killed herself with lethal face powder, or some such.

Mrs. Tisdale—let us call her Eunice for brevity—met the sisters at the very beginning of their careers, so to speak. She was originally Eunice Sheridan, the daughter of the very same theater manager who provided the Gunnings with costumes—they were too poor to possess dresses that were fine enough—to make their presentation to the Earl of Harrington.

Beyond fascinating, isn't it?

According to Eunice's diary, Maria wore the costume of Lady Macbeth and her sister, Elizabeth, that of Juliet. Make what you will of that information, I have nothing clever to offer.

Incidentally, I feel as though I should be charging you for this letter—at least the price you pay one of your many subscription libraries.

But I will give you this first installation at no cost.

Alas, it seems I have come to the end of the page, my dearest, lovely Joss, and I think I have given you enough entertainment for one day. You must be shocked I have not had time to pen a detailed description of the rural beauties that have soothed my jaded urban sensibilities. I'm afraid you will have to wait for both that joy as well as the Further Adventures of Eunice in London until next time.

Yours in domestic bliss,
Mel

She sealed her letter with one of the rose wafers the prior resident of Halliburton Manor had left in her writing desk and put it in her reticule. If she walked quickly enough, she could ensure the letter went out on the next mail coach.

After delivering the letter she would stop in and visit Mrs. Tisdale and see how Sarah was faring with her cantankerous charge.

**

Magnus was loitering—there was no other word for it—in Mrs. Tisdale's kitchen.

He should have been on his way to Sir Thomas's, where he had an appointment to discuss tutoring the squire's eldest son before he went off to school in a few months.

Instead, he'd come to see Mrs. Tisdale and learned she was eating while her temporary servant—Miss Griffin's maid, Sarah—cleaned the kitchen and baked bread. Everything was under control. Magnus should leave and do the hundred other tasks on his constantly growing list.

"Can I make you something to eat, Mr. Stanwyck?"

Magnus looked down into warm brown eyes and smiled. "Thank you, but no, Sarah. I've eaten."

Her smile turned into a grin: a very knowing, wicked grin that made his neck and face hot.

Just like the maid at Halliburton house—Jenny—Sarah made Magnus feel oddly aware of himself—his body, the fact that he was a man. With a man's needs.

He gritted his teeth against the foolish thoughts that seemed to be assailing him more often lately.

"I'm going to pop up and see Mrs. Tisdale," he said, unnerved by her effect on him.

"Oh, aye, she'll like that, *Reverend*. Still fancies the lads, she does, even at 'er age."

Magnus's jaw dropped, but Sarah just chuckled and went back to her cleaning.

"Where is *she*?" The old lady demanded the moment Magnus stepped into her room.

"By *she* I assume you mean Miss Griffin?" He took the chair from the wall and set it closer to the bed.

She snorted. "Is that what you call her?"

"That is her name, Mrs. Tisdale."

She made a skeptical sniffing sound which Magnus chose to ignore. He was tempted to ask her exactly who she thought Miss Griffin *really* was but didn't want to encourage her sniping.

49

"Doctor Bryant said your leg is healing nicely and that you'll be up and around in no time."

"The doctor is a fool. I'll die in this bed."

Magnus heaved an irritated sigh. "Why would you say such a thing?"

"Because I'm old—ninety-two on my next birthday—and people who are almost ninety-two can be sure of only one thing: they will die sooner rather than later."

Frustration—and something else—burned in his chest. Before he could decide what it was she laughed at him. "You'll never make vicar if you refuse to accept death, Magnus."

"I can accept death, ma'am, just not when a person wills it. Other than your leg you are as healthy as a horse." She *harrumphed* at the comparison and Magnus smiled. "Pardon the expression."

"I most definitely shall *not*."

"I'll strike a bargain with you—I won't liken you to equine beasts and you don't talk of dying in bed?"

She glared at him but jerked out a nod.

He leaned down to open his satchel. "I've brought you a new book."

"What is it?" She squinted suspiciously. "Some improving tract sent by the vicar?"

Magnus grinned. "No, though that is exactly what you deserve. It is something my mother sent in her last care package." He held it up, even though he knew she wouldn't be able to read it. "*Sense and Sensibility,* by A Lady."

"Sounds like drivel."

He laughed. "You haven't even heard any of it yet." He handed it to her, but she didn't take it.

"Will *you* read to me? Or are you too busy for an old lady."

He *was* busy, but he could hardly say so. "I shall read a bit to you."

And so he read for a quarter of an hour, until she drifted off to sleep.

After putting the volume on her nightstand, he went below and hauled in some coal for the uncomfortably appreciative Sarah.

And now he was standing in Mrs. Tisdale's small foyer, clutching his hat, and loitering. Waiting for *her.*

"You idiot." He mashed his hat down on his head, jerked open the door, and strode down the path like a man who wasn't hoping to

Melissa and The Vicar

encounter Miss Griffin before he had to turn off to head toward Sir Thomas's house.

Magnus didn't encounter her or anyone else before he took the lane that led to the squire's manor. It was a good half-hour walk and by the time Magnus arrived the air was dense with moisture and the sky rapidly turning a gunmetal gray. He predicted he would be caught in in a deluge of biblical proportions on his way home.

The squire's elderly butler, Quarles, opened the door. "Ah, Mister Stanwyck, Sir Thomas is expecting you."

"And how have you been, Quarles?" Magnus asked, slipping out of his coat and handing over his hat before following the older man up the worn stone steps.

"Very well, thank you for asking. Mrs. Quarles and I greatly enjoyed your last sermon, by the way—the one about removing the beam from one's eye first."

"Thank you." Magnus had to admit he was rather proud of that sermon, himself. He'd written it hoping to subtly prod Mrs. Pilkington and Miss Philpot into examining the source of their mutual animus. As far as he could see, it had yielded no success in that area, but several parishioners had commented positively on it.

Quarles led Magnus to the second floor and opened the door to the bookroom, which Magnus had been in before and greatly admired.

Sir Thomas was sitting at his massive Tudor desk reading what looked to be a newspaper. Magnus was, quite frankly—and perhaps ungenerously—surprised to find out the man read anything at all. He knew his thoughts were not befitting to a member of the clergy, and it grieved him to admit it, but he could not bring himself to *like* Sir Thomas. Part of that was due to persistent rumors that the squire made free with not only his servants, but with at least one of his tenant farmer's daughters. If it had been mere rumor then Magnus would have been more vigilant in scouring his mind of such accusations. But, unfortunately, there were several physical manifestations of his suspicions. The most recent was a set of twin boys. Their mother, Etta Felix, had been only fifteen and had died in the process of birthing her children. Before she died, she'd told her mother who the father was. Magnus only knew this because Mrs. Felix had collapsed in his arms a month later, approaching him, rather than the vicar, for guidance.

S.M. LaViolette

When Magnus had approached Mr. Felix—a farmer for the squire and father of ten children, not including his daughter's twins—and offered his assistance, the older man had gone half-mad telling him to mind his own business. The next time Magnus saw Mrs. Felix she had a swollen jaw and refused to meet his eyes, begging him to forget her ill-advised imaginings.

Without their word, he could hardly accuse the squire and put a stop to such behavior. So, here he was, answering the squire's summons like a good, obedient curate.

Sir Thomas didn't look up until Quarles cleared his throat.

Magnus found the affectation amusing rather than humiliating. They both knew Magnus was the son of a marquess and, therefore, several rungs higher on the social ladder than a mere baronet. Sir Thomas also knew Magnus was not financially dependent on this position—or any other—which made him more difficult to torment than an average, impoverished clergyman.

"Ah, Stanwyck." He gestured to a chair across from his desk. "Have a seat." He cut a glance at his butler and said, "Fetch Master William and bring him to the library."

The door clicked shut behind the butler and Sir Thomas stood. "How about a drink, Mr. Stanwyck?"

It was not yet three o'clock. Besides, Magnus felt a visceral reaction at the thought of sharing a drink with this man. "No thank you, Sir Thomas."

"Suit yourself." The squire strode to a console table with several decanters. He was a barrel of a man who liked to dress in riding clothes, regardless of the fact that he was a dreadful equestrian and too heavy, clumsy, and unfit to ride to hounds. Magnus had only seen him astride once, his mount a magnificent stallion. The squire had ridden him hard, sawing at the horse's mouth brutally enough to leave pink foam on his lips and bloody flanks from his spurs.

"Never trust a man who would inflict pain on an animal," his father's old stablemaster, Belkin, had said more than once. And Belkin was a man respected throughout West Yorkshire for his skill with both horses and hounds.

Sir Thomas lowered himself behind the desk, raising a half-full glass of amber liquid to his lips and draining at least a third of it.

"So," he said, setting down the crystal with a loud thump. "How are things in New Bickford since I've last been here? I understand there is a new tenant at Halliburton Manor?"

Melissa and The Vicar

"Yes, a young lady and her aunt."

The squire gave him a leer that made him feel dirty. And hostile.

"Comely?"

Magnus forced a smile onto his stiff lips. "Miss Griffin has come to New Bickford to convalesce."

"Ah, one of those—a malingerer." Distaste and disinterest replaced lechery and he grunted, putting Miss Griffin from his mind, which was just as well because Magnus's hands had already tensed and an anger he was unaccustomed to feeling had begun to surge through him.

"Still, I'll wager any new female has put the rest of your flock into a flutter." The squire gave a rude laugh and a doubly rude look. "When are you going to marry one of 'em?" His smile widened, exposing yellowed, crooked teeth. "Or do you like havin' 'em all panting after you? Like so many bitches with—"

"Sir Thomas."

The other man blinked, as if he were surprised that Magnus wouldn't join in with his crude insinuations.

For a moment Magnus thought he might take issue with being the object of such a chiding tone from a mere curate—no matter his connections—but then he burst out laughing.

"Sorry to ruffle your feathers, Reverend. I'm not accustomed to men of God and I'm afraid I keep company that isn't nearly so . . . er, pure."

The library door opened and a boy of about eleven entered, his body as stout as his father's, his expression sullen and unpleasant.

"Ah, here he is, the young savage." The squire sounded proud to have produced such a son. "Come and greet the reverend like a proper gentleman."

The boy came to stand before him, his gaze scathing as it flickered from Magnus's collar up to his eyes. "Mister Stanwyck."

He'd had run-ins with Master William on more than one occasion. Each and every time he'd seen the boy, he'd either been tormenting a younger child or breaking something or abusing an animal. Like father, like son.

Again, Magnus forced himself to smile. "Good afternoon, William."

"Will is headed off to Eton come the end of the summer. You're an Eton man, aren't you, Mr. Stanwyck?"

He was, but it wasn't something he took excessive pride in, nor was he interested in rehashing his school days with this man.

"Are you looking forward to school?" he asked William, instead of answering his father.

"Yes, Mister Stanwyck." A sly expression entered the boy's eyes and Magnus knew he was the type who would enjoy the brutish entertainments of boarding school.

"He's looking forward to gettin' up to trouble, is what he's doing," the squire said, his words an unpleasant echo of Magnus's thoughts. "But he's an ignorant clod when it comes to his letters and needs a few months of tutoring to whip him into shape." Sir Thomas's small piggy eyes turned mean. "Or it'll be a real whip I'll use on him."

Magnus fought a wave of revulsion. If physical punishment of an animal was disgusting to him, physical punishment of a child was anathema. Even a repulsive child such as William.

"I'm afraid I have no time to offer any tuition, Sir Thomas. However, you know Mr. Dinkins in the village is a retired schoolteacher and takes pupils. I will enquire and—"

"I don't want old Dinkins, I want you."

Magnus met his belligerent stare with a cool look. "I'm afraid I don't have the time. As I said—"

"You don't have the time? Or is it the inclination you don't have?"

Magnus frowned. "I beg your pardon?"

"Think you're too fancy to tutor a mere squire's boy, *Lord* Magnus?"

"I assure you, Sir Thomas, that is the farthest thing from the truth. But my schedule is—"

The squire came around the desk, his posture menacing. "Make time in your schedule."

Magnus stood. The squire might outweigh him, but Magnus had no doubt he would be able to turn the other man inside out with his fists.

He flinched away from the unusual violence of his own thoughts; just standing near Sir Thomas was enough to poison a person. It was past time to end this encounter.

"I'm sorry, Squire, but I cannot."

The room crackled with emotions and Magnus wondered for a moment if the other man would strike him. What shocked him was that he would welcome it; he would welcome the opportunity to respond in kind.

Melissa and The Vicar

But the squire—a man who was essentially a bully and a coward—must have seen that in his eyes. He laughed and jerked his chin at his son. "We'll not keep you, seein' as how you're so *busy*. Show the reverend out of my house, William."

The journey from the library to the front door took place in silence. Magnus had just put on his hat and opened the door when the boy spoke.

"You'd better have a care, *Mister Stanwyck*," he said with a tone more suited to a boy five years older. "People who cross my father don't prosper."

Magnus looked down into the boy's sly, too-knowing eyes. "I wish you the best of luck at school, William."

Chapter Six

Mel kept missing him.
 She'd arrive at Mrs. Tisdale's to learn he'd just left. Or he would call on Halliburton House while she was out wandering and exploring. Their second Sunday in New Bickford he'd not been in church because he'd been called to a sick parishioner's house.

Even yesterday, when she'd had the ill chance to encounter Hector on the pathway—and the little brute had chased her halfway to town—Mr. Stanwyck didn't appear to rescue her. Her valiant protector seemed to have abandoned her.

Mel felt as though fate was conspiring against her and then reminded herself that fate—or God, if you leaned in that direction—was more likely to be *protecting* the curate by keeping them apart.

When Mel finally encountered him, it was at the vicarage. He was returning just as she was leaving, naturally. Mrs. Heeley had invited Mel and her "Aunt Daisy" to the weekly ladies' tea. This week's tea had been especially well attended as everyone was preparing for the upcoming fête.

In the spirit of being a better aunt, Daisy had dressed in her "aunt clothing" and accompanied Mel without complaint.

The hour had not been nearly as tedious as Melissa had feared, although she could see Daisy's patience had worn thin with topics like whether Mr. Skiperson should be allowed to make the punch after last year, whether they should have an alternate, indoor location for the dance that would take place that evening because Jemmy Henderson—the village's oldest resident at ninety-seven (Mrs. Tisdale was nipping at his heels, so to speak) had predicted rain and he'd only been wrong once, back in '71.

And so forth.

Daisy's thin veneer of civility was cracking by the end of the hour.

They'd just said their goodbyes and closed the lychgate when Mister Stanwyck came striding toward them, coming from the direction of town.

Melissa and The Vicar

"What a delightful surprise." His face lit up in a way that made Daisy nudge Mel in the ribs with her elbow.

"Stop it," Mel hissed through a smile.

"Good afternoon, Mister Stanwyck."

Mel wanted to roll her eyes at Daisy's distinctly un-aunt-like tone of voice.

"You ladies must have been at the meeting Mrs. Heeley was hosting. Did you settle all the details for the fête?"

"Oh, was it a meeting?" Daisy asked with exaggerated innocence. "It seemed more like a riot with tea and biscuits."

The curate grinned. "Patience, Mrs. Trent—the Devil is in the details."

Daisy gave a sinful, throaty chuckle. "Oh, is that where he is? Because I've been—"

"Yes, we made the final arrangements for the fête, thanks to Mrs. Heeley's patience," Mel interjected, vowing to strangle Daisy at the first opportunity.

He smiled at what she'd left unsaid: that Mrs. Pilkington and Miss Agnes Philpot's wrangling had taken its toll.

There was an awkward moment of silence as they all struggled for something to say.

Daisy finally broke it. "I'm going to take a walk into the village, Melissa," Daisy said, giving the curate an insufferably gracious smile that warned Mel what was coming. "Perhaps you might walk my niece home, Mister Stanwyck."

Mel's face heated. "Really, that's not nec—"

"I'd be delighted." And he actually *looked* delighted.

Still, she hesitated. "I'm sure you must be terribly busy."

"Actually, I was just going to pop in at home and fetch a book I was meant to deliver to Mrs. Felix." He cocked his head charmingly. "Have you met the Felixes? They are your nearest neighbors to the east."

"They must be the only people who haven't paid a visit in the past two weeks," Daisy said with heavy irony.

This time the curate's laugh was a little uncertain.

Mel edged slightly in front of Daisy and looked into his perfect, clear blue eyes. "If you're sure it wouldn't be out of your way—"

"Of course not, I've loads of time to spare."

S.M. LaViolette

Mel was pretty sure he was lying—people were constantly calling on him for something or other—but she wanted to spend time with him; she wanted it with an intensity that frightened her.

"It'll take me only a half a jiffy," he said, his teasing smile telling her he remembered very well the last time he'd used the phrase.

Mel watched him stride away, trying not to let her eyes wander all over his tall, muscular, loose-limbed body. And failing.

Daisy poked her in the ribs. "There, you owe me for that one, Mel."

She turned to find Daisy smirking at her. "I thought you were going to town."

"A more appropriate response would be, 'Thank you, Aunt Daisy.'"

"Try to control yourself, Daisy—and remember you're supposed to be the mature one."

Daisy snorted. "Maybe *you* should have played the aunt."

"Yes, well, I'll know better next time."

Daisy's eyes widened. "Next time—"

"Now who can't take a joke?" Mel made a sweeping motion with her hands. "Shoo, go away."

She was grateful to have a few moments of peace to collect herself before the reverend returned. Mel knew she should be walking into town with Daisy right now. This attraction she felt for the glorious curate was nothing but a severe disappointment in the making. All she had to offer him were lies—or disgrace if he were ever to find out who she really was. And exposure, she knew, became more likely every day. Daisy wasn't the only one misbehaving. One of the two footmen they'd brought with them was debauching a maid from the local squire's house. Jenny had sneaked out twice that Mel knew of to meet with the innkeeper's son. Her household was beyond her control.

Her dream of staying a little longer than the five weeks she'd originally planned was seeming less and less like a wise idea, and not just for her. She could see how Mister Stanwyck was coming to like her—to care for her. He wasn't the kind of man to play games or hide his feelings. Everything he did was honest: she'd never met another person, male or female, with so little guile.

While everything she did—everything *about* her, down to her name—was nothing but a lie.

Melissa and The Vicar

Just what would the handsome, kind, and honest Reverend Stanwyck say if he knew he was offering to walk home the most notorious madam in London? She already knew he thought her far younger than she was—not an uncommon mistake given her diminutive size.

As flattering as that was, she knew she should have corrected him when he made the passing reference to young ladies in the village and included her among their number. Lord, she was pretty sure she was actually *older* than him.

"Are you ready?"

She turned away from her misery to find him holding a small bundle of twine-wrapped books in his hands.

Yes, she was as ready as she'd ever be.

She didn't wait for his arm because having contact with him right now would not be good for her state of mind. So, they walked side by side, not touching.

It was Mr. Stanwyck who broke the somewhat awkward silence. "How has Hector been treating you?"

Mel couldn't help smiling. "I think we've reached an accommodation. I bring him stale bread and let him pretend that *he* was the one who actually brought it to his hens, and he lets me pass unmolested."

He laughed, the sound warming her. "I'm pleased to hear you've taken his measure so quickly," Mister Stanwyck said. "Tell me, you've been here coming on two weeks. How are you finding country life?"

"I'm enjoying myself." Mel was surprised to realize that was true. She *did* enjoy the slower, quieter pace of life. She also enjoyed shucking off the burden of operating a business, but she could hardly tell him that. "At first I thought I'd never get used to the silence, but now I like it."

"This is really the first time you've been out of London?"

"Yes, it really is."

"And have you lived with your aunt long?"

"Most of my life—since my parents died in a carriage accident." She'd made up this part of her story before coming.

"Oh, I say—I'm terribly sorry."

Melissa felt bad for making *him* feel bad. "Please, do not apologize. I was too young to remember them." Which was not entirely a lie. She certainly had no memory of her father.

"You are made of stern stuff if you can tolerate the London summers."

"My uncle's business kept him in town," she said, making up this new chapter of her story on the spot.

He turned to her. "Oh, and what business was he in?"

Melissa was transfixed by his sweet, blue stare. "Um—"

His tanned cheeks flushed. "I don't mean to pry. I was—"

"You aren't prying—and his business is certainly no secret." Except to Melissa, whose brain was spinning like a butter churn to come up with something. Joss's face flashed into her mind and she said, "He was a butcher."

"Ah." He nodded, his forehead slightly furrowed.

Mel felt like a fool: just why would a butcher not be able to leave London during the summer?

"He owned several butcher shops," she added, digging herself in deeper. "He always said he'd take a holiday but his employee problems were constant." That was certainly true with a whorehouse—why would it be any different in any other business?

The curate nodded, seemingly convinced by her argument. "And does your aunt still have all those, er, shops?"

"Thankfully no—or we'd not be here." Before he could pursue the subject of her life in London she gestured to the bundle of books. "What have you got there?"

He held them up so she could see the spines. "These are just a few novels my mother sent to me. She is a voracious reader."

"How kind of her to share her books."

"Yes, she is a very kind lady as well as being a wonderful mother."

A vicious punch of yearning made her stumble, and he was quick to take her arm.

"All right?" he asked, glancing down at her with a look of concern.

She nodded and he released her.

Because she wasn't suffering enough, she went back for more. "You sound very close to your mother."

"Yes, we are." He grinned at her. "My brothers tease me that I am her pet, but I think they are just jealous."

What must it be like to have parents one loved and respected? Not that she hadn't loved her own mother. Once.

"Where is your family?"

"I am from Yorkshire."

Melissa and The Vicar

That surprised her. "You don't sound like any of the Yorkshiremen I've met."

"And have you met many?"

Mel didn't think he'd care to hear just how many. "A few."

"My mother is a southerner and was adamant about stamping out any of the local dialect—not that we all can't speak it, anyway."

"How did your father feel about that?"

"He adores my mother and left the raising of the children in her hands."

"It sounds like you had an idyllic childhood."

He must have heard something in her voice, because she felt his eyes on her. "Yes, I was happy. Very happy and I know that makes me lucky. I'm fortunate in both my family and my good health." He paused. "The Felix family," he lifted the books, "the people I'm giving these books to, well, they're an example of a not-so-lucky family."

"Oh?"

"Their eldest daughter died last year—after delivering twin sons." He hesitated. "I'm afraid the boys were born out of wedlock."

Mel took a moment to absorb that.

"Mr. Felix is a tenant farmer who has ten—well, nine, now—children of his own to feed. Mrs. Felix sells eggs and milk and takes in laundry, but they barely have enough to feed and clothe everyone, not to mention afford luxuries like books."

They walked for a while in silence. "You still visit them even though their daughter had children without being married?" It took her a moment to realize that he'd stopped walking. She turned and looked up at him and his expression stunned her. "What is it?" she asked.

"Do you really believe it is the place of a vicar or curate to heap misery on people like the Felixes by judging them—by withholding aid?"

Mel was taken aback by his vehemence. She opened her mouth, but before she could answer his cheeks flooded with color.

"I *do* beg your apology, Miss Griffin. That was ill done of me to snap at you. I'm afraid I'm only so vehement because there is some truth in what you say. I'm ashamed to admit there are people in our community who shun the Felixes."

Mel could guess who some of those people were, but she left the subject alone. She was more relieved than she would have believed to discover he was not angry with her.

"It was a foolish question, Mister Stanwyck, you were right to be annoyed."

"There are no foolish questions."

"I imagine I could contrive a few."

That surprised a laugh out of him.

This time, she took his proffered arm and they resumed their walk.

After a few moments of companionable silence he said, "I must confess that I often become angry at how little I'm able to help some members of the congregation."

Mel was too surprised by his confession to answer.

"It eats at me that I cannot do anything to help the Felixes, even though I know their daughter was gravely wronged."

"Do you mean she was—"

"Yes, I believe she was forced—" His words were hurried, as if he didn't want her to have to say the dreadful word.

"She told you this?"

He shook his head, his jaw so tight she could see the clenched muscles beneath his skin. "No, but she told her mother before she died."

Mel wished she could say she was surprised, but she'd seen it too often. Most of the women—and men—who came to work for her had started selling themselves after similar incidents. Although she had to admit that she hadn't expected rape to be common in a community as quaint and seemingly happy as New Bickford.

"I'm afraid I have shocked you with my plain-speaking. I apologize. It is hardly a suitable subject for a young woman."

"I would have thought young women—or any women—were *exactly* who the subject was for." Mel could tell by his stiffening posture that her statement was the last thing a young, innocent female would have made. Well, it was too late to change her words now. She plowed on. "Do you know who is responsible?"

She felt his hesitation—the struggle inside him between what was proper to divulge and whether he had already said too much. It did not escape her attention that this man who everyone else brought their troubles to was considering unburdening himself to her. The thought warmed and frightened her at the same time.

"I do know." He paused for a long moment. "But I have no evidence and to accuse this particular man—even *with* evidence—well, it would be difficult to get justice for the Felixes. In fact, it would likely make their situation even worse."

Melissa and The Vicar

"Worse than a dead daughter?" Even as the words left her mouth, she wanted to pull them back. He did not deserve her anger.

He stiffened at her words and the anger in them, but he did not back down. "Yes—worse for *her* children and the nine children of Mr. and Mrs. Felix who are still alive."

He was right—she knew he was, even though it tore her up inside to admit it. Her anger drained from her as quickly as it had flared. Why would she—of all people—believe that justice waited for the poor and powerless? The only way to protect oneself in this world was to have money—a lot of money.

***

At her insistence, Magnus left her at her front gate.

"Thank you, Mr. Stanwyck. Please, you needn't walk me all the way to my door." She was no longer angry and her lips curved into the lazily amused smile he'd begun to look forward to. But this time the smile did not reach her eyes. Magnus couldn't help wishing she didn't feel like she had to pretend for his sake.

He could see she wanted to get away, so he bowed over her hand and watched until she reached the front door, which she entered without looking back.

Magnus walked away feeling like a coward, a thief, and a brute.

A coward because he'd been relieved when she'd let the subject of the Felixes drop.

A thief because her aunt had carelessly tossed out her Christian name and he'd snatched it up like a greedy squirrel with a nut, tucking it away: Melissa. She was Melissa.

And a brute because he'd brought up a subject no gently raised young lady should have to think about.

Most women—young *and* old—would have blanched or flinched away, but she had met the issue head on. Magnus groaned. Rather than finding her reaction insensitive or brash, he'd found it indicative of intelligence and unflinching resolve to say what was right.

He knew what was happening: he was falling in love with her. It was possible he'd *already* fallen. However, never having been in love before he couldn't be sure. But if love meant wanting to be with one person more than anybody else or thinking about them when you weren't with them or wanting to know everything about them . . . Well, if that was love, he'd definitely fallen into it.

Of course, there was also his physical reaction to her. *That* feeling Magnus was painfully certain of—not that he was ashamed. He believed God had designed man and created all the emotions he felt—even lust. It was man's place to decide when, and if, a particular emotion was appropriate.

Magnus agreed the act of physical love was for procreation, but he also believed it should be *enjoyed* by both husband and wife. What he'd been thinking and feeling the brief time since meeting Melissa—*Miss Griffin*—was not appropriate.

Last night, when he'd not been able to sleep, he'd dressed himself and gone to the church. He loved the intense quiet and peace of the building at night almost as much as he loved seeing it full and alive on Sunday.

Sometimes, just sitting in a pew and *being* was enough to clear his mind of the petty distractions of life. Yes, Mrs. Heeley was a dreadful cook who insisted on preparing part of every dinner she invited Magnus to. Yes, the vicar tended to leave the unpleasant tasks that accrued for Magnus to handle. Yes, Magnus sometimes became irritated with the backbiting and gossiping that happen among the parishioners whenever more than two people assembled.

But all those small things could build up and get in the way if a person was not vigilant; if a person did not remind themselves what truly mattered.

Last night Magnus had reminded himself what mattered. He'd become a cleric because of a desire to serve God by serving his people. It didn't matter where he was or which of God's people he found himself among, he could always serve God.

But the depth of emotion that was beginning to build inside him for Miss Griffin was becoming a distraction from his chosen purpose and he did not want to view either her, or his feelings for her, as a distraction. So, he'd gone to the church to ask God for guidance.

Magnus knew both members of the clergy and a few laypeople who claimed God answered them—and he believed them. During his first year in seminary he began to think that perhaps he was deficient—unworthy—because God had never spoken to him. His anxiety at the lack of divine communication had grown until it was a crisis of confidence: was he God's chosen instrument or merely a pretender?

Luckily, an older and wiser man—a retired vicar who'd been a bit godlike himself when it came to age and wisdom—noticed Magnus's growing agitation and misery and intervened before he did something that would be difficult to undo.

Melissa and The Vicar

The man had, quite simply, explained that God's answers—his voice—came in an infinite variety of forms. Like the flash of enlightenment so often spoken of in novels, Magnus understood that he'd fallen into that trap of the young and taken what he'd heard literally.

The realization had been lightning-like, but it had taken years for Magnus to recognize that the sense of peace God sometimes granted in response to a prayer was his answer. Last night his answer had been a decision that he must declare himself to Miss Griffin. He would have no peace until he made his heart known to her. If she rejected him, he would go on. But if he didn't speak—to spare his pride—he'd be doing himself a disservice and would also be less of a man. Pride, he knew, had no place in love.

Magnus accepted the very real possibility that her regard for him had not progressed as rapidly as his for her. Oh, he knew she *liked* him, enjoyed his company, and found him physically attractive—this last because she had said as much. But those things were a far cry from love. Was it wise to approach her so soon?

In the general scheme of things, he would never have thought of being so hasty. But she was leaving in a few weeks. While she hadn't stated an exact date, she wouldn't be here beyond another month.

What he had to work with was a month. After that she'd return to London and his place was here.

He shifted the books he was bringing to the Felixes from one hand to the other, staring at the gilt spines, the sight of which reminded him of what he was going to do. Would Miss Griffin *want* to be the wife of a curate?

He thought of the way she'd taken responsibility for Mrs. Tisdale without even being asked—that certainly demonstrated an interest in caregiving.

But then Magnus considered her impassioned, and rather unconventional, response from earlier; was she the type of woman who would be accepted by the rather parochial society that made up most of rural Britain? She was a young woman, but she was no chit fresh from the schoolroom. The fact that she was so personable and attractive and yet unmarried at her age must mean she wished to be unwed. Perhaps she had expectations that many men could not fulfill?

He left the road and climbed the stile that led to the Felix farm, his mind sifting through the few instances he'd seen her with others. It was true she got along with Mrs. Tisdale better than anyone other than her servant, Sarah, but Mrs. Tisdale was an outsider. How would a woman of such strong character deal with the likes of Mrs. Pilkington?

Magnus grimaced at the thought, which was perhaps unfair. After all, who *would* deal well with Mrs. Pilkington? Even Mrs. Heeley, the most unflappable of people, found the woman taxing. But Mrs Heeley's response was to ignore her and smile. He could not see Melissa doing such a thing. Wouldn't he be wiser turning his attentions to a woman who was more biddable, retiring, and suited to his life's work?

Magnus tried to think of the young ladies who'd made their interest in him abundantly clear since he'd come to the parish three years earlier. But the only face he could summon was Miss Griffin's, Melissa's. Yes, a curate owed his parishioners some consideration when it came to taking a wife. But what about *his* wants? Didn't *he* deserve a say in his life's companion?

The thatched roof of the Felix cottage came into view and Magnus was relieved to turn his thoughts to more immediate and mundane matters.

Chapter Seven

*D*earest Joss,
     I am going to choose to believe the silence on your end is due to the fact business is so brisk and not because some catastrophe has over-taken you.

No doubt you have been on tenterhooks waiting for *The Further Adventures of Melissa in the Country*. All jesting aside, I've been having a rather adventurous time.

I'm sure you remember the old lady I mentioned in my last letter—a certain Mrs. Eunice Tisdale? And I know I mentioned that Sarah accepted double compensation to act as nurse/housekeeper. You will scarcely believe what I am going to say next: Sarah has decided she will stay in New Bickford when I return with the others to London.

Yes, it is the same Sarah we both know—she who has been scolded times beyond counting for sneaking out to the stables, sneaking out of the house, for—well, I shall speak plainly—for sneaking in general.

It would seem Eunice is a sort of pied piper of whores because Sarah is not the only one taken in by her rough charm.

But the most amazing part? Eunice has decided that she likes *me*. Even though I come between her and her beloved Reverend Stannwyck, she cannot deny she has come to enjoy my company.

She is old, but she is sharp and it didn't take her long to take my measure.

"Like birds, whores of a feather flock together," was her testy response to me when I told her she was in danger of becoming my friend. "Just don't expect to do any flocking with our local curate," she cautioned me just yesterday, not unkindly.

I know you would be crowing if you were not such a kind person, Joss. Yes, it's true: I've become heart-struck by the local curate. Before you jump to any conclusions you should know that I do not speak in jest when I say that <u>every</u> female in the area, marriage minded or not, is at least half-way in love with him. How could they not be?

Mr. Stannwyck is not only angelically handsome, he is quick-witted, humorous, kind, and universally accepting of his fellow man and woman, no matter how trying many of them (Mrs. Pilkington!) might be.

I've been gradually insinuating myself with Mrs. Heeley, the vicar's wife (I can hear your gasp from here) as she likely has the most information to impart *regarding Mr. Stanwyck. I'm confident I will have his entire story from the lady—just as soon as I can determine how to start her talking!*

But if all these tales of his kindness have you thinking him lacking in fiber, you would be wrong.

Although he deals with those around him with unfailing courtesy and good humor, he is possessed of an iron spine and a dangerous, albeit very slow burning, temper. Yes, I have caught a glimpse of it.

Have I piqued your interest? Or are you gnawing on your arm in envy that I have encountered such a specimen of masculinity? Oh, and how very masculine he is. No, it is not all tea cakes and fêtes and sermons for Mr. Stanwyck.

I will give you an example which should serve to illuminate just what I mean—I beg you will not allow it to drive you over the edge into jealous obsession. You are still first in my heart, dearest Joss, even though you are no longer in my bed . . .

But I digress with my taunting.

Two days ago I was exploring the lane in the direction opposite of town (you see what a fine countrywoman I have become?) stomping through the underbrush and risking life and limb in the name of adventure and good health when I came upon a most fascinating sight.

At least a half-dozen people had assembled around a fence and were staring at something near one of the few trees that had been allowed to remain in the pasture.

One of the people, a woman, was particularly agitated, wringing her hands (yes, people actually do that, it seems) and crying. When I inquired if there was anything I could do (see what a Good Samaritan I have become?), she explained. It seemed her son, a young boy of four years of age, had wandered into their very own pasture. Before I could ask her why this was upsetting, I saw an enormous beast lazing near the opposite fence, currently engaged in eating, but switching a small, whip-like tail in a manner that reminded me of a stalking cat.

Yes, you've probably guessed, being the rural gent that you are—the boy had wandered into the pasture reserved for the tenant farmer's prize bull.

And guess who had wandered in after him?

The farmer, whose son it was? No.

Certainly not the mother, because two of the other men were restraining her.

It was, of course, Reverend Stanwyck.

He was in the process of slinking toward the tree, staying along the fence-line as long as practicable. But the time was rapidly approaching when he'd need to cut across the field to get to young Robbie, who had, unbelievably, fallen asleep not far from the tree.

The bull, whose name is—are you ready for this?—Odysseus, was chewing a mouthful of grass, his posture deceptively relaxed. Except for that tail.

Melissa and The Vicar

I won't keep you in suspense any longer. By the time the reverend reached the young boy, Odysseus was more interested in what Mr. Stanwyck was doing than what he was eating. He'd begun to make the restless movements that indicated—according to the growing clutch of bystanders—an interest that would quickly become unhealthy for Mr. Stanwyck.

I can jest about his now, Joss, but at the time I was frozen with terror.

Mr. Stanwyck slipped off the little boy's shirt—a patchwork thing made of pieces of brightly colored fabric. I didn't know why he was doing it at first and wanted to yell at him that the bull was beginning to wander closer.

But it turns out Mr. Stanwyck is not only brave (in addition to all those qualities I listed above and will not irritate you by restating) but intrepid. Before he picked up the boy, he did something with the shirt and then held it in one hand while he propped the waking child on his hip, using his other arm.

By this time the bull was . . . sauntering . . . toward him.

Reverend Stanwyck is—in case I've neglected to mention—a rather sizeable man. He is not anywhere close to your size, of course, but then who is, dear Joss?

Never would I have imagined a man so large and muscular could move so quickly. Of course Odysseus is also large and muscular.

The reverend ran toward the nearest section of fencing rather than heading for the turn-style. Odysseus gained on him in horrifying time.

Just when the bull had lowered his head in a menacing fashion, Mr. Stanwyck hurled the boy's shirt sideways. He must have tied it up around rocks or dirt because the shirt fluttered through the air, far enough to distract Odysseus, who—amazingly enough— veered off to follow it!

The reverend scrambled rather ingloriously over the fence and tore his holy blacks in the process. (Before you ask, nothing shocking was exposed. Unfortunately.)

Like the true hero he is, he merely smiled at the grateful, weeping mother and accepted the praise of his spectators with humble thanks.

Melissa paused, brushing the soft barb of her quill back and forth across her chin as she decided whether or not to share the next part. While it was true that Joss was her closest friend in the world, she wasn't certain she wanted to share everything.

No, perhaps she would keep what happened *after* the Odysseus Affair to herself. It wasn't anything shocking, but it had been an hour she'd enjoyed more than any other she could recall in recent history. Which was probably a sad reflection on the lack of enjoyment in her life this past year or so.

Once the reverend had returned Robbie to his mother and endured the gratitude of the dozen bystanders, Mel had managed to work up enough nerve to make her offer.

"You have a large tear in your waistcoat, Mr. Stanwyck."

A charming notch appeared between his sky-blue eyes as he examined the front of his garment.

"It is up the back—where the seam runs up the garment—you cannot see it from your vantage point. You must have pulled it just the right way to tear."

He met her gaze with a good-natured grimace. "That is unfortunate. I'm afraid I'm not very careful with my clothing and this is my last respectable waistcoat." He picked up his coat, which he'd tossed carelessly on the ground along with his hat, both of which had been kicked and scuffed during the excitement.

She watched as he casually beat his hat with his hand to knock of the dust.

"Nor with your hats, either. You are going to ruin it if you continue on that way," she added in a chiding tone.

He looked up from the battered head covering and grinned before dropping it on his startling fair hair—which was sticking up in all directions and somewhat sweaty from his valiant exertions. "Which way are you headed, Miss Griffin?"

"I was on my way back to the manor," she lied.

"May I walk with you? I was headed back to the vicarage."

"I would like that."

So they'd made their farewells to the others and set off together.

"Do you make a habit of such dramatic rescues, Mr. Stanwyck?"

"No—only one per month, I'm afraid."

"But that isn't true." He gave her a curious look. "You can't have forgotten that you rescued me from Hector not long ago."

He grinned. "If I recall correctly, you were rescuing yourself when I got in your way and you ran me down."

"A true gentleman wouldn't remind me of my cowardice."

He pressed his hand over his heart. "You are correct, that was ill done of me."

"I shall forgive you. This time."

"Tell me, have you found the water yet? When I stopped by yesterday Mrs. Trent told me you were venturing that direction."

"I didn't know you'd called yesterday," Mel blurted. "I'm afraid my aunt neglected to mention it. She's been distracted lately." The

Melissa and The Vicar

distraction was in the form of a groom she'd met from at the Sleeping Ferret, Mel could have added, but chose not to. Instead she said, "Were you looking for me for some specific purpose?"

When he didn't answer immediately, she risked a glance at him. His cheeks had colored—now why would that be? What was he thinking? Or was it merely from his earlier exertions? After all, he'd been running and the day was exceptionally warm. Or was it because—

"I was on a mission from Mrs. Heeley. It seems there is a bit of competition for the largest two booths this coming Saturday. I was sent to ask how much space you would need for your wares?"

Mel swallowed her disappointment at his prosaic question. What had she been expecting him to say? Why was she acting like a besotted fool rather than a whore of almost thirty?

They'd discussed the logistics of booths and tables until they reached the turnoff to the manor.

"Well," he said, removing his hat. "I guess this is where we part ways."

"If you come inside I can get Jenny to mend your waistcoat." She didn't even know if Jenny was home. She'd been just as bad as Daisy lately when it came to gallivanting about town.

He hesitated. "Are you certain that wouldn't be an imposition?"

"Not at all. Jenny is a wizard with a needle." That was true enough. She'd been a seamstress for a tailor before he'd cornered her one day and taken more than her job from her.

"Well, then, I'd be grateful." He held up his hands, which were long, well-shaped, but also bore cuts, scrapes, and burns, signs of his daily labors. "I'm afraid I'm all thumbs when it comes to such things."

They walked up the path toward her house. "You have nobody to mend for you at the vicarage?"

"Mrs. Dennis, the vicarage charwoman, is always glad to do so, but I'm afraid she has been stretched rather thin lately with all the preparations for the fête."

He opened the door.

"Jenny?" Mel called out as they removed their hats in the small foyer. When nobody answered she tossed her hat and gloves on the console table. "Make yourself at home in the sitting room, Mr. Stanwyck. I'll go find Jenny and arrange for some tea."

She left him and made her way to the kitchen, which was at the very back of the house. Mrs. Bunch looked up from the bread she was kneading.

"Are you alone?" Mel asked, glancing around.

Mrs. Bunch frowned, shaking her head. "No, the village girl is here—she's out beating a carpet right now—but that blasted Jenny disappeared the moment I turned my back."

"Drat."

"Why, what is it?" The older woman slapped the loaves into shape, giving a low groan as she straightened her back and wiped her hands on a cloth.

"I've got Mister Stanwyck in the sitting room."

Mrs. Bunch was suddenly awake and aware. "I'll have a tea tray ready in a trice."

Mel cocked her head and smiled, amused by all her employees attempts to throw her together with Mr. Stanwyck. It was true there was nobody so hopeful as a whore.

"Thank you, Mrs. Bunch." She didn't mention about the mending—she could do such a small thing herself.

She found him in the sitting room examining the large landscape above the dormant fireplace.

"I say, this is rather hideous, isn't it?"

Melissa laughed and he immediately looked horrified. "Lord, please tell me it isn't something you brought with you?"

She gave him a look of mock severity. "I'm going to ignore that not so subtle insult to my taste, Mr. Stanwyck. No, it was here when I arrived, along with a library full of books and even clothing in some of the cupboards. Speaking of clothing, Jenny is on an errand." She glanced around and spied a mending basket. "But I can attend to it."

"Oh, are you sure?"

"Do you doubt my ability to do mending?"

He laughed. "It cannot be worse than mine."

"Now, take off your coat, which I will give to Mrs. Bunch when she arrives with our tea. She can brush away all the dust and sponge it clean."

He complied and then hesitated, his hands hovering above the buttons on his waistcoat, as if suddenly sensible to the fact he was about to strip down to his shirtsleeves and cravat. His beautiful face once again flushed. Lord, what an adorable man.

Melissa and The Vicar

"I cannot stitch it while it is on your person, Reverend," she teased. "Or at least I could, but it would be far more shocking to anyone who might walk in on us."

He looked relieved at her levity and nodded.

Mel busied herself with digging through the mending basket for what she needed rather than staring at him like some hungry child outside a sweet shop window.

He handed her the garment and she looked up at him as she took it. Her breath froze in her chest. His eyes—his friendly, amiable, kind, sunny blue eyes—were a dark blue, the pupils huge as he looked down at her. She recognized the expression in them—it was an expression that was her stock-in-trade: desire. Or lust, to put it in raw terms. And oh, how very raw he looked in that instant.

"Thank you, Miss Griffin." There was a harshness in his voice she recognized, as well, and he cleared his throat, his color deepening.

"My name is Melissa, Mr. Stanwyck."

He nodded slowly, as if in sudden understanding. "And I am Magnus."

"Magnus," she repeated. "How. . . unusual." Her voice was breathy, tentative—in other words, completely unlike *her* voice.

And then he smiled and, in a flash, the pleasant, sunny Reverend Stanwyck was back again; gone was the intense, dangerous man she'd caught only a glimpse of.

"It is both unusual and unfortunate. I would tell you all the horrible names I was called in school if I wasn't still suffering from all the scars."

Mel scrambled to gather her wits as he turned and went to the chair across from her.

The garment in her hands was still warm from his body and she almost raised it to her face and inhaled but caught herself in time.

As Melissa recalled her reaction, she stared unseeingly down at the letter she'd been writing to Joss, her mind stuck back in that moment, which remained as clear as crystal in her mind.

Oh, God, she'd thought. *Oh, God. I am lost.*

She shuddered at the memory. What a disaster for a woman like her to fall in love with a man like him. She absolutely could not share either the incident or her true feelings with Joss, no matter how close they were.

Melissa scrawled her name across the bottom of the letter before setting aside her quill.

No, she thought, her heart aching hard enough to break, some things were better kept to oneself.

Chapter Eight

Magnus took out his handkerchief and mopped his brow.

"You could call Jem Brown to do this, Mr. Stanwyck."

He smiled at the vicar and tossed his handkerchief onto the pile of clothing he'd taken off, piece by piece, while he'd struggled with the blasted lychgate. "I've almost got it, Mr. Heeley. You see here." He pointed to the massive hinge, which had somehow become bent and now made a rude snapping sound whenever the gate was opened.

The vicar peered at the gate and nodded. "It's Mrs. Dennis's twins. They like to stand on it and swing back and forth."

Magnus knew that but hadn't wanted to tittle-tattle on the charwoman's sons.

"Well," he said, picking up the metal bar he'd brought to bend it back. "I think just a bit more of this." He inserted the bar and carefully pulled. The hinges were old and he suspected the metal had become brittle with age so he didn't want to handle them too roughly.

He stepped back and moved the gate. There was still a bit of a grinding sound, but nothing to what it had been.

"There. I think that will hold it until we can get Mr. Brown to look at it. I think it may need to be taken off and pounded into shape properly."

The vicar gave the gate an experimental push while Magnus returned the tools to the large wooden box he'd taken from the generously sized stable that served both the vicarage and the curate's cottage. Right now there were only three horses in the twelve-stall building: the vicar's old carriage horses and Magnus's chestnut gelding, Friar.

"Hello, old man," he murmured when the horse came trotting over. "I'm a bad master, aren't I?" he asked, stroking the velvet-soft muzzle. "You need a good hard ride and I've been neglecting you."

"Why don't you take him out?"

Magnus jumped at the sound of the vicar's voice. He'd not realized he was behind him.

The older man leaned against the rail and scratched the big chestnut under his jaw. "He's a fine beast," he murmured, an almost acquisitive tone to his voice. He must have heard it because he cast Magnus a flushed, slightly embarrassed look. "I used to be accounted something of a goer when I was younger."

Magnus hoped he hid his surprise. "Perhaps you would like to take him out for a jaunt, sir?"

The vicar laughed. "No, I'm afraid those days are long behind me."

"They say riding a horse is something you never forget."

"That might be true, but my old bones wouldn't care to remember it. Neither would Mrs. Heeley."

They laughed.

"But you go ahead." Mr. Heeley stroked Friar wistfully. "I'll wager there's a cool breeze down by the water."

Magnus was nodding his agreement when he remembered. "Mrs. Pilkington is expecting me. I, er, spend half an hour with her son every Thursday about this time."

"Ah yes, the one who wants to take orders?"

Well, his mother wanted him to. "Yes, sir."

"You run along; I'll talk to young James." He turned from Friar. "It's been a while since I've spoken to the younger members of the flock." Magnus hesitated and the vicar made a shooing gesture. "You've not had a day to yourself in a while. Go on."

"Thank you, sir." Magnus collected his discarded clothing and changed into his riding togs. It felt odd to be wearing his buckskins and top boots and out of what his brothers teased him as his "God suit." The vicar was right—it had been over a month since he'd taken a half-day to himself. Mr. Heeley was getting on in years and Magnus tended to pick up the duties that involved traveling to the various parishioner households. That kept him busy and this recent trouble with Mrs. Tisdale had just added to his schedule. Still, he enjoyed being with parishioners more than he did studying theology or attending to the managerial aspects of the parish. That was where he and Reverend Heeley diverged—which made them a good team.

Thoughts of Mrs. Tisdale just led to thoughts of Miss Griffin.

He'd not seen her since walking her home after what the villagers were calling the Odysseus Affair two days earlier.

No, he'd not seen her, but he'd certainly thought of her enough. And the things he'd thought. Magnus tried to hold back the vivid

Melissa and The Vicar

images, but he couldn't. You would think he'd watched her dance the Seven Veils rather than mend his wretched waistcoat. But the prosaic action had somehow been both domestic and wildly exotic.

"You idiot," he chided.

Perhaps a good hard ride would tire both body and mind and he could get some sleep tonight.

***

Melissa groaned with pleasure as she lowered her hot, sore feet into the freezing water. Joss had been right—yet again: There was nothing like taking off your shoes and stockings on a scorching day and dipping your toes in the water.

She lay back on the sun-warmed boulder and closed her eyes. She had the fair-skin of a redhead—although mercifully without the freckles—and would burn terribly if she remained uncovered for too long. But just for a moment she wanted to enjoy the sun.

Her morning walk from the manor to Mrs. Tisdale's had been more tiring than she'd expected. The day was heavy and humid and it felt like the white puffy clouds that floated overhead wanted to rain.

She'd wanted to rest for an hour before resuming her journey home but—after enduring five minutes of abuse from Mrs. Tisdale, who'd been in a *mood*, as Sarah called it—Mel had slapped her hat on her head and left a grinning Sarah to deal with the discontented old woman.

She'd felt remarkably like poor Dori must have felt that day; she was too irritable to go home, where she would most likely snap at Daisy—provided Daisy wasn't off in a hayloft with her new beau.

So, instead, she'd marched toward the path Mr. Stanwyck had told her about several days earlier. She recalled, too late, that he'd warned her it was not the nearest beach, but it was the most private.

It had been even farther than she'd thought and she'd been about to turn back when the scraggly trees gave way to seagrass.

And suddenly there it was—an endless, breathtaking expanse of water.

She'd chosen her spot not far from the sheer cliff face, a collection of big round boulders that were partially shaded by the steep rock wall behind them.

Even five minutes of blazing sun was too much and Mel felt her face beginning to redden. She propped herself up on her elbows before tying on her hat and then backing toward the shaded part of the rock.

S.M. LaViolette

Before her, the beach stretched out in a long, gentle curve, the water lapping a shoreline that was made of tiny pebbles rather than the sand she'd been expecting. Not that she'd ever been to a beach, but everyone knew there should be sand.

Stunted trees grew on bluffs that mirrored the curve of the shoreline and her only other company was noisy shorebirds that appeared to live in the cliffs and run back and forth with the action of the waves.

Mel had never believed she'd enjoy solitude as much as she did. Growing up in London—especially the cramped, filthy warren in St. Giles where her mother had settled and eventually died—didn't give a person much opportunity to be alone.

As she gazed toward the endless horizon, she knew coming to New Bickford had been the right thing to do. When the expensive Harley Street doctor had come to see her last year and told her she would die if she didn't take care of herself, she'd needed to consider his words seriously. Did she want to die?

She'd been stunned—and frightened—to realize she didn't know the answer to that. Oh, she was good at the job of living—or at least surviving—but she couldn't recall the last time she'd found true joy in anything. Apparently, her lack of joy had taken its toll on her body and she'd begun to get ill.

It had crept up on her so slowly that she hadn't noticed until she'd coughed up blood. The doctor had called it *gastric ulcerates* and said it was serious enough to kill a person. He'd put her on a diet that was bland enough to kill her, but it had made her feel better almost immediately. He'd also told her that rest was the key to getting better.

Mel had felt so much better after a few weeks on his dreadful diet that she'd forgotten the second part of his prescribed cure: going to the country to rest.

And then, around the New Year, she'd begun to cough—along with several of her employees. Not long after everyone had been sick, some for weeks. But, by the end of April—four months later—she'd noticed she was still coughing. And then she'd coughed up blood. Again.

"I'm not sure you comprehend what I mean, Mrs. Griffin, so let me state it as baldly as I can: it is not a matter of *if* you will die, ma'am, but *when*," the doctor had told her after administering a vile-tasting tonic.

Melissa and The Vicar

So, she'd grudgingly made plans, taking far too long to leave. Instead of departing in the spring she'd not left London until—

A flicker of movement caught Mel's attention and she turned just as a horse and rider leapt from a bluff.

"My God," she whispered, her hand at her throat as man and beast sailed through the air for an impossibly long moment before fluidly making contact with the shore, their movements not stuttering for an instant as they churned up the fine rocks and gravel.

Mel sat up and tilted her hat to shield her eyes, not wanting to miss even a moment of the magnificent display. She'd seen riders in the various London parks and drunken young bucks coming and going from The White House, but she'd never seen anything like this.

The power of the horse's magnificent body was awe-inspiring. And the man mounted on it rode as though they shared one mind. Just as they reached the point where pebbles gave way to the water he reined in and leapt off the horse's back. He leaned forward and took the beast by the harness, giving it what appeared to be a kiss on the nose.

Mel covered her smile with a hand, as if somebody might catch her enjoying the sight of a man being kind to his horse. He removed what she thought was the bridle and then did something to the saddle before turning the horse loose. And then he plucked off his hat and tossed it onto the shore while the horse wandered toward the nearest clump of sea grass.

Mel had suspected it was Mr. Stanwyck, but the sight of his ash blond hair confirmed it. So, he was an excellent horseman to add to all his other skills.

And then he began to remove his clothing.

"Bloody hell," she muttered, sitting forward and twitching her hat even lower, not wanting the bright sunlight to interfere with what she was seeing.

His movements were sure and quick and he gave no care to his garments, which he tossed behind him without even looking.

Even from her lamentably far distance she could see his naked torso was every bit as well-formed as it had felt that first day when he'd rescued her from Hector.

He pulled off a boot while still standing and then the second, hopping around on one stockinged foot, his howl audible even from her vantage point. Mel grinned. Yes, the pebbles might be hard on a bare, tender foot.

His hands disappeared around the front of his body and Mel realized she was holding her breath. It came out in a hiss, along with a vulgar word, when he shoved down breeches, drawers, and stockings in one abrupt motion, stepping out of them as naked as the day he'd come into the world.

But *oooh,* how much more majestic.

He ran to the water, his compact, muscular bottom and impressive thighs flexing as he leapt and then dove into an oncoming wave. Mel held her breath yet again as she waited for him to surface. The seconds ticked past . . .

And then he burst from the water with a yell.

The next quarter of an hour was one of the more enjoyable that she could remember. He played in the water like a joyous sea creature and Mel caught too-rare flashes of water-slicked flesh as he gamboled and cavorted.

She was torn between wanting him to continue his playing and wishing he would emerge. Mel soon noticed that he drifted along with the water. That meant that in order to reach his clothing he'd have to walk not quite—but almost—toward her. She was duplicitous enough to mold her body between the cliff and the rock, deep enough into the crevice to be hidden but still have an excellent vantage point.

What a despicable voyeur she was. She'd long thought her clients who paid to watch were not quite right in the head. Now she realized there was an excitement associated with knowing you were doing something bad, but then doing it anyway.

Mel wriggled to get comfortable, wishing for tea and biscuits—or perhaps even a glass of the fine brandy she often enjoyed even though a lady wasn't supposed to—so she could appreciate the show properly.

She also gave a brief but fervent moment of thanks to whatever deity had made her persevere and walk the extra three-quarters of an hour to reach this rarely used section of water. A beach that *he* had mentioned.

She shifted against the hard rock and squinted to find him but it was too blasted sunny to see anything but the blinding reflection off the water.

As if somebody had heard her complaint a cloud slid across the sun and the glare from the water lessened, giving her an uninterrupted view.

"Praise the lord," she said beneath her breath.

Melissa and The Vicar

It appeared that her luck was in. The sudden lack of sun must have cooled things off for the bather. He'd been swimming arm over powerful arm out toward the horizon but now turned and headed toward the shore. Once again, Mel held her breath as he came closer and closer and—

She was glad nobody else could hear the noise she made.

To say he looked like a water god out of mythology was trite, but, oh, it was so very, very true.

He strode from the waves like some male version of The Birth of Venus. Or The Birth of Adonis or Zeus or one of those randy Greeks or Romans who was always getting his kit off at the drop of a hat.

Melissa realized she was sliding off the rock because she'd leaned forward so much and pushed herself back into her crack, briefly disgusted by her own avidity but quickly suppressing it.

He bent at the waist and slicked water from his legs with both hands.

She swallowed.

When he stood again, he did the same with his arms and then, Great God Almighty, with his chest. Even from this distance she could see he had the smooth, nearly hairless, chest that exceedingly fair men often possessed. He walked toward his pile of clothing and again bent, this time with his bottom toward her.

A humiliating mewling sound escaped her, reminding her that it had been a long time—almost a year—since she'd last taken a lover to her bed. And it had been even longer since she'd taken a *male* lover.

Mel swallowed twice as he dropped into a crouch, his hands doing something with his clothing. How she wished she were close enough to see clearly what she could only imagine at this distance.

He shook his head like a big dog and diamonds of water glinted. And then he turned and flopped onto his clothing, his arms and legs spread to dry in the sun.

Melissa dropped her head into her hands. Good. God.

Beneath the thin summer muslin of her dress her sex was wet and pulsing in a way that made her want to take care of her body's nagging urges this very minute. It wasn't as if moral qualms were holding her back; no, it was that she was engaged in a violent mental argument. Her body wanted release, but her mind wanted a closer look.

Mel knew she should take a third fork—one suggested by the faint voice of conscience—that led back to the manor.

The sun resumed its relentless beating and she looked up to see the cloud had disappeared entirely. She was . . . hot, and not only between her thighs. She was hot everywhere and more than a little sweaty. If she was hot and sweaty, he would be . . .

As if in a trance she pulled on her stockings, tied her garters, and laced up her ankle boots. It would have been easy to slip back up the trail without being seen, but her body was moving toward him, just like she knew it would. The sound of pebbles crunching beneath her shoes was mostly swallowed up by the pounding surf. Still, she was astounded he didn't hear her.

Although the soles of his feet were the first thing she encountered, she forced herself to look at his face before examining the rest of his body. His lips were slightly parted and his breathing deep and even: he'd fallen asleep.

Melissa briefly closed her eyes and said yet another prayer—that he would stay sleeping—since her last had been so effective.

And then she opened her eyes and feasted.

Her jaw dropped lower as her eyes made their way from his face down. He must play in the sun often; although his forearms and face were darker than the rest of his body, his chest and legs were also browned. He did have hair on his torso, just a scattering around his small coral-pink nipples, more in the area between, and then that fascinating thin golden trail that pulled one's gaze south.

Melissa loved a man's upper body, especially when the body was like Mr. Stanwyck's. She swallowed; like *Magnus*. It was the first time she'd said the name—even in her mind—since the day he'd told it to her. She'd avoided even thinking it, as if that was some kind of restraint.

Well, so much for restraint now . . .

He was devoid of fat, his muscular torso ridged and corrugated in ways that made her already watering mouth even wetter. She let her eyes wander over the rounded muscles of his shoulders, the powerful resting bulge of his biceps down to the V of muscles that began at his taut belly and went down and down and . . .

She took her time before arriving at her final destination, her eyes widening at what lay on his flat abdomen, jutting proudly between his compact hips.

My, my, my.

Melissa grinned; the angelic curate possessed a *devilish* weapon. And it was tumescent, as if he drifted in some erotic dream world, his

Melissa and The Vicar

eyes darting restlessly beneath his eyelids, his magnificent body slick with quickly evaporating drops of water beneath the beating sun.

He shifted slightly and made a barely audible sound, his hand coming to rest on his shaft. Mel stared as he grew longer and thicker and hardened. The contrast between his tanned, golden-haired forearm and long, thick, ruddy cock was . . .

Well, it just *was*.

She made a loud gulping sound and it was all she could do not to drop down and take him in her mouth and—Mel froze, horrified. She'd actually begun lowering herself to her knees. She felt woozy at what she'd nearly done and whom she'd almost done it to: a curate, for God's sake.

What a bloody disaster that would have been.

She bit back a groan, her frustration and lust looming as high and powerful as a tidal wave. But she swam against the current of her nature because something told her he wouldn't be happy to wake up and find her attached to his body.

It was a shame, because she could make him so very, very happy.

Mel swallowed both the moisture in her mouth and the carnal thoughts as she gazed down on him, one last look before she left him here. *Oh, Mr. Stanwyck, what a wonderful surprise you turned out to be.*

Mel didn't realize she'd spoken out loud until he twitched and shifted, his hand tightening around his stiff shaft. And then his eyes opened and met hers. For the tiniest fraction of a second his beautiful lips curved into a lazy welcoming smile and his heavy, hooded eyes creased at the corners.

An instant later, he yelled.

***

Magnus was having the most delicious dream. He was naked, hot, and hard and sitting in Mrs. Tisdale's kitchen. That should have been alarming, but it was Miss Griffin and not Mrs. Tisdale who was in the kitchen with him. She was cooking something on the small cookstove. And she was wearing that same apron. But nothing beneath it this time.

A throb of pleasure traveled from his tight, aching balls to his erection as he stared, mesmerized by the way the apron strings met at the base of her spine, the ends dangling between a smooth, rounded bottom that looked like two halves of a peach. And just like a peach, it demanded to be touched, tasted . . .

Magnus sank to his knees behind her, his mouth lowering to one velvet cheek, his hand sliding between her slightly parted thighs. He grunted at the damp, swollen heat, his erection hard enough to cut glass.

She turned and looked down at him, as if he'd called to her, her beautiful face languorous and smiling.

"Oh, Mr. Stanwyck . . . "

Magnus smiled up at her while stroking between his thighs. But the sun behind her blazed so brightly he couldn't see her expression when—

And that's when he realized that he wasn't dreaming.

His body folded into a jackknife position as he brought his knees to his chest. "What the bloody hell?" he yelled, his voice at least three octaves higher than usual.

She didn't move or turn away.

"*Miss Griffin!*"

She cocked her head, as if confused, but she didn't stop staring. Indeed, she lowered her eyes to where his arms wrapped around his knees. He suddenly imagined the view she must have of his exposed rod and jewels only a moment earlier.

"Miss. Griffin." He repeated the words slowly and sternly—using the tone he employed on the disobedient boys he often tutored.

His words seemed to snap her out of whatever shocked state she was in.

"Oh," she said, sounding and looking blank, as if her attention were a thousand miles away, rather than on his erect, exposed—Good Lord—*dripping,* erection. But then she turned around.

Magnus made an embarrassing sound—like a startled hen—and scrambled for his clothing. He seemed to be moving in treacle and his actions were clumsy as well as slow. He missed sticking his foot into the leg of his buckskins three times before he could pull the damned things on.

He yanked on his damp, wrinkled shirt, realized it was on backwards, pulled it over his head so roughly he heard something tear, and then tugged it back on the right way. A cravat was beyond him so he just hung the tortured strip of fabric over his shoulders. He was hunting around for his stockings when he saw she was standing on one of them.

He closed his eyes. If he was stunned, shocked, and rattled how much worse must it be for *her*? While it was true that she was a woman in her twenties rather than a girl fresh from the schoolroom, she was still a maiden. The poor thing had been positively *frozen* in shock looking at him.

Although he had no personal experience with nude women, himself, at least he'd seen renderings of the female form in books. And of course there was that one occasion at seminary when the man he'd roomed with had sneaked a woman into their rooms and then—

Good God! What was he doing thinking of that at a time like this?

Poor Miss Griffin. The most she'd probably ever seen of a man was two days ago when he'd removed his waistcoat. And she'd kept her eyes modestly fixed on her sewing then, he recalled. Magnus could only hope he'd not frightened her for life when it came to the male body.

He needed to calm himself, to approach this rationally, to not frighten her any more than she already was, he needed to—

She bent down and picked up his stocking. "Are you decent, Mr. Stanwyck?"

Magnus gaped. She didn't *sound* ruined . . . In fact, she sounded . . . *amused*?

She shifted from foot to foot and he realized she was waiting. Impatiently, apparently.

"Ah, yes," he said, his voice hoarse as he slipped his arms into his coat. "Quite decent."

She turned and looked up at him, as unreadable as the Sphinx.

They stared, and it was Miss Griffin who broke the silence. "Your stocking."

He glanced down at her hand. "Er, thank you."

A soft knicker made them both turn. Friar had come over to see what the commotion was about. The blasted horse. Why hadn't he done the job of a faithful steed and let him know earlier that he wasn't alone? Why hadn't he watched over Magnus while he slept and—

"May I pet him?"

"Hmm?" He glanced at her as he hopped on one foot, pulling up his stocking. "Er, yes, of course." She turned to Friar and Magnus gave in and sat down in the gravel with an inelegant thump.

"He's beautiful."

He pulled on his boot, his eyes on her long, slender hand as she stroked Friar's neck. Lucky horse.

"What's his name?" She turned to him. "Or is he a she? I haven't been around horses much," she added, when she saw his surprised expression.

"Friar is a he."

"Ah, so a stallion." She nodded, as if storing this piece of information.

"Well, he's a gelding, but you know—" He stopped when he realized what he was saying.

Her mouth pulled up into a half smile that made him look away. Lord. They were sitting here talking about geldings when she'd just seen his—

"Friar?"

Magnus heard the humor in her voice. He pulled on his second boot and got to his feet, brushing off his breeches. "Yes, well, I had originally named him Flyer but my brothers decided it would be amusing to change it."

She cut him a shy smile and he stared. *Now* she was shy? Now? When they were both clothed and speaking of horses? He didn't think his face would ever be a normal temperature or color again.

"That *is* quite amusing," she said, breaking their staring contest.

Magnus snorted. "They certainly thought so."

"You mentioned you had five brothers," she said, not taking her eyes or hand from the horse. "And are they younger, older—"

"I am the youngest."

That information made her look at him. "The youngest of six boys. They must all dote on you."

"Yes, well, I'm actually more of a family pet than a sibling—at least that's what my brothers would say if you asked any of them."

She laughed, and the sound warmed him as well as reminded him of the oddity of their conversation. She'd just seen him naked and sprawled and, well, *erect*. And yet they were talking about siblings? Perhaps she was in shock?

"No sisters?"

"No, much to my mother's chagrin." He stroked the other side of Friar's neck, earning an approving nicker.

"Are you close in age?"

"I'm seven years younger than Philip the closest to me in age—and seventeen years younger than Cecil my oldest brother." They stroked Friar in silence while she absorbed that information. "Do you have any brothers or sisters, Miss Griffin?"

Melissa and The Vicar

She shook her head slowly back and forth. "No, just me."

"I know your aunt raised you—did she have no children of her own?"

"They were unable to have children."

"They must have enjoyed having you with them."

She dropped her hand and turned to him. "I'm sorry, Mr. Stanwyck."

His face, which had just begun to feel normal, flamed. "Er—"

"I shouldn't have been staring while you were, um—"

Magnus cleared his throat. "Ah yes, quite so." He fiddled with Friar's halter. "Well, there's no harm done. I'm fine. And so are you, at least—" He bit his lower lip hard enough to taste salt and metal. "At least it seems you are fine, but—"

Magnus, you idiot, shut up!

He cursed—thankfully only in his mind—and clamped his jaws shut to prevent further idiocy from pouring out of his mouth. Instead, he busied himself with Friar, the whole time aware of her stillness—which was made all the more noticeable by his flapping about like a landed fish. Was she in a state of shock? Was that why she was so quiet? *He* was bloody well in shock. Just how long had she been standing there? And what about him? In his dream he'd been kneeling between her—

"Mr. Stanwyck?"

"Yes, Miss Griffin?" Magnus was pleased to hear he didn't sound like a squeaking rodent.

"Do you forgive me? For invading your privacy?"

He saw humor and a little regret in her face, but no embarrassment. Just how could that be when he was all but choking on mortification? Or perhaps she was simply better at hiding it?

He dredged up a smile from somewhere. "Of course, Miss Griffin. I mean, there is nothing to forgive. It is I who was—" He grimaced, stopping himself before the words "naked and erect" slipped out. "In any case. Were you heading back?"

She nodded.

"I will accompany you."

She glanced at the horse.

"I'll lead him and walk beside you."

They walked toward the path she must have taken—not the one he rode down, which was wider and longer and not as convenient for those from town. But he'd been out for a ride and unconcerned about time. It had been his half-day of freedom, after all. Well. That had ended in embarrassment, hadn't it? And probably more than one actionable crime, come to think of it. Public indecency? Endangering the morals England's women?

"May I ask you a question?"

He turned to find her looking up at him. "Of course."

"When did you decide you wanted to be a vicar?"

As questions went it wasn't anything new. Still, he couldn't help feeling she was asking it for different reasons than he was accustomed to. But it was better than stewing on what had just happened.

He helped her up over the bluff before answering. "I was at a funeral—I must have been nine or ten." He glanced at her and grimaced. "I hate to admit it, but I don't even remember who the funeral was *for*. What I do recall is that my father and my brother Cecil and I were the only mourners at the graveside. It seemed the deceased had been alone in the world—no family, no friends, except we three and the vicar. In any case, I recall the vicar's words quite distinctly. He said the afterlife was something every person had to face alone, but death itself was not. He went on to say that one of a clergyman's important duties was to deliver the last rites but that wasn't his only—or even most important—duty, which was to keep a dying person from being alone. I recall thinking to myself—why, what an honor that must be, to be the last person to see another human on their way out of this life—to make sure nobody felt alone, even if they *had* been, in life, very lonely." He shrugged and looked down. She was staring up at him, her mouth open.

His face heated. "You are looking at me as if I have just said something . . . shocking."

"Oh. Well, I don't mean to." Her beautiful face wore a puzzled expression. "It's just—" Magnus stared: now *she* was blushing. Well, it was about damned time. But why *now*?

She shook her head, as if to dismiss whatever it was she'd been about to say. Magnus stopped and laid a hand on her forearm to stop her. "Hold a moment. Tell me, it's just—what? What were you going to say before you stopped yourself?"

Her lips tightened, as if she wasn't going to speak, but then, "It's just that I thought your reasons would be leading people to God or saving souls or something of that nature."

Magnus laughed. "You must think I'm dreadfully pompous if you believed I would say such a thing."

Melissa and The Vicar

Her flush deepened and she looked away, staring at her hands. "No, no, I don't think that at all."

He leaned toward her, feeling bad about laughing at her response after he'd pried it out of her. "I know you wouldn't think such an uncharitable thing, Miss Griffin. I was just teasing you a little."

She looked up just then, her face barely an inch from his; there were flecks of gold in her green eyes. An expression that looked like pure agony contorted her perfect features and then, suddenly, her hands were on his face and her lips were pressing against his.

Chapter Nine

Melissa felt like she was outside her body, watching as a disaster happened. Watching as *she* caused a disaster.

She'd begun to feel oddly light when he'd described his reasons for entering the Church: because he never wanted anyone to die alone. She'd been a hair's breadth away from bursting into tears. Melissa *never* cried. Or at least she hadn't since that day: the day her mother had sold her for less than Melissa now spent on a pair of gloves.

But she'd certainly felt like crying today—not from grief, but from the unrelenting beauty of the man beside her. He wasn't just beautiful on the outside, he was beautiful within. And like the wicked destroyer—the despoiler of anything good or pure—she couldn't keep her hands, or in this case, her lips, off him.

He stood as still as a statue—a warm, breathing statue—as she slid her hands from his jaw to the back of his neck, inexorably pulling him lower. She angled her head and stroked between his slack lips, the action making him shudder and pull away. At least he tried to pull away, but Mel held him tight, drawing her body closer to his when she couldn't move him. The second time she stroked into him his hands landed on her upper arms. Gently, but firmly, he set her away from him.

Their eyes locked. She was pleased to see he was breathing hard, his fair skin darkly flushed, his normally sky-blue eyes the deep navy of the ocean. He swallowed hard, his gaze flickering from her mouth to her eyes and then back. And then he let out a low, animal groan, his expression tormented as his arms drew her closer, as if his limbs rather than his will, were controlling his body. This time he was not tentative. He crushed her against him, his mouth slanting over hers, his tongue plunging into her.

Mel thrust her hands beneath the unbuttoned flaps of his coat, wishing desperately there wasn't a shirt and waistcoat between her questing fingers and his body. An image of what he'd looked like, naked, slick, and hard, lying in the sun—like some pagan offering— flooded her mind and she groaned and latched on to his tongue,

Melissa and The Vicar

sucking as suggestively as she could. Which was more than most men could stand without crumbling.

But Mr. Stanwyck, it seemed, was made of sterner stuff.

He thrust her away and took a staggering step back, breaking contact, only stopped from getting even farther away by the big body of his horse.

He snatched off his hat and grimaced, squeezing his eyes shut before opening them again.

"I am *terribly* sorry, Miss Griffin. That was ill done of me."

The laugh burst out of her before she could help it and she bit her lip, grieved that she'd made him look so mortified. She reached out to take his hand, to squeeze it, to tell him she wasn't mocking him. But the freezing expression on his face stopped her.

"Dishonoring young women is no laughing matter to me, Miss Griffin." He spoke in a tone she'd never heard—a hollow, coldly angry, almost Godlike tone that would be perfect for preaching fire and brimstone.

She'd somehow managed to turn this affectionate, warm man into an Old Testament preacher.

"I know it isn't," she said, lowering her eyes from his—which burned the same blue as the hottest part of a flame. "You are correct."

They stood in silence, hearing only their breathing and the tweeting of birds.

He clapped his hat on his head. "Right then. Shall we walk?"

"You don't need to escort me back. I'll be—"

"Nonsense." She looked up at his tone, which was once again light, sunny—and determined—even if there were now clouds covering his blue eyes.

Mel looked from his forearm to his face and laid her hand on his sleeve.

They walked in uncomfortable silence for a few minutes, until Mr. Stanwyck spoke. "I haven't been to Mrs. Tisdale's yet today. Have you seen her?"

The topic of the old lady brought the mood back to earth rather quickly. "I have. I'm afraid I left in a bit of a snit."

He chuckled and the sound loosened some of the stiffness between them. "Well, it's a rare person she has *not* done that to."

"Certainly not to you?"

"Oh yes," he said, his free hand absently looping and unlooping the reins as they walked, the restless gesture giving lie to his calm words and tone. "She's even managed to make the vicar lose his almost legendary placidity."

Mel laughed. "I must know what she did."

The next few moments—until they came to the fork in the road—passed in only slightly stilted conversation.

"I thought you were going to Mrs. Tisdale's?" she asked when he turned in her direction.

"I am, but I'll see you back to Halliburton Manor, first."

"But that will take you out of your way," she protested.

"Yes," he agreed, "But on Friar the journey will take only a fraction as long."

She could tell by his tone that he was determined.

"I've heard a rumor," he said, changing the subject.

A frisson of fear shot up her spine. "Oh?"

"Yes, I understand you will be selling some of your stylish London garments at the fête."

Mel exhaled with relief. "Yes, you heard correctly."

"The news has caused much joyous celebration among the female population."

"Well, I hope nobody sets their expectations too high. I'm afraid I shan't have anything like ball gowns."

He cut her a glance. "Oh? You are retaining all of those?"

"I do not own any ball gowns."

"That surprises me."

"And why is that?"

"I thought one did nothing in London but attend balls, eat ices at Gunter's, and go on the strut every day in Hyde Park."

Mel smiled. "I hate to disappoint you, but I do none of those things."

"Surely you had a Season?"

She detected a note of uncertainty in his tone, as if he wanted to know more about her but didn't want to pry. Luckily this was a topic she'd given some thought to, lately.

"Not as such," she said. "My aunt and uncle had a small social circle but my uncle was ill for a long time and it didn't seem right to revel in the midst of that."

"Ah, that does sound difficult." She could almost hear the cogs spinning in his head as he sought another subject. "So how *do* you spend your time?"

Melissa and The Vicar

Mel wondered what he'd say if she told him the truth. The memory of his kisses—passionate, but not particularly practiced—told her that he'd clearly had very little experience in that department, which made sense given his profession. He didn't seem like the type of man to frequent brothels; Mel would have wagered a good deal of money that he believed sex before matrimony was a sin.

"Have I stumped you or are you just ignoring my impolite prying?" he asked in a teasing voice.

"Neither. It's just that I do nothing unusual," she lied. "I visit the subscription library, occasionally attend the theater or eat dinner with friends." That much was true—although all her friends were whores and the theater boxes she attended belonged to men who brought women who were not their wives. "Nothing exciting."

"Certainly more exciting than New Bickford."

"Yes, perhaps. But I came here to rest, and New Bickford is perfect for that."

"I'd almost forgotten that you were ill," he said, "You look positively blooming now."

An awkward silence followed his earnest declaration. Melissa realized it was the type of thing he probably said to women all day long, without any discomfort. But now, with her . . .

Once again, he was the one to break the silence. "I do know what you mean about not missing the city—I confess I find myself missing few of the things town life has to offer."

"You lived in London?" She risked a glance at him, relieved to see he was looking straight ahead. His profile was just as perfect as the rest of him.

"No, but I lived in Oxford while I attended university."

"Ah."

"Spoken with the derisiveness of a Londoner about any other city." He nudged her with his elbow and she stiffened at the casual touch. He must have noticed, because they walked in silence until they turned the corner and saw Halliburton Manor.

"Well," she stopped not far from the rose arbor that led to the front walk. "Here we are."

"Indeed." He looked at her with eyes that were guarded and no longer sparkled with easy affection.

"So," she said, swallowing back disappointment and pasting a smile on her face while she held out her hand. "Thank you."

"My pleasure." He bowed over her hand, the gesture smooth and practiced, almost as if he did it all the time.

Mel watched him mount Friar and then waved as he rode away, looking until he disappeared around the corner and she could see him no longer.

***

Magnus stared into the darkness above his head, unable to sleep, reliving the events of yesterday afternoon over and over in his mind's eye. Just as he'd been doing almost constantly since it happened. He was usually able to marshal his thoughts and think rationally. But not when it came to her—to *Melissa*.

He thought about getting up and dressing, going to the church, and dropping to his knees and *begging* for strength. But he was so bloody hard and something about carrying his erection into a sacred place felt . . . profane.

Besides, he needed to sleep. He'd been so weary today that he fell asleep while at his afternoon tutoring session. And had woken with an erect cock. Thank God he'd been seated behind a desk. He could just imagine the enjoyment two adolescent boys would've gotten from witnessing their curate with an erection.

He groaned, his hands fisted tightly at his sides, cock throbbing, ballocks full to bursting.

It was pointless. He would have to get some relief or he would never fall asleep. Yes, that is what he would do—not revel in the act, but simply employ a practical, workmanlike approach that—

"Oh *shut up*, Magnus, you pillock," he muttered as he sucked in a harsh breath and took himself in hand. He was so bloody close it shouldn't take long. He stroked, gripping his shaft hard enough to hurt, as if causing himself pain might make what he was doing less sinful. Like some Catholic monk mortifying his disobedient flesh with a whip.

Magnus gritted his teeth but it failed to keep out the images of her that began to coalesce in his mind's eye. Every time he eradicated one, another three would pop up, like persistent weeds in a lawn. And all of them were the product of lust. God, the *feel* of her when he'd taken her into his arms and kissed her! Generous, firm breasts, a waist so tiny his hands almost met, and then there had been the way she'd sucked his tongue . . .

Magnus's body twisted into a painful, familiar, and delicious arch, his buttock muscles thrusting and thrusting and—

Melissa and The Vicar

"Ah," he grunted, his muscles going rigid until the violent pulsing of his penis was the only movement in his body. In the cottage. In the world.

He spent hard enough to reach his chin, the splash of hot liquid bringing him down to earth with vicious speed. As he slumped back on the bed, his hand still cradling an erection that was not, by any means, finished, he knew there would be no sleeping—at least nothing worthwhile. Not tonight, nor the next—not until he could make her his wife. He should have told her his feelings today, had he not been such a bloody coward. Soon, though. He would have to tell her soon.

Chapter Ten

Dear Mel:
 I apologize for the delay in answering your letters. Yes, I am aware you've written four to my one. I should have realized sooner this was a contest.
 You will be pleased to hear life goes on—for the most part—without incident. Laura has taken to her bed with a sudden illness. She is certain Hugo poisoned her. Naturally Hugo found that accusation highly amusing.
 "Poison is a woman's weapon, darling," he said when she flung her accusation at him after she finally came down to breakfast. "If you wake up one morning to find your head has been severed, you'll know that was me."

Mel couldn't help it; she laughed.

Although his words were—I must admit—highly amusing, they were not the kind of thing to smooth her feathers. Therefore, I have sent her for a week of enforced recuperating at the Clarendon, the price to be borne by The White House.

Mel slammed her teacup down so hard the saucer cracked. "Bloody fucking hell."

Daisy, who'd come into her dressing room uninvited to ransack her clothing, just laughed. "Hugo or Laura?"

"Both," Mel growled.

I can hear your howls of rage all the way in London. I know it is not an inexpensive way of getting her out of the house, but it will allow the dust to settle. Besides, she was too ill to work and was only spending her time stirring the pot.
 Hugo, of course, is thrilled.

"Naturally," she muttered.

Much to my eternal gratitude and delight I've discovered that a happy Hugo is a cooperative Hugo. He has taken up Laura's part of the operations without complaint.

"I just bet he has."

On another, more serious, note, I feel like you should know there has been a certain royal duke spending a lot of time here lately.

Mel sat up straighter, clenching her jaw against whatever was coming.

I know Hugo is responsible for his own, er, actions, but I did strongly caution him against this. Of course he did not listen. Nothing has happened—well, nothing out of the ordinary for such a situation—nor do I have any reason to suspect anything might, but it does seem to be a degree of danger you do not need to encourage.

Mel was grateful Joss could discuss such an explosive topic so discreetly. The truth was, allowing sodomy to occur beneath her roof was a danger to all. At the same time, a number of very powerful, wealthy, and influential people had become invested in the future of The White House for the very reason that she *did* allow the activity to take place.

Personally, she did not care who fucked who. In fact, she believed there would be fewer wars if men would divert more of their energy to fucking rather than fighting. Sexual frustration and repression, she was certain, were a good part of all the trouble modern civilization faced.

But her opinion was neither popular nor legal.

The punishment for what went on in some of her rooms was death. But these were adults and they all knew the stakes. At the same time, toying with a royal duke was a good way to end up at the bottom of the Thames. Those in power made it their business to keep track of the royal brood. They also believed it was their business to rectify any . . . *problems* that might develop. Preferably *before* they developed. Mel knew that a royal duke engaging in homosexual activity would qualify as a problem that had *already* gotten out of control. If anyone was going to suffer, it would be Mel, her employees, her business, and— most certainly—Hugo. This was simply—

"There, how does this look?" Daisy asked, pulling Mel from her thoughts. *And* standing in front of her, wearing Mel's newest straw hat.

S.M. LaViolette

"How does it look?" Mel repeated with a scowl. "It looks like it is *mine*, that's how it looks."

"*Pffft!* Don't be so stingy." Daisy headed toward the door.

"Where are you going?" Mel asked. Not that she couldn't guess.

"To town."

"You will be discrete, I trust?" It was no point asking her to hold off her activities entirely, but discretion . . .

"I promise." She wet her index finger and drew it in a pattern Mel supposed was meant to be a cross.

"Have you taken care of all the garments we are to sell tomorrow?"

"Yes, they are already crated and waiting in the inn's assembly room—along with everyone else's."

"And you will be there tomorrow morning to help set up and—"

"Crikey, Mel! Yes, I'll be there."

Her head throbbed. "You might want to start wrapping things up with your lover, Daisy. And tell Jenny and Sarah to do the same. We shall be leaving as scheduled—at the end of the month."

Daisy gave her an unreadable look and for a moment Mel thought she would argue. Instead she said, "And are you going to tell the curate that, or should I?"

Mel clenched the letter in her hands. "Why do you ask?"

Daisy rolled her eyes. "Because while you've been avoiding *him* he's been stalking *you*. As if you didn't know that already."

Mel *did* know he'd been looking for her ever since that day at the beach—almost a week ago. But she couldn't face him—not because she was embarrassed, but because she simply wanted to touch him so badly it hurt. That scared her. It scared her more than Hugo and his royal-shenanigans, or the thought of Joss finally leaving, or anything else she could think of. She'd fallen for the first time in her life, and she had fallen hard. She realized Daisy was examining her like a surgeon with a patient who had a fatal disease.

"I shall tell him tomorrow. No doubt I'll see him at the fête."

Daisy gave her a hard look, but she left without another word, slamming the door behind her to make her point.

Mel sighed with relief. She was in too much turmoil to be around anyone, especially anyone as smug as Daisy. She knew all of them—from Mrs. Bunch to the footmen—were enjoying the sight of their employer in an emotional turmoil. The notorious madam of The White House, a woman rumored to have turned Wellington away (a

Melissa and The Vicar

greatly exaggerated story she'd never bothered to correct). A woman who was infamous for her habit of only taking either two men or one woman, when she did take lovers to her bed. This latter rumor was true but had happened so infrequently in the past five years it might as well be a lie.

Mel had to admit she found it amusing, as well. She was brought as low as a schoolroom miss. She—Hannah Baker—a woman who'd had so many lovers she could not count them even if she'd wanted to.

"You fool." She savagely folded Joss's letter and then thought better of it. Instead, she held the corner to the nearest candle, holding the pages until they were mostly consumed before tossing them into the cold fireplace. No matter how carefully worded the letter was, it was still better to erase it from existence.

***

Magnus did not see Miss Griffin for six—almost *seven*—days, and not for lack of trying. Indeed, he visited Mrs. Tisdale every day—triggering suspicion with his assiduous care. He would have liked to have said it was out of good Christian piety, but the truth was that he wanted to run into *her*.

But he didn't.

Nor did he see her in town. He saw her aunt, who, after careful prodding, disclosed that her niece was not ill, just busy with something vague and London-related.

It was probably best he didn't see her because he'd likely make a fool of himself. As it was, he'd planned out his approach with the care of a general planning a campaign. He would be giving the sermon tomorrow and was going to find her today at the fête and ask if she wouldn't mind waiting for him after the service. She would have to know what that meant. She could either put him out of his misery by flat-out rejecting him or she could leave him hanging in the breeze until tomorrow afternoon.

That had been his plan a couple days ago, but he'd begun to question the wisdom of this approach by the morning of the church fête. Distance and absence had not calmed him; it had left him half-mad from thinking about her. It had also made him a danger to himself and others. He'd walked in front Mrs. Peevy's gig, slammed his thumb in the lychgate, and allowed his attention to wander while Mrs. Tisdale was speaking to him—this last being the most dangerous to his health.

S.M. LaViolette

His days had been desolate, but his nights? Well, those had been worse.

When his body wouldn't allow him to sleep, he'd light a candle and try to read. When his body wouldn't allow him to read, he would take out his sketchbook.

That led to dozens of sketches of one subject, many of which were, to say the least, *imaginative*. Which, in turn, led to his body being even less interested in sleep.

He'd given up resisting the relentless demands of his body. He had two choices: masturbate or harm either himself or somebody else through sheer exhaustion.

Unfortunately, masturbation didn't seem to clear his thoughts. At least not longer than a few hours. By the sixth day after their interlude he'd worn himself raw and there was no relief in sight.

He'd also almost filled up his sketchbook.

Well, today it would all be over, one way or another. It was the morning of the fête and he'd woken extra early to pay a visit to Mrs. Tisdale. Today his visit was legitimately for the older woman's good rather than other, more questionable, motives.

He knew the day would be hectic and it would be impossible to see her later. He also wanted to check with Sarah to make sure she had somebody to watch the old lady when she went to the fête.

He arrived to find Sarah washing up from breakfast.

"Good morning, Reverend," she called over her shoulder, shooting him one of her saucy smiles—a smile that reminded him very much of Miss Griffin's aunt, come to think of it. Magnus shook the pointless thought from his head.

"Good morning, Sarah. How is she this morning?"

"Full of p—" she grimaced. "Ah, full of vinegar, sir." She set aside a clean pan and brushed her damp hair from her forehead with the back of her wrist, the action drawing his gaze toward her low-cut neckline. He immediately jerked his eyes back up to find her grinning. Magnus thought it rather odd that Melissa's servants were so earthy while she appeared—for the most part—rather proper.

"You were saying, sir?" Sarah asked, jolting him from his musing.

"When will you be leaving for the fête?"

"Oh, I ain't goin'."

"You aren't?"

"No, I'll stay here with herself."

"Is something wrong? Is she not feeling well?"

Melissa and The Vicar

"Nah, she's all right and tight. But she don't like the other woman." She jerked her chin in the general direction of the vicarage—ah, Mrs. Dennis, the charwoman.

"Well, that may be so, but you can't stay here days on end. You need time to enjoy yourself, too."

She shot him a cheeky grin. "Oh, I enjoy myself right enough."

Magnus's face heated for reasons unknown to him. "Er, well, good, then," he finished rather lamely.

"Besides, I get enjoyment out o' listening to the old bird's stories."

Magnus winced. "I'm not sure I'd let her hear you call her that, Sarah."

She laughed and the action caused her tight bodice to jiggle.

He forced his eyes up to hers. "Are you sure you don't mind? I've already spoken to somebody about spelling you."

"No, I'm fine."

"If you don't mind me asking, what kind of stories does Mrs. Tisdale tell?"

"Oh, just this and that. You know, about her younger days." An evasive look slid across her normally open features but was just as quickly gone.

"Well, I'm glad you are staying. I believe she likes you, too."

He'd left her to her cleaning and popped upstairs to confirm Mrs. Tisdale was doing well. She'd waved him off, her attention focused on a box of old letters, and Magnus headed to the village green, where he was to help set up for the fête.

He'd hoped he might run into Miss Griffin, but he didn't meet a soul until arriving in town. Once he got to the green the morning flew past in a maelstrom of last-minute crises and it wasn't until eleven that he saw her. She and Mrs. Trent were in their booth sorting clothing into different piles.

Magnus was about to go say hello when Mrs. Pilkington pounced on him and dragged him away to help with the umbrella that shaded her daughters' booth. The three girls were selling more dolls than he'd ever seen in one place.

"These were all part of our collections," Emily, the youngest, volunteered.

He eyed a particularly vile-looking doll with curly blonde hair that was shockingly like his own. He squinted; it looked as if the hair had been—

"Marie burnt her hair with curling tongs," Susan, the middle girl, volunteered in an undertone.

"*Susan.*" Marie's homely face flushed the color of a poppy.

"What? It's the truth."

"You don't mind selling them?" he asked, hoping to head off an argument.

"Mama said we were too old for dolls," said Emily.

He didn't know their exact ages, but he knew Marie and Susan were old enough that Mrs. Pilkington had made it clear to Magnus that it was his duty to choose one of them for his wife. Emily, he suspected, was close to sixteen.

"Emily, hush." It was Marie again, the self-appointed enforcer.

Emily looked so chastened and forlorn it pulled at his heartstrings.

"Which is your favorite?" Magnus asked.

She looked at Marie and then shook her head, her eyes settling on a doll that was only a fraction the size of the rest. A cute little thing that wore a tiny tiara, like a princess.

"How much is that one?" he asked, pointing to it.

Susan scoffed. "Oh, Mr. Stanwyck, why would you want a doll?"

"Shut up, Susan," Marie said, mortified. "Perhaps he has a niece, or young cousin."

He ignored them. "How much, Emily?"

She mumbled a price and Magnus took out his small leather coin pouch. "Here," he said, handing her two small coins. "I don't need any change back."

Her lip trembled as she handed him the doll and he smiled and shook his head. "I bought it for you, Emily."

"You can't take that," Marie chided, reaching for the doll, which Emily hid behind her. "Mama will be livid."

"Oh, Mister Stanwyyyyyyke!" Miss Agnes Philpot's piercing voice was—for once—music to his ears.

"I'm afraid duty calls," he said, escaping before Emily either started crying or her sisters tattled.

Miss Philpot needed him to level out the table where she and her sister had set up their house plants. Once he'd finished that he had to help the vicar settle a dispute about which group of musicians—two had shown up—would play at the dance and which would play during the fête. By the time he had a spare moment it was time to set up his own small booth, which really was no more than a table, two chairs, and an umbrella he could tilt to keep out the sun.

Melissa and The Vicar

He'd waited so long that his booth, such as it was, had ended up at the very last spot, which prevented him from being able to watch Melissa's booth. Miss Gloria Philpot—his first customer—arrived before he'd had a chance to take out his pencils and sketchpad.

"I'd like a portrait, Mr. Stanwyck."

Magnus recalled doing one of her last year but he did not think it politic to point that out. Instead he pulled out the chair for her and picked up his book. The first page he turned to was filled with a naked Miss Griffin. He slammed the book shut.

"Ah, that one is full." He moved to put it back in his bag but her voice stopped him.

"Might I take a look at your sketches?"

Horror slithered down his spine at the mental picture that conjured. He gave her a smile of regret. "I'm afraid these are just rough pieces not finished enough to share." A lie, that. These were some of the best damned sketches he'd ever made—even though they were all from his imagination.

After Miss Gloria, came the innkeeper's son, Joe Biddle, a quiet man who'd said no more than three words in the time Magnus had been in New Bickford. When Magnus gently teased him about whom the portrait was for Joe had turned an alarming shade of red and the remainder of the sitting had been conducted in silence.

Mrs. Heeley, surprisingly, was next. "I want to have one done for his birthday. It is to be a surprise." The vicar's birthday was in the middle of next month.

"I haven't had a chance to walk about—how is the turnout?" he asked her, smiling as she unwrapped something—a sweet of some kind, no doubt—and nibbled while he worked.

"It is an excellent turnout—better than last year. Miss Griffin and Mrs. Trent are quite the most popular." Her gaze slid sideways to where Lady Barclay's booth sat. The squire's wife had a pinched expression and was gazing jealously in the direction of Melissa's booth.

Magnus grimaced. "Perhaps I will go and give Lady Barclay some commerce when I've finished with your portrait."

"Excellent idea, Magnus." She gave him an impish smile. "You have all the instincts of an excellent vicar."

After he'd finished her portrait, he told the two people who approached next that he'd be back in half an hour and made a sign for his table to that effect.

There was a woman buying cut flowers when he went to Lady Barclay's stall, but the squire's wife all but shoved her aside when she saw Magnus waiting. Like her husband, she was both snobbish and unctuous. He tried not to judge her harshly; having such a husband could not be pleasant. But she did not make his good intentions easy.

"Ah, *Mister* Stanwyck!" She said *Mister* in a way that indicated it was private jest the two them shared. Magnus knew people like Lady Barclay could not comprehend a person preferring the title of *mister* over *lord*. "I understand you paid us a call last week. Shame on you for not coming to see me."

"I do apologize. I'm afraid I was in a horrid rush that day," he lied, his gaze slipping away from hers to the buckets she had filled with fresh-cut blooms. "I do believe I'd like some flowers."

"For somebody special?" She cooed suggestively.

"Actually, for several somebodies. I'd like a few small arrangements as a thank you for some of the ladies who've done the lion's share of work for the fête."

Her face fell and he felt almost guilty for depriving her of some new gossip.

They chatted about general matters while she assembled four nosegays. She was just wrapping up the last of them when the squire arrived.

"There you are, Stanwyck." Sir Thomas cut an amused, slimy glance at the flowers. "Goin' courtin' are you? Who's the lucky lass?" He snickered. "Or it looks like you have several."

His wife tittered and Magnus handed over the required coins. "Thank you, Lady Barclay." He turned to her husband, to whom he *had* to say something. "Have you come to help with sales, Squire?"

He snorted. "I've come to judge the livestock fair."

Ah, yes, Magnus had forgotten about that part, which was handled by several of the local farmers and their wives.

He glanced at the sky, which was beginning to darken. "Rather late, isn't it? Will you wrap things up before the dinner and dance?"

The squire was staring at something over Magnus's shoulder.

"Thomas," his wife said, prodding him, "Mr. Stanwyck asked you a question."

Sir Thomas pulled his gaze away from whatever had held it, his forehead rippled with something that looked very much like disbelief.

"What's that?" he asked his wife in a rude tone.

Melissa and The Vicar

Magnus answered. "I just pointed out it was rather late to begin the judging. After all, the dinner and dance begin in an hour."

The squire seemed to shake himself. "Aye, I know. But I'm only doing the horse judging. Mr. Leveret did the other animals." His gaze flickered again over Magnus's shoulder, and his jaw tightened. "Well," he said, cutting Magnus a brusque glance and ignoring his wife altogether, "I'd better be off."

Once he'd gone another couple came to the table and Magnus was free to turn and look to where the squire had been staring. Mrs. Trent must have gone off somewhere and the booths on either side of her were temporarily unmanned. The only person facing them just now was Miss Griffin. She was chatting with two young girls who were clutching a garment a piece, and she must have felt eyes on her because she looked up. For a moment her expression faltered, but then she smiled and waved.

Magnus strode toward her, feeling a bit like a fool with his armload of flowers. "Hello Miss Griffin, hello Sally, June."

"Hello Mister Stanwyck," the girls responded in a singsong and then broke into giggles. He knew them both from Sunday school—where they spent their time giggling and gossiping.

"What have you purchased?" he asked politely, making all the correct noises when they showed him their wares. "Well, these are for you." He handed each girl a nosegay, deciding the young girls would probably appreciate them more than either Mrs. Pilkington, the woman who'd done the most work, or the vicar's wife, the woman who'd made sure Mrs. Pilkington didn't drive away all the other volunteers.

The girls took the bouquets and the giggling was joined by blushing and mumbled words of thanks.

"And these two are for you and Mrs. Trent," he said to Melissa when the girls had run off, no doubt in a hurry to show all the other girls what Reverend Stanwyck had given them.

She smiled at him and cocked her head. "These weren't really for me or those girls, were they?"

Magnus grinned. "Now, what is a man supposed to say to a question like that?"

She laughed, her expression far more merry than he'd ever seen. "You are right—I will just say thank you." She held up the nosegay and inhaled deeply. "These are lovely. A product of the squire's greenhouse, I understand."

"Yes, have you met his wife—Lady Barclay?" They both turned to the flower booth, which was now crowded with customers.

"Not yet."

A new pair of gigglers drifted up and began to sort through the few garments that remained. "You don't seem to have much left."

"No, I believe all of my clothing sold in the first ten minutes. What is left is my aunt's." She gave him a sideways grin. "I shall make certain to point that out to her."

Magnus laughed.

"And how is the portrait booth?"

He pulled back a foot and glanced down to the end of the booths, where there were people milling. He grimaced at her. "They are circling—I'm afraid I have been shirking and must run."

She held up the flowers. "Thank you." She hesitated and then said, "I do hope you'll join me and my aunt at our table for dinner."

"I would be delighted."

She flushed and turned away, as if embarrassed. For his part, Magnus felt as if he floated back to his table.

**

It was Daisy who saw him first.

Dinner was served out under the stars, which was all that was in the sky, despite the dire warnings of rain.

There were tables set up all over the green and the tables used for booths had been commandeered. Lamps and colored lanterns provided the light, and laughter and eating and the tuning up of musicians filled the night. Melissa had to admit it was magical.

She was looking about for Daisy, whom she'd sternly warned against abandoning her for her beau, Joe Biddle—at least until halfway through the dance—when a hand gripped her arm hard enough to hurt.

"We have trouble, Mel."

When she would have turned around to face her, Daisy stopped her. "No, don't turn around. Come with me." She all but dragged Mel to the small covered pavilion that had been set off to one side as a ladies' retiring area.

Once inside, they both pretended to examine Mel's hem until the three women who'd been in the small area left.

Melissa dropped the hem and turned to Daisy. "What in God's name—"

"I saw one of our customers here."

Melissa and The Vicar

She could only stare.

"And not somebody who will be happy to keep to himself, either—it's that wretched Sir Thomas."

Mel raised a hand to her mouth and closed her eyes. "What an idiot I am! I heard the name but Thomas is such a common one I never imagined—"

"I know," Daisy said. "I didn't, either."

Sir Thomas was one of the handful of men over the years Melissa had needed to ban from the brothel. It happened after he'd become rough with one of the newer girls—a timid woman who'd insisted she'd worked before. But she must have been green, because instead of making a racket and running from the bastard, she'd endured a savage anal rape that Mel only learned about when the woman needed a doctor.

After that, the men at the door had twice told Sir Thomas—Mel didn't believe he'd ever given his last name, most did not—that the house was too busy to admit him and had turned him away. But the third time, he'd caused a stir and demanded to see Mel. When she'd told him why he was no longer welcome he denied it all and called the girl, Lucy—who was so damaged from the incident that Mel moved her permanently to the kitchen—a slut and a liar.

If there was one word that bothered her—far more than *whore* ever had—it was the word *slut*. A man like Sir Thomas would force himself upon a woman and then call *her* a slut. The word was like a match to a fuse and Melissa had done something she rarely did and raised her voice, telling him exactly what she thought of him. In the end it had taken Hugo and another man to drag him out.

"We both need to go," Daisy said, echoing what Mel was thinking. "Now."

It would look odd to simply leave without saying anything, but the alternative was unthinkable.

"I've already told Joe we'll need a ride—he's gone to fetch his father's carriage and meet us just outside of town."

"Oh, Daisy—do we really need him? It is a full moon and surely we could walk—"

"I will want to say my goodbyes."

Mel looked into Daisy's usually smiling face and saw pain and regret. She nodded. "Of course."

"We can leave in the morning—Mrs. Bunch and the girls can take care of any packing. Sir Thomas won't know any of them." She hesitated. "But I want tonight for me and Joe, Mel." Her eyes were both adamant and pleading. "Just tonight."

"Of course," Mel said again. Daisy held out her hand and Mel took it. They embraced, as if they were parting.

"It was fun while it lasted, being a normal woman," Daisy whispered in her ear.

Mel's eyes stung at her friend's despairing tone. "We knew it would end eventually, darling."

"I just didn't think it would hurt this much," Daisy confessed.

Mel felt a hot tear slide down her cheek. "Neither did I, Daisy. Neither did I."

Chapter Eleven

Magnus was looking for Melissa but trying not to be too obvious about it. His search was made more difficult by the fact people kept stopping him and asking him to join their table. He'd just extricated himself from the Philpot sisters when a heavy hand landed on his shoulder.

He turned to find the squire and had to struggle to put a pleasant expression on his face. "Sir Thomas, were you looking for me?"

"No, actually, I was looking for the woman who was selling used clothing. My wife did not know her name."

"Oh, you mean Miss Griffin?"

The squire looked arrested. "Her name is Miss Griffin? Not *Mrs.* Griffin?"

"No, she is definitely a miss. Perhaps you are thinking of her aunt? Although her surname is Trent."

"Her aunt?"

Magnus wondered if the squire was intoxicated and subtly sniffed the air. He smelled the odor of beer, but nothing stronger.

Sir Thomas snorted, gazing at nothing in particular, his expression one of amazement. "Well I'll be damned."

"Squire?"

The older man seemed to remember Magnus's presence. He gave him one of his leers—the ones that always made Magnus feel like he needed a hot bath to scrub himself clean.

"You'll have to excuse me, Mr. Stanwyck, I need to go see somebody."

Magnus watched him walk away and shook his head. The man wasn't merely revolting, he was also strange.

"Ah, there you are, Magnus."

"Hello Mr. Heeley. Were you looking for me?"

"Come and join us at our table."

Magnus hesitated a moment before saying something that would no doubt make his intentions clear. But he was going to ask her tomorrow in any case, so . . .

S.M. LaViolette

"Actually, I was hoping to find Miss Griffin and her aunt—I was to join them for dinner."

The vicar blinked, and then gave him a regretful smile. "I'm afraid you missed her—I saw her and her aunt getting into Joe Biddle's carriage. They must be going home." He paused and chewed his lip. "I do hope she has not taken ill again. She came here to convalesce, but I've never really heard from *what*."

She'd *gone*? And without saying anything. But—

"You should pay a call on them tomorrow."

Magnus nodded.

"Will you join us?"

He looked up from his thoughts and smiled. "Yes, yes, of course I will. I just need to put away my things and fetch my satchel and then I shall be back."

The vicar ambled away to where his table waited and Magnus stared after him, stunned. He'd just lied blatantly to the vicar. He had no intention of coming back. He was going to Halliburton Manor. He could not stand waiting until morning to find out if she was ill.

***

Only Mrs. Bunch was at the manor when Mel returned home and she was already in bed.

Daisy came inside to fetch something in her room and then came back to the entryway, where Mel had sat down.

"Oh, look at you—still in your hat and cloak," Daisy said, stopping in front of her, a cloth bag clutched in her hand. "You have it bad for him, don't you?"

Mel didn't bother denying it.

"Should I stay? I could—"

"No, go to Joe." Mel hesitated and then said, "You are going somewhere private?"

"Aye, he keeps a small cottage. That's where he lives when he isn't helping out at the inn."

Mel stood and walked her to the door. "You should go. I'll be fine."

"If you're sure?"

Before she could answer there was a loud knock.

Daisy clutched her arms. "Oh God, do you think it's him, come after you?"

Fury bubbled in Mel's chest at the thought of that man forcing his way into her house—especially since he was already driving her out of

Melissa and The Vicar

the village. "There's only one way to find out." She yanked open the door.

Magnus stood outside, his hand poised as if he'd been about to knock again.

"Thank God," Daisy breathed.

Immediately Magnus was alert. "Is something wrong?" He glanced over his shoulder. "I see Joe is waiting out front. He said he was waiting for his orders."

Mel turned to Daisy. "You'd better not keep him waiting."

Daisy left without another word.

"Come inside, Mister Stanwyck."

His forehead was wrinkled with concern. "Is aught amiss?" he asked again as he shut the door.

"All is well," she lied. "Daisy just forgot she'd promised Miss Philpot a book and wanted to run home and get it. And I . . ." she faltered as they entered the sitting room. "Well, I was just tired." She turned to find him standing in the open doorway. "Come in, reverend, and shut the door."

"Perhaps I should leave. Especially as Mrs. Trent is gone."

Mel sat down on the settee, suddenly bone tired and too tired to argue. "If you feel you should."

But instead of leaving, he came to the settee and lowered himself to his haunches and then reached out and touched her chin, tilting her face until she had to meet his gaze. "What is wrong, Melissa?"

She would later tell herself that it was hearing her name on his tongue that undid her. But that was a lie, he'd undone her from the first day they met—her golden-haired knight protector.

Whatever he saw on her face made him slide his arms around her as he came up to sit beside her, holding her as if she were as fragile as fine china. His hand stroked her back and she realized he'd taken her in his arms because he believed she needed comfort. While she wanted him for far earthier reasons.

He sat back just enough that she could see his face, his expression as gentle as it had been when he'd lowered the little boy Robbie into his mother arms. "You look so—"

Mel kissed him, a light, sweet kiss that said everything she could not. His blue eyes were startled, but then his lids lowered and he took her mouth in a deep, unhurried kiss that shook her to her bones. His exploration of her was patient and thorough; it was the kind of kiss she'd always imagined young innocent people enjoyed the first time they made love. Young people who'd not been sold to a man thirty years older, a man for whom kissing had been the last thing he wanted.

Magnus's tongue caressed her, worshipped her, learning the curves of her lips, her mouth, and even the ridged, oddly sensitive roof of her mouth.

He leaned back, smiling. "Did I tickle you?"

She nodded, unable to speak.

He smoothed her hair back from her temple, his expression one of unsuppressed joy, and all because he had kissed her and was holding her. Destroying her.

"I shouldn't be doing this, Melissa, I know that. But I simply could not wait to ask you—" he broke off, took a deep breath, and then said, "When I heard you might be ill—well, to be honest, I used it as an excuse to behave badly and come here at such a scandalous hour." He kissed her forehead. "I love you, Melissa. I know it has happened ridiculously fast, but I want you to be—"

Mel couldn't. She simply could not hear him speak the question she could only ever answer one way. He was openly and innocently offering her his heart and would want hers in return. She had no way to tell him that the only thing she had to give him was her body; her heart had shriveled to dust and blown away a long time ago.

She should send him away, but she couldn't. Not without giving him the only thing she had to give: a night of pleasure. Years from now, when he was happy with a caring wife and a large brood of children, he would recall tonight fondly, even if he could no longer recall her name.

***

One moment she was in his arms, the physical manifestation of all his dreams. The next, she'd pulled away.

"What is it, Melissa? Have I frightened you?"

The look she turned on him was not the guarded look she'd greeted him with at the door. This was different than anything he'd seen on her face and it sent a frisson of shock up his spine—a tingling awareness of danger.

But it sent another bolt to his groin.

She lowered herself to the floor, the motion as fluid and graceful as a ripple of water.

"Magnus?"

Melissa and The Vicar

He swallowed as she laid a hand on each of his knees, looking up at him through her lashes.

"Yes?" he said, sounding just like a croaking frog. She slid her hands up his thighs and he almost jumped out of his skin. "What—" She paused and cocked her head. "Don't you like that?"

His eyes dropped to her lips, which were suddenly slick and pouting. He wrenched his gaze away, looking up. But she wasn't looking at him, she was looking at his groin, which was very conscious of her attention.

She began kneading his thighs, her slender hands far stronger than he would have imagined, her touch . . . exquisite. Magnus shook his head, took her wrists in his hands to still her, and said, "What did you say?"

"You said you loved me, Magnus."

It wasn't what he'd been expecting and her voice was a shaky whisper.

"I *do* love you Melissa."

Something flickered in her eyes but before he could identify it, she stood, straddling his lap but not breaking his grasp.

"Magnus." She lowered herself onto his thighs, her bottom warm and firm through their combined clothing, her position was . . . well, quite frankly her position was shocking.

"Melissa, I don't think—"

"Shhhhh," she whispered the word in his ear just before she began nibbling, kissing, and—yes—licking him.

"This is wrong, Melissa." He'd meant to sound firm, commanding—but it came out more of a question.

She gave a throaty chuckle, working her way down his jaw to his neck. "How can something so wonderful—between two people who love each other—be wrong?" Her lips pushed into his cravat and her mouth settled over his Adam's apple. And then she bit him.

Magnus groaned, his head falling against the back of the settee. And then he heard what she'd said: between two people who love each other. He struggled through the sensual haze that was becoming thicker by the second.

"You love me?" he asked, realizing her hands had come free from his grasp at some point and she was removing his cravat.

"I do, Magnus. I love you." She shifted slightly and her soft, plump bottom accidentally brushed his cramped, swollen cock.

He almost leapt out of his skin. "Ah, God, Melissa, you mustn't, you're—"

She did it again, and then again; Magnus realized she was doing it on purpose. Before he could absorb the meaning of that, her hands, warm and soft, slid across his chest. She'd somehow managed to get his waistcoat open without him noticing. It was as if she'd sprouted a second set of hands.

"You are beautiful, Magnus." She kissed her way down his throat, lingering on his collar bone, her bottom now moving almost . . . rhythmically. "And what we are doing is beautiful."

Her words pierced the heavy fog of arousal and he blinked his eyes, using his hands—which had been lying limply at his sides—to gently take hold of her, pushing her back until he could see her face. Which might have been a mistake because she was flushed and her lips were swollen and darker red, her eyelids were so low only narrow green crescents were visible: she was gorgeous.

Magnus wanted her so badly he ached with it, but . . .

He shook his head. "Melissa, darling, I can't do this with you. It isn't right to—" She tried to lean closer, but he held her firm.

"Please, Magnus, I want to tell you something."

He hesitated. If he let her near, he wasn't sure he'd be able to find the strength to resist her again.

"Please?"

He released her and she pressed herself against him in a way designed to torment.

"Magnus?"

He exhaled shakily as he felt her breasts pressing against his chest. "Yes?"

"I'm not a virgin, Magnus."

They both went still. Magnus, because he was not expecting her words and Melissa—he supposed—because she feared his reaction.

What was his reaction? He didn't really know. It wasn't just *one* reaction; it was like his old nurse's knitting basket, dozens of strands of tangled yarn. There was profound disappointment that they wouldn't be each other's first, resignation, acceptance, and a hope that whoever had taken her maidenhood had done so with love and tenderness.

"Do I revolt you?" she whispered, her words hot on his ear.

He thrust her away, his hands tight on her upper arms. "How could you ask me a thing like that?"

Melissa and The Vicar

***

Melissa was shocked by the anger and pain in his face. "I didn't mean—" She stopped. How could she say what she meant? How?

His expression softened. "I should not have become so angry at your question. Perhaps it's because a part of me is angry that this is not something we'll experience for the first time together." He shook his head. "But I'm not angry; we'll have a lifetime to explore our love for one another."

It struck her like a mallet between the eyes—she must have been stupid to have missed it. He was talking about sharing their virginity: *he* was a virgin.

He brought her forward again and kissed her forehead. "I know it's a sin to make love to you out of wedlock, Melissa—but I'm human and weak. If we're to be married, it does not feel like it is so wrong." He kissed her again, laughing softly ruefully against her skin. "What a terrible thing for a man of God to say. I'm just greedy and selfish and—well, I want you."

Mel shuddered at the raw longing in his voice. A tiny part of her mind told her that to make love to him with no intention of marrying him was worse than lying.

But she just didn't care.

She was still straddling his lap. "Touch me, Magnus. Please." Her gown had ridden up to her knees and she moved them apart, took his hand and slid it beneath her skirts, leading him up her thigh.

His body shuddered and he took control of the exploration, his fingers questing and stroking her skin ever higher, his touch gentle, but not tentative.

Melissa groaned softly when the tips of his fingers brushed the sensitive skin of her upper thighs.

His breathing was ragged on her temple as his hand came to rest on the damp curls covering her sex. "I've imagined touching you like this dozens, if not hundreds of times, Melissa. In my imagination it is daylight and I can see you—all of you." She felt him swallow, his finger stroking the seam of her swollen lips. She opened herself wider, sliding lower. He groaned, the next caress grazing her peak. It was all she could do to keep from thrusting against his hand like a crazed animal.

"Do you like that?" he asked, pausing his stroking. "You must tell me what you like, sweetheart. Everything."

"Harder," she murmured, stunned when her face heated at the single word: sweetheart. She, a woman who'd done and said unspeakable things yet had never been anyone's sweetheart.

His finger probed her slick heat. "Ah, Melissa." He sounded reverent, his hand not shy about learning the feel and shape of her. "You are so wet—that is your arousal . . . for me." He tone was wonderous, and his words were the most sensual thing a man had ever said to her.

His finger again touched her peak and she jolted. She felt his lips curve against the thin skin of her temple. "This is your clitoris, the source of female pleasure." He circled her bud and again she jolted. He chuckled. "I've done some research—although only with books." He kissed her temple. "I never imagined it would be so pleasurable as this."

He *had* done his research and Melissa relaxed into his touch as he fell into a rhythmic motion, his thumb stroking the base of her pearl, his other fingers teasing the entrance to her body.

The familiar tightness began to build in her, her body tensing and flexing in anticipation.

"Yes," she whispered, her single syllable of encouragement earning a low rumble from him. "Yes, please, Magnus" She began to shudder, the sensation overwhelming all thoughts. When the explosion came, her body stiffened and then shook as the waves pounded her. He cupped her mound and held her as her inner muscles convulsed.

"Oh, Melissa." His voice was barely a whisper. "I can feel your pleasure."

She rode out the most glorious climax she could remember, held tightly by him, like a precious possession.

God, she loved him so much it hurt. She wanted—no, *needed*—to feel him inside her body just once before she had to let him go.

Mel shook the sensual fog away and pushed up onto her knees. "I want you inside me."

It was his turn to freeze. For a moment, she thought he'd resurrect the same tired argument from before. But it seemed she'd worn him down, and both their clumsy hands fumbled with his fall. Once he'd opened the catches and buttons, he stood, effortlessly lifting her and then tenderly laying her out on the settee.

Melissa lay sprawled and shameless like the wanton she was, her knees cocked, her dress rucked up to her hips, and her thighs spread to expose her sex.

Melissa and The Vicar

He sucked in a harsh breath; his huge pupils riveted on her sex.

She lifted her hips in encouragement. "Touch me again, Magnus."

Their eyes met as his hand slid up her leg, not stopping until he reached her mound.

She groaned, her eyelids fluttering.

"You're magnificent." He shook his head in wonder, his face twisted in an expression of near pain. "You're so beautiful—and already so dear—it hurts to look at you, Melissa."

His finger parted her lips and he entered her. Her back curved into a tight arch, her jaw clenching as he withdrew, and then entered her again and again, pumping her with slow, steady strokes.

"Does this feel good?"

Melissa opened her eyes to find him watching her, his attention only for her. She'd performed sexual acts in broad daylight, in front of a room full of men, naked, clothed, dressed in all manner of costume—but never had she felt this exposed.

She couldn't bear his loving, curious scrutiny a moment longer. "I want to see you, too, Magnus," she said, when it seemed he would finger her to orgasm yet again.

He removed his hand from her body with obvious reluctance before toeing off his boots and then shoving his clothing down in one push, the way he'd done that day by the water.

"Your coats and shirt, too," she said when he would have knelt with his torso still covered.

He flashed her a grin. "Bossy." He freed himself from his garments as quickly as he'd done with his breeches, drawers, and stockings.

And then he stood before her in all his godlike glory.

Mel wanted to make him stand there—to pose for her—but he was already lowering himself between her thighs, his shaft long, hard, and thick and his tiny slit weeping freely. For her.

He kept one knee on the settee, the other foot firmly planted on the floor. She could see between his muscular thighs, which had an odd hairless pattern on the front and inner thighs which she knew was from the friction of his riding leathers. His sac was fuzzy with dark blond hair and snug to his body, his cock rigid and wanting, the thick blue vein pulsing so insistently she could see it. He was primed and ready and he looked as if he might explode when she touched him. It made her own body throb when she thought about how he'd denied himself while seeing to her pleasure.

She would make that up to him ten-fold before the night was through.

***

Her body created a ferocious yearning in his chest that Magnus couldn't recall feeling since he'd been a young boy going to the sweetshop with his nurse. He was allowed to pick only one thing—just one. How could he choose what part of her to touch first?

"Magnus?"

"Hmm?" He was finding it difficult to pull his gaze away from her pink slickness. He'd seen illustrations—both scientific and artistic—but none of them did justice to the real thing. Over the years he'd read more than a few books; books that went into great detail about pleasuring a woman with his mouth. All those times he'd sat with some coveted, wicked tome open, his breeding organ hard and weeping, he'd told himself he was doing his duty and studying for the day in the distant future when he'd have a wife of his own—a woman he'd need to tutor in the erotic arts. It had never occurred to him that a woman might come to him with knowledge and experience of her own.

Magnus was grateful he'd known enough to make her shudder and come apart with his fingers; he knew he could do the same with his tongue—if she'd allow it. His cock hurt at the memory of her climax. It had been . . . exquisite. And he wanted to make her do it again. And again.

"I want to see you."

Her low, insistent words shook him from his selfish reverie. He knelt high, letting her see his body and inspect it, even though he had a suspicion she'd done as much the day she watched him on the beach.

"Stroke yourself."

He could not have heard her correctly. "I beg your pardon?"

"I want to see your hand wrapped around your erection. Show me what you've been doing while thinking of me in your little curate's cottage."

Magnus was surprised that his eyeballs didn't roll from their sockets. It occurred to him that perhaps he wasn't the only one who'd been reading books and doing research. He looked at her slack lips and heavy eyelids and slid a hand around his shaft.

Melissa and The Vicar

Her lips curved into an unspeakably sensual smile and he almost spent all over himself. He stopped his stroking and she shot him a haughty glare.

"I'm afraid that if I continue to do that I will . . ." He searched for the least vulgar term.

She held out her arms. "Come into me, Magnus. Please, I want you." She opened her thighs wider in invitation.

His body knew what to do; his muscles and sinews moved with a confidence that was as natural as breathing and as ancient as humankind. She lifted her hips and Magnus placed himself at her entrance and hesitated.

"Please."

He pushed inside but stopped with only his crown breeching her, savoring the exquisite sensation. "Oh, Melissa."

"More." Her inner muscles contracted and he shuddered and pushed deeper.

Her hips rose to meet him and she grasped his buttocks and pulled him with remarkable strength, grunting in animal satisfaction when he was hilted.

He was inside her—as deep as he could be. He wanted to stop, to take time and marvel at the wonder of their bodies so intimately joined—but she tightened around him and his hips bucked. He pulled out with torturous slowness, and then plunged into her, making them both moan.

He knew what she wanted—what they both wanted—and began to stroke into her with deep, powerful thrusts. He could feel himself losing control before he'd hardly even started. It would all be over before it had even begun if he didn't—

"Take your pleasure, Magnus." She wrapped her legs around him and they fell into a rhythm, Melissa tightening when he entered, and relaxing when he slid out. Their bodies already knew each other and he was awed by the perfection of their fit. It was exquisite; it was unlike anything he'd ever imagined.

Magnus looked to where they were joined—to where his length, red and slick, plunged into her auburn curls, stretching her delicate pink lips.

The erotic sight catalyzed him and he began to buck and thrust, unable to stop the climax that seized control and barreled through his body. White explosions went off behind his eyelids as he clutched her hips in a cruel grip and slammed into her one last time, holding her body still as he poured himself deep inside her.

***

He'd fallen asleep while still inside her.

Melissa wanted to stay this way forever. He fit her so perfectly it filled her with wonder. And fear. And a wrenching pain that twisted her insides into a tight knot.

You can't have him. Ever.

She pushed away the horrid thought and concentrated on the moment. Right now she was lying beneath her lover—the man she so foolishly allowed herself to love—and he was buried inside her.

Although he'd ejaculated, he hadn't gone completely soft. It was as if his body was ready to make up for lost time.

Oh, and what a body. He was heavy on her—crushing her—but it was delicious. She would let him sleep for a while and then she would wake him slowly.

For a while, she drifted in a shallow, sensual doze with him. But the mantle clock's ticking was a grim reminder that this night was passing. She didn't want to waste even a moment of it in sleep.

Instead, she stroked him lightly, her touches making him shift and mutter in his sleep, his body settling more heavily and covering her.

Tomorrow was Sunday, and he would soon wake up and remember that. And the moment he did, he would begin to pull away. In his mind, it would be a temporary separation—just until they were man and wife. He might have slipped tonight and given in to his body's demands, but this would be the first and last time for such weakness. Only when they were joined in matrimony could they be joined in body again. Melissa knew that as well as she knew the sun would rise.

He'd capitulated tonight, his physical needs overwhelming his conscience. She also suspected that one of the reasons he'd given in to his lust was murkier than the thoughts he was accustomed to dealing with: if he lay with her, it would bind her to him.

She'd recognized the thought as it flickered across his open, honest face and she'd latched onto it tightly and used it to get what she wanted: his body inside hers.

Mel closed her eyes. She couldn't let him go away—not yet. The best way to keep him when he woke was to overwhelm his senses with pleasure and that was something she was an expert at doing.

Melissa and The Vicar

So, she began to move her hips in minute, undulating motions while controlling her inner muscles as she'd been taught to do so many years ago. She knew from experience that the subtle movement was enough to harden even the least responsive of male organs—which Magnus's was most certainly not.

She wanted to arouse his body, but not awaken it. Not yet.

She allowed herself a smug smile as his cock twitched inside her. Ahh, there it was.

All too soon he came to full hardness, the thick vein in his shaft pulsing against the sensitive skin of her inner passage. Perhaps she could make him climax in his sleep?

But one look at his beautiful face and flickering eyelids told her that was not to be.

Melissa watched hungrily as he made his slow, languorous journey to the surface of consciousness. His eyes moved rapidly behind his lids, the way they had on the beach. A moment later, his heavy lids lifted and surprise flashed in his eyes. But instead of shock, this time the corners crinkled and his lips curved into a lazy, lusty smile. "I am so grateful I didn't sleep through this—you are wicked to begin without me."

She offered her mouth and he took her in a deep, languorous kiss that went on and on while his hips began to move. They locked eyes, their bodies working like one mechanism, thrusting and flexing and thrusting and flexing.

Melissa had never climaxed with a lover inside her.

The man who'd bought and trained her all those years ago had not wasted any time on the needs of her body: why would a man care if his whore attained satisfaction?

Their lovemaking, if you could call it that, had been simple: she'd made him hard—not an easy task—and then rode him to his pleasure. He then fell asleep and she left him until he wanted her again.

Later, when she'd been older and free to pick and choose lovers for herself, she'd achieved orgasm, of course, but never during the act itself.

But as they worked in tandem to please one another, sensation gathered and built from her very toes. Her own feelings were heightened by watching his transformation. His skin took on a telling sexual flush, his breathing quickened, and his body—already hard and muscular—became even harder as his blood pumped faster and faster, his velvety skin sweat-slicked and taut beneath her hands.

Mel catalogued his responses to store and enjoy in the dry years ahead—greedily memorizing each breath, shudder, and thrust. She wanted it to go on forever, but she felt his control slipping away. For the first—and probably last—time ever with a lover, she released the strangle hold she kept over her emotions. She gave herself up to him completely, meeting him thrust for thrust.

"I love you, Melissa," he gasped in her ear as he drove them both over the edge.

They held each other so tight that she couldn't tell her heartbeat from his.

A thought wiggled through the physical sensation, struggling as hard as a fish fighting the river's flow: *if this never ends, I never have to leave him.*

But the thought, like a fish, was there and gone in an instant.

***

Magnus felt like the clock was chiding him. Its rhythm sounded eerily like a voice: *Go now, go now, go now.*

So, reluctantly, he exhaled and opened his eyes. She was looking right at him.

He smiled and kissed her nose. "I hate to say this, but I must go, my love." She looked so forlorn he added, "Only for the next few hours." He kissed her again. "Will you walk with me after church today? We can go see Mrs. Tisdale together." He grinned. "Do you think she'll be surprised when we tell her our news?"

She returned his smile, but it was sad.

"Come," he said, sitting up and holding her in his arms, his tone cajoling. "You knew I would have to leave. We've been fortunate, but your aunt may be back any moment." He glanced at the clock and frowned. "I'm surprised she isn't back yet."

She shifted from his embrace and stood.

Magnus looked up at her. "I'm afraid your gown is rumpled beyond repair—will you hate me for that tomorrow?"

Her laugh was half-hearted and she began to collect his clothing, which he'd thrown all over the room in his haste.

Magnus took his shirt from her and shook it before pulling it on. His neckcloth he just slung around his neck.

She handed him his waistcoat, her smile finally a real one. "This waistcoat has a tear in it, too. Do *all* your waistcoats have tears?"

Melissa and The Vicar

He reached for the waistcoat but grabbed her instead, pulling her close and stealing a kiss. "Yes, and most of my breeches, and coats, and unmentionables. I shall keep you busy mending."

She kissed his chest where his shirt was open and then turned to hunt the rest of his things. He was dressed and ready in far too short a time.

As they walked to the door he stopped and turned to her. "I can't help feeling you are sad. Do you regret what we—"

"No!"

The sharp word surprised them both. She shook her head and repeated, softer this time. "No. I don't regret a moment." Her mouth pulled into a half smile. "Except that it is over so soon."

He took her face in his hands and kissed her soundly. "We shall see each other in a mere," he checked his watch, "nine hours." He kissed her one last time. "Although I have to admit it will feel like a lifetime."

"Yes," she said as she opened the door. "It will feel like a lifetime."

Chapter Twelve

London
Six Weeks Later

It was astonishing how quickly Mel fell back into her daily routine. A week sped past before she knew it. And then another, and another. Soon a month had gone by.

Although Daisy never said a word, Melissa knew the other woman was shocked by her ability to cut Magnus out of her life and out of her heart.

Part of Mel—the part she kept locked away in the dark recesses of her mind—agreed with Daisy's assessment: Mel *was* inhuman.

But then again, it was also the way she stayed sane. Because the moment she opened her mind to memories of Magnus was the same moment she would begin unravelling. And Mel was terrified she'd come completely undone if she ever allowed that process to start.

So, instead, she turned every thought toward her business.

She speedily hired several new employees in preparation for the expansion into the new building, grateful—now—that Laura's behavior had pressured her into moving along with the plan. Laura and Hugo were behaving with admirable restraint, as were the rest of the servants—apart from Daisy, who'd gone back to work, and then succumbed to an influenza Mel suspected had more to do with listlessness than actual illness. But Daisy paid for her lodgings so Mel didn't need to exert pressure on her, although they both knew there would be no retiring yet. Another five years on her back at least, Mel believed, until her friend could stop working and have enough to carry her through.

As for herself? Well, the best way to lead was by example, so she was considering taking clients for the first time in years. After all, why had she been saving herself?

She was a whore who owned a whorehouse, lived in a whorehouse, and only associated with other whores and the men who paid them. It was past time she accepted that. The distance she'd attempted to maintain between herself and the others who worked for her had been hubris—or at least snobbery.

Nobody who worked at The White House—well, except perhaps Hugo, because who knew what the devil *he* thought—enjoyed exchanging sex for money. But that was life, wasn't it? Everyone had to do things they didn't like. Even the royals weren't exempt. Look at Prinny, forced to marry a woman who hated him so much she would just as soon stick a hatchet in his forehead as even look at him.

Thinking of Prinny made her think of the *royal issue* Joss had warned her about in his letter all those weeks ago. She'd been putting off speaking to Hugo because she knew it would be a difficult, and probably unpleasant, conversation. But she'd been here almost six weeks; it was time.

She pulled the bell and a servant answered almost immediately. "Tell Hugo I'd like to see him."

The maid—a new girl whose name Mel couldn't seem to keep in her mind—dropped a curtsey and scuttled away.

She went to the sideboard and poured herself a generous brandy, but when she raised the glass to her mouth she recoiled. She sniffed the glass—but it just smelled . . . off.

The door opened and she turned to find Hugo slouched in the doorway.

"Please, come in," she said dryly.

He grinned and shut the door behind him. "You wished to see me?"

"That was . . . fast."

He shrugged, the gesture sinuous, as all his movements were. If his behavior had been conscious, it would have been less effective, but his body was solid muscle and he moved with a grace that was surprising in a person whose manners were so very grace*less*.

She lifted her glass. "Does this smell off?"

He took a sniff with a nose that was far bigger than his face required. "Smells fine to me."

She shuddered. "Do you want it? I haven't touched it."

He took the glass, his expression speculative. "Is it your stomach again?"

"No." Mel hated that everyone knew her private business, but that was what happened when you coughed up blood while eating dinner with your employees.

She gestured to the heavy leather armchairs arranged in front of the fireplace. It was barely September, but she was cold for some reason, so she'd had the charwoman keep big fires in all her rooms.

"I think I know what this is about," Hugo said.

"Oh?"

"Mmm-hmm. Your surly associate—*Joss*—was deeply unhappy about my new friend. Which I find highly ironic for a man who has recently absconded with one of the most notorious aristocrats in Britain."

"I'd shut up about Joss and his business if I were you," she said, shifting irritably in her chair, unable to get comfortable. "And let me assure you, Hugo, Joss was a lot more sanguine about your behavior than I am."

His thin lips pulled into his idea of a smile. "Well, you don't have to worry. Our *special guest* has moved along."

She snorted. "If you think that means we don't have to worry about him then you are not as smart as you hold yourself out to be."

He shrugged and took a sip, his expression one of pure sensual pleasure as he swallowed the expensive brandy. "I know there are people who've suffered from the vigorous cleansing ritual my friend's powerful keeper employs, but this wasn't the kind of thing *my friend* would *ever* want to get out." Hugo smirked, "Trust me, he'll take our little secret to the grave."

Mel studied him while she considered what Hugo was really saying: he'd not just let the duke fuck him, he'd also rogered a member of the royal family.

She had to admit he was right, even a royal would have difficulty evading harsh punishment for something like that.

Hugo cocked his head and eyed her from beneath his habitually drooping lids—one more thing that could have seemed like an affectation if she didn't know he naturally looked this sleepy no matter the time of day or what he was doing.

It struck her, in a flash of terror, that he might be *blackmailing* his royal duke to ensure his silence.

Her eyelids fluttered shut at the thought. No, she could not even begin to contemplate such a possibility.

"You're curious, aren't you? You want to ask me questions."

Mel opened her eyes to find his mouth tilted in a wicked smile that united his mismatched features into something hypnotic and compelling. "You'd like to know all the details . . . how it felt to have

Melissa and The Vicar

so much power at my mercy. How it felt to have a man who might one day be king on his knees sucking me off."

Mel had to laugh and his sensual smile shifted into a self-mocking grin.

"I'll tell you, darling, but only over my pillow."

Melissa snorted. "I don't sleep with my employees, Hugo." Especially not ones she couldn't trust any farther than she could throw them.

"You slept with Joss."

She straightened in her chair. "Who told you that?"

"The man himself." She gave him a look of disbelief and he laughed. "All right, that was a lie. I was just guessing, but I can tell from your reaction that I guessed right."

Mel stretched her neck, wondering why she was so stiff.

Hugo leaned forward and put his glass on the table. He'd spread his knees, the black leather riding breeches that *were* an affectation stretched taut as he rested his forearms on his thighs, leaning toward her. He wore black boots polished to a glass-like shine, a black muslin shirt, a dull silk waistcoat of . . . yes, black, and a black cutaway coat that fit him like tar poured over his lean but broad back and shoulders. As affections went, Melissa thought it was more than a little effective. A successful whore always needed a signature, or trademark, and this was Hugo's: the whore in black. As for Mel's trademark? Well, it had always been her reserve. That, coupled with her selectiveness, had made her a commodity that men made fools of themselves to acquire.

"I'll pay you."

She blinked and stared at his face, which was no longer smiling. "Excuse me?"

"I understand you're considering taking on clients again, I would like to be one of them—preferably the only one."

Mel threw back her head and laughed. "You'd like to get your hands on my share of The White House, not on my body."

He grinned, not insulted by her accusation. "Can't I want to get my hands on both?" He stood and came toward her, the front of his breeches distended in a fashion that said maybe he *did* want her, after all. Or, perhaps he was just the sort of man who became aroused by money.

"And who told you I was considering taking on clients?" she asked.

"I'll never tell." He perched on the arm of her chair, somehow able to get away with the maneuver without her shoving him off. He leaned toward her and ran a finger down her jaw, his heavy eyes close enough that she could see they looked solid black. Mel stared into them, trying to get some sense of the man behind them. But Hugo was a dark horse both inside and out—and he kept himself so far behind a wall of illusion she wondered if he even existed independently of his façade.

His thin, sneering lips curved into a smile that somehow managed to be one of the most sensual Melissa had ever seen. Not that it could compare with Magnus's sweet, clear-eyed, joyous expression of love, of course.

Oh, Melissa, darling . . . don't open that *door*, a mocking voice in her head chided.

No, she'd better leave Magnus just where he was: far, far away from *her*.

Hugo's next words jerked her from her miserable thoughts. "I want to pay you; I want to be your client."

Mel's hand was lying on the small bit of chair Hugo wasn't occupying with his body. He encircled her wrist with his fingers, and they both looked down. The one part of Hugo Buckingham's body that was undeniably beautiful—well, other than his cock, which was, Mel had to admit, quite something to behold—were his hands. Like the rest of him they were long and shapely, the power in them latent as he squeezed her wrist and brought her hand to rest on his impressive erection.

Mel curled her hand around it, gripping him hard enough to make him hiss, his nostrils flaring with either pain or excitement or both; a person never knew with Hugo. She smiled and he leaned down toward her, his lips parted to take her.

"You can't afford me, Hugo darling." She gave his prick a sharp squeeze that got him off the arm of her chair quickly enough. He was momentarily surprised, but not angry. She'd never seen Hugo angry and hoped she never did.

Instead he laughed, a throaty, sensual sound that managed to make even her lifeless heart beat a little faster. "I adore you, Melissa. One day you'll realize I'm the perfect man for you—your perfect mate. We are two sides of the same coin. You'll see the light eventually."

Mel watched as he sauntered from the room, hoping to God he wasn't right.

Melissa and The Vicar

Meanwhile, in New Bickford . . .

Magnus knew he should have waited for the rain to pass before starting back to the vicarage, but some urgent compulsion always compelled him to get back, as if there was something waiting for him in his lonely cottage.

He wiped the moisture from his face with the back of his hand and stared through the almost impenetrable combination of dark and rain. There was some moonlight—he would not imperil Friar's health, even if he had little care for his own.

Some part of him wondered if he wasn't hoping to get sick—to die. It was a sin against God to think such a thing, but it wouldn't be the first time Magnus had sinned.

He'd thought the weight on his chest would become lighter as time passed. It had been eight weeks, yet things seemed no different from that very first day—when he'd gone to Halliburton Manor to look for her after she'd not come to church. Surely *that* day should have been the worst?

The house had been a hive of industry when he rode up, and he'd wondered what she was doing. But it had been the cook who'd answered the door, her lined face kind as she told him that her mistress was gone—along with her aunt—back to the city.

His brain had spun like a toothless cog. "When is she returning?" He'd known as the words left his mouth that his question was foolish—that he was only asking something that would bring more pain.

"I'm afraid she's not coming back, sir. Something important called her back."

The information was like a piece that simply would not fit—an extra piece in a puzzle—and he had no place for it in his brain.

"Would it be possible to get her direction in London?" he asked when he realized he'd been standing still and silent for a socially unacceptable amount of time.

The cook's expression had been worse than her words. Her eyes had filled with pity. "I'm afraid I'm not at liberty to give out such information. I'm very sorry, sir." She'd looked it.

When he'd stood mute and stupid, she'd reached out and laid a hand on his hands, which he saw were clenched together in front of him, his knuckles gone white.

She gave a squeeze and turned away, shutting the door quietly and leaving him standing on the front steps while servants bustled around him.

He'd had mad visions of clinging to the top of the carriage that was taking her baggage back to London. Or bribing the postilion to fit him in the box on the back. Or simply riding Friar all the way to London behind the carriage.

Ultimately, he had turned around and gone back to the vicarage, finishing his normal Sunday tasks like a dead man walking. The vicar and his wife both told him he looked ill, that he must have picked up an influenza on one of his many house visits. Go to bed, they said, get some rest. He'd obeyed them because it was easier than explaining why that wouldn't help.

He'd prayed, and prayed, and prayed. Nothing came to him anymore. His actions—his requests of God—felt self-serving and hollow.

So, when the vicar had said he was going to pay a call on a farm that was several hours journey by gig, Magnus had jumped at the opportunity.

The people he'd visited today were grindingly poor. Their farm had the well-worn feel of a tattered garment and even their fields had looked bloodless and dusty as he'd ridden through a weed-choked lane to reach the ramshackle cottage.

A few chickens scratched dispiritedly in the dust and a pig rooted unconvincingly near the corner of the house. Two children sat quiet and motionless under the eaves, their eyes too large for their faces.

"Hello," he'd said, smiling as he swung down from Friar. The vicar said the dying man had a family but hadn't mentioned how young they were; these children could not have been more than three or four. If Magnus had known, he would have brought one of the carved toys the vicar's stablemaster kept him supplied with. He cursed himself for having nothing in his satchel other than his bible and three jars of Mrs. Heeley's dreadful preserves.

He crouched down in front of them. "Do you want to pet my horse? His name is Friar and he's very friendly."

They looked from him, to the horse, to each other. Some message seemed to pass between them, and they nodded.

Melissa and The Vicar

"Let me lift you, he likes to have his nose petted."

Again, they nodded, and he scooped one up in each arm. They sat almost perfectly still, completely unlike the children he was accustomed to, who usually climbed him like a tree and mauled him like their favorite toy until their parents despaired. But he loved children and adored how at ease most were with him. Perhaps it was because he was the youngest and had never had a young sibling of his own to follow him about and pester him.

"Go ahead," he told them as Friar stood without moving, his big dark eyes meeting Magnus's, as if he knew these children were not like those he normally carried about on his back, the boisterous, happy boys and girls who begged Magnus for a ride whenever he took Friar on his rounds.

They petted Friar's velvet soft nose and chin, tentative smiles fluttering across their narrow, pale faces. The door to the cottage opened and their postures stiffened.

"Mr. Stanwyck?" The woman in the doorway looked as beaten down as her children, her hopeless eyes not only exhausted, but shadowed by the unrelenting fear of what would happen to her when her husband was gone and whoever owned their land learned there was nobody left to work it and pay the rent.

Magnus took the children back to the step and set them down before standing and greeting her.

"Would you like to take me to your husband first, Mrs. Jones? Perhaps we might talk after I meet him?"

She nodded, her eyes red and raw, as if she had no more moisture left to cry.

The house had the moist, sweet, sickly odor he'd come to associate with illness and death. The little cottage was only two rooms and a blanket separated them. Mr. Jones lay on a pallet on the floor, a nearby basin making the room so foul Magnus's eyes watered.

The man on the pallet had wasted to nothingness and his breathing was so shallow that at first Magnus believed he'd already died. But then his chest rose and a weak cough racked his body. He turned to Mrs. Jones, who was staring at her husband with dead eyes.

"Would you like a few minutes to go rest? Perhaps have something to eat? Or spend a moment with your children?"

She turned away without answering, leaving him alone with a living corpse.

Magnus took out the accouterments that usually gave him strength, the ritual of preparing another for death usually brought him purpose and focused him. But today, he felt like an actor assembling his props—a man merely playing a role.

This is not about you. The grim inner voice made his spine stiffen and his face heat with shame.

No, it *wasn't* about him. It was about Mr. Andrew Jones, a farmer who'd been struck by a chain that had snapped while he pulled a tree stump. The vicar said the man had never regained consciousness, but his body continued to function, slowly wasting away. That had been almost a month ago.

Magnus closed his eyes, took a deep breath, and began to pray.

***

The vicarage was dark and quiet by the time Magnus rode into the stable. It was still raining, and he was drenched through and had been for hours.

He saw to Friar's welfare first. It wasn't his mount's fault that his mad master had ridden for hours in the rain. After removing Friar's saddle and bridle he gave him a triple portion of oats, and rubbed his sore, wet body with a rough cloth as the horse happily munched away. Once the big gelding was warm and dry, Magnus switched to a curry brush.

The repetitive motions were hypnotic, freeing his mind and allowing it to wander. It chose the same path it always did.

What had happened that night after he left? Why had she left? Was it because of what they'd done? Had he disgusted her with his raw lust?

No answer his mind composed made any sense to him. His imagination was insufficient to come up with a reason for what she'd done—how she'd left him.

When his arms were too rubbery to move any longer, he oiled Friar's tack and then—when he could avoid it no longer—made his way to his lonely cottage.

As weary as he was, he couldn't sleep, so he ate some of the shepherd's pie the vicarage housekeeper had left him, not bothering to warm it up.

Tonight he'd crossed over from self-pity to self-awareness. Yes, he was in considerable mental anguish. Yes, it would take him time to come to terms with what had happened. And, yes, he would not treat his love as if it had been a mistake—a weakness that had led him to

Melissa and The Vicar

sin, to break his vows to God. He would go on—unlike poor Mr. Jones, whose breathing had finally stopped an hour after midnight. He hadn't wheezed, whimpered, or made any sound at all as he left his body. His struggle was over, but his wife and children's struggles were just beginning. If they could continue against such perilous odds, surely Magnus could?

He'd ridden into the small village closest to the farm and woke the local innkeeper, who was also the undertaker, and had paid him from his own pocket to provide what was needed, letting him know that he would return to perform the service.

Tomorrow morning he would speak to the vicar about the poor fund and perhaps finding a position for the woman. A farmer's wife would make a good housekeeper, there had to be something for her.

He closed his eyes and leaned back in his chair. A mixture of food, warmth, and exhaustion sent a wave of lassitude through him. He'd just drifted off when a sharp knock made him jump a good foot in the air.

When he jerked open the door, he found Sarah outside, her wool cloak dotted with moisture. Her cheeks were stained with tears and her laughing eyes were, for once, serious.

"It's Mrs. Tisdale, sir. She's . . . well, you'd better come."

Chapter Thirteen

Melissa was working on the plan for the new supper room. She wanted to remove two walls to make a room that could be used for either more card tables or one of the masked "balls"—which were really just orgies—she offered from time to time.

While many of her clients came and went hatted and cloaked or even masked, some enjoyed the more exhibitionistic pursuits. Many of them liked to imagine themselves as Roman senators engaging in a bacchanal, so she catered to those whims on occasion. She didn't care if they wanted to dress in rabbit suits and hop down Saint James in the middle of the day—as long as they were willing to pay for it.

She took a sip of milky weak tea and grimaced. Her stomach had been sensitive, although she hadn't had the wrenching pains or—God forbid—the blood. Still, she'd been throwing up in the mornings and Daisy said she was losing weight and looked pale.

Ha! She was one to talk. Her erstwhile most popular whore was now her housekeeper. Melissa hadn't even known she *needed* a housekeeper. But it seemed to give the older woman a sense of purpose, and also keep her from moping.

But it hadn't kept her from prying.

"Are you sure you're not increasing, Mel?" she'd asked just last week when one of the maids must have tattled that Mrs. Griffin's wash basin was once again filled with something other than used wash water.

Melissa had been assailed by shock, terror, fear, and anger in rapid succession. And lastly, filled with an almost crippling bolt of hope. Which she'd swiftly crushed.

While it was true that she'd not employed her usual precautions when laying with Magnus, she'd always had intermittent courses, sometimes going as much as half a year without bleeding. No, she was not carrying a child, and that should be a relief to her.

"It is my stomach condition, Daisy. And I'd thank you to stay out of my business."

Melissa and The Vicar

Daisy had merely raised her eyebrows, but at least she'd dropped the subject.

But the subject had wormed its way into Mel's mind like an eel writhing its way under a rock. She knew what her friend said was a possibility. It was *always* a possibility, especially when a woman was such an idiot that she allowed a man into her body without a sheath, and then failed to cleanse herself.

But that had not been an option that night nor had she wanted any such thing with Magnus. In the week since Daisy had planted the idea, she continued to be ill in the mornings and have a sore back. And her pelvis felt oddly . . . heavy. She'd been a whore since she was fourteen but never had she become pregnant. When she'd been with Lord Vanstone, he'd put the fear of God into her, warning her he would toss her out onto the street without a penny if she quickened. He'd taken her to an old woman, a courtesan who no longer took lovers, but whom many wealthy and powerful men went to for conversation. Dorothy had been the most composed, confident, and wicked person Mel had ever met; she'd also became Mel's idol over the two years they were friends—before the older woman died.

Dorothy had taught Mel something even in death, as her funeral was bare of any of the great men who'd come to her salons for amusement, entertainment, and even advice.

That was her last lesson to Mel: a whore should never expect loyalty or friendship from the men she fucked.

In any case, Mel had adhered to Dorothy's strict cleansing regimen while she belonged to Lord Vanstone. After him, she'd required any man who wanted to bed her to wear a sheath. She didn't care if they didn't like it; she'd seen too many victims of the pox to allow anyone to change her mind.

She'd never been careless and allowed herself to fall pregnant. But now Daisy had made her consider the possibility—something she'd never thought of before. If what she was feeling was not more gastric trouble—if she really *was* with child—what would that mean for her? Would she—*should* she bring a child into the world? If she did, she knew she could find a home for it. She'd seen it happen—she had helped women find proper homes—she didn't need to bring the child up with the shame of having a whore for a mother.

Melissa had never thought of herself as the maternal type, but she had to admit to a certain sense of something—all right, perhaps it *was* a yearning—at the thought of a baby.

A sharp rapping interrupted her musing and she looked up. "Yes?"

It was one of her footmen, Herman, who was as haughty as a lord and had the good looks to pull it off.

"A man to see you, Mrs. Griffin." He presented the tray with a flourish and a bow.

Melissa looked at it, and then looked again. "What?" she muttered, picking up the small rectangle as if it were a venomous insect. She looked up. "He is downstairs?" she asked stupidly.

Herman gave a moue of disapproval. "Yes, madam, and he appears to have leapt straight off his horse. He is garbed in a drab coat and mud-spattered leathers. He said he is not leaving until he sees you."

She stared at the name on the card and shook her head. "Lord Magnus Stanwyck"? He was a bloody *lord?* How could she not have known that?

Mel knew that shouldn't surprise her. How much did she know about him, really? Only that he had five siblings, a loving family, and that he was kind and—

She shook away the pointless dithering and stood. "Has he said what he wants?"

A look of apprehension crossed the servant's features and Mel realized she was speaking sharply.

"No, he's only said he wished to see you. Shall I ask him and return?"

"No." She looked up from the card in her hand. "Leave me for a moment—wait outside until I call you."

He nodded, his expression no longer haughty, and quickly shut the door behind him.

She wasn't surprised that he'd found her. She'd suspected Sir Thomas of being unable to keep his exciting surprise to himself—it sickened her to imagine the conversation. But she hardly expected that Magnus would seek her out. Sarah had certainly said nothing in the few brief letters she'd written to Daisy—and which Daisy had shared with Mel.

He could only be here because he'd discovered who she was and had come to confront her. Perhaps not shame her—no, he was not that kind of man—but he would want to face her. She ground her teeth at the thought of discussing anything with him—of seeing him at all. He was so . . . so loving and kind, she could just imagine him

Melissa and The Vicar

trying to help her, to get her out of this profession: to save a fallen woman. Hadn't somebody done that in the Bible?

Mel didn't think he would do it in the spirit of superiority, but because he really had loved her—or at least he'd once loved who he believed her to be: Miss Melissa Griffin, a youngish spinster of independent means who lived a proper life with her aunt.

Mel dropped her head into her hand and groaned. God, the stories there were about her—and most of them, unfortunately, true. If Sir Thomas had filled his ears there was no telling what Magnus knew about her.

Well, Mel would just have to make sure he saw her as beyond saving; that was the only way to get rid of him for good. If she could disgust and revolt him, she could make sure this would be the last time she ever had to see him. If that didn't work, well . . . she looked down at his card, sickened by the thought that came to her.

If that didn't work, she had something even worse.

She tossed the card onto the table and strode to a door, jerking it open so abruptly Herman jumped.

"Fetch Hugo."

Herman hesitated. "I believe he might be with—"

"I don't care if he is rogering the Queen Mother herself. Bring him. And make haste."

***

Magnus didn't know what to expect after what he'd learned from Mrs. Tisdale that night, but it certainly wasn't a place like this.

"I'm here to see Melissa Griffin," he told the richly liveried footman who greeted him at the entrance to The White House. It was a house that was indeed white and took up the greater part of one side of a street. It was as meticulously and tastefully maintained as his father's London house, which sat on Berkeley Square. And he believed it might actually be larger.

"Is she expecting you?" the haughty bastard demanded, pushing Magnus's already strained patience to the limit.

Magnus reached into the pocket of his greatcoat and took out a gold case his mother had given him on his eighteenth birthday—a case containing cards she'd printed for him and which he'd not used in years—well before he took up his living at New Bickford. He snatched one out and slammed it onto the salver that rested on the table in the entry hall. "Take her that."

The footman merely lifted an eyebrow at his theatrics before glancing at the card. He did not appear to be impressed by Magnus's title, but then Magnus supposed the men who could afford to walk through these doors were far more august personages than he.

The footman sauntered from the room with the salver and card. Magnus slumped against the wall, chancing to catch a glimpse of himself in the mirror that hung beside the door. Good God! No wonder the footman had looked at him with such derision. He appeared deranged; he *was* deranged. His eyes were wide and red-rimmed from a lack of sleep and his hair stuck out in all directions. What little he could see of his cravat made him cringe.

He tidied himself as best he could. He could do nothing about his eyes and dirty, rumpled clothing, but he could at least school his features into an expressionless mask.

And then he waited. And waited.

He was just about to get up and open the door the servant had disappeared through, and continue opening doors until he found her, when the door opened.

"Mrs. Griffin will see you now."

Magnus snorted softly to himself, *Mrs. Griffin*. He stood and followed the footman without speaking a word. The interior of the building was even more elegant and tasteful than the grand entry hall. Melissa—or somebody she employed—certainly knew their business when it came to creating an expensive, elegant environment that would make most aristocrats feel right at home. Nothing in the house was new or flashy; indeed, the carpet runner was an ancient, almost threadbare antique that bore the look of Savonnerie and the chairs and tables scattered in the small seating areas they passed looked like furniture you might see in Brooks or Whites.

They traversed through several different areas of the house and up two flights of stairs before they entered a part of the house that felt subtly different—less . . . practiced, although the décor was still that of an aristocrat's town house rather than a brothel. Or what Magnus had imagined a brothel would look like, having never been inside one before.

The footman stopped before a set of double doors and flung one open.

"Lord Magnus Stanwyck."

At first Magnus didn't see anyone—and when he did, he wished that he could unsee her.

Melissa and The Vicar

Melissa was at the far end of the room, reclining on a chaise lounge and wearing a diaphanous dressing gown that did more to outline the details of her lush, magnificent body than if she'd been naked.

And she wasn't lounging alone.

A glass of wine dangled from her fingers. "Why, Mr. Stanwyck—or should I say *Lord Magnus*, what a . . . surprise."

The man lying behind her had an arm negligently tossed over her side, his fingers playing idly with her breast—with her nipple, which Magnus could see was hard through the thin silk. His entire body became hot, the blood throbbing so loudly in his ears he wouldn't have been surprised to feel it running down his jaw. He was like a captured animal, unable to tear his gaze from the sight of the man's long, elegant hand, cupping and stroking, cupping and stroking.

"Is this the man you told me about, darling? The vicar?" His amused words were like a punch in the face, but at least it allowed Magnus to break away from the horrible sight of this man caressing her breast, and Melissa . . . *letting* him.

Magnus felt rooted in place. This couldn't be happening.

She smiled; a wicked, sinful smile that simultaneously made him begin to harden while causing his gorge to rise. The reaction left him confused, sick, *angry*.

"Hugo is teasing you, Magnus. He knows full well you are a curate."

The man grinned at him, a loathsome, hateful, smug grin that sent the flames of his rage soaring, an inferno he welcomed. Something flickered across her face as her hand settled over the man's stroking fingers. She made the gesture appear like an embrace, but suddenly Magnus saw the truth. And it cooled his fury like a bucket of ice water.

Melissa was doing this on purpose—she was humiliating him with this degenerate swine so that he would go *away*.

"I would like a moment alone with you, Melissa."

The other two chuckled at his request, Magnus's tormentor sliding free of her grip, his hand moving over her waist, to her hip, and then inching toward her mound.

Magnus took two long strides toward the chaise. "Remove your hand from her person or I will break it."

The man froze, his expression amused and curious rather than afraid.

Magnus looked away from his leering smirk. "Melissa, please, I wish to speak with you. Alone."

"You are not the master of me, Magnus." Melissa deliberately took the man's hand, which had been hovering just above her body, and slid it to her mound, spreading her legs to give him access to the most private part of her, and then she paused, meeting his gaze.

She cut him a smug, hateful smirk. "I fuck who I want, how I want, when I want. And if you continue to stay, you are going to have a front row seat."

Magnus flinched as though she'd kicked him in the face, his body frozen, his fists clenched at his sides, his mind reeling.

"I think you shocked him, Mel."

Again, they chuckled, the man's hand beginning a rhythmic stroking, his long, thin finger tracing the darker outline of her cleft, which was visible beneath the silk. Melissa's eyes were heavy, her hips gently thrusting.

"Look, darling, we're making him hard."

Magnus felt like a prisoner inside his own body—over which he'd lost all control. The other man, as hateful as he was, wasn't lying. Magnus was as hard as pig iron from watching another man fondle the woman he loved. He was—he must be—

His brain stuttered, unable to process what he was seeing, feeling. Was he a deviant? What the hell was wrong with him? How could he—

"Perhaps he'd like to join us?" his tormentor murmured, his hand slid from Melissa's sex up her belly, to her mouth. Melissa was waiting and she sucked a long, masculine finger between her lips.

Magnus couldn't have said what shocked him more: the other man's words, or his own body's response. Because suddenly he saw them in his mind's eye—the three of them—spread across that lounge, their bodies naked and writhing and—

Magnus shook his head hard enough make him nauseous and dislodge the horribly erotic image. It was this place—it was like a disease, like a black creeping mold that infected everything that came into contact with it. It was infecting him and Melissa was caught in its thrall as well.

"Melissa. I want five minutes of your time—alone." It was not a request—she could accommodate him, or he would begin to dismantle things: starting with the man touching her.

Melissa and The Vicar

Her lips curved around the man's finger, which she'd been sucking like a pornographic sweet, sliding her hand around his wrist and removing his hand. "What do you think, Hugo?"

The man eyed Magnus with open amusement, the moment stretching forever before he finally shrugged. "Why not?" He slid from behind her, his movements sinuous as he rose from the chaise, turned, and helped Melissa to her feet.

"Thank you, darling." She offered her lips to him and he claimed them with brutal swiftness.

Magnus swallowed hard and jerked his head away, but not before he saw her hand lower to the obscene bulge in the man's black buckskins and give him a possessive squeeze.

Hugo strolled toward Magnus and stopped.

He was perhaps two or three inches shorter than Magnus, who stood just at six feet, but the other man was as lean and hard as the snake he resembled and probably weighed a good three stone less.

In addition to leather breeches that fit him like a second skin he wore tall black boots of supple leather that molded to his long calves and a shirt of whisper-thin black lawn that did nothing to hide the slender but muscular torso beneath. He wore no waistcoat or coat and his appearance was that of a man who'd been interrupted in the middle of sensual pleasure. The look he gave Magnus was not one he'd ever received from another man. His eyes *smoldered*, his expression of raw lust creating pictures in Magnus's head of things he never would have believed he was capable imagining. The graphic, erotic thoughts left him breathless, hard, and terrified: what if this stranger just released primitive desires within Magnus's mind that had always lurked beneath the surface?

The other man's harsh face—so angular and hard it was actually ugly—leaned closer to his and his thin lips twisted into a sneer, his irises so dark in color they were indistinguishable from his pupils.

"I'll give you a quarter of an hour before I return."

It was a threat and a promise and Magnus did not bother telling him what was really going to transpire. He waited until the door clicked behind him before turning to the chaise.

Melissa's eyes snapped open, her sensual smile disappeared, and she crossed her arms. "You wanted to talk. So, talk."

"Is that man your lover?" It was the very last thing he wanted to say, but the seething hatred and jealousy inside him could no longer be suppressed.

"Was that what you wanted to talk about?" She sneered. "Then, yes, he is. Although we are not exclusive. I have *lots* of lovers, Magnus."

"Why are you saying these things to me? To drive me away?"

"Is it working?"

His rage and jealousy subsided as he looked at her beloved face, so twisted and angry—with him.

"I love you, Melissa, don't you understand?"

Her laughter was like an acid that made his face burn. "I would have thought that leaving without telling you who I was or where I was going would be answer enough for you. But instead you have somehow tracked me down, in spite of my very obvious wishes."

He shook his head. "Why are you behaving so cruelly?"

"Because I'm not interested in your love or your way of life. Go back to your little village—to where all your female worshippers believe you are without sin—to where you are perfect. To your flock who would never believe their precious curate could *fuck* a whore in the middle of her sitting room. Don't worry, I shan't tell anyone you slipped, Reverend."

The fact that her words were true only hurt more. "You have every right to think badly of me, Melissa."

"Why, thank you so much for telling me what I am allowed to think, *my lord*."

He took a deep breath and reminded himself he had no right to the anger he was currently feeling. She was right that he had stalked her and come here without her permission. He had also used her body outside the holy bounds of marriage just as surely as any of the men who'd paid her for the privilege. The fact that he loved her hardly changed that.

He met her angry gaze. "Mrs. Tisdale died two nights ago." He knew it wasn't fair, but it did disarm her—enough that they might be able to speak rationally.

Her eyes widened in surprise and flickered around the room restlessly, on anything but him. "I'm sorry to hear that," she finally said.

He nodded, his silence forcing her to look at him.

"I'm saddened to hear that," she repeated. Her expression changed as quickly as a flash of lightning. "Surely you didn't come all this way to tell me that?"

"No. I came to renew my offer of marriage."

Melissa and The Vicar

She blinked and her jaw dropped. "*What?*"

His face heated at her disbelief and scorn; he should have expected that. "I want you to be my wife."

"Are you mad?" She bolted to the small writing desk and snatched something up—his card, he saw. "Who *are* you? Who is your father?"

Magnus sighed. "The Marquess of Darlington."

Her green eyes bulged. "Darlington! A bloody *marquess*. You *are* mad," she yelled.

The door opened a crack. "Is anything amiss, darling?"

"Shut the door, Hugo," she shouted at the cracked door and then whirled on Magnus. "I can guess how you found out my whereabouts."

Magnus opened his mouth to tell her that Mrs. Tisdale had only given up her identity because she'd been feverish with pain and delirium.

But Melissa held up a staying hand. "No, shut up—I don't care what you have to say. You have no business following me, Magnus."

"I beg to disagree."

"Beg all you like—I happened to enjoy the sound of men begging." She flung the card toward the desk but it fluttered to the ground. She stalked toward him, her movements certain and dangerous, not stopping until she was so near that he felt the heat of her body. "Listen carefully. You'd better take your kind offer of marriage and go back to New Bickford and give it to some innocent young virgin. If you don't, I will contact Lord Darlington *myself*. How do you think your mother—who loves you so much, and whom you adore—would react to hearing her most favored son has been cavorting with a whore?"

Magnus shook his head in horrified amazement. "I know this is not really you, Melissa—to make such ugly threats."

"This is *exactly* who I am and you don't know a thing about me. I'm giving you a chance to leave, to get as far away from me and our unfortunate night together as you can."

Magnus didn't fool himself that he saw love lurking on her face. She was looking at him with raw . . . something. Fury? Anger? Hatred? She was so committed to her goal—that of driving him away—that he felt pity for her. He knew it was his fault that she underestimated his tenacity and believed him to be nothing but gentle and kind. Magnus had only ever shown her one side of himself. She didn't know about the rest of him—about the willful, spoiled parts of his character that he fought so hard to keep at bay.

Magnus almost felt bad about what he was about to unleash. Almost.

***

Melissa died a little more with every second he stared at her and ugliness poured out of her mouth.

Please go, Magnus. Please don't make me say all these ugly, horrid words. Please . . .

But he was as pale, white, and unmoving as a statue. His anger—jealousy, she supposed—at Hugo had drained away and all she saw now was compassion and understanding and—she didn't think she was mistaking it: pity.

He took her hands and she jumped. When she would have yanked them away his grip tightened. His hands were like a gentle, iron vise. "I'm going to leave this place, Melissa." He paused and her heart stuttered.

He is leaving you! a voice inside her head shrieked.

Magnus's lips curved into a sad smile. "But I will return by six o'clock. At that time, I will collect you and whatever possessions you care to bring with you. I will arrange for us to be married by a friend who is the vicar at St. Olav's. It is an unusually hasty request, but he will make an exception for me."

Mel felt her jaw sag open but couldn't summon the strength to pull it closed.

"Afterward, we shall stay a night in London, at my family's house. After that we will go to Yorkshire, where I will introduce you to my family. We will stay for two weeks before returning to New Bickford. The curate house is small, but we shall manage until I either find something more appropriate in the area, or perhaps I might take a living I've been offered in East Anglia." He gave her hands a squeeze. "It is something we can discuss and decide together." He released her. "But for now, pack your possessions and be waiting for me when I return." His voice was still soft and kind, but there was something else. Something beneath his words that she'd never heard before—something she never in a lifetime could have imagined: it was iron. Pure, inflexible, unbreakable iron. She could only stare.

He lowered his mouth to her forehead and kissed her before turning away and heading for the door.

"You are insane," she managed, her voice weedy and weak.

Melissa and The Vicar

He turned and cocked his head.

"You are," she insisted, as though he'd argued. "I *won't* be waiting for you, and you *won't* gain entry to my house again. This is the last time we will speak."

His expression was one of sadness mingled with regret. "Please, Melissa. Don't make me insist."

She laughed and was horrified to hear a tinge of hysteria in the sound. "Insist all you want, just don't do it here. Your fifteen minutes are almost over. I suggest you leave before Hugo comes back."

He took a deep breath, held it, and then exhaled, his expression that of a tolerant father who must—although he was reluctant—punish his recalcitrant child.

Melissa stared: who *was* this man? This stern, commanding Magnus standing before her? An unwanted—and unexpected—spike of lust struck her as she took in the confident, commanding expression on his beautiful face.

"If you do not leave with me and marry me, I will destroy this place." His mouth pulled into an almost embarrassed half-smile.

Melissa's heart stuttered. "You are talking like a lunatic."

He continued, undeterred. "I don't mean I will physically destroy it; I mean I will see that the entire enterprise is brought down. I don't intend to harm any of the unfortunate people who are employed here, but I would imagine lives, futures, and prospects will be damaged in the process. The men who make use of your business will not gather round to save you, quite the opposite. I would never incite such chaos and leave lives in a shambles; I will be around afterward to help those who want it, but it will be an unpleasant business for all involved. But you—"

He took a step toward her, his eyes suddenly on fire, like the burning blue gaze she'd seen in a Renaissance painting once, some martyr who'd been lashed to a post and was about to face a fiery death with an expression of eagerness that was almost erotic.

"You." He slid a warm hand beneath her jaw, his size and restrained power making her feel small and vulnerable, just as she suspected he intended. "Suffice it to say you will not be able to resume this type of work anywhere in England. And if you leave the country, I will follow you."

She shuddered, awestruck at the quiet finality in is voice, the inevitability. His hand slid down her cheek to her throat, his fingers at the back of her neck flexing as he pulled her close. He didn't kiss her; he just held her lightly against him while he spoke.

"I come from a wealthy and influential family, Melissa." His words were warm puffs of air on her temple, but they sent chills throughout her body. "I know aristocrats do not wield the power they did even a half a century ago. But I think you know the displeasure of a marquess—especially one who has the King's ear—can be heavy, indeed. I think you know I am not the kind of man to issue idle threats. I told you that I loved you the night we were together and you answered in kind. I asked you to marry me that night and you accepted. Based on your words and my expectations we came together as man and wife." He made a sound of frustration. "What could you expect would happen? I told you that you were my first and only lover; surely you must have guessed such an action meant a great deal to me." He paused. "But you *lied* to me so that I would abandon my convictions and lie with you. You lied to get what you want, and now you will marry me." He kissed her temple, the gesture less like a benediction and more like a seal. "And you will do so because you gave me your word."

Mel closed her eyes.

If he had yelled and blustered, she would have disbelieved him—and she would have yelled and blustered in response. But this . . . this declaration of his, an almost reluctant willingness to go to such lengths to keep her to her word—his iron-clad resolve to go to war. No, he was not lying.

The fight, which had kept her upright since she'd first glanced at his card, left her body in a rush. She told herself it was the inevitability which caused her to capitulate, but the raw truth was that she wanted him so very, very much. Even though she knew they would both suffer dearly for their wants.

He must have sensed her submission because he stepped back, his hands gripping her shoulders to steady her, his face once again the kind, gentle, and concerned face of the man she loved.

"I've been fortunate enough to be granted an audience with His Grace, the Archbishop of Canterbury. I will need your full name for the special license."

Melissa met his clear, honest gaze and opened her mouth, curious as to what name would come out. "Melissa Griffin, no middle name."

Melissa and The Vicar

He smiled and nodded and a leaden sickness settled in her stomach at the ease with which he accepted her lie. "Thank you, my dear. You will be waiting when I return?"

He could have ordered her to be waiting, they both knew that. But he'd asked instead.

She swallowed, and then nodded. "Yes, Magnus, I'll be waiting."

Chapter Fourteen

Magnus was concerned for his wife of less than two hours. As he'd asked—very well, ordered—she had been waiting for him when he returned with the carriage his father kept at the London house.

Acquiring the special license had been far easier than he'd expected. Deciding to hew as closely to the truth as possible, Magnus had confessed his lapse to the archbishop, whom Magnus knew only slightly but believed would be sympathetic to his situation given his history of scandalizing his family by eloping with his own bride.

License in hand, he'd dropped in on his very surprised friend, Thomas Wilkins, who had—after some rather intense persuasion—agreed to marry them that evening.

He'd next gone to Darlington House. Although the knocker was off the door he'd gone around to the servants' entrance.

Mr. and Mrs. Dawks, who'd worked for his father since before Magnus was born, appeared genuinely thrilled to see him, although he could see they were curious as to why he was not wearing his blacks and had brought so little with him—nothing other than one small traveling bag.

But when he told them he would be bringing his new bride to stay they were ecstatic. And, like the good servants they were, began to make the house ready, although he'd told them they needn't go to any great bother. They prepared a meal, removed the Holland covers, and stoked fires in the best adjoining guest chambers.

He'd gone down to the kitchen to help with the bath he'd requested, putting aside their protests that the ancient Dawks could transport the required hot water.

Clean and dressed in a suit of clothing he'd found in the bedroom he kept, he set out to collect Melissa.

He'd been shocked at his own behavior after he'd her standing in the middle of her room, almost too shocked to notice the lurking Hugo as he'd left.

Melissa and The Vicar

"Hugo."

The other man had turned away from Melissa's door, which he'd apparently been about to open.

"Don't go in there." He'd closed the distance between them. "And never lay a hand on her again."

The man—some manner of whore, Magnus assumed—merely laughed. "The only one who gives orders about Mel is Mel."

"And now her husband." He'd turned and left, more pleased than he should have been by the man's expression of utter shock.

But his amusement had worn away the longer he contemplated what he'd said, how he'd behaved, whom he'd *become* in that room. Magnus abhorred violence of all kinds, and the things he'd said to her—the coercion he'd used to force her to live up to a vow she'd obviously never meant seriously—left him disgusted with himself and horrified.

He knew the cause of his beastly behavior was seeing her with *that* man. It had made him want to flex—to demonstrate that he had *some* power. She had prodded him with a flyswatter and he had responded with a twenty-pound mallet.

But it was too late for regrets. They were here, at the home where he'd run and played with his brothers as a child; the place where he'd dressed in ridiculous finery for his first trip to Carlton House with his father; the place where he'd held his grandmother's hand as she died—the same night he told his parents he was entering the clergy.

He and his new wife sat in the smaller of the two dining rooms surrounded by an impressive array of food. They'd come directly from the tiny church, where only Thomas and his wife had been their witnesses. His interaction with his friend had been, naturally, somewhat stilted. He supposed it would have been natural to invite the couple to celebrate with them, but he could hardly let his friend see them in their current state of armed neutrality—well, at least on her part. For his? He had exhausted his anger—his jealousy—and now he wanted to begin their married life on the right footing.

But of course he was not the one who had been threatened and coerced into this marriage. He looked across the food, most of it untouched, to where she sat.

"Melissa?"

She looked up from the plate he'd served her and saw she had eaten none of it.

"Won't you eat something?"

"Will you threaten and force me if I don't?"

He flushed. "I should apologize for my earlier, er, bombast."

"An apology costs you nothing now, does it? And it is worth just as much to me."

"I deserve that," he conceded. If he'd hoped his mild words would appease her, he'd been dead wrong.

She flung up her hands. "Oh, all is well, then. So." She shoved away her plate and cutlery with a noisy clatter and then propped her elbows on the table and leaned toward him in a distinctly unladylike pose. She was wearing a gown he'd never seen before; a gown cut so her breasts, which he knew were lovely, were displayed more prominently than he'd seen before. It was not gaudy or unsuitable, merely nothing like the proper pastel muslins she'd worn in New Bickford. It was a deep rose color that flattered her skin and hair and made her appear positively edible. Magnus blinked at the sudden thought; he'd do well to put such amorous images from his mind for the foreseeable future. Perhaps for the remainder of his married life.

He realized he was staring at her chest and glanced up. Her expression was mocking—unpleasantly so.

"So," she repeated, "now that you've taken me from my home with all the finesse of a Viking dragging a woman by her hair, what do you intend to do with The White House?"

Magnus didn't believe he'd heard her correctly. "I'm sorry?"

"It is yours now, isn't it? As well as my person, of course."

He realized that he'd begun to tense, to breathe faster, to become angry at her hostile, accusatory, *mean* tone. And then he realized he had no right to that anger. Everything she said was true: her person and her possessions now belonged to him under the law.

"I want nothing from your business. But neither will I permit you to continue profiting from it." He watched as she became redder but ploughed forward. "I'm inclined to ask that you close it immediately, but I'll give you a month to contact your man of business and end things."

She lunged to her feet, swatting violently at the wine glass that sat untouched and sending it whizzing past Magnus's shoulder and shattering against the black-and-white marble floor.

"Are you trying to make me hate you? Because you needn't bother—I already do."

Magnus pushed back his chair and went to her. Spirals of auburn hair, which he knew possessed a beautiful curl when unbound,

Melissa and The Vicar

escaped from the stern chignon she favored, floated around her angry face; her eyes were like the phosphorescence he'd occasionally seen in the water off New Bickford Head.

"Melissa." He raised his hands to touch her but then froze when she flinched away from him. "Please," he said, lowering his arms to his sides. "I deeply regret the words I spoke in anger to bring you to this point. You will never know how much I grieve them. But we are man and wife, now. We will be with one another as long as we live—don't you think it behooves us to make the best of our situation? After all—" He couldn't help himself and reached for the gentle curve of her jaw; this time she let him. "After all," he repeated, his body throbbing at the mere touch, "I *do* love you, and I believe you care for me—or at least you did before today. Perhaps . . ."

He broke off when she leaned toward him, her eyes heavy, her lips parted, tilting her face up to be kissed. Magnus obliged her, their lips barely meeting, but enough to bring him to complete arousal. She kissed him teasingly, her nibbling reminiscent of that night, of the loving they had shared. "I did say I loved you, Magnus," she whispered, her words thrilling him, "but I only said that to get what I wanted. You know how that is, darling, but I apologize *now* for what I said to you *then*."

He stiffened, and not in a pleasurable way.

She pulled away and smiled up at him, one eyebrow cocked in amusement, the sultry look in her eyes nowhere in sight, her expression that of a pugilist spoiling for a fight. "I didn't really mean it," she said, just in case he'd missed her point.

Magnus suppressed the flare of hurt and anger he felt at her words. Instead, he nodded. "Very well, I will accept you lied when you said you loved me. Will you be seated?" He had the satisfaction—slim—of seeing her eyes widen in surprise at his cool acceptance of her cruel words.

She dropped gracelessly into her chair, her expression wary and uncertain. Magnus gave the bell pull a tug.

When the Dawks arrived, he gestured to the broken glass. "Would you please have someone clean up the mess and bring a new glass for my wife? I'm afraid I was rather clumsy with this one."

***

Melissa glared at him from across the confines of the post chaise. It was the second day of traveling. She'd not spoken a word to him since dinner on their wedding day. She smirked at the word *wedding*. Her husband was reading, his expression fixed enough for her to believe he was not merely acting. No, he'd read for an entire day yesterday. And then last night, when they'd stopped at an inn and he'd procured chambers for them: two *separate* chambers.

He'd ordered her a meal for the private parlor—not consulting her, of course—high-handed behavior she was beginning to realize he must have possessed all along, but had merely kept hidden—and then he bid her good night and took his own meal in the public dining room.

She'd been furious. It had been her plan to ask him to let her have her evening meal in peace because she wanted to see that hurt, pained expression that he'd shown her the day he'd begged for her hand. Instead, he showed her nothing but courtesy, kindness, and polite concern. He was a perfect husband.

And she? Well, she was as sharp-tongued as the proverbial fishwife, everything she said sarcastic, or veiled, or just outright rude. And he never rose to the bait.

But beneath her anger was no small amount of worry and shame. She had lied to him about her real name—lied to the Archbishop of Bloody Canterbury—and she'd concealed her growing suspicion that she was likely pregnant.

He had bullied and threatened and she'd done what she did best, well, second best—she'd lied.

You lied because he forced *you to lie!* her furious inner voice said, the truth of the statement stirring the embers of her anger but not enough to burn away her guilt at what she'd done.

Even so, her shame wasn't strong enough to make her forgive him. She knew it was childish, but her desire to bait and draw a rise out of him increased with each hour they spent together. Just what did it take to ruffle his hateful placidity and composure? Two days ago she'd found the answer to that question: Hugo. Yes, Hugo had gotten through Magnus's veneer of kindness and civility.

Unfortunately, she couldn't pull Hugo out of her valise to taunt him with, but that didn't mean she couldn't introduce his apparition.

So last night, in her room all alone, she'd written Hugo a letter, addressing it to him in a bold hand and giving it to her *husband* when he'd come to lead her downstairs this morning.

"Will you see this is posted for me, darling."

His pupils flared at her affectionate tone and his answering smile was instant. And then he'd looked down at the letter in his hand. His beautiful lips tightened but he still managed one of the smiles she now thought of as his *curate mask*. "It would be my pleasure."

And those were the last words they'd exchanged since they'd entered the carriage this morning.

He looked up, as if aware of her brooding stare, and smiled at her. "Are you comfortable, my dear?"

He asked questions like this at least every few hours; she ignored each and every one of them. At first, she'd believed it was for the sake of the servants, or just to batter her with his vapid courtesy. But she'd begun to realize he was genuinely concerned for her comfort. Which only annoyed her more.

She ignored his question yet again and turned to look out the window. Not much to see: it was gray, rainy, and the wind howled.

"I'm afraid you won't be seeing Bodmin Moor at its best," he said, apparently not caring whether he spoke to her or a blank wall. "But there is a certain bleak beauty that one can enjoy at any time of year."

She studied her cuticles as if there was no more interesting sight in the world.

"You are probably wondering how it is that I have a cottage in such a remote area?"

Mel moved to her other hand.

"It belonged to an aunt on my father's side. She was rather a rebel who refused to marry and spent her time on the Continent, until the War drove her back home. She spent her last years here and I often came to visit her when I was in school."

Mel sighed.

"She died three years ago."

She looked up at the pain in his voice, but his expression was bland and contemplative.

"I suppose I should tell you a bit about my family. We are relative newcomers to the aristocratic table. My great-grandfather was a shipbuilder in Liverpool during the wars of the last century." He paused, his tone musing. "Although it is difficult to see where one war begins and another ends." He shrugged, the movement of his broad shoulders elegant even in his poorly fitted blacks, which he'd reverted to the morning they left London. It annoyed her that she even noticed his bloody shoulders or what he wore.

"Great-grandfather William Stanwyck made two of the ships in the squadron that destroyed the Spanish fleet in Vigo Bay. King George—our current king's grandfather, rewarded him with a barony:

William, 1st Baron Stanwyck. Naturally my great-grandfather immediately packed his bag, removed himself to the small town of Branford where the King's generous grant of land awaited him, and commenced laying flagstones for the baronial manor almost the moment he leapt from the carriage."

Mel realized she was smiling and put a stop to it.

"He soon had a hall to go with his title, but no wife and no son to carry on. He married Lady Anne Portnay, the thirteenth child, and seventh daughter, of the 5th Earl of Sheringham. It wasn't a mere step up the social ladder for William, it was a prodigious leap. His son, the 2nd Baron and my own grandfather, was not so well placed—in spite of his maternal connections—that he could ignore the family business. He, too, provided the accouterments every monarch needs to wage a successful naval campaign. He was rewarded with an earldom and marquisate in quick succession, but neither of these titles came with land. Not bothered by that oversight, James, my granddad, immediately began expansion on his baronial hall, a project which kept him busy and happy as he and my grandmother—the daughter of a baron—were fruitful and multiplied." He paused and glanced at her, catching her openly listening. She yawned and opened the book that sat beside her on the seat. He didn't laugh, but she could feel his amusement.

"Which brings us to my own father. Ships were a distant memory when my father, David, appeared on the scene. He was born the third son out of five and survived all but one of them." The humor had drained from his voice. "My father, his elder brother, and two of his sisters also survived the smallpox epidemic, but all four siblings were scarred.

Mel put down the book.

"My father grew a beard to cover the disfiguring scars but his brother—the eldest but one—had been left both scarred and blind and took his own life. One aunt still lives at Stanwyck Hall and has never married. The other is the one I mentioned earlier—Aunt Eudora. Although she never said so, I believe she avoided marriage because of her scarring. She was also a very . . . how should I put this? Aunt Eudora simply did not accept her role as a spinster aunt who stayed at her married brother's house and knitted stockings. She was a free spirit; I suppose is the best way to describe her. It is from my aunt that I learned to follow my heart and join the clergy rather than embrace a future as a gentleman farmer."

Melissa and The Vicar

This time, when he caught her looking, she did not yawn or look away. He held her gaze for a long moment and then continued, turning to gaze out the window.

"My mother was the youngest daughter of the Duke of Southmorland. She was, what the *ton* so vulgarly phrases, a diamond of the first water. My parents' marriage was a love-match. My father says it was love at first sight—he fell in love with her when she didn't run away at the first sight of him."

Mel smiled; how could she not?

"My brother Cecil, who is Earl of Sydell, lives at home. He is horse and hunting mad and you will never see him without a pack of hounds at his heels. Michael, the eldest but one, has his own very pretty property only an hour away. He is engaged to be married to his childhood sweetheart, our nearest neighbor's daughter—an unholy terror who tormented all the boys in the neighborhood growing up." He grinned at her. "I believe you will like Molly when you meet her."

Mel could only stare. Didn't he know what he was saying? She was a *whore* and an infamous one, at that. And he thought he could merely stroll into his family house and introduce her to the daughters of dukes, earls, viscounts? It was at times like this that she found it difficult not to scream at him like a shrew—how could he be so bloody *naïve*?

"The next in line is Henry, who is with his regiment on the Continent. After him is James, who is with the Duke of Wellington's diplomatic core, and then there is Philip who lives on one of my father's estates up in Scotland." He gave her the same sweet smile that had unraveled her in New Bickford, but which she now knew was a façade for a man who did not shy from ruthless behavior to get his own way. "And then there is me."

"Their baby and favorite," she said.

He did not deny it.

"The one who has married a whore."

"Enough!" he bellowed.

Melissa almost jumped out of her skin, and even the carriage seemed to shudder.

She could see, by his wide eyes and flaring nostrils, that he had stunned even himself. She was beginning to suspect his temper was triggered by specific things—and when it happened . . . well . . .

"I won't tolerate that word. If you have no respect for yourself, at least have some for me."

"What," she jeered, sounding nothing but spiteful even though her heart was hammering in her chest, "you prefer another word? Prostitute? Harlot?" she hesitated and then, "*slut.*"

He stared at her through pupils that had shrunk to pinpricks, his irises a chilling, frosty blue. "That will be the last time you speak those three words, either."

"You are very fond of giving orders, *my lord.*"

"I am your husband, Melissa."

"And that is a husband's job, to issue orders?"

His jaw worked from side to side. Who would ever have guessed this stern, commanding man inhabited the same body as the other Magnus—the caring, loving, laughing man who'd entranced every female in his vicinity with his gentle sweetness? Of course, she'd been goading him for days. Most other men would probably have beaten her by now.

He looked away, gazing out the window. His profile was achingly beautiful. Her husband was a magnificent man. If her life had been different—if she'd not spent the last fifteen years as a whore—marriage to Magnus would have been her greatest dream.

But this? He'd behaved rashly, spurred by jealousy at the sight of her stupid games with Hugo. And he'd taken a step he would live to regret. Deeply, and sooner rather than later. And when that happened? When they found themselves sitting at a table with a man she'd spread her thighs for—which would happen, it was only a question of how soon—he would start to hate her.

And that would be the best outcome.

The worst possibility was that he would challenge some man who dishonored her—or *him* rather—with a throwaway comment about something she'd done that would most likely be true. Which would only make him angrier and hate her more.

Likely he would meet said man on a foggy morning with pistols. That encounter would either end with his death or banishment from England. Banishment would be just the same at that point because he would be ejected from the Church faster than a bullet from a pistol when they learned about his marriage. They might not be so kind as to discharge him. No, they would probably make his existence a living hell, until he finally did the dirty work for them and quit.

And he would hate her for all of it.

So, all his efforts since they'd married—his apology for behaving like a primitive brute and threatening her business with disaster; his

Melissa and The Vicar

solicitousness for her care and comfort; his loving behavior and looks, nay, his *love* itself—because she knew he loved her—all of those efforts were for naught. He couldn't make her love him—she already did.

Melissa told herself that she'd entered this marriage knowing it was not legal *because* of her love for him—not that he would see it that way when he eventually found out her deceit. But sometimes you had to do things for those you loved even though they would not thank you for it.

She would stay with him only as long as it took to see to the sale of The White House—an action she could take without subterfuge as he'd already indicated he wanted her divorced from the business. With the money from the sale and her savings she would be able to leave him and live a comfortable if not luxurious life. She might stay in England and find another small village like New Bickford—she found she enjoyed the country. Or she might simply leave England altogether and begin anew somewhere on the Continent. She could raise their baby in peace. He would be devastated for a while, but he was resilient and would heal, in time. After all, it would be better to be the victim in a tempest in a teapot than trapped in a marriage that could only end in unhappiness and pain, most especially *because* they loved each other.

He could not see that, nor could he see that she would destroy his life, and her love for him would destroy hers. That's what they were to each other, whether he saw it or not: mutual destruction.

Chapter Fifteen

In front of other people—innkeepers, servants—Melissa was polite and pleasant.

But the moment they were alone together, she became a stranger: a hostile stranger. Unfortunately, they were alone together for the better part of two days and she'd not even begun to thaw.

Last night they arrived at his aunt's cottage—more of a manor house, Magnus supposed—and it had been too late to do much but introduce her to Mr. and Mrs. Hixon, the couple who lived at Moor House and acted as caretakers.

Despite the tension between himself and his wife, Magnus had felt at peace the moment he'd stepped into Moor House. Of course, he'd felt pain and loss, as well, but it was still the place where he could feel traces of his beloved aunt's presence.

Magnus had considered leasing out the house, but he'd loved his Aunt Eudora deeply and couldn't bear thinking about somebody else using her things or—even worse—replacing them. Eventually he'd have to do something with the place; it wasn't right to leave it as a shrine.

But for now, he'd been grateful there was somewhere he could take his new wife that was not London, not his family's home in Yorkshire, and not back to New Bickford.

After the angry incident at dinner that first night Magnus had quickly realized that his initial plan—to take her to visit his family—was beyond foolish.

No, they needed to spend some time alone together—somewhere they would not be bothered by outside distractions—and learn to rub along before he settled her into the curate cottage.

He'd learned that very first evening of their marriage that the place to learn about his new wife most certainly was not London.

At Melissa's request, Magnus had left her alone at Darlington House after they'd finished their disastrous wedding dinner. No doubt his abandonment of her had shocked the servants, but Magnus had been too bruised by her obvious hatred to care how it might appear to others. Mingled with his pain was guilt and shame at his high-handed treatment of her and the mess he'd made of both their lives.

His father, a staunch Whig, maintained a membership at Brooks for all his sons, despite the fact Magnus hadn't been to London in years. So, he paid a visit to the club for lack of anything better to do.

Of course, he'd encountered people that he knew, friends of his brothers mostly, and also a schoolmate from Eton. He'd had several drinks while they'd teased him about casting off his blacks for an evening of debauchery. He'd not had the courage to tell them he'd just married that very day. Besides, that news was for his family first, not a bunch of drunken bucks.

They'd been mocking him mercilessly when somebody suggested, "We should take him over to The White House and show him what a good time is all about!"

The name set Magnus's head buzzing.

"I hear Mel Griffin is back in the saddle and taking new customers for the first time in years."

Magnus's head jerked up then.

"Look," one of the others said—he hadn't known or cared who it was—"Even curates from rural counties have heard of our Ice Madam."

"Ha, not yours, Devlin. You're too bloody ugly for the likes of her."

"Dev's too bloody poor, is more likely," somebody else said, causing laughter all around.

"But seriously, Mag," John Taylor—one of his brother Michael's friends—said, "is it against the rules to enjoy a little carnal pleasure?"

"Yes, old man, surely you need to know what to preach *against* before you can be persuasive," another man said, setting them all off into gales of laughter again.

"Mag? You all right?" John leaned closer, his forehead creased in concern. "Don't be angry, it's just a bit of teasing. I didn't mean any disrespect."

Still, Magnus couldn't seem to speak. The others were describing something one of them had done during his last trip to Melissa's—his *wife's*—place of business. Perhaps they were even describing something *she* had done.

"I swear, Peggie," said Viscount Royce, a man closer to Magnus's age and one whom he'd never particularly liked, "that girl could swallow a cricket bat. And having the two of 'em going at me at once, well, it was—"

"Who?" Magnus's rough word surprised him more than the sweating, rotund lord, who merely blinked.

"Er, what's that, Stanwyck?"

"I said, *who*? *Who* could swallow a cricket bat?"

The men had gone still around him.

Royce blinked while John set a hand on Magnus's shoulder, but he shrugged him off.

"Don't you know the girl's name?"

Royce's laughter was nervous. "Not that I can recall," he glanced around at the others, as if looking for guidance. "I mean, she was a whore, Stanwyck, not a girl in her first Season who expects chit-chat."

"The White House isn't where we go for pleasant conversation," another one added. "It ain't bloody Almack's."

A few of the men chuckled.

Encouraged by his friends' laughter, Royce relaxed, his sly, disgusting smile returning. "The women at The White House have been trained up right and know how to serve a man just the way I like it—which means they *can't* talk."

The others laughed heartily and equilibrium was restored. Magnus glanced around at these men—his peers—while they told increasingly raucous stories, one-upping each other and boasting about their sexual prowess.

Had one of these men been inside Melissa? Had any of them done these things with *his wife*? His head had become so hot—his vision so blurry and red—he'd actually worried about his sanity.

He'd left then. Right bloody then, lurching to his feet and making a beeline for the door, ignoring their calls, not stopping until he was three streets away. Only then realizing he'd gone in the wrong direction.

He'd hoped to enjoy the luxurious surroundings of Darlington House for a few weeks since going North was now out of the question. But less than an hour at Brooks made him accept that he needed to get the hell out of London before he did something irreversible and foolish.

When he finally arrived back at Darlington House he'd immediately written a letter to Mr. and Mrs. Hixon, the couple who managed his Aunt Eudora's house, telling them to ready the house for him and his new wife's arrival.

Melissa and The Vicar

He'd also needed to send a message to his own wife the following day when she'd not come down for breakfast and again at lunch. He'd told her to prepare to travel early the next morning, once again displaying a high-handed manner but seeing no way around it.

He'd had hopes for the ride to Bodmin Moor, reasoning that being in an enclosed space would throw them together so they'd *have* to talk. He'd clearly been wrong on that score. He told himself that he must keep hoping and trying, but it was getting more difficult to come up with ways to interact with her.

Today had been their first full day at Moor House and he'd spent most of it in his aunt's study going over the ledgers Mr. Hixon kept for him. He didn't see Melissa leave the house; in fact, he didn't see her at all until dinner. Although the dining room was considerably more intimate than Darlington House, the dining experience was exactly the same; well, minus the broken wine glass.

They ate their meal with Magnus asking questions and Melissa giving monosyllabic answers. She'd left him alone to his port—which he didn't drink—and refused his invitation to join him in the library.

As they'd done the night before, they each retired to their respective quarters, the master and mistress's chambers. He supposed she would have like the room farthest from him but Magnus would be damned if he'd embarrass himself in front of the Hixons, who already must wonder at their less than amiable behavior toward each other.

Magnus paced his room as he listened to the activity next door. Neither of them had brought body servants with them and were doing for themselves. It sounded as though she was putting the contents of her trunk into the dressing room.

It was an hour before the room became quiet, but a line of light beneath the door indicated she'd not yet gone to bed. Magnus inhaled deeply and went to the connecting door, giving it a sharp rap. The pause was so long he thought she was going to ignore him. What would he do then? What would—

The door jerked open and she stood in the opening. "Yes?" Her eyes were hard green stones in her pale face. She wore an emerald green negligee that caused him to immediately begin sweating.

"I would like to speak to you," Magnus said, wishing his voice was not so harsh.

"You are speaking to me."

He clenched his jaws. "May I come in?"

She made him wait. And wait. And wait. Eventually, she spun on her heel and went back into her room, leaving him to follow.

There was a sofa and chair in front of the crackling fire and she draped herself on the loveseat, tucking her bare feet beneath her. Her pose reminded him, uncomfortably, of the way she'd been lying on her chaise with that bloody Hugo. His groin stirred at the thought and he wanted to howl: how could he possibly find such a memory arousing?

"What do you want, Magnus?" She was studying him with a dispassionate gaze that gave him a hopeless, falling feeling. Was this it, then? This life of anger and animosity?

He sighed and lowered himself into the chair. "I'm well-known in the area and Mrs. Hixon has already said our neighbors to the south, the Tenleighs, are eager to meet you. I would like to pay them the respect of calling first. Will you accompany me?"

"Of course, I will."

Magnus was nonplussed; that had been easier than he'd expected. "Thank you."

She heaved an exaggerated sigh. "Anything else?"

He cut her a glance that she returned with a blank stare. So, she was going to make him work for every inch.

"There are a few important matters I'd like to discuss with you—matters I do not wish to decide alone."

She snorted. "Really? I thought you would be doing all the decision-making for the both of us."

Calm. Stay calm. Remember, you deserve all of this and more. "This has to do with my family. I was contemplating writing them a letter. I believe we should tell my parents the truth."

She bolted upright, swinging her feet down to the floor with a loud *thud.*

"Are you mad?" she asked, the question reminding him of the last time she'd asked him the exact same thing: the day he'd forced her to marry him. "Do you think because your parents are viewed as the beloved eccentrics up in the North that they are so removed from the influence of the *ton* they would embrace a *madam* as a daughter-in-law?"

So, Magnus realized, she *had* been listening to his long, droning stories about his family in the carriage while pretending to read a book or examine her fingernails. The thought gave him hope—if only a little.

Melissa and The Vicar

"Just because your mother paints landscapes and wears the clothing of an artist and your father holds meetings where he shocks the other wealthy, country gentlemen with his radical intellectual notions does not mean they want to acknowledge a *whore* as their favorite son's new wife." Her eyes narrowed when he winced. "You may not like the word, Magnus, but that is what I am. If you can't accept the truth, perhaps you shouldn't have threatened me into marrying you."

"Of course, I accept your past—enough to wish to deal truthfully with my family. I cannot leave them in the dark on this matter forever, Melissa. Although they don't often go to London my father *will* go to partake in the Session, and my mother will accompany him. And then there is the fact I wish to take you to my brother's wedding next month in London. I would like to tell them the truth before then."

She snorted, the sound slightly hysterical. "Did you marry me with the intention of heaping humiliation on me?"

"No, of course not, Melissa." Magnus was so tired—so *very* tired of bickering. "Why do you say things like that? I've married you—does that seem like the act of a man bent on humiliation?"

"Ha!" She stood and strode to her dressing table in a cloud of silken fabric and subtle, intoxicating perfume, dropping onto the padded silk bench and snatching up her hairbrush.

Magnus stood behind her and met her furious gaze in the glass.

Her hair was a froth of dark, curly auburn that hung to her waist. It was shiny and thick and each stroke of her brush filled the air with its clean fragrance. They had not slept in the same bed and it did not appear they ever would. He knew he was a swine to want her when she was so angry with him—justifiably, he admitted—but, heaven above! She was so beautiful and desirable.

And of course there is the fact you want to claim what is yours—to wash away any memory she might have of Hugo-of-the-fondling-hands-and-stiff-cock.

Magnus closed his eyes and heaved a sigh.

"Of course, I should be grateful you have deigned to marry me—not only a—"

His eyes flew open and he moved toward her, taking her shoulders in a gentle, but firm grasp. "Please, not tonight. Please."

She was breathing heavily, her eyes burning into his, her expression as hard as granite. Magnus tried not to see their lives stretching before them, a repeat of this day forever, but that was all his tired mind could seem to offer.

Her eyes dropped to where his hands rested on her shoulders and he removed them, stepping back.

"I shan't say anything to my parents, or anyone else, until you agree it is time."

"Which will be *never*," she flung at him. She snatched up her brush. "May I finish?"

"Of course. I'm sorry for the interruption."

She went back to her brushing and he left her, closing the door and leaning against it while he stared at the bed, *his* bed. Thankfully he had no valet to bear witness to the state of affairs, although he'd made a fool of himself mussing bedding that morning for the maid's benefit.

He wrote a letter to his parents, as planned, but left out anything that had to do with Melissa other than telling them she was the orphan daughter of a well-off merchant who'd died when she'd been a child. She'd been raised by her aunt and uncle, another London merchant. Her uncle died several years earlier and her aunt brought her to New Bickford after a bout of illness the prior fall.

As he sealed the letter Magnus realized he didn't know much more about Melissa Griffin than his parents did; aside from the obvious.

They'd been married six days and he'd hoped to know something about her past by now, about where she came from, who she really was, and how she'd ended up at The White House. Of course, he'd reckoned without Melissa's ability to hold a grudge.

Magnus shrugged out of his black coat and tossed it over the back of a chair, toed off his dress shoes, and slipped out of his dress breeches and small clothes before donning one of the flannel nightshirts he'd found in his old chambers. And then he pulled back the covers and climbed into the cold, lonely bed. He'd put a book his mother sent him on the nightstand, but he was too miserable to read. So, he blew out the light and tried to sleep.

But images of the last week, and the miserable month that preceded it, filled his head. Here he was married, the woman he loved in the next room, and he was further away from her than ever.

Be careful what you ask for, his old nurse had chided him when he'd been spoiled or greedy.

Well, he'd not asked—he'd *demanded*—and it was far too late to be careful.

***

Melissa and The Vicar

Melissa put down the brush as soon as Magnus shut the door. She stared at her reflection in the mirror, hating what she saw. She was such a horrid, cruel shrew and she was not sure how much longer she could maintain her act.

He looked so beaten down. She knew he was the architect of his own misery but causing him pain was making her life hell. And not touching him . . . well, that was becoming its own special torment.

Add to that were her rough mornings and unusual aches and pains. Yes, she was pregnant with his child. When she'd missed her first cycle a few weeks after returning from New Bickford she'd thought nothing of it—even when she'd missed her second. But now. . . There was no doubt in her mind. Part of her was overjoyed: she would take a part of him with her when she left.

Thinking about his child growing inside her just made her more aroused for her husband and it also made her aware of how little time they had left together.

She might try to tell herself that she hated him—to protect herself for the day when she would have to leave him—but the truth was not easily smothered. She loved Magnus with all her heart and wanted him—in every way. And soon she would need to leave him.

Melissa knew her body as well as any woman in her business and was familiar with her cycle of arousal. During a month she climaxed more easily or wanted sex more at different points. But the sensations she'd started experiencing recently? They were different. Deeper, more . . . primitive.

As she'd been sitting here tonight, and making him miserable, a thought occurred to her: whether or not she enjoyed herself now, she was still going to leave him. So why was she working so hard to make herself—and him—so miserable *now*? Why not enjoy herself for as long as she could? Wasn't that a far smarter approach? It was clear that tormenting him and resisting him was doing nothing to lessen her love and desire for him. She wasn't fooling herself; she was only making them both miserable.

She stood and pulled off her dressing gown. Beneath it was one of nightgowns she'd always worn; it was provocative, but not cheap or lurid. And she had a body she had never shied from showing off. Why not? What else did she have that was of any value?

But tonight she didn't want even a nightgown between them. She pulled it over her head and went to the connecting door, laying her ear against it: nothing.

She twisted the handle, surprised that he hadn't locked her out for being so beastly. The room beyond was dark and she hesitated a moment to allow her eyes to adjust.

"Melissa?" The voice, wide awake, came from a dark mass on the far side of the room. "Is something wrong?" She heard the rustle of fabric and realized he must have sat up.

She closed the door and navigated her way slowly toward him, not stopping until she bumped up against the bed.

"Mel?"

It was the first time he'd used the diminutive of her name and it made her smile. "Can I come in bed with you?"

His stunned silence was palpable, and then, "Of course, here." She heard a light thumping sound—a hand patting a mattress. "Come in, I'm holding back the covers."

When she slid in beside him, she realized he was wearing a nightshirt and the knowledge rocked her to her core. She'd never been in bed with a man in a nightshirt. Ever. But he was her husband, and that's what married couples wore. It was both domestic and wildly erotic at once and she wished she could see him.

He made a choked sound as he dropped the bedding over them. "You are naked," he wheezed.

She smiled at his sudden labored breathing.

"You not wearing any clothes at all," he added, just in case she didn't know the meaning of the word naked. "Lord, I sound like an idiot."

Melissa grinned in the darkness and turned toward him, running her hand up his cloth covered body and letting it rest over his half-erect organ.

"May I take off your nightshirt, Magnus?"

He sucked in a breath and stiffened. All the way.

She had to bite her lip to hold back a giggle as he ripped his nightshirt over his head and sent it sailing into the darkness. Melissa leaned toward him and kissed the first thing she could find, part of a nipple and his lightly haired chest.

He hissed and his arms slid around her but she held him back, "No, I want to explore you first. Lie back."

He complied without speaking.

"Are you cold? Do you mind if I pull back the covers?"

"You can do anything you want," he said in a strangled voice.

She shook with suppressed laughter.

"Are you laughing at me?"

"Yes." This time she couldn't hold it back.

"I don't blame you. Your hands on my body are making me a pitiful wreck."

"Shhh." She smoothed her hands over said gorgeous, muscled body, which she swore was thinner than it had been only weeks ago. He was leaner, but still sculpted perfection.

He groaned as she massaged his shoulders.

"You like that?" she asked, even though she knew he did.

"No. I love it."

Her hands roamed his torso, kneading and stroking, his body becoming warm and supple beneath her fingers, his breathing deepening as she worked her way down the tight musculature of his abdomen. He was exquisite—one of God's masterpieces, although he'd probably consider such a thought blasphemous. That was fine; she would keep it to herself.

She wanted his body inside her so badly her thighs were sticky as she knelt and pushed apart his legs, kneeling between them, her hands moving the whole time, touching every part of him but the one he wanted most. Tormenting him yet again, but this time for their mutual pleasure.

She dragged her fingers over the thin skin over his hip bones, jostling his erection and causing him to groan.

"Melissa, please," he begged.

Her body was so primed that his pleading alone could have sent her over the edge.

Instead, she backed up and lowered her mouth to the place where his erection sprouted from his body and joined to his sac, which was a tight pouch of need.

She breathed on him, her hot feathery touches making his hips buck for more.

Her eyes had adjusted to the gloom and she could see the outline of him, long and thrusting. She smiled and ignored his erection, sucking his taut jewels into her mouth, instead.

He groaned something that sounded like her name. His hands tangled in her hair and she she felt the struggle inside him, the desire to pull her up to where he wanted her and use her for his own pleasure.

But Melissa held his hips firmly, making love to his tight, sensitive sac before moving up the silky skin of his shaft, licking, sucking, and nipping her way to his head. By the time she reached her destination he was salty and slick and trembling. He needed to come badly. She knew from the last time with him that he would be ready again soon. She took his length into her mouth. Even though she relaxed all her muscles and opened her throat to him, he was long and her eyes watered as she struggled to take him all the way to his root.

"Oh, Melissa." It was a strangled moan, as if to keep himself from screaming. He gripped her head now, his fingers flexing, tightening, guiding. She knew what she was doing and could have done it far better without any help, but she loved the feel of his hands on her. And she adored the tension in his body as he struggled to control himself, fighting the primitive urge to fuck her mouth.

She relaxed and opened completely to him, giving herself up to which ever urge won out.

***

Magnus couldn't control his own body. His hips were jerking and no longer obeying him. Her mouth—an impossibly slick, hot, and tight tunnel—closed around every inch of him. He could feel the head of his cock as it rubbed the back of her throat—how could she *breathe?*—and his own throat constricted in sympathy, but his hands tightened and his hips bucked into her, savagely pounding the yielding softness which she offered him, her body pliable and accommodating around his girth.

Her position was wildly erotic and submissive; she'd made herself a vessel, waiting to be filled by him.

Magnus crested on this last thought and froze, buried deep inside her while he pulsed, spending in luxurious ripples into her throat while she hummed her pleasure, her tongue and lips caressing him, coaxing every drop.

Shame at how he'd used her crept beneath his euphoria.

"Shhh," she whispered, as if she could read his sudden tension.

He opened his mouth to apologize but her gentle massaging between his thighs made forming words impossible. He must have drifted off—only for a few moments—and he woke to the feel of her tongue, licking his belly, probing his navel, and then settling on his chest while she lowered her body on his.

"Melissa." His arms wrapped around her. "I'm sorry," he mumbled into her hair, which was tufted and messed from his brutal grabbing. "Did I hurt you?"

Melissa and The Vicar

"I adored it." She bit his neck so hard he winced. "I love the feel and taste of you, I loved feeling you inside of me."

"I didn't choke you?"

She gave a low, earthy chuckle that made his ballocks clench. "You did. And I *loved* it."

His face was so hot he was surprised it didn't glow in the dark. He realized now—rather foolishly—that she'd been vocal about her pleasure the first time they'd laid together. He had been a fool to think she'd learned everything she knew from books, as he had. He wished he could please her with as much skill. He hated to think of that smug, evil man doing more for her. What if—God, what if he could not determine what she needed? What she liked?"

"Magnus?"

"Hmm?" he said, not trusting himself to say anything else.

"You have gone still, but your heart is pounding. What is wrong? Did I disgust you with my behavior?"

"No, of course you didn't. You—you—tore me in two. You humbled me. I was lying here thinking," he bit his lip. There was such a thing as too honest—was what he was about to say *too* honest?

"Tell me, Magnus—what is it? If we are to deal honestly with each other and to—to make something of this marriage, we will have to discuss subjects other couples might not. We are not like other people—at least I'm not—so perhaps it will take more care and effort."

She was right.

"I wish I was more experienced," he blurted, and then chuckled wryly, "or even that I had *some* experience. I wish I could bring you pleasure the way H-Hugo must have."

She began shaking her head before he'd even finished. "No, please don't think that—ever. I'm grateful, honored, even—that I was your first. I wish you had been mine but wishing for things long gone is pointless. As for Hugo," she hesitated.

"What?"

"You are going to hate me."

His heart clenched. Good God, what was she going to tell him now? Magnus forced down the fear and said, "I could never hate you."

"Hugo and I were never lovers, Magnus. I used him to make you despise me enough to go away."

A laugh broke out of him. "That doesn't make me hate you. I am so very, very relieved to hear it."

She nuzzled closer. "I thought you'd be furious that I'd done such a thing."

He gathered her close and squeezed her. "Trust me, darling, I'm a lot happier knowing you were only play acting than believing he'd actually been your lover. Although I have to admit that was very wicked of you." He kissed her. "But about that other part—about my lack of, er, well, experience."

"We can learn together."

"You already know so much."

"But it is different with somebody you love, Magnus."

His heart lurched into a gallop—it was certainly being put through its paces tonight.

"Thank you for saying the words, Melissa. I knew you loved me, but I longed to hear you say it."

She ran her hand up and down his sides in a way that made his sleeping organ begin to harden again. "Oh, you *knew* it, did you?"

"Mmm hmm, you told me. Remember?" He nuzzled her, hoping she'd associate that night with positive things, rather than his dreadful words to her that day at The White House.

"What's that?"

Magnus froze. "What is what?"

Her hips, which were pressing against his, began to pulse. "I feel something."

Magnus laughed, his face hot with joyous embarrassment. "I'm sorry, is that terribly rude? To get an erection while somebody is talking to you?"

"No, not if that somebody is your wife. Who you left wanting when you drifted off to sleep."

He rolled her over before she could protest. "You didn't give me much choice, did you?" Magnus wished the room was lighted, as it had been their first time. He could only see her outline, although he could certainly feel her soft, warm body well enough.

She spread her thighs beneath him. "I want you." The laughter was gone from her voice and he slid his hands beneath her bottom and lifted her, she tilted her hips and guided him to her entrance and he pushed himself inside.

"Ah, you are heaven," he murmured.

Melissa and The Vicar

"Isn't that sacrilege?" she asked, the tremor in her voice letting him know she was not unmoved.

He gave a shaky laugh as he positioned his body himself more securely. "Not if it's true." He thrust into her, harder this time. She grunted with pleasure. He pulled all the way out and entered again.

"Yes, Magnus, please. Hard."

"As you command," he said, thrilling at the need in her voice.

Yes, this—he could do this: take her to heaven and go with her.

***

Magnus knew he should ask his wife what was responsible for her sudden turn about, but the balance between them was so tenuous he simply could not take the risk of upsetting it.

What he wanted—more than anything—was to make this marriage a success. Right now, if that meant living in ignorance about her past or the inner workings of her mind, he was willing to do so. For now.

Everything changed after that night.

They did call on their neighbors, and not just the Tenleighs, the sweet older couple who'd been the best of friends with his Aunt Eudora. Over the course of the ten days they spent at Moor House they ate dinner out three times and even attended a small country assembly, where nobody knew anything about his wife because the last people to have been to London were the two of them. It was, he knew, cowardly to be so grateful the denizens of the area were homebodies and that he and Melissa did not need to fear exposure. But their emotions were so battered they simply needed some time to heal.

"You should see the area on horseback," he said one day after they'd had to hurry back because of an impending rainstorm. "There is no better way and we could cover a far greater distance."

Melissa's wicked lips curved into a smile of regret. "I'm afraid I don't ride."

"You have *never* ridden?"

"No, never."

"How is that possible?"

Melissa had chuckled, a sweet, rich laugh that was like honey. "I simply never had any opportunity in London, Magnus."

"But there is a sizable stable at your, er, business. I know because I left Friar there that day."

The conversation suffered a momentary hitch, but then Melissa went on, clearly as interested as Magnus not to strain their tenuous peace. "All carriage horses, and only a few of those. I lease out some of the spaces to a few of the neighboring buildings."

Magnus had to smile; she was certainly a very savvy woman of business. He knew most of his friends and family would view a woman conducting business as far beyond the pale, but he respected anyone who could support themselves.

He realized she was waiting for him to answer. "Well, we shall remedy this dire situation immediately. I shall go into the village and inquire about engaging a couple hacks."

Melissa's eyes widened. "You mean I can simply get on a horse and start riding?"

He grinned. "We'll spend the first part of the morning going round in that small arena beside the stables. It's not been used for ages but will work fine for our purposes."

Her eyes sparkled in a way that almost robbed him of breath. "So, tomorrow after breakfast?"

"Yes, if they've got a suitable mount for you. If not, we'll have to go further afield, but we'll find something."

"Oh no, Magnus." Melissa's face fell. "I do not possess a habit."

He grimaced. "Oh, blast. I'd forgotten about that." They stared at each other in silence for a moment, the light in her eyes dimmed. Magnus snapped his fingers. "Lord, I'm daft. My aunt's clothing is all here and she was a bruising rider."

"You wouldn't mind?"

He was touched that she understood his reverence for his aunt's house, but it didn't extend to her clothing. "Of course not, darling. And I know my aunt would have been happy to see somebody get use out of her things. She was a bit taller and stouter than you, but not by too much. I'm sure Mrs. Hixon could either take it in or knows somebody who could. Never fear, we shall make something work," he assured her.

Mrs. Hixon *was* a wizard with a needle and the habit needed only minor alteration. It was a plain black wool that looked striking with her fair skin and auburn hair.

The King's Head Inn did indeed possess hacks for hire and one of them was of a placid temperament that even a child could handle.

And so that was how Melissa came to receive her first riding lesson.

Magnus saddled up the gentle mare with one of his aunt's several sidesaddles and spent an hour leading her around the small arena.

Melissa and The Vicar

"This is not hard at all," she said, grinning down at him as walked the horse in circles.

He stopped. "Would you like to hold the reins?"

"Oh, yes, please."

After another hour she was ready to test her mettle on the driveway.

"You'll be a horsewoman in no time," Magnus told her as he helped her dismount after she'd gone up and down the drive at least a dozen times. "Tomorrow we shall go out for a short ride. Just around the park, nothing too difficult."

"I can hardly wait for tomorrow—but then I can hardly wait for tonight, either." Their eyes met and he knew she was recalling their passion in bed the night before.

He loved her so much it frightened him. But, he told himself, that fear was nothing but a residual emotion from the time when he'd been without her—and also from the rocky first days of their marriage when everything had felt as though it could come crashing down around them in an instant.

Now everything had changed—he loved her and she loved him. There were no more lies between them, nothing but love. He never had to fear losing her again.

Chapter Sixteen

The carriage ride back to New Bickford passed far too quickly—as had the days at Moor House. It frightened her how much she'd enjoyed the time they spent together, even though they'd done nothing more than ride horses, walk the moors, and take dinner with a few older couples who'd known Magnus all his life.

It had all been so very . . . normal. How was it possible that normal could be so enticing? At the back of her mind was the unspoken thought that she'd better not become too accustomed to normal. When would she begin to show? Already she was approaching three months and—

But she had made the decision to live for now and knew it could not be for too much longer.

The journey was a delight and, though neither of them spoke of it, there seemed to be an agreement to leave any serious matters behind them and enjoy the last of their wedding holiday.

They laughed like children during the day and made love at night at the inns they stayed in, even managing to squeeze into a tiny trundle bed when they could only get one small room. It was the most wonderful night so far, in Mel's opinion, and they'd needed to sleep almost on top of each other.

But always at the back of her mind was the fact they were drawing ever closer to New Bickford. She had never asked him exactly what Sir Thomas had said about her, and she knew the time would come when they would need to discuss the ugly tangle that was her past—unless she was fortunate and they could avoid the horrid squire altogether before she had to leave Magnus. She knew that was likely a fantasy and it was best to broach the topic now but destroying their newfound happiness was not something she was eager to do.

Besides, she was married now to a man from a powerful family—or at least Sir Thomas would believe she was legally married, along with everyone else—surely he would think twice about spreading stories about her? She could only imagine Magnus's response to hearing such rumors.

She looked at her happy, beautiful husband, who was so excitedly telling her about the horse he would buy her. He was contented and pleased and at peace. She couldn't bring up the squire just now. They had plenty of time for that discussion when they were back in New Bickford.

***

Magnus had written to the vicar to tell him the good news the day they'd married so he wasn't surprised when their carriage rolled into the village to see his parishioners lined up along the street, some throwing flower petals, some grain, and some merely waving and smiling.

"Oh, Magnus. This—" She shook her head, red-faced and uncomfortable. "This is a mistake."

"Hush, darling, you are one of us now. They just want to make you welcome."

She just frowned, and then said, "Oh, look, there is Sarah."

Magnus saw her wearing her distinctive red cloak but looking sober. He knew the death of Mrs. Tisdale had struck the girl hard. He'd been happy that the older woman had found such a kindred soul to spend her last days with.

"I wonder that she is still here," Melissa said.

Magnus turned to her. "Mrs. Tisdale left her the cottage, and everything else she had, which apparently is not insubstantial—surely you knew that?"

Her brow wrinkled and she shook her head. "No, I received no word."

Magnus found that surprising but shrugged it off. This was one of the many matters he wanted to discuss after they'd settled in a bit at the curate cottage.

There were several things he needed to make clear to her—he did not want her thinking he begrudged her friendships, and he was afraid that was the way he'd left things. He also wanted to talk about his demands when it came to her business. As much as he abhorred what The White House stood for, it would not be fair of him to demand she act so hastily if that meant she lost the money she'd worked so hard for. He would insist on the dissolution of the business but give her all the time she needed to find a purchaser for the actual structures. But, again, that discussion could wait.

He waved as they passed the last of the villagers, his gaze sliding to his wife's profile, his cock stiffening as he recalled the nights since she'd come to him. He felt a twinge of guilt at how eager he was to get her into his snug bed at home.

"I hope you'll not find the cottage too small," he said, when she continued to stare out the window at nothing.

She turned to him and smiled, her hand going to his cheek. Magnus loved her touches, absolutely adored that she felt free to express herself physically.

He leaned into her hand. "I especially hope you won't find the bed too small."

She gave him an arch look along with a quick kiss. "No matter how small it is I know I can find a comfortable position.

He threw back his head and laughed. Life, he decided, could not possibly become more perfect.

***

Magnus woke up just before first light every day and often worked until dark. Melissa had known he kept busy, but she'd never understood just how much of the vicar's work he shouldered.

Mel went with him when it was acceptable—to call on homebound parishioners, to visit the outlying areas that took a gig to get to, and of course she sat beside him in church on Sunday.

She knew he was taking care to make sure they had enough time together, even though the demands of daily life were always pressing on him. For her part, she was learning quickly how to be a curate's wife, no matter that it was a position she would not hold for long.

It had been her intention to bring up the subject of Sir Thomas and how they would manage him, but the news that the squire was off on an extended visit to some hunting box in the north was a reprieve she simply could not ignore. So, for better or worse, they simply kept going on the way they had been: ignoring her past and living in the moment.

Mel decided she could enjoy another two months of her fairytale existence before she would need to abandon him to raise their child—a child he could never know about.

Just thinking it made her ill. So, she *didn't* think about it. She savored each day to the fullest.

She discovered that she loved being the mistress of her own house, no matter how modest. The idea of preparing a meal for him, again, no matter how modest, was something that warmed her heart.

Melissa and The Vicar

A few days after they moved into their little home—after they'd eaten several meals at the vicarage—she'd told him about her plan to learn to cook.

"Oh, darling—you needn't become a drudge," he said. "If you wish to learn how to cook, that's your choice. But I can afford to hire help to clean and cook for us." They were lying in each other's arms after making love for the second time that evening. "Lord knows I don't wish to eat at the vicarage every night. What *was* that desert tonight?"

Melissa couldn't help laughing with him. "I think it had tentacles."

He snorted. "Poor Mrs. Heeley. I really don't think there can be a worse cook in all of England."

"I wouldn't be so sure," she'd teased.

While Magnus had been pleased about her decision to learn to cook, he'd insisted on engaging a full-time domestic.

It was perhaps two weeks after they'd settled in when Melissa first saw the household accounts. She had always managed her own books at The White House, so it hadn't been difficult to read his legers and discern that Magnus was wildly wealthy.

He'd apparently inherited a house with extensive property from a bachelor uncle which he kept leased, as well as the significant inheritance from his Aunt Eudora. He certainly did not need his curate wages and she realized, more than ever, how much he genuinely loved his work.

Despite his wealth, he lived frugally. The clothing he'd worn in London at his parents' house had been exquisitely tailored. But his regular clothing, what Mel thought of as his curate uniform, consisted of loose-fitting and not particularly well-made suits which she suspected he wore so as not to flaunt his wealth in front of his parishioners.

His only true extravagance was keeping Friar. And it was an extravagance he wished to expand.

"We need to get you a horse," he said. It was a chilly day but she'd insisted on joining him on his walk out to the Felix property. They were both hatted and gloved and wrapped against the weather and his voice was muffled by the thick, ugly scarf he wore.

Her heart hurt at his lovely offer—oh, how she wished she could one day ride beside him on his rounds of the parish. She evaded the issue. "And we need to do something about your scarf, which is beyond hideous."

He gasped. "Mrs. Stanwyck! I'll have you know my old nurse made this for me."

"If half the things you claim about her are true, the woman is a cross between a saint and the queen."

"It's almost as if you've met Nanny Potter already, darling."

She rolled her eyes. "Doesn't it cost a great deal to keep a horse?"

He shrugged her question away with his customary response to anything that did not fit with his plans. Mel had learned that her new husband was accustomed to getting his way. It was only lucky for the world that Magnus's impulses were generally so selfless and kind.

"You need a horse in the country," he said by way of answer.

"But I'm not a horsewoman."

"You are well on your way after your time in Devon."

She was opening her mouth to argue when a horse and rider came bursting out of a road she knew led to the squire's house.

Even with her inexperienced eye she could see the rider lacked the skill to control his mount, a massive, glorious black beast who looked like something from a fairy tale. Until he came closer.

"Oh Magnus," she murmured, taking a step closer to him. "Is that poor thing *bleeding*?"

"He is."

She turned at his grim voice and he squeezed her hand.

"Let me deal with this." He raised his eyebrows at her and she nodded.

The squire, for that was who it was, pulled up brutally on the bridle and Mel saw that the bit he was using was not only larger than the one Magnus used on Friar, but it was cinched cruelly tight.

"Mr. Stanwyck, well, what a pleasant . . . surprise." Barclay's eyes slid to Melissa and his fat, moist lips twisted into a smile that made her stomach lurch. "I returned last night to learn congratulations are in order, Mr. Stanwyck. This must be Mrs. Stanwyck—or should I say Lady Magnus?" He grinned and continued. "I just came from up north, where I was hunting with a few mutual friends." His slimy gaze drifted between them. "Good friends of both of you—I would almost say *intimate* friends," he added with barely suppressed glee.

Mel glanced at Magnus; did he know what Sir Thomas was hinting so heavily about? But Magnus remained immobile, his blue eyes as chill as the weather, his gaze fastened on the distressed stallion.

"I believe your horse's bridle is not properly adjusted, Sir Thomas. Would you like me to fix it for you?"

Melissa and The Vicar

Barclay's smile grew and he lazily shifted his amused gaze to Magnus. "This is a method I heard about for breaking a willful animal." His hands tightened on the reins until the horse's eyes showed white.

"I think the only thing this practice will yield is a *broken* animal." Magnus's voice was like the cold blade of a knife. Even when he'd been furious at Hugo—and her—he'd not sounded so grim.

But Barclay just grinned. "Well, thank you for your expert opinion, *Lord Magnus*. But the animal belongs to me, so that makes it my affair, doesn't it?" He chuckled suddenly, his eyes swiveling back to Melissa. "You just take care of your own animals. I'm sure you'll have your hands full." He nodded to Melissa and smirked at Magnus before digging his spurs into the horse's bloody sides.

Magnus vibrated with rage as Barclay charged down the dirt road. "That man is an abomination."

"He is. But nothing he is doing is against the law, Magnus. He could bridle his wife with the same mechanism and get away with it." He turned to stare at her, his expression one of horror.

Melissa shrugged. "It is life, Magnus. Come," Mel slid her arm through his. "We'll be late."

But he didn't move. "You don't think somebody should do something—try at least to stop him from tormenting that animal?"

"By somebody do you mean you? Then, no, I don't."

He shook his head at her, his eyes clouded with disappointment and disbelief.

His expression angered her. "His cruelty is abominable, Magnus, there is no denying that. But that is a *horse*. All over this country, as we stand here, worse is being done to women and children every minute of every day."

"So, we should do nothing?"

"No, I am merely saying we should choose our battles." He stared down at her and she pulled on his arm. "Think about it, Magnus. What *can* you do to stop a man from abusing his animals? What power does the law give you in such matters? None. And you know that."

He glared at her, his jaw moving from side to side.

Mel squeezed his arm. "I'm sorry. Sir Thomas is a despicable man—but there is nothing you can do in this instance."

He stared at her for a long moment, but finally nodded, his shoulders slumping in defeat.

Mel kissed his cheek. "We should make haste, the Felixes are expecting us."

Finally, his expression softened and he nodded, allowing her to pull him away.

***

That night, after dinner, Magnus worked on his next sermon—even though he was not to give it for almost two weeks—while Melissa looked through a book of recipes from their new cook, Mrs. Hawkins. Melissa liked the older woman, who came during the day to make their meals and do the other chores. Melissa was learning a bit more about cookery than she previously knew—which had only been the coddled eggs and toast she'd made for Mrs. Tisdale.

Thinking of Mrs. Tisdale made her realize she'd been here for over two weeks and had not yet gone to see Sarah since waving at her on the day of their arrival.

Mel was torn about wanting to see her, wanting to know what was happening in London, because she knew Sarah would have received letters. Most likely because she'd *written* letters, something Melissa had yet to do.

But, at the same time, she wanted to forget all about the outside world and stay wrapped in the warm cocoon with Magnus. Although he spent a great deal of time away and they often dined with the vicar and his wife, their nights together were magical and private.

She had so little time left with him she did not wish to spoil it. Not only that, but her letters to London would likely create questions she did not wish to answer. Cognizant of how little time she had left to conduct her business, Mel had sent letters to both her man of business and Hugo and Laura. She knew Hugo did not gossip, but could not feel as sanguine about Laura, who had a tendency to drink copious amounts and become indiscreet.

So, all of that had combined to keep her away from Mrs. Tisdale's—or Sarah's, she supposed she should now call it.

She wondered if Magnus had been to see Sarah. Perhaps he would like to go with her tomorrow. She looked up to find him staring—his expression intent, his blue eyes burning.

"What is it?"

He shook his head slightly, as if coming out of a dream. "It's nothing." To her surprise, his cheeks reddened.

She closed the book of recipes and went to where he sat in the plain wooden chair that served the writing desk. He laid down his quill

Melissa and The Vicar

and gestured to his lap, so she sat, her arm around his shoulders, her bottom resting on his hard thighs. He kissed her neck.

"Tell me what you were thinking, Magnus."

He pressed his face against her throat and she could feel the heat. He chuckled, the sound husky. Melissa shifted subtly, moving her bottom higher until she felt his cock: he was hard. He hissed in a breath.

"You have been thinking about me, I hope."

"Yes." The word was muffled by the quickly heating skin of her throat.

"Magnus?"

He pulled away and looked up at her, his face positively flaming. "I was wondering about that man—Hugo."

"I've already told you I never—"

"Shh, I know. I wasn't thinking that. I was wondering what he does there?"

Mel blinked. "You mean at The White House?"

"Yes."

"Well, he is . . ." She bit her lip and then shook her head in frustration. "I know you don't like the word whore, Magnus, but I'm afraid I'm at a loss as to how else to describe it."

But her husband wasn't interested in semantics. "I understand about needing to use the word. I don't understand about *him*."

Magnus was, she realized, curious about Hugo. Perhaps even titillated by the notion of what he did, but too innocent or embarrassed to know how to articulate it. Melissa realized, rather late she supposed, that this was at least one way in which she could help her husband: sexually. After all, what was the good of being the most sought-after whore in London if you couldn't share some of your hard-won skills with the man you loved?

She saw he was waiting. "Part of The White House caters to women."

He blinked. "You mean as customers?"

"Yes."

"Women go to a *brothel*?"

Mel couldn't help it, she laughed.

"You are laughing at my naïveté. Yes, yes, you are Mel," he insisted when she opened her mouth to argue. "That's all right, I *am* naïve. However, I'm not completely unaware and I'm positive I've never heard of such a thing."

"That's because it's not something I advertise. It is a service that sells itself by word of mouth alone."

He just stared.

"Everyone knows men go to prostitutes—aristocrats, poor men, and—*yes*—even members of the cloth on occasion." He opened his mouth and she shook her head. "You asked, Magnus. Will you let me finish?"

He made a show of shutting his mouth tight.

"Just what do you think women do when their husbands keep mistresses and live their entire lives with them—complete with a half-dozen children like our very own royals do?" She didn't wait for an answer. "Some women *like* the pleasures of the flesh. But even the wealthiest women are the property of their husbands or fathers or brothers or whatever man controls their lives. Women must satisfy any needs they have in utter secrecy or risk being beaten, committed to an asylum, or divorced. That is what I offer: discreet sexual pleasure for women. And Hugo is the most popular of my employees."

His jaw tightened at this last piece of information and his almost childlike inability to hide his emotions on such a subject made her love him even more. He was truly without guile.

"So, women pay to lay with him?"

"Among other things."

He perked up at that, jealousy of Hugo forgotten, at least temporarily. "What kind of other things?"

"Whatever women want, Hugo will do."

His eyes went dark at both her words and her tone. He swallowed. "When he left the day I visited your chambers, he looked at me. I would swear his expression was sexual."

"It probably was, knowing Hugo. I don't want to shock you, but he also services male clients."

He didn't look shocked, he looked amused. "I went to Eton, darling, I'm perfectly familiar with the things men sometimes do with each other."

She hadn't considered that. "You must view such a thing as a sin." I wasn't a question.

But her ever-surprising husband just shrugged. "In the scheme of things, men perpetrate much more heinous actions upon one another. As long a man is not forced—which I know sometimes happened at school—I do not believe it is anything to crusade about."

Melissa and The Vicar

"This cannot be the attitude of the Church?"

"No, positively not. And to speak of it isn't encouraged. Not only is it considered a sin against God, but man as well. And, as I think you know, man's punishment would be swift and sure. But enough of that," he said, his expression growing sensual in a way that made her body tighten with anticipation. "I want to know more about what a woman wants."

"Oh, you do?"

"I want to know what *you* want. I want you to teach me how to please you."

"You already please me."

His mouth pulled up on one side, his expression impish. "Thank you. But I should like to keep pleasing you; I do not want to be the type of man whose wife wanders."

She laughed. "What would you like to know?"

His eyelids lowered. "I've read about cunnilingus."

Her jaw dropped.

"That is not how it is said?"

"No, that's correct. I just didn't expect—"

He grinned. "I believe you might be blushing for the very first time."

Melissa laughed. "You *have* embarrassed me."

"Why?" he asked, suddenly serious. "Don't you like it when a man does that to you?"

Melissa didn't know how to tell him that none of the men she'd serviced over the years had wanted such a thing. She especially didn't know how to tell him that only her *female* lovers had ever performed such acts on her.

He cocked his head. "Mel? What is it? You look . . . odd."

She sucked her lower lip into her mouth. Yes, he knew what she'd done for a living. But this . . . for some reason, she shied away from this part of her sexual life. Perhaps it was because she'd been closest to her female lovers—they had usually been her choice, rather than her business.

"I *do* enjoy it," she admitted. "But I have never received such a gift from a man."

The moment stretched and she could practically hear his mind whirring. And then, "Ah, Sapphic love." She didn't say anything and a worried V appeared between his eyes. "Do you mean you prefer women?"

She smiled and shook her head. "I prefer *you*. You are the only person, male or female, I have ever loved, Magnus. But when it comes to sexual experience—Well, I'm afraid there is probably nothing I've not done."

"Except received satisfactory cunnilingus from a man."

She chuckled at his doggedness. "Well, yes, except that."

"That is one thing I can give you that no other man has."

"It isn't a contest, Magnus."

He slid his arm beneath her knees and stood, groaning and giving a theatrical stagger. "Have you gotten heavier, Mrs. Stanwyck?"

"I know you did not just ask your bride of barely a month if she was getting fat, Mister Stanwyck."

He laughed, unabashed, and took her back to their bedroom and set her down inside the door.

"Now, take off your clothes," he said, no longer smiling, his own hands already going to his waistcoat buttons.

They were naked and breathless in mere moments. He took a step toward her but stopped.

"I shall be back in half a jiffy, now get on the bed." He jogged to the other room before she could answer, affording her the arousing sight of his firm bottom flexing its way into the other room.

She'd barely laid down when he returned with the big candelabrum from their dining room table.

"What—?"

"I want to see."

Once he had lighted *five* candles he came to the bed. She was laying with her legs slightly apart, one leg bent at the knee and falling outward. His eyes were fixed on her, his lips slack, and his tongue darted out to moisten his mouth.

"I know I'm a savage," he said, without looking up, "but I need to taste you immediately—before I receive instruction."

She chuckled and let both knees fall open into a splayed, immodest position she knew would expose her completely.

He muttered something that sounded like a prayer and dropped to his hands and knees to crawl toward her.

"So beautiful," he murmured, looking rather beautiful himself as he leaned low, the powerful muscles in his back and arms flexing, his tight bottom thrust in the air. His hands were warm and strong and gentle as his fingers parted her lips. He didn't hesitate when he had her open but lapped her from her opening to her bud with a flat, hard stroke of his tongue. And then he moaned, the sound shuddering through her body.

Melissa let him play and get a sense of her, thrilled that her body could be this much of a delight to the person she loved. And then there was watching her saintly husband perform such a very earthy and erotic act. A saintly husband who turned out to be a remarkably fast learner.

With his tongue pointed into a tip, he probed at her opening, entering her with suggestive thrusts of his hot slick organ, his elbows pushing her wide while he fucked her with his tongue. She smiled at the vulgar word, deciding she might use it on him sometime and see if—

He stopped abruptly and licked toward her already stiff peak, which he circled with maddening precision, coming close, but never touching. She thrust her fingers into his hair and was just about to issue an order when his lips surrounded her clitoris, their pillowy warm wetness gentle but firm as he sucked her into his mouth, massaging her with his lips and tongue until she was half-mad.

Mel's hips bucked, chasing his mouth when he pulled away. He looked up the length of her body, his face expectant, his lips slack, wet, reddened; his cheeks, chin, and even his nose slick from her juices. He was *drenched* in her.

"You must tell me how to make you climax like this."

Her eyes rolled back in her head and she laughed weakly. "I don't think you need any help from me."

***

She refused to help him, so Magnus had to experiment on his own. He had to admit he did not mind at all. He could see all of her, all the lovely places he'd felt with his hands and fingers. She let him explore, her body spread wide open to him under the light of half a dozen candles.

He knew she believed him to be naïve, but he certainly wasn't stupid enough to think this was the type of activity men and their wives typically engaged in. But Magnus, contrary to what many people believed, thought a strong belief in God did not negate a strong desire for carnal relations with one's wife. He refused to believe God would create such beautiful, fascinating creatures as women and want them to be hidden away. He planned on spending years getting to know every part of Melissa's body. And he could make an excellent start in that direction tonight.

At first, he'd thought there were only her soft, swollen lips that concealed her jewel, the small fleshy nub that drove her mad. But when he spread her with his fingers he saw there was a second set of lips that were far more delicate and sensitive.

He licked them, alternating sides, sucking gently, using his lips, tongue, and even his teeth to nibble her gently, the way she did with his sac and shaft when pleasuring him.

He almost ejaculated onto their bed when he realized his licking was causing her flesh to swell and produce the lubricant that made their joining so slick, pleasurable, and erotic.

Her clitoris, he saw, had also grown, pushing back the protective covering he knew was called a hood, exposing skin of unsurpassed softness and sensitivity. He prodded the base of her bud with his pointed tongue, swirling around it in circles, until her hands slid into his hair and her hips pushed up at him; just as he did to her when she took him so deep in her mouth that he couldn't help nudging her throat. And like him, she held his head, grinding against his mouth for her pleasure.

Magnus renewed his sucking while she used him, his tongue concentrating in areas that made her moan and thrust the hardest. When she bucked and ground against him hard enough to pull the hair from the roots, he slid the two middle fingers of his right hand into her sheath, curling them the way she'd taught him and searching for the small, rough spot that brought her extra pleasure.

Her body arched when he found the correct place, her back lifting off the bed so high that only her shoulders and feet still touched the bed. Magnus knelt high so that he could watch her expression of near pain as she gave in to her orgasm, her sweat-slicked breasts shuddering as she jerked with each savage contraction. Magnus stroked a hand over her midriff, stroking the gentle, feminine swell.

Her contractions began to come farther apart and were less violent in nature. When she shuddered and lowered to the bed, he used his knees to push her thighs wider and then bent low to guide himself to her entrance. She was so wet and swollen that his cock slipped to her back entrance and he'd accidentally pushed against her before he realized what he'd done.

He was about to pull away but she said, "Yes, Magnus, yes . . . that." She reached between their bodies, her eyes opening lazily and latched on to his—most likely stunned—eyes. "Take me back there, please."

Melissa and The Vicar

He throbbed so hard at her begging he was worried he would not last to do what she was asking—something he had never even considered before but suddenly wanted fiercely.

She spread the wetness from her climax lower, until Magnus realized what she was doing. His erection was so wet and slick he wondered if he'd spent without realizing it.

She lifted her hips and reached blindly over her head. He saw what she was doing and pulled a pillow beneath her hips.

"Another," she said, her breathing hoarse and ragged.

With two pillows thrusting her hips up high she was presented like a gift to him. She pulled her knees to her chest, the action opening exposing her fully to his gaze. And then she took his hand and sucked his middle finger into her mouth.

They stared into each other's eyes as she slicked his finger and then moved it between her thighs. "You need to prepare me." She pressed his finger against the tight pucker.

Magnus's blood pounded in his ears so hard it was difficult to hear her. He took his hand from hers and pushed his body back, away from her. Her eyes widened and he smiled.

"Shhh," he whispered, lowering himself back into the position he'd assumed earlier. "You know how I like to watch what I'm doing."

He lowered his mouth over her, giving her jewel some attention before tracing the seam of her, spreading her with his hands, dragging his tongue back until he could explore this taboo part of her body.

She shivered beneath his licking. "Yes, Magnus. Yes . . ."

He smiled at her pleasure and commenced to lick and probe and nibble.

She was wet and musky with the mingled smells of their bodies and he shook with impatience to sample this unknown part of her. It took all his will to open her gently and slowly, thrusting his tongue deeper and deeper until he gently breached her opening, using tongue and finger together, stroking into her until she was groaning and grinding against him.

"More," she ordered in a hoarse, desperate tone.

He slid in another finger, pushing more deeply, pumping her, sucking the tender skin of her inner thigh, reading the clues her body gave before allowing a third finger to join in.

His erection rubbed against the soft bedding, his organ hard and sticky as he anticipated the tight tunnel he was preparing.

Her hands scrabbled at his shoulders. "Now, Magnus. Please."

He was up in an instant, kneeling between her spread thighs, positioning himself at her back opening.

"Slowly," she breathed, her head thrown back. He put his slick, hot crown against the impossibly tight entrance, pushing until he just breached her.

"Oh, Melissa," he groaned, the tightness exquisite. Her thighs quivered as she tilted, her position of supplication and need making him push deeper. It was certainly unlike anything he'd ever felt. The tightness was close enough to painful to make him cautious, but the knowledge of what he was doing—of how he was taking and possessing her—irresistibly erotic.

He kept pushing until their bodies touched and he was fully sheathed inside her. He hesitated, not wanting to hurt her. But she flexed her muscles and he gave a yelp of surprise, withdrawing far faster than he'd gone in.

"Hard, Magnus. Use me hard."

His brain exploded at her words and he thrust into her just as she'd commanded: hard and deep, seated all the way to his tight bollocks. He groaned; she was slicker now, primed by his juices. Again, he withdrew and then slammed all the way in. And again. And again. Pounding her without mercy, her grunts of guttural pleasure chipping away at his control. His jaw clenched teeth-crackingly tight, as if that would hold back his release and prolong his pleasure. He wanted to do this for hours—for days—but his control slipped away and he pounded into her, keeping her almost bent in half as he used her body without care or consideration.

When he emptied himself deep inside her she clamped so tight around him that he could feel the pulse of his cock against her skin as he filled her, his body contracting and straining to spend every last drop.

As ever, he lost track of time in the pleasure-filled haze after he climaxed. When he woke from his brief death and saw he was still holding her knees to her chest, he moved to pull away.

She held him. "Don't go," she said, her legs lowering and wrapping around his waist.

"But I'll crush you."

"Then crush me."

He lay back down, keeping his weight on his forearms, which also allowed him to see her glowing, beautiful face.

Melissa and The Vicar

"That was . . ." He gave a weary chuckle. "Well, I don't have the words to express myself just now."

"Good." The look she gave him was smug and it made him throb for her—both in his groin and his chest.

He opened his mouth, hesitated, and then closed it.

"What is it?"

Her expression was lazy and her smile slack.

"I want you to meet my parents."

The ease disappeared from her face in an instant. "Oh, Magnus . . ."

"They know we're married and I've received two letters asking if we'll be attending Michael's wedding in London—that's less than a month away, darling."

"Couldn't you go?"

"What, alone?" He frowned down at her. "No," he said before she could answer. "Of course I would not go without you." He shook his head, a familiar, stubborn feeling taking hold of him. "I want us to go—together. I'll tell the vicar we need a week to attend. He'll understand. You'll enjoy meeting everyone, Melissa. You just need a few weeks to settle into the idea."

She stared at him, her expression unreadable. He knew he was behaving high-handedly, and any number of other unpleasant adverbs. But she was his wife, for heaven's sake—she needed to meet his family.

"You know what will happen the moment I step into the public eye, Magnus? Your brother's wedding will involve a good number of people, won't it? Do you understand the danger?"

He nodded. "I understand."

She took a deep breath, expanding beneath his body, and finally exhaled. "Very well, I will go."

Magnus's heart stuttered at the expression of resignation on her face. He knew this was hard for her—it would be difficult for both of them. "Thank you, darling."

She gave him a half-hearted smile. "You're welcome, Magnus."

"I love you, Mrs. Stanwyck."

Her smile tightened. "I dearly hope nothing happens to make you stop loving me, Magnus."

He kissed her hard. "Hush with your foolishness. Nothing can come between us and our love."

He would remember those words later.

Chapter Seventeen

Melissa waved as Magnus rode down the drive. He would be gone most of the day, visiting a family on the far edges of the parish. She'd arranged to meet Mrs. Heeley to discuss the upcoming fall church schedule that morning, take a tour of the vicarage garden, and also decide which duty she would rather take off Mrs. Heeley's hands: the children's choir or decorating the church once a week with flowers. Since Melissa knew nothing of singing or children, she thought she would take the flowers. But when she'd told Magnus he'd cajoled her into the choir.

"Musical knowledge is not really necessary. In fact, if you were musical, it would be unbearable torment. It would actually be best if you were tone deaf. Are you tone deaf? Let's hear you sing."

"Very droll. But how can I manage a choir if I don't know what I'm doing?"

"This is the children's choir, darling, they are none of them older than five or six. You will mainly be keeping them from eating prayer books or bits of the church during practice. You'll be able to choose a helper. Pick Miss Gloria Philpot, she has a glorious voice to go along with her name and is excellent with children. Besides—" He'd taken her in his arms, his hand going to her belly, and he'd stroked her with a look of possession that had almost broken her heart. "You need to start getting comfortable with children—I'm hoping we'll have one of our own one day soon. And it's best to practice on somebody else's children first."

"That's a dreadful thing for a curate to say."

He'd chuckled and she'd somehow managed to laugh with him—a true testament to her ability to lie and scheme while her heart broke inside her.

Luckily, the subject of children had given way to a bit of wrestling and she'd used the other of her specialties: her body. And then . . . well, suffice it to say, he'd convinced Mel to take the choir by shamefully using his own body as an unfair method of persuasion.

Melissa and The Vicar

But always at the back of her mind was the knowledge that she would leave him and he would never know about their child.

***

Melissa finished her daily cooking lesson with Mrs. Hawkins and changed into her walking boots. She put on her heavy wool cloak and then headed to Sarah's for the visit she'd been putting off for reasons she didn't wish to think about.

It was cold and windy—the natives to the area said it was unseasonable and warned of a long cold winter—and she had to stop twice to re-tie her bonnet, which the wind tugged and tossed.

Astonishingly, she'd discovered that she missed her long rambles when she'd gone back to London. She could have walked in the park—and sometimes did—but it wasn't the same as a vigorous tromping through the country.

The truth was, she loved being a curate's wife. She'd worried that living such a quiet existence would become tedious after a life of constant activity—albeit a good part of those activities not things she enjoyed—but she adored the slower pace.

Thinking about London made her think about what she'd agreed to do: go to Magnus's brother's wedding.

By agreeing to his request she'd chosen the exact date of her departure.

Some part of her mind shrieked away from the knowledge they now had only a few weeks left together. But the greater part of her brain—the part that had gotten her through the horrific years with Lord Vanstone—continued to function as if nothing was wrong. One thing she knew about herself was that she would always survive, no matter how little she might wish to.

She'd received a message from her man of business and he'd already had two offers for the property. She knew the offers were from Laura and Hugo. According to Magnus, she was not allowed to—

The pounding of horse hooves interrupted her thoughts. Whoever it was, they were coming toward her fast. Melissa staggered clumsily to the side of the path to get out of the way but the horse came around the corner at breakneck speed and its rider had to pull up brutally to bring the creature to a stop.

She looked up, her heart pounding in her ears, unsurprised to find Sir Thomas leering down on her. He was seated on a different horse today, but this one did not seem to be faring any better. Like the black stallion from the other day, this one had foam around its mouth, some of it pink.

"Well, Lady Magnus."

She looked from the unfortunate horse to its repulsive master. "Sir Thomas."

"And where is your husband? The hoity-toity Mr. Lord Magnus?"

"Attending to his duties." She glanced to both sides but he was blocking the path. Probably deliberately. "As will I, Sir Thomas, if you would let me pass."

He sat back in mock surprise. "My, my, it's the hoity-toity Mrs. Lady Magnus, I see."

"Is there something you want of me, Squire?"

His fishy lips curved into an unpleasant smile. "Look at you—pretending as if butter wouldn't melt in that pretty mouth of yours when both of us know you've sucked more cock than a wharf-side whore. Now, I wonder what that husband of yours would say if he learned you weren't really Miss Prissy So-and-So with her proper *aunt* and pretty manners."

Luckily, he mistook her stunned expression for one of anger rather than surprise. If Sir Thomas hadn't told Magnus who and what she was, then who had?

She couldn't believe Sarah had betrayed her trust. Could it have been Mrs. Tisdale? They were the only two—other than the squire—who'd known.

Sir Thomas fisted the reins tightly in one hand and leaned closer, his eyes burning with . . . anger? Jealousy? Spite? Or all those emotions and more.

"You like to act the grand queen, don't you? 'The Ice Madam' is what some young fools call you. Too fine a whore to take just *any* man between her legs. But I know something most of those poor, dumb blokes don't know." His smile spread. "I know about you and Vanstone"

The name echoed in the cold air between them. It was all she could do to maintain her expression. How, in God's name, had this swine heard about Vanstone?

"Some of the men in his lordship's little group still talk about you, Mrs. Melissa Griffin—although they use another name, of course. Your real name, I 'spose." He shrugged. "Yes, Vanstone's bosom beaus do like to reminisce about the young whore who could throat them as smooth and deep as velvet even while two other gents

Melissa and The Vicar

mounted her from the other end." He grinned and chuckled. "Quite the prize you were—a plum out of reach to most mortal men, until you got too old and Vanstone tired of you."

He grinned at the revulsion she must have shown. "Yes, I heard about the fun he had with you those last few months before he brought in a newer, fresher piece to replace you." His smile hardened. "Do you still remember those days with a quiver?"

Melissa merely stared.

He shrugged. "Maybe you don't—it was a long time ago, what? Twelve years, I'd wager, and you've probably sucked a mile's worth of cock since then."

She didn't care about the insults; it was the information itself she had to know about.

"How do you know about Lord Vanstone—he went to great pains to keep his activities private. At least he used to."

"Oh, he still does, at least outside our little group."

Our? Melissa couldn't help it, her eyebrows shot up.

He saw it before she could stop herself. "I see your surprise, such fine gents associating with the likes of Sir Thomas—a baronet so new his title still squeaks." He shrugged again, but Mel saw the anger behind the uncaring gesture. "But that don't matter if you have enough money, girlie. I would have thought *you* would've known that: money is all that matters, these days."

She knew Sir Thomas spoke the truth—about that, at least.

"I've only been part of the elite circle this past three years or so." His smirk shifted into a frown. "Not long after *you* turfed me out of your precious whorehouse, if you recall."

Melissa could see by the gleam in his piggy eyes that he wasn't going to forgive her for that.

He snickered. "I probably should thank you for throwin' me out or I wouldn't have been so persistent with old Vanstone." His tongue darted out and he licked his lips in a way that nauseated her. "Mmm mmm, I have to say I get *exactly* what I need from his pretty little fillies."

Bile rose in her throat but she had half-a-lifetime of experience schooling her features. He would get *nothing* from her.

"Yes," he said, meditatively, looking at her with an appraising, hungry expression she'd endured thousands of times. "Even after all that cock you look as fresh as a daisy. I can see why the curate couldn't resist you. I'll bet you were as pretty as a picture when you were just a lass. Of course, you're nothing to the girls Vanstone has had since I had the good fortune to join his club. I believe he's wised up about putting all that money in a tart he'll only want for a few years. Not only is this newer *missus* top shelf in looks, she also started out a good deal younger."

He laughed at her expression, which was not as well-guarded as she'd believed

"Yes, you set the bar high for your sister whores. I can vouch that not only is she even lovelier than you, but she's quite accomplished at pleasing whatever need a man might have." His eyes narrowed. "And I have to admit I might have learned about a few new fetishes since I joined the old man's club. You see, he's been more than accommodating to me since I made him a sizeable loan. Especially since he's had to ask twice for longer terms to repay. Indeed, Vanstone is so close to going under the hatches that a person might almost accuse him of being a whoremaster the way he's using this latest chit.

"It seems he's learned he can keep his investors quite happy if he throws those little parties a bit more often and is a tad more . . . generous. Think of what you missed out on, my lady—all the fun you could have enjoyed."

His eyes watched her with the close avidity of a tormentor and his victim, hoping for blood, for signs of pain and anguish. Well, he wouldn't squeeze any from Melissa—at least not when it came to Vanstone and what he'd done to her those last months, when he'd begun to lose interest in her.

She almost laughed. What Sir Thomas didn't realize was that nothing he—or anyone else—could say to her face would bother her. Did he think she hadn't *been* there during those nights? Evenings of debauchery so shocking that Vanstone and his cronies—all titled men with family and position to protect—didn't want word to get out.

Mel looked up and saw he'd been watching and waiting, no doubt hoping she would breakdown. Instead, she smiled coolly. "I assume there is point to this journey down memory lane, Sir Thomas."

His features shifted into a vicious mask at her tone. "You'll not use that voice with me again, *slut*."

Mel stiffened at the hated word and he smirked.

"Ah, you don't like that, do you, my little *slut*. I remember the last time I used it on you—you were acting high and mighty while denying me access to your bloody whorehouse. And why? Just because I enjoy

Melissa and The Vicar

a bit of slap and tickle. Because I sometimes employ a bit of the whip and spur while I break in a filly." He lowered his crop to his boot heel and sent the wicked metal disc spinning. "You listen good, *slut*. You'll give me some of what Vanstone's cronies reminisce about. And if you're good and please me—if you're properly broke to bridle—I won't need to raise any stripes on that fine hide of yours." His nostrils flared in anticipation. "At least not much." He jerked his chin over his shoulder. "You and Miss Sarah, back there. Yes, I'd fancy the two of you at once, I reckon. I know you two *sluts* would like to have at each other. After all, I've heard you haven't let a man come between those thighs in years—well except your precious curate, of course. You must have been getting it somewhere all that time you sat alone on your throne, in your little kingdom." He snickered, becoming red and aroused at his own words.

"Why would I agree to such a thing?"

"You'll do it because I'll tell your sainted husband the whole gruesome story of your past."

It was her turn to smirk. "He already knows."

He snorted. "That's a bloody lie."

"Feel free to ask him." She shrugged.

They locked eyes, his face tightening into a mask of thwarted fury when he realized she was serious. And then, in an instant, his expression turned to one of unholy glee and he slapped his thigh, the sudden motion causing his mount to startle. Sir Thomas wrenched back on the reins so hard Melissa was surprised the poor beast's neck didn't snap.

"So," he said, once he'd resettled the horse, whose eyes showed white all the way around. "His lordship decided he'd get himself a wife trained up in more than making calf's foot jelly and reading scriptures, did he?" He shook his head and chuckled. "I have to admit, the idea of having a piece who looks like you, and with your skills, to use each and every night any way I choose does appeal." He wore an expression of mixed lechery and admiration. "I never would have expected it of the young moralizer. But that just goes to show how deep hypocrisy runs in some people. You say he knows about you bein' a madam, and I'll believe you. But I'll bet every pound and pence I have the he knows nothing about Vanstone's little parties. He probably thinks he won the Ice Madam, the woman all of London fought for. There is no way a man like him would ever have married any woman who'd done even half of what you did for Vanstone."

She couldn't control the flutter of her eyelids, and he pounced on it.

"Ah, yes." He stroked his chin theatrically with one leather-gloved hand. "I guessed right, didn't I? He. Don't. Know. At least not the worst of it. It was a long time ago and he's, what? Five and twenty at most?" He laughed, looking genuinely amused by his words. "Lord Magnus would have been at Eton yanking on his Man Thomas while you were servicing Vanstone's exclusive little club—some of whom are probably even related to his august lordship."

He grinned and shrugged. "And if it turns out I'm wrong and he *does* know the worst, well, I can tell the vicar just as easily. What do you think the vicar and his wife would think of that? Perhaps you could buy the good vicar's silence the same way you are going to buy mine?"

Melissa could only stare, imprisoned so deep within a cage of frustration and loathing that she as if she were looking through bars.

"So," he said, when she didn't answer. "Our other playmate wasn't home when I knocked earlier, which means we'll not have our fun today. It's just as well, really, I don't want to rush things. It can't be tomorrow since I've got business I can't shirk, not even for this much pleasure. And then there's a quick trip out of the area the day after that, which will take me away for a damnable five or six days. Lord! That means . . ." He made a show of contemplating the dates. "You'll have to wait 'til next Friday for your fun—which gives you more than a week to put a shine on that gold-plated cunny and have it ready for me." His eyes narrowed. "Since you're a lady of leisure, just like your little slut friend back at the old slut's house." He hooted at her widening eyes and slapped his thigh. "Ha! Didn't think I knew about the old bird? Well, I know a lot more than I need to tell, don't I? I guess you whores take care of your own because she certainly left young Sarah all right and tight, didn't she? That's a pretty little cottage with a pretty little piece of land—wouldn't mind having it myself." This last part he said as if it had just occurred to him, which she knew for a lie even before he spoke. "In fact, I told Sarah the last time we were together how her land comes all the way out to the road, lots of nice timber. Seems she might be interested in selling it, once I spend a little more time convincing her."

He chuckled.

"But there I go digressing. As for you and her and me and our afternoon of frolics—well, I guess noon would work fine. That way we'd get a good half-days' worth of fun before I send you back to your husband all satisfied and well-pleasured." He cut her a dangerous look, his smile gone. "Don't mistake me, *slut*. You and the other one had better be lying naked on your backs with your legs wide open and waitin' when I come 'round next Friday. Don't make me lose my temper, my *lady*."

He touched the brim of his beaver hat, spurred his horse with the same viciousness he did everything, and rode on, casually dragging his crop over her chest as he passed, a hint for her to consider.

Melissa watched him go, staring long after he'd disappeared. If she were the type of woman given to weeping—which she was not, having used up all her tears a long time ago—she would have started crying right then.

***

Magnus had missed her terribly today. He felt like a lovelorn idiot, but he couldn't help it. Perhaps this is what a lifetime of abstinence had done to him—made him into an insatiable beast? But he didn't like to think of his feelings that way—only physical in nature. He'd not just missed her beautiful face and body, he'd missed her cleverness, her dry humor, and her unexpected enthusiasm for becoming the wife of a curate.

So, his need for her had overwhelmed decorum and he'd behaved like a sailor home from a year-long voyage when he stepped into their cottage, all but tearing off her clothes.

"I couldn't stop thinking about last night—all day long," he said, his breath coming in harsh pants as they both fumbled with the fastenings on his buckskins. "Did you miss me today?" he demanded, shoving his clothing off in one messy lump.

"No."

He laughed. "It's a sin to lie, Mrs. Stanwyck. I'm afraid I shall have to punish you."

And then he'd taken her twice. Once on top, and the second time he'd lifted her above him, telling her to practice riding him for when her *other* mount arrived.

He'd been gone all day on Friar to visit a family three hours' ride away. He'd meant to come home and write to his mother, telling her they'd be coming to London for the wedding. But then he'd seen her, her hair mussed from her fingers, her shoulders hunched over some recipe she was studying. And he'd had to have her immediately.

As they lay in bed, after, their bodies sated, Magnus's thoughts of horses recalling what she'd said when they'd run into Sir Thomas abusing his poor mount.

He'd tried to put the repellent episode from his mind, but he'd recalled it, and several other unsettling matters, again today. He hadn't lied when he'd said he'd thought of last night all afternoon—but he'd thought of other things, too. And he needed to ask some questions, questions that had teased him often lately.

They'd left a candle burning because they both enjoyed seeing each other while they made love. He turned to her, kindling again at the sight of her sweat-slicked profile. She had been wild tonight, too, almost as if something were driving her.

She must have felt his gaze because she turned and smiled. "What is it, Reverend?"

He grinned. He loved it when she called him that—especially during their bouts in bed. Did that make him wicked? He did not believe it did. After all, she was his wife. And Magnus believed God took pleasure in joy. No, the feelings he had for her could not be bad.

He pushed an auburn spiral behind her ear. "I have some things I'd like to ask you—things I've put off, but which I've thought of more often than I'd like."

Her expression, light and happy a moment earlier, became wary. "Yes?"

"Will you tell me how you came to be . . . well, in your line of work?"

She gave him a small, sad smile at his cowardly use of such a weak euphemism. But he could not use words like whore or prostitute to describe her.

"Why do you want to know, Magnus?"

"It's your past, Melissa. I've talked about my past—and when you meet my family, *they* will tell you mortifying tales of me when I was young. But I know nothing about you." He hesitated. "I've held off from asking, not wishing to pry, but you are my *wife*. I know what you did for a living, I just want to know how you started down that road. Whether you like it or not, we shall have to tell my family at least part of your past—and we shall have to do so sooner rather than later. I cannot allow them to find out from someone else."

She stared at him with opaque eyes and he had no idea what to expect. Finally, she nodded. "I daresay you should tell them when you go for the wedding."

Melissa and The Vicar

Relief flooded him and he took her hands and kissed her fingertips. "You mean when *we* go for the wedding."

She smiled. "Of course."

"Thank you," he said.

"For what?"

"For understanding what we must do, no matter how uncomfortable it will be. I cannot say they will not be shocked, but we are married now and they will come around." He could see from her face that she doubted that. Well, so did he, but he hardly wanted to admit it. "Now, please, tell me your story."

"It is not an uplifting story."

"I understand that. I hope it doesn't upset you—I don't want to cause you pain—but I want to know you."

"It doesn't hurt me to talk about it, Magnus. I came to terms with my past a long time ago." She smoothed her hand absently across his chest, the light caress leaving his sensitive nipples hard. Magnus had never given a moment's thought to his nipples until he'd met Melissa. "No, I do not mind telling you about it, but it will change the way you look at me."

He kissed her cheek. "Nothing could do that. I love you with all my heart."

She made no comment, but removed her hand and turned onto her back, looking at the ceiling. "I have to begin a few years before I became a—well, just so you will understand my mother and maybe not judge her so harshly."

Magnus opened his mouth to say he did not judge, but then closed it. Yes, he did judge, as much as he tried not to. And already he judged a mother and father who'd allowed their daughter to fall into such work.

"I grew up in a decent area in London—at least for my first years—where people were neither poor nor rich. My father was a merchant sailor and I have very little recollection of him. One year, he simply did not come home. I know my mother sought information about him from the man who owned the ship, but there was nothing. The assumption was that he'd decided to start a new life in some foreign port."

He lightly caressed her arm, wanting to be in physical contact as she recounted what was surely to be a difficult and unpleasant tale.

"My mother worked many small jobs to keep body and soul together. She did mending, washing, cleaning—anything she could find. Our neighbors were very kind, especially the butcher's family who lived just down the street." She turned to him and smiled. "I am still very close with their youngest son, Jocelyn Gormley. I hope you will meet him one day—he is my closest and dearest friend."

Magnus squeezed her arm and smiled. "I would like that, too." The jealousy that stirred inside him was worrying. He was not, by nature, a jealous man. Or at least he had never believed he was. But he'd quickly realized he was possessive and territorial when it came to Melissa. Asking God for help with his jealousy had begun to factor regularly in his nightly prayers.

"The Gormleys and other neighbors helped us in small ways. Charging us for only a half-pound of something but giving us a pound. They were kind people who I know felt badly for us. But it was never enough."

Her hand caught his and she laced fingers, as if she needed closer contact for what came next.

"When I was thirteen, we were evicted from the room we rented. My mother had already sold everything we had of value. We lived in a narrow street not far from our prior home for almost two weeks. There were other families—decent people—those were hard times. But there were not-so-decent people, too."

Magnus heard her swallow.

"One day I came back from a day of selling oranges—something I did for a fruit and vegetable vendor—to find that my mother had found us a place to live. The kind woman who owned the house was sending a cart to collect us. They would take me first, and my mother would follow with our things." She turned to him, her eyes bleak. "I asked why? Why were we being separated? She made up excuse after excuse. But I wore her down. And just before the woman arrived, she told me: *He's a rich man and will treat you kindly*, she said. *He will dress you in pretty things and you'll live in a beautiful house.*"

She stopped and bit her lip before meeting his gaze. "Although I was a maiden and only thirteen, I was a woman by the standards of the streets and I knew plenty about what went on between men and women. I'd seen streetwalkers plying their trade in broad daylight. I knew what my mother meant. I was terrified and I begged her to tell them no—or if not that, at least to come with me."

Magnus closed his eyes; pity, frustration, and rage prickled his lids. He felt the touch of her lips on his.

Melissa and The Vicar

"Don't, Magnus. Please, don't be sad for me. I should have never begun—"

"No, I want to hear it. All of it."

"It is so . . . I don't know, worse than sordid—really, just sad."

He pulled her against him, their bodies like spoons in a drawer. It was easier not to see her while he listened to her grim story. That might be cowardly, but so it was. "Tell me the rest, my love."

She sighed. "The woman who'd bought me had been doing her job for a long time. She brought two big men with her. It was not pretty and I fought like a wild animal. But I remember one thing—she told my mother an address, a place where she was to go. Not until I a few years later did I find out it was a brothel, a place that was only one step up from the street."

"Did you see your mother there?"

"I didn't go until a year later. By then, nobody knew where she'd gone. My guess is she either moved on to a worse place or ended up on the street. She'd not been well the last time I saw her. I believe she must have had consumption. I can never forgive her for what she did, Magnus, but the one thing she did manage was to negotiate a decent contract when she sold me."

He kept his mouth shut; he had no right to comment on her mother's behavior one way or another.

She inhaled deeply and slowly exhaled. "As for me, Mrs. Pelham took me to a very proper looking house and had me deposited in her sitting room. When I tried to run, she had one of the men hit me, but not in the face—never in the face."

Magnus's temperature shot up, his head so hot his vision seemed to waver with the heat. She squeezed his arm but did not comment.

"It didn't take much to convince me that I'd better obey Mrs. Pelham. She sat me down and fed me a tea complete with biscuits and cakes and sandwiches of a quality and amount I'd never had. And then she'd said to me: *This is what your life can be if you are obedient. If you are not, you will get beaten, and, in the end, you will wind up in the same place but with bruises rather than cakes. The decision is up to you.* Mrs. Pelham said I was to call myself a widow—as asinine as it was for a girl my age to behave like a widow. It was the way things were done—to prevent the man who would be my protector, an aristocrat who'd paid a great deal for me—from appearing to be debasing a minor and—"

"Who?" he grated, "Who was it."

She twisted around in his arms, until they were facing one another. "No, Magnus. I will never tell you his name. Ever."

"Melissa, it is entirely possible—probable, in fact—that I know this man. You must—"

"Yes, it is. And that is why I *won't* tell you. You can order me to tell you, I know I am legally bound to obey you, but you will have to beat it out of me."

His jaw dropped in horror. "How could you think I would—"

She gave him a quick, hard kiss and a smile. "Hush, of course I know you would not beat me. I cannot tell you, Magnus. Just the same way I cannot tell all the other men's names."

Magnus wanted to close his eyes, to hide the fury her words evoked, but he couldn't. It would shame her. So, he just clamped his jaws shut.

"Do you want me to go on?"

"Yes." *No!*

But how could he *not* know what happened to her? Even though he knew that hearing it all would bring him nothing but heartache. He should have never opened this door, but now that he had, he could not close it. He had to go inside.

***

It is happening, a relieved, weary voice in Mel's head said as she watched her beautiful, kind, sweet, and—ultimately—innocent lover discover what kind of woman he'd chosen to marry.

She'd hoped to leave him without having to tell the whole sordid story of being sold, and she knew she could lie to him—she'd thought about it when he'd asked her—she probably *should* have lied to him, at least for his sake. But with the squire's threats today she'd realized he needed to know something of her past—because later, after she'd gone, somebody was going to tell him. Even if it wasn't Barclay, he would come face to face with the truth of everything—perhaps even the worst of it. Melissa knew there was no escaping it. Even in a backwater like New Bickford there was a man who knew what she was. Or what she had been. At least she could make sure that Magnus wouldn't be surprised when some nameless person confronted him about the whore who'd not only tricked him into a false marriage but then abandoned him.

She looked into his eyes. He'd steeled his expression, like a man who was determined to see something through, something unpleasant.

Melissa and The Vicar

"I will call the man John, for simplicity's sake. As dreadful a woman as Mrs. Pelham was, she never lied to me. Right from the beginning she made sure I knew what would happen to me. First, I was taken to a lovely town house. It had been furnished tastefully. There was a lady's maid, a butler, a footman, and a cook. In time, when I could be trusted to go outside my gilded cage, I would have my own carriage, horses, coachman, and groom. I lived in the house alone for a few days. Mrs. Pelham had told me a woman would come to see me. She was somebody chosen by my protector to—" She glanced up to Magnus, who was watching her with a mixture of revulsion and dread curiosity on his angelic features. "This woman had been a famed courtesan in her time. She was old then, but men still came to her for advice on all manner of subjects. John had sent her to me." She hesitated, not sure of how much to tell him about Dorothy, whom she'd come to love a great deal, no matter that she'd been complicit in sacrificing her to Lord Vanstone.

Well, in for a penny, in for a pound.

"She taught me many things—things that would keep me from getting with child, protect me from diseases, when possible, and, of course, she taught me how to pleasure a man."

His eyelids fluttered but did not close. "Go on," he said through clenched jaws.

"I was to be fed, groomed, and prepared—it seemed my new owner was in no hurry. My hair, which had been brittle and dull, became luxuriant and shiny. My skin, which had been insect-bitten, rough, and raw, became soft and supple. My body, which had been spare and angular, became healthy and plump, although I had been underfed for long enough that I did not begin to develop a womanly form until I was seventeen." She felt her mouth pull into a grim smile. "Whether by design or by malnutrition, I remained small and slight for longer than most girls my age. Almost as important as my physical grooming was the grooming of my voice, manners, and behavior. I was not an ignorant urchin, but I'd had very little schooling and I spoke with the accent of the streets. Dorothy is responsible for the way I speak today, although I have employed various others over the years to further smooth any rough edges. I did not meet John until two months passed."

She reached out and took her husband's face in both hands, locking eyes with him.

"More?"

He swallowed before nodding. "Yes."

"It was no surprise what he wanted from me and I was able to perform as he wanted. He was so pleased with me that he soon began taking me around with him—to the theater, to dinners at other mistress's houses." Magnus shuddered, but said nothing. "And, eventually, to the parties such men enjoyed having. Time passed in a blur. I settled into my life and accepted my lot. To be honest, Mrs. Pelham and my mother had been correct. I was one of the lucky ones."

He shook his head, but she stopped him.

"No, it is true. There were girls—far younger than I'd been—being sold every day for far less and into far worse conditions. John was not demanding or rough or cruel. He was gone for the summer every year and I had that glorious time to myself. I had holidays to myself also, as he had a family he was expected to be with. I had a family of my own by then—other women and even a few men—who were in my position, people who would not judge me for what I did, for what I'd become. My life seemed to have settled into a pattern."

She paused, but then continued. "Then, a few months after my seventeenth birthday, I began to notice a change. John came to me less frequently. When he did, it was usually to take me out to . . . parties. These were functions we'd often attended through the years. But there was a difference." She stopped and sighed. Every time she thought she'd said the worst, she'd forgotten there was something even more dreadful. She'd only ever told this story to Joss and there'd been no need to soften things for his consumption. She paused, almost believing she could work up the nerve to tell Magnus at least some of what Barclay had boasted of knowing today. But she couldn't. She simply could not describe what had happened at the end with Lord Vanstone, no matter that Sir Thomas might eventually take care of educating Magnus for her.

She realized there was a tension in his body; he was waiting.

"Go on, finish it."

She inhaled deeply. "What was happening had happened before: John was tiring of me. It was Dorothy, rather than John, who eventually told me. I was to be provided with a generous settlement—what my mother had negotiated for me, even though I was leaving his employ early. The amount would be enough to allow me to live for several years without working. But I was to vacate the townhouse in a month's time, to make room for another occupant."

Melissa and The Vicar

He shook his head, his expression appalled. "Another young girl?"

"Yes, this was something he'd done for years. Dorothy told me I was the fourth girl, and now I was to make room for the fifth."

A vein in Magnus's temple was pounding so insistently she thought he might do himself harm. "The swine. Is he still—"

"I've already told you, Magnus. I will give you no information. The last thing I want is for you to show up on his doorstep the way you showed up at The White House."

He looked grim and she knew this was not the last she'd hear of this. "Go on."

"There isn't much more to tell. I went to The White House because I knew I didn't have enough money to never work again, even if I lived frugally. But I did have enough money to invest with the woman who owned The White House at that time. Mrs. Hensleigh was a legend—a madam who paid her girls well, abhorred the virgin trade, allowed in no girls younger than sixteen, and permitted no violence. She had more people wanting to work for her than she could ever accommodate, so I was fortunate I had money to invest. At first, I was still required to work, but I could be selective." That much, at least, was true—although she was slightly overstating things. "We never became close friends, but she was a good employer and business partner to me. When she accumulated what she needed to stop working, she offered me the first option to purchase."

He was studying her, his eyes no longer frantic, but pensive. "I want you to know this, Melissa, I do not judge you for what you've done, but—as much as it shames and pains me to admit it—I've found myself feeling jealous. Even after hearing your painful story, I suspect I will still feel threatened that you have such extensive sexual experience while I only know what I've overheard from boasting young men and a few books. That jealousy is the product of my own insecurity and is a problem of mine, not yours. I'll continue to grapple with it, probably for a long time. If I ever seem to be taking out my own frustration on you, you must bring me up sharply. Do you understand?"

She smiled at this very Magnus-like statement. "I understand."

He didn't return her smile, but stared over her shoulder, as if seeing something else.

He looked so . . . determined, so willing to tackle his demons head on. That made her ask something she swore never to speak out loud.

"Why did you marry me, Magnus? When you found out what I was you must have been appalled. Why?"

He exhaled noisily and rolled onto his back. "I won't lie to you, Melissa—I was deeply shocked. Horrified, would be more like it."

She swallowed, glad he wasn't looking at her when he admitted to such feelings.

"I was furious with you for lying to me—for using my proposal to manipulate me that night at Halliburton Manor. But I came to realize I'd wanted you every bit—more, I'm guessing—as you wanted me. I was hurt that you would just run off without saying anything. Even when I knew who you really were, I couldn't believe you'd think me capable of being the type of man who'd stop loving you because of what you'd done."

"But you didn't really *know* me, Magnus. I lied so much—"

"Were you lying when we laughed together over some absurdity?"

She parted her lips. "But—"

"Were you lying when we discussed our impressions of books, arguing and bickering and—once again—laughing together in spite of our differences?"

"No, but you don't—"

"What you did is not who you *are*, Melissa. I know now that you have little exposure to scripture." That was kind of him. She'd actually confessed to him that she'd never even stepped foot in a church until New Bickford. "But surely even you have heard the story of Mary Magdalene?"

"The wh—prostitute who gave comfort to Jesus."

"If my God—a gentle, loving, and *forgiving* God—does not judge such matters, who am I to do so?"

She could only stare in amazement. It was, even after she'd been married to him and seen him angry, difficult to believe this man was not a saint. He certainly did not deserve to be stuck with her as a wife. "I know you are of a non-judging and forgiving nature, but even you must realize that the truth of who I am will cause catastrophic damage to you, your family, and most likely the profession you love and are so very good at."

He did not answer her immediately, giving the matter some thought. In fact, he thought for so long, she began to feel anxious. Had she introduced the subject in a way that had finally made him see how disastrous their union was? Was he regretting—

Melissa and The Vicar

He gave her a wry, lopsided smile—the expression surprising her. "I was trying to come up with an answer that did not make me appear such a spoiled brat, but I cannot lie to you. You see, the decision to marry you—which you think so catastrophic—is really my family's fault."

"*What?*"

He laughed. "Yes, it's true. They raised me with so much love, so much support for my every endeavor, so much admiration for my decision to enter the clergy even though not a one of them is overly devout—well, they made me the person I am. A man who cannot conscience that any decision or desire of his could possibly be a bad one." He gave a sharp nod. "So, there. There is your answer of why I married you: because they spoiled and pampered me and I cannot bear not having my way. Well, also because you are irresistible and I love you."

"You're mad, Magnus. Utterly barking mad," she said, laughing, but not entirely without a bit of hysteria.

He demonstrated his barking, along with a little howling, for good measure. Melissa laughed and played along with him, but she knew he was not telling her everything.

She tried one last time. "I'm happy you came after me, Magnus, and—yes—I'm happy to be your wife. But I hope you will be as satisfied and happy about our marriage when—"

He laid his index finger across her lips before leaning low to replace his finger with his mouth. "Hush, love of my life, we will deal with things in their own good time—and not before."

"Very well," Melissa said when she saw he wanted her assent. "I will not raise the subject ever again."

"Good. Now, you'd just told me about your investment."

"There isn't much else. I began to expand the business, buying the nearby buildings, for example." Melissa knew it was an odd thing to boast about—especially to her curate husband—but she couldn't help adding, "In the almost twelve years I owned The White House it tripled in revenue."

Magnus pushed himself up onto his elbow, his forehead furrowed. "Wait—if my addition is correct that would make you—"

"I will be thirty on my next birthday, on the last day of the year." She frowned at him. "Why are you looking at me that way?"

His smile was somewhat sheepish. "I thought you were closer in age to me."

Melissa cut him a narrow-eyed look; dear God, could the loathsome Sir Thomas have been *correct* about Magnus's age?

She heaved a sigh. "I'm almost afraid to ask."

He grinned. "I will be four and twenty on my next birthday, next Wednesday, as a matter of fact."

She groaned and dropped her head back. "I am six years older than my husband."

Magnus laughed and lowered his face to her breasts, his hot mouth closing over one nipple and sucking hard before he chuckled wickedly and said, "Oh come now, darling, it's closer to seven."

Mel could not let that stand. They wrestled and, of course, their playful wrestling turned into something more passionate.

After she made love to her beautiful husband, and as he slept beside her, his big body warm, his breathing deep and even, Melissa finally let herself consider the matter of Sir Thomas Barclay.

Sarah had not been at the cottage when she arrived. Mel had thought that odd, but it had also been a good thing as it gave her time to consider her options.

That night at Moor House, when she had gone to Magnus's bed, it had been with the intention of enjoying their lives for as long as possible, until she had to leave.

The more she slid into this life, the less willing she was to give it up—no matter how unrealistic that was. Whatever fatalism that had ruled her when Magnus had forced her into marriage had fled. Now she saw that they were a good husband and wife team, and that she would, if given the chance, make an excellent vicar's wife.

Every day she spent with him she loved him more. Every day she spent made her less willing to let go of this life. She'd begun to hope, at the back of her mind, there might be some way they could be together.

But that had been foolish. Oh, so very, very foolish.

She would have to leave him. Sir Thomas's threats had made that clearer than ever.

But that did not mean she had to let Sir Thomas have his way.

She had over a week to consider his threats. If a lifetime of struggle had taught her anything, it had taught her patience. It had also taught her that very few people planned out their actions to the rational conclusion, but Melissa was one of them.

Sir Thomas believed there were only two options open to her: public humiliation or doing what he wanted.

Melissa and The Vicar

He was very wrong.

Chapter Eighteen

The weather the next day was wretched and Magnus decided he would take the gig out to the Felix place rather than walk. Besides, he could visit two other families that lived farther out that way and distribute the vile jellies from Mrs. Heeley. He'd already decided he would give all three jars of delicious potted beef that their housekeeper had made to the Felixes, who needed it more than the other two families.

Just as he was climbing into the gig Melissa had come running after him.

"This is for Una." Her hair was whipping around her pale face, the auburn strands the only vibrant color on such a gray day.

Magnus took the brown paper-wrapped package. Una was the Felixes' oldest daughter, a girl of fifteen who Melissa had taken a liking to on their first visit to the dreary Felix farm.

"It's just a fleecy shawl and a day dress I no longer wear." She'd hesitated. "Are you sure I can't come wi—"

"It's far too cold, darling." He leaned down and gave her a kiss, not caring who might see. "Now get back into the house before you catch a chill."

She'd watched from the dining room window, waving to him as he rode away. He would have loved to take her with him, but he was not about to take foolish risks with her health. He hadn't forgotten that she'd originally come to New Bickford to convalesce, although she'd never been specific about what ailed her.

Magnus grimaced. How could he not know such a thing? Was he really such an incurious, uncaring louse? He should ask her questions like that rather ripping her clothing off and throwing her into bed the first thing he entered the house. Memories of that immediately brought a smile to his face and a thickening in his groin.

Or at least he should ask her those questions rather than the one he'd asked last night. Both his smile and groin deflated at that

Melissa and The Vicar

thought. He wished he'd not heard any of it, although he knew that was weak.

Because if she could live through being sold to a monster, then certainly he could live through hearing it.

He'd not said anything last night, but he would most certainly find out who this man was. He was not a fool; he knew that his wife's past was a notorious one. That night at Brooks had proven it. But he refused to dodge her past everywhere he went and he knew her past would eventually come to New Bickford. When that time came, he would learn what the parishioners would tolerate to keep him. Also what the Church would do. He loved his chosen profession and he loved worshipping God in the bosom of a congregation. But he would not be destroyed if he had to move Melissa to his estate, Briar House, in Lincolnshire. They could make a life there. He was the largest landowner in the area and people might learn who his wife had been, but none of them could afford to behave in an openly unchristian way toward him.

But that was borrowing trouble. The truth was that nobody in New Bickford—with the exception of Sarah, who wanted to keep the secret as well—knew anything.

***

Over the next five days Melissa braved the weather and trudged over to Sarah's cottage only to find it empty each day. On the sixth day, just when she'd begun to give up hope—and as the meeting with Sir Thomas loomed large—she arrived at Sarah's cottage to find the wagon from the Sleeping Ferret in front of the house. Joe Biddle was there and he was stacking crates carefully into the bed of the wagon.

"Joe, what is going on here?"

He yelped with surprise and spun around so fast he almost fell.

"I beg your pardon. I didn't mean to startle you."

"Hello, Mel."

She turned to find Daisy standing in the doorway, wearing a huge apron and large cloth around her head, managing to look wicked, all the same—like the Devil's own charwoman.

"Daisy, what are you doing here?" Melissa hadn't realized how much she missed her and the two of them almost broke each other's ribs embracing.

But it was Daisy who pulled away first. "Come inside, it's a misery out here. No—don't shut that. You can leave the door open, Joe will be hauling for a while, yet."

As Daisy led them through the small house Melissa couldn't help noticing there were boxes in various stages of fullness everywhere.

"Where's Sarah?" Melissa asked when they reached the kitchen.

"Upstairs packing. Sit. I've put the kettle on." Daisy hung up Melissa's hat, scarf, and cloak and then bustled about making tea, in silence.

Mel was in no hurry to learn what was probably not going to be good news, so she waited patiently.

In a short time, they had cups of tea and even a few biscuits.

"So," Daisy began. "I guess you can see Sarah is leaving."

Mel snorted. "I'd gathered that."

"Don't take that high-and-mighty tone with me, you ain't my employer no longer," Daisy snapped, her slipping accent no doubt a sign of rebellion. After all, it was Melissa who forced everyone who worked for her to take elocution lessons. "I'm not sure what you expected—leaving us all in a lurch while you ran off with your Prince Charming."

Melissa opened her mouth to answer but Daisy raised a hand. "No, just let me say my piece. And then you can talk circles around me and bend me to your will, just like you do to all of us."

That *hurt*.

"That pig Barclay came here and forced himself on Sarah. It wasn't just that, but he made noises about how he'd like to buy the land from her. For cheap."

Melissa grimaced.

"Aye, he's right secure in his position. How would it be if the villagers learned what Sarah really was? And what about Joe and me? His father's inn would be finished. So, Sarah fetched me down here and we talked it all out. Way we figure it, there's no future here for the three of us. Joe agrees."

Melissa hadn't heard Joe speak yet, so she found the thought of him "talking" anything out astonishing. But she kept that to herself.

"What will you do?"

"Sarah will sell the place and we'll take the money and start up somewhere else, fresh."

"Start up doing what?"

Daisy's checks colored. "We figure—me and Joe—that we could run an inn like his Da's. I've got a little saved up, and with what Sarah gets from Barclay—"

"Wait a moment, what? You mean she'd sell to him?"

Melissa and The Vicar

Daisy startled at her tone and then frowned. "Don't think we'll cut off our noses to spite our faces like some might."

Mel sighed. "Yes, you're correct, I often do things on principle that I probably should not but—"

"Ha!"

"Don't sell it to him—especially not at a bargain price."

"It so happens we don't have all the time in the world to linger and loiter and wait for another buyer to come along. If you haven't noticed, the squire is the only one in these parts who looks to be acquiring land these days. Joe said his Da has been trying to sell the small place he has on the outskirts of New Bickford for over five years. We can't wait five years, Mel. We can't. I've already waited my whole life. I'm forty-one years old—a washed-up old whore—"

"Daisy—"

"Yes, a *washed-up old whore*. I knew when I went back to London with you that I didn't have the stomach for it anymore. Each night was a struggle. After the first week I knew I'd end up hangin' from a rafter if I kept at it."

Melissa closed her eyes briefly, horrified that her good friend had been in such pain and she'd not noticed.

"No," Daisy said, shaking her head when Melissa opened her eyes. "Don't blame yourself for it. You were too miserable in your own little hell to notice mine. And I can tell by the way your nostrils are flaring that you'd like to dispute that."

Melissa laughed.

"But it's true and we both know it. And now it seems The White House is at sixes and sevens—and I heard rumors there is buyer and a sale soon to happen. I can't get an answer out of Hugo or Laura and I'm afraid they'll burn the house down one night in a rage, killing all of us along with them. Besides, I'm guessing Mister Stanwyck might draw the line at profiting from sin." She didn't wait for an answer. "But that's neither here nor there. The three of us don't want to work in a brothel. Not even if it ain't on our backs. We have a good chance at something new. It's not like people care if their innkeeper was once a whore." She cut Melissa a curious look, "Not like it must be for you and the reverend."

Melissa had no interest in discussing that with anyone, not even somebody she liked as much as Daisy. Instead, she put on her bargaining hat—so to speak—and topped up both teacups.

"There *is* a buyer for the London properties," she said, smiling at the other woman's look of surprise. "But that needn't concern you. Because it just so happens I might know somebody who could afford to give you maybe even a little more than what this property is worth. Do you think you'd be interested?"

***

Magnus had visited the Felix property twice in the past six days and each time he'd found Mr. Felix unavailable. He was determined to talk to the man—to get him to take action against Sir Thomas. He'd been surprised it had taken him so long to come up with the solution: the Felixes could have a farm on Magnus's property in Lincolnshire. It required a move, of course, but they could live on a property where he *knew* they'd not need to worry about the lord molesting their daughters. Besides, the tenant houses on his property were all in excellent shape and the soil was fertile and well-tended.

Armed with this brilliant idea, he'd saved the Felixes until his last call of the day, reasoning he'd be able to catch the man as he wouldn't be working the farm in the darkness.

The last people he'd visited had just had a new baby and wanted him to take a glass of their homemade wine to celebrate. By the time he made it to the Felix property it was well after dark.

He'd just turned off onto the narrow drive when he heard something shrill, like a girl screaming. He paused the gig and heard noises coming from behind one of the hayricks that bordered the road. He saw the squire's horse before he saw the man himself.

Sir Thomas had his breeches down around his ankles, and had bent the girl over, holding his hand over her mouth while she made choking crying sounds and tried to get away. He fumbled between their bodies with one hand, struggling to mount her.

Magnus's head exploded.

Never in his life—not even at Eton—had he struck another person. He'd simply never felt the need to resort to violence. He'd believed he was close to it that day at The White House, when Hugo had touched Melissa.

But that day was nothing compared to this.

When he had time to think on it later, Magnus realized he must have lost touch with himself for a period of time. He had no recollection of what transpired between seeing the squire's naked arse and sitting on bastard's chest, pounding his face.

Melissa and The Vicar

"'Ere then, Mr. Stanwyck. That's enough, sir. You've got to stop. 'Ees out like a snuffed candle." John Felix was a big man—but not as big as Magnus. It took him and two of his young sons to pull Magnus off Barclay.

Una was in the arms of another girl, her next younger sister, he thought. The two of them holding each other and crying, their horrified eyes telling Magnus it was his mad violence, rather than the squire's behavior, which was terrifying them now.

"I'm all right now," he said when Felix and his sons kept hold of him. They were reluctant to release him. And when he looked down at the squire's mashed, bloody face, he could understand why. But it must have looked worse than it was because Barclay sputtered, and blinked, wiping bloody hair from his eyes.

"Pull up your breeches and cover yourself," Magnus snapped.

Even beaten to a pulp Barclay would not back down. He must have been in pain, but he mustered a nasty grin, not bothering to tuck himself in. He paused, coughed, and then spat. Magnus saw a tooth along with the mass of blood and mucus. Good. He hoped to bloody hell he'd knocked them all out.

Barclay's next words broke in on his murderous thoughts. "What's the matter, Lord Magnus, come here to get your revenge defending the honor of your wife? Ha! The honor of a whore. She told me last week that you knew and I didn't believe her. Have to give you some credit for that. I guess she decided to 'fess up herself." He gave a gruesome chuckle. "That's a damned shame, I was lookin' forward to havin' one of those orgies she was so famous for. But I 'spose this means she won't be joinin' me and that little slut over at Tisdale's place on Friday. Unless you was plannin' on joinin' us, too, of course." He gave an ugly laugh and then winced, his hand going to his ribcage. But it wasn't enough pain to stop his venom from flowing. "I have to admit I like having a bawdy house just down the way. Quite a nest of them around these parts, isn't there? Almost like whore calls to whore, doesn't it? What's the old saying? A leopard can't change its spots? Well, your bloody precious wife is still a whore, no matter that she's now got a curate for a husband and a marquess for a father-in-law."

Magnus could only stare as the full impact of Barclay's poisonous words sank in. Melissa *knew* this man. Had he . . . oh God . . . had he been a *customer*?

As thrashed as he was, the squire had a nose for misery—no doubt from spreading it around enough. He laughed, dropping his head back to the ground and holding his sides. "She didn't tell you the whole of it—did she? How the hell did you find out, that's what I want to know? By God, that's rich though—it wasn't your wife who told you about the little tryst we had planned. Maybe she was hopin' to meet me this Friday. You ain't giving her what she needs, I guess."

Magnus turned away, unwilling to listen to another word, and encountered the stupefied faces of not only Mr. Felix and his sons—twelve and fourteen—but also his wife, who must have heard the commotion and come running. They were not staring at the man on the ground in horror, but at Magnus.

And that's when he realized his life, as he'd known it, was as good as over and had been since the day he'd married. Melissa had known that all along, but he'd been too much of a bloody fool to even understand the half of it.

But the worst part of all? The woman he'd lost everything for had—at the very least—lied to him, and at worst, had been planning to meet another man to keep her secret.

Chapter Nineteen

Melissa opened the little door in the stove for the fiftieth time in the past hour.

Magnus was supposed to have returned at an hour ago. It was dark outside but the wind had died down around sunset. Still, there was too much cloud cover for it to be safe to—

Her thoughts were interrupted by the sound of wheels on the crushed gravel drive that led past the curate house up to the barn. There, she was worrying for nothing.

She adjusted the table linen although it was perfect and polished the tine of a fork, although it didn't need it. She was so excited; not only had she thwarted Sir Thomas today, but she'd also successfully cooked her first Yorkshire puddings. Of course, those had gone out to the hens as they weren't fit for eating cold.

She was waiting until Magnus arrived to start the new puddings in the hot pan. She planned to pour him a glass of brandy—which Daisy had brought from London as a wedding gift—and talk while he watched her prepare their meal.

The brandy wasn't much of a gift when the bottle had been pilfered from The White House. Still, she supposed it was the thought that counted. Besides, she'd seen Magnus enjoy fine brandy when they'd been in Devon, but he kept nothing that special here.

When she'd asked him why, he'd jested it was because he was a humble curate. Melissa thought it was because he didn't want to appear wealthier than the vicar by consuming luxury goods.

Mel looked at the clock that sat over the blazing fireplace. Why, she'd heard the wheels of the wagon at least fifteen minutes ago. He should have put away the horses and gig by now.

She twitched back the kitchen curtain, which allowed her to see the vicarage. There was Magnus's familiar form, standing on the front step of the vicarage. The door opened and he went inside.

She sat back, staring at the messy heap of dishes she'd used to make this simple meal. Mrs. Dennis, the charwoman, said she'd get better with time, although they both knew the curate would not let his wife become a kitchen drudge. Cooking this meal tonight had somehow reminded her of that first time, in Mrs. Tisdale's kitchen, when they'd begun to know each other.

The minute hand had moved a full thirty minutes and still Magnus had not returned. By now she knew something had gone wrong. It was after nine; he'd never come home this late before. And when he'd been late, he'd always sent word.

By ten o'clock she had taken the roast out and put it on the bakery rack just outside the back door, in the cold area where they stored apples, potatoes, and other hardy food items. Everything else, the side dishes, the batter for the puddings, and the pie she'd made—her first—she left out on the counter. It would go to the pig and chickens tomorrow.

She extinguished all but one candle in the front hall, so he could find his way when he decided to come home. She banked the fire, undressed, and bundled up in bed with a book Lady Darlington had sent in what Magnus called her "care packages."

She must have fallen asleep because she woke up to find the candle guttering in the socket. The clock on Magnus's nightstand said it was almost one.

When she went to the kitchen and looked out the window she saw the vicarage was completely dark. Wherever Magnus was, he wasn't there.

She climbed back into bed, staring at the left side, Magnus's side. The fire in the bedroom was still burning, the hot glow from the coals keeping the small room warm and cozy. Even so, Melissa suddenly felt very, very cold.

**

Magnus knew he was lucky not to be confined in the root cellar the village kept for the few criminals they encountered. His face and hands weren't the only thing that got cold on his ride from the Felix farm back to the vicarage. As his anger against Sir Thomas and John Felix cooled, he realized that he'd broken not only man's law, but God's as well.

The curate house was ablaze with lights when he rolled down the drive. He thought he saw a figure moving behind the lace curtains of the room Melissa called the sitting room, even though it barely qualified for the name of parlor.

Melissa and The Vicar

Thinking about her in there, waiting for him—no doubt eager to take him in her arms as she had every night since coming to his bed that first time in Yorkshire—caused a queer blend of anger, frustration, disappointment, and sorrow in his chest. No, he could not go to her. Not yet. He would raise his voice and he would behave like a savage—which he now knew he was capable of. Besides, he didn't have time to fight or do anything else with her. He had to warn the vicar and he had to confess to things that would, likely, get him not only removed from the curacy, but also from the Church.

He put the gig away, currying old Nancy better than she'd been brushed in years, dragging his feet to go and begin what was surely going to be one of the worst nights of his life.

The vicar answered the door with his welcoming, vague, dear smile. A smile Magnus was about to obliterate.

"Come in, come in. Just back from the Felix and Johnson houses?

Magnus dropped his hat on the table beside the door and removed his greatcoat, hanging it on a peg, before answering.

"Yes, I saw both them and the Morgans, as well."

"Goodness, you have been busy." He smiled up at Magnus, a slight notch forming between his gray eyes, his expression faltering. "You've not come for idle chit-chat, I think."

"No, sir."

"Well, let us go to my study. You go make yourself comfortable and I'll ask Mrs. Loftis to make us up a tea tray."

Magnus smiled with a gratitude that was not feigned.

The vicar's study was a room Magnus loved. Book-lined and warm, it was a room that embraced a person. Or at least it always had him. It was the kind of room he'd one day hoped to have, himself.

He sat at the chair farthest from the vicar's desk. He thought the other man would appreciate the distance once he began speaking. The door opened and Mr. Heeley entered, rubbing his hands together, which he did unconsciously whenever he finished even the smallest piece of business.

"She'll have a tray for us shortly. I'm pleased to say she just baked a large batch of macaroons, so we'll have something delightful to take with our tea instead of—" He stopped abruptly, suddenly aware of his near disloyalty.

Magnus smiled. He would miss the vicar, but even this heavy fog of regret was not enough to make him regret Mrs. Heeley's cooking.

"I've come to talk to you about some things that aren't very pleasant. First, I know Sir Thomas has forced himself on at least one of his tenant's daughters." Magnus hadn't known *exactly* what reaction to expect from his disclosure, but it certainly wasn't the one he received.

Heeley's features screwed up into a tight knot, as if faced with something deeply distasteful. "Yes, yes. I'm afraid he has always made a habit of such, er, well, unpleasant behavior."

Magnus's mouth opened but his brain wasn't providing any words.

The vicar appeared not to notice. "Is it one of Felix's daughters, again?" Twin slashes of red colored his pale cheeks.

Magnus cocked his head, unable to believe what he was hearing. "You *knew* about this?"

The vicar's hands fluttered somewhat helplessly, two brown-spotted leaves blown by winds over which he had no control. "Well, I knew about the other girl. Er, the one who had the twins. The girl came to me some months before and told one side of the story."

Magnus could scarcely believe he was hearing him correctly. The vicar had finally recognized Magnus did not look like a particularly receptive audience.

"I can see what you are thinking, Magnus. You think I should have taken up the cudgels on her behalf, marched over to Squire Barclay's house and accused him—our local magistrate, largest landowner, and the most generous benefactor to Saint Botolph's—of molesting and impregnating a tenant farmer's daughter?"

Magnus gave a helpless snort of disbelief. "Well, yes, Mr. Heeley, that is exactly what I think you should have done."

Fortunately, the door opened and a maid entered with the tea tray or Magnus might have once again found himself sitting on a man's chest after having pounded him. His fury frightened—no, *terrified*—him. What was *wrong* with him? When had he become so volatile?

Even as he wondered the question the answer came with it, like the two halves of a seashell: he was angry because he couldn't punish who he really wanted to punish, the men who'd used his wife—starting with the one who'd defiled her to begin with. When he thought of this mystery man, which he'd done far too often in the brief time since she'd spoken of him, it was Barclay's face he pictured. Oh, he knew it wasn't Barclay, but only for lack of opportunity rather than lack of intent.

Melissa and The Vicar

The vicar faffed about with the teacups. "Two sugars, isn't that right?"

Magnus has as much intention of drinking the vicar's tea as eating the chair he was sitting in, and he'd lost patience with the whole façade.

"If I were to tell you I came upon Barclay in the very *act* of raping Felix's daughter, would that be enough to spur you to act?"

The vicar stared at him, his mouth a gaping black hole. "You must gain control over your emotions, Mr. Stanwyck. It is most unbecoming for a man of the cloth to behave this way."

Magnus almost fell out of his chair. "It is unbecoming to get upset about a girl getting raped by the very man who is supposed to protect her—the man who owns the house she lives in, the land her father farms, *everything* they have belongs to the squire. So, by that reasoning, I suppose his daughters do as well."

The vicar shot to his feet. He'd obviously forgotten his advice from less than a minute earlier because he was shaking with anger. "Do you think I am insensible to the squire's depravity? Do you? Do you think I am so ignorant that I don't know he possesses not a shred of moral fiber?"

"Then why the hell don't you do something about it?"

The room rang with his words and vicar's face turned a dangerous shade of red. "I will *not* be spoken to this way by my own curate!

"I serve at the pleasure of the Earl de Longue, whose right it is to appoint both our livings. I am not *your* curate, I belong to the people of this parish—and I owe them a duty to protect them."

The door to the study opened and Mrs. Heeley stood in the doorway. That's when Magnus realized they must have been yelling.

"Charles, what is going on? Why are you raising your voices at one another?"

The vicar obviously had to struggle to compose himself. "It is nothing, my dear. We merely became rather excited expressing our opinions."

She smiled uncertainly, her eyes drifting from the vicar to Magnus. "Very well, then. I shall leave you to it." The door shut behind her.

"Does Mrs. Heeley know about Sir Thomas's *unpleasant* proclivities?"

The vicar's deep-set eyes looked ready to pop out of his head. "Are you mad? That is hardly the type of thing I would ever tell my wife. She is a gentlewoman and to inflict this type of thing on her would be savage and cruel."

Magnus stared, arrested. He'd said the same thing to Melissa and he remembered her response clearly, *it was exactly the type of thing every woman should think about.*

It struck him like the proverbial bolt of lightning what an incredibly naïve fool he'd been. Melissa had been trying to tell him this all along and he'd refused to see it. No, it was worse, he hadn't refused to see it, he'd failed to recognize what she was talking about at all.

"Who else knows about this?"

Heeley's jaw worked side to side.

When he did not answer, Magnus's heart felt as though some giant fist was squeezing it.

"Others in the Church know." It was not a question and the vicar did not nod or answer.

Magnus shook his head, his jaw sagging in disbelief. "It is well-known, isn't it—what he does. But the money he gives has bought more than new windows for St. Botolph's."

Heeley's expression softened and leaned toward him. "You are a young man, Magnus, and full of righteous indignation, willing to take on the world and right the wrongs you find. You're—"

"Isn't that what we're supposed to do? Right wrongs, Vicar?"

The vicar made a noise of frustration. "You are willfully choosing to misunderstand me. I am trying to help you—to save you from potential embarrassment if you think to go over my head on this matter and—"

"Even if the entire Felix family, and I, write out sworn, signed statements you will do nothing about this matter?"

The vicar opened his mouth. It hung open for half a minute before he closed it again.

Magnus nodded. "Just as I thought."

"Mr. Stanwyck, you are judging me unfairly."

"This is not a cricket pitch, Mr. Heeley, we are not children to toss around words like fair and unfair. You have said more than once that we are the shepherds of our flock. Should we turn our backs and let the wolf take his fill?"

"You believe I don't wish to stop him?" The vicar's entire body quivered. "Barclay is an obscenely wealthy man with half the aristocracy and gentry beholden to him for loans—some of those

Melissa and The Vicar

people are *extremely* powerful individuals who determine *our* futures, Magnus. They all despise him, but they will not go against him. And Barclay will *crush* me, Mr. Stanwyck. Just like an insect. And what will I do, a man of eight-and-sixty, when he tosses me out of the only home I've ever known? What will my wife do? You come from a wealthy powerful family and can weather the displeasure of the Church and I *know* you possess an estate of your own to go to if you no longer have a church living. I do *not* have such a luxury."

It was Magnus's turn to stare with his mouth open, and the silence hung heavily between them before Magnus spun on his heel and headed toward the door.

The vicar's voice stopped him. "Mr. Stanwyck."

He turned.

The vicar's expression had gone from outraged to terrified to supplicating. "We will be most successful with this issue if we go about it slowly, and subtly. Churning the waters never yields anything good. Nothing can be gained from confronting the squire directly."

Magnus laughed and the vicar flinched at the humorless sound. "I'm afraid the time for subtlety has passed, Vicar. I beat Squire Barclay bloody tonight, in front of half a dozen witnesses. But don't worry, I'll not be remaining at St. Botolph's. Most likely I will be asked to resign to avoid what you call *churning the waters*. And in my letter of resignation rest assured I will mention the vicar of St. Botolph's has known of the squire's *unpleasant* activities for years. I'm going to hand it to the bloody Archbishop himself. And if he is involved in this, well, he should know his position is not unassailable."

Magnus left the door open behind him, no matter how much he wanted to slam it.

Outside he looked at his watch. He'd only been inside the vicar's study a quarter of an hour—it felt like years had passed. He'd believed his world had shifted dramatically earlier, with Barclay. But this—he glanced at the curate cottage. The windows all blazed with light, all of them; she was still awake. He could not go there, not now. He would yell at her worse than he'd yelled at Heeley and he did not want to repeat the mistake he'd made at The White House, when he'd threatened her.

He shoved his hands in his pockets and hunched his shoulders against the cold mist that had begun to fall and was perfect for cooling his hot temper. The moon was near full although occasionally shrouded by the low-lying clouds. Still, he could see well enough.

Magnus needed to calm down, because he was rapidly learning everyone around him was perfectly satisfied to play their part in this charade. The vicar acted like nothing untoward was happening, John Felix made his family act like nothing happened, and the squire acted whatever bloody way he wanted.

And Magnus? Well, he'd acted like a fool. Or, worse, he'd not been acting and he really *was* a fool. After all, what should he expect from a wife he'd had to threaten to marry him?

He didn't think she'd planned to meet the squire on Friday because she wanted to. But he *did* think she would meet him if she thought it would protect him: poor, innocent dunce Magnus, so happy in his pampered cocoon of ignorance and privilege. He *knew* she could give her body to another man without caring, but that didn't make it any better. If anything, it made it worse. Didn't she value herself at all? Didn't she value the things they did together? Or was bedsport just sport to her?

He ran his hands through his hair and groaned, his wet head making him aware that he'd been so busy being outraged he'd forgotten his hat at the vicarage. He should go home or he'd soon be soaked through. But he couldn't.

His mind slipped to the other subject that had occupied him ever since leaving the Felix farm. He'd asked John Felix straight out if he would give evidence if Magnus offered him a tenancy on his land and the man had said no. It was just . . . inconceivable.

But then, it wasn't. Felix had nine children, two grandchildren, and himself and his wife to feed and support and the notion of moving to Lincolnshire was as frightening as transportation to Australia to such people.

The house where they lived was ragged and small and Barclay did nothing to keep it up. And the land where Felix scratched out his living was fertile enough, but there wasn't enough of it.

Perhaps the vicar was right; perhaps the only way to deal with this problem was to find every pretty young girl in the area a job somewhere far away from here. Perhaps he was not just naïve but tilting at windmills.

Magnus desperately wanted to talk to his father. He'd never given much thought to the management of the huge Darlington estate, but his father owned over fifty thousand acres and employed hundreds of people on that one property alone. But his father was a beloved master, or at least the people who worked in the house and worked

Melissa and The Vicar

his land appeared satisfied. Certainly Magnus had never seen any families as desperate as the Felixes. But had he really looked? He hadn't lived at home—except in the summers and on holidays—since he was nine. And the last thing he did when he visited his parents was inspect their tenant farmers. Perhaps there was poverty everywhere?

He thought of Cecil and his love of the outdoors; did that extend to seeing to the people who would one day be his? Or did he just see to his own pleasures?

Good Lord. Each door he opened just led to another. He'd been living in his own little world and he'd been doing it for a long time.

Magnus looked through the misty moonlight and saw his feet had taken him toward Mrs. Tisdale's cottage. The little house sat not far ahead, looking exceptionally sad and lonely. He squinted—to be honest, it looked almost . . . *abandoned.*

Magnus could see even before he reached the front steps that the windows were without their coverings, and when he looked inside, he found the front parlor was utterly empty. Everything save for the fireplace screen was gone. He walked around the house, a foolish action—what did he expect to find? That only the parlor had been stripped?

He tried the back door and found it was unlocked—not unusual in their small community, where thievery was rare.

His feet echoed eerily as he walked the bottom floor and then climbed the stairs. The rooms up here were just as empty. He stood in Mrs. Tisdale's room and stared out the window into the quiet of the night. What had happened? Where had Sarah gone? And why did he feel this was yet another thing his wife might know about and withheld from him?

Well, there was only one way to find out just how—or if—Melissa was involved in this mess, and that was to talk to her.

It was time to go home and speak with his wife.

Chapter Twenty

Melissa felt him slip in beside her. She did not move to look at the clock; she did not want him to know that she'd remained awake, unable to sleep, worried.

He must have been exhausted because his breathing was almost immediately deep and even. Unlike what had been his practice, he did not touch her. In fact, he stayed at the very edge of their small bed. She knew something was very wrong. One of the first things he'd insisted on after the night she'd gone to him in Devon was that they always share a bed.

"Why would I ever want to sleep anywhere else but with you, Melissa?"

She'd smiled at the time, realizing it never occurred to him that *she* might prefer privacy, at least occasionally. But the truth was, she'd become accustomed to another person in her bed, to Magnus. He was a tactile man and reached for her often, not just to take her sexually, but to hold her. And now he could not seem to lie far enough away.

She must have fallen into an exhausted, uneasy doze because when she woke just before first light, she was alone. Wrapped in her dressing gown and slippers she found her husband at his writing desk, fully clothed but not in what she teasingly called his vicar suit. She swallowed, lightheaded. It had come, and far sooner than she'd expected.

He must have heard her because he looked up. He did not look like Magnus—at least not as she knew him. His sky-blue eyes had become wintry and opaque, like a wall of ice. And his beautiful face seemed to have changed overnight, the elegant, soft lines now hard and chiseled: it was almost as if he'd been transformed in some way.

He turned back to whatever it was he'd been writing. "I am resigning my curacy effective immediately. I've arranged to have the Sleeping Ferret's post chaise come round at noon. That should give you plenty of time to pack and get ready. It appears their wagon is not available, so anything larger that is ours will have to be collected later."

Melissa and The Vicar

The room fell silent but for the scratching of his quill. Anger began to seep in along with shock. Why was he behaving this way? Hadn't she told him this would happen? And now he was acting as if she'd sprung some new scandal without his knowledge.

"And is this all the explanation I am to get, Magnus?"

She had already known just how furious he was when he did not stand when she entered the room; Magnus was the most courteous man she'd ever known. Ye he remained seated and kept writing. "I didn't know you needed me to tell you anything. I assumed you'd get it all from Barclay when you met him on Friday."

Melissa closed her eyes. How, just *how,* had this happened? She opened them to find Magnus staring at her, his anger white-hot now.

"I'm sorry. I was—"

"You are sorry about keeping things like this from me? Or sorry about getting caught?" His tone was like the cruel, hard point of a whip. He signed whatever document he'd been writing—his letter of resignation? And sanded the piece of paper before turning back to her. "I expected that one day somebody who knew you from your past life would surface. But I never thought I should have to endure the added humiliation of it being *him.* And you have known for some time, have you not?"

Melissa could only stare. His anger was like a blast furnace—she would become consumed if she came closer, if she engaged him. Besides, she could see he had no interest in listening to her right now.

"As I walked last night, trying to wrap my mind around this—around why you would keep such a thing from me—it occurred to me why you left so suddenly back in July. You must have seen him—or he saw you—at the Summer Fête." He stopped, his blond eyebrows arched as sharply as scythes.

"Yes. Daisy saw him and came to me. That is when we decided to leave."

He nodded, his nostrils pinched and white while he folded his letter, his hands shaking. "So, knowing you were leaving, you accepted my offer, told me you loved me, and then *fucked* me."

Melissa had never heard him swear before. Even when he'd been angry at The White House, he'd not resorted to raising his voice or vulgar language. She'd heard the word countless times in her life but never before had it sounded so . . . harsh.

"Magnus."

His head jerked up.

"Will you let me speak? Will you let me at least try to explain?"

He sat back immediately, folding his arms over his chest and resting one top-booted ankle on his opposite knee. "Please do."

Melissa leaned against the wingchair, not ready to sit. "I *am* sorry I didn't tell you about the squire knowing who I was. But the reason I never mentioned it is because until recently I thought you knew."

An unpleasant expression took control of his face. "And you think I wouldn't have said something if I knew? That I would have come back here, blithely, if I knew?"

She sighed. "I don't know what you would have done. But the reason I believed what I did is that I couldn't think where else you would have learned who I was. I know Sarah didn't tell you."

"No, she didn't say anything until—" He stopped, uncertainty and discomfort joining the other emotions flickering across his face.

"Don't worry about Sarah's part in it—I know now what happened. It must have been Mrs. Tisdale who told you."

"I thought you knew," he said, confusion joining the other expressions clouding his face.

"Not until I encountered the squire, several days ago, while walking to see Sarah. It was then that I learned you didn't learn the truth from him. I know this because he used the threat of exposing me to—"

"To force you into having sexual relations with him."

She grimaced. Good Lord. Just what had Barclay told him? "I didn't do anything, Magnus. I was—"

"You were to meet him on Friday—*today*—to tryst at Sarah's cottage. Yes, Sir Thomas told me in some detail what the three of you would do."

"I would never have done that, Magnus. You must know that."

"What *were* you going to do?"

That was the sticky part. Well, the stickier part—and the agonizing part, as well. She could hardly tell him she'd planned to be gone by Friday—both out of Sir Thomas's range and out of Magnus's life. She was torn between gratitude she didn't have to leave him just yet and fear about whether she would ever be able to make herself do the right thing.

"I don't quite know," she said untruthfully. "I was working on something."

"And did that something include Sarah leaving Mrs. Tisdale's?"

She blinked. "You *saw* them?"

Melissa and The Vicar

"Them? Who, them?"

Well, that answered that question. At least this was one thing she could tell him the truth about. "Daisy and Joe came to help her move. They were there only yesterday but they wanted to be gone before the day was out. It sounds like they were."

"What is going on, Melissa?"

She slid into the chair with a sigh. "I bought the house and land from Sarah."

"*What?*"

"Barclay knew who Sarah was and he'd—" She bit her lip. Why did it always seem so difficult to tell her husband ugly things? Things she wouldn't have blinked about telling Joss or Hugo or Daisy?

"I can imagine what he did if he had leverage over her," Magnus said, interrupting her thoughts. "Go on."

"He was going to buy the land for a fraction of its worth and Sarah was going to take it, just to get away from him. She and Daisy and Joe have some idea of opening an inn and posting house and they are going to pool their money. So, I offered them full price for the property."

It was his turn to blink. "You have enough money for such a purchase?"

"I had an offer for the buildings in London. I didn't sell the business," she added before he could ask. "Just the buildings." When he said nothing, she cut a nervous glance at him. "You told me I could do what I wished with the proceeds of such a sale. So, I did."

"That is a very kind thing to do for your friends."

She shrugged. "I owe Daisy and Sarah this much at least—this chance at a new life. This way they'll have enough to purchase a decent inn."

"And The White House—who purchased that? Do they understand it can no longer operate? I told you I wanted it closed—I want no connection existing between that place and you." Thunder had rolled back into his eyes, which had begun to clear only a minute earlier.

"I don't know who the purchaser was." That was, as far as it went, the truth. "But I know there will be no business called The White House." That was also true.

His jaws worked as he stared holes through her. "It seems you think of everything."

Melissa hoped he would always continue to think that way. Unfortunately, she suspected he would one day learn that she had actually left one large loophole in the deal she made with Hugo, Laura, and their other, unknown, investors. They had to close The White House, but they could open for business under a new name. While she felt guilty for lying, she also felt anger at Magnus. Who was he to say what other people could do to earn their crust? And she'd haggled hard for the price on the building so it was not as if she'd given them a bargain. They'd paid for it, it was theirs, they should be able to do what they liked.

"And just what were your plans for the property you acquired here?" he asked, pulling her back to their conversation.

"My immediate goal was simply to keep Barclay from exploiting Sarah any further. But I had thought that—"

"Yes?"

"Well, perhaps it would be nice to keep the cottage for a woman, or women, who might need a place of peace. The way Mrs. Tisdale needed it."

He nodded his head slowly, his eyes never leaving hers. "And what about Barclay? What was your plan for him? Especially since you would now be going to an empty house without even another female to help if you should need it."

She took a deep breath and prepared to tell him yet more lies. "The truth—in all honesty—is that I didn't have anything planned yet. I expect I would have let him go there and become angry. And then he would have come to the vicar, which is what he threatened. I'd like to think I would have told you by then, so you were not unpleasantly surprised, but I'll admit I was in no hurry to destroy our life here."

"It is not *you* who has destroyed our life, Melissa—if, indeed our life *has* been destroyed—it is Sir Thomas, or—likely, the vicar—indeed the *Church*—and the good people of New Bickford."

Melissa wanted to weep for the bitterness she heard in his voice; it was the first time he'd sounded so resigned, so . . . jaded. So much like *her*. She leaned forward and caught his attention. "Won't you tell me what happened yesterday? Please."

He glanced at the clock on the mantle. "We must get ready—there are still a few things I have to do. I will tell you in the carriage on our way to London."

She sat back in surprise. "We are going to London?"

Melissa and The Vicar

"For the time being. I would take us to my property in Lincolnshire, but it is still under lease. I shall have to see if the tenant can be compensated to leave early. If not, it is a yearly lease which renews each January."

"But . . . *London*? Magnus, are you sure? If there is ever going to be a chance of somebody seeing me, it would most certainly be there."

"That is rather the point, Melissa."

"*What?*"

"My parents will soon be in town, if they are not already there, having come to engage in wedding matters. It is time you meet them and it is time they know how things stand. Especially now that a man like Barclay is on the loose with such information. I will not run and hide from the fear of exposure. The truth is either already out—or soon will be. I would like to prepare my parents rather than having them learn your identity at a dinner party."

He hesitated, his eyes searching her face for something.

"It is my intention that we will live at Briar House. I have never liked society, even when my mother convinced me to live in London for a Season. I have no interest in the vapid existence of Town life. I suspect you are not eager for socializing in London, either. So, we shall keep to ourselves after my brother's wedding."

The longer he spoke, the hotter her face became. This. This is what she'd known would happen: horror, rejection, judgment, and— eventually, although he might not understand this yet—isolation as even those people whom he believed loved him set him at a distance, if not giving him the direct cut.

"But—"

"Please, Melissa. Do not belabor this point. We are married and the lies must stop. We were going to tell them in any event when we went for the wedding. What difference does a week or so matter?"

She didn't tell him that she'd not planned to *be* in London in a week or two.

"Telling the truth to my family is the first step in our new life together. Will you come?"

She met his weary, deadened gaze and said, "Yes, I will come."

He nodded, his expression lightening slightly. "Things appear rather dire now, but I have faith in you, us, and our chances for a life together."

Melissa looked at his beloved face, knowing he was desperate for an answer from her. So she said, "I also have faith, Magnus."

After all, what was one more lie?

***

The ride to London had been mostly silent, but not bristling with hostility as their last carriage ride had been. Melissa knew that was because her husband was not as immature and grudge-bearing as she was. Magnus's anger burned white hot but only briefly.

By the time he finished telling her the whole sordid tale of his interaction with Barclay, the Felixes, and the vicar he no longer looked angry with her, merely exhausted.

She hadn't commented when he'd finished. What could she say? And so they had lapsed into silence for the remainder of journey, each of them busy with their own thoughts.

She knew Magnus thought that beating on the squire and arguing with the vicar meant the end of his career, but Melissa suspected the money and power that worked so well to protect Sir Thomas could also be employed to bring Magnus back into the Church. He might have a living in the Outer Hebrides for a few years, but he was part of the ruling class and they took care of their own.

It was terribly unfortunate that Lord and Lady Darlington were already in town and were there to greet them when they arrived at ten past seven that evening.

She'd hoped for at least a day to settle in and get her bearings, but they were in the act of removing their cloaks and hats when Magnus's parents came down the sweeping marble stairs into the stately foyer.

"Darling!" Lady Darlington said, running toward her son with an undignified haste that Mel found endearing.

While mother and son clung to each other in greeting Lord Darlington smiled down at Melissa, his expression cautious, but not unfriendly.

"And you must be my son's mysterious bride." He took Melissa's hand and bowed over it. "Welcome to Darlington House."

Magnus came toward Melissa, his mother's hand in his. "How rude I am, darling. Mama, this is my wife, Melissa. Melissa, my mother, Lady Darlington."

The marchioness hesitated only a moment before drawing Melissa into a soft, lavender-scented embrace. "Welcome, my dear, welcome." She put Melissa at arm's length and studied her, her expression far more difficult to read than her husband's. "You have brought home a beautiful wife, son."

Melissa and The Vicar

Magnus beamed at her, his hands clasped behind his back, rocking on his heels like a pleased young boy.

"Come," the marquess said, one hand on his wife's waist, the other gesturing toward the stairs. "Let us show you to your chambers. Maybe once you've had a chance to freshen up you'll join us for tea?"

"That sounds lovely," Mel said, feeling tired, disoriented, and almost dreamlike as she followed her faux mother and father-in-law up the stairs.

"Did Cecil come with you?" Magnus asked. Melissa could hear the hope in his voice.

"No, he will be here the evening before the wedding," his mother said, heaving a sigh before cutting Melissa a look of maternal asperity. "Our eldest son is rather difficult to pry from our country house," she explained.

Magnus laughed. "Cecil should have been born a horse and then he'd never have to leave the stable."

His mother gave him a playful swat. "Hush."

"I should tell you that Mel and I were already here, Father. We came to stay a few nights after our wedding."

"Ah," the marquess said in a noncommittal tone, gesturing to Melissa to proceed him once they reached the landing.

"This is your *home*, darling. You must come and stay whenever you wish, you know that," the marchioness said, leading the way, the gorgeous georgette of her gown billowing behind her like a mauve specter. "I'm *so* happy we were engaged to dine out this evening with Lord and Lady Phelan. You know they are our dear friends so they did not take umbrage when I told them we were begging off to spend the evening with our son, the cleric."

"Oh, Mama, you didn't need to—"

"Yes, son, she did," the marquess stopped, his expression serious as he regarded his youngest son before opening the door in front of his wife.

"I put you in the grandest guest suite—I do hope this is where my son put you on your last stay, Lady Magnus?"

Hearing the title only added to the unreality. Before she could answer, Magnus spoke.

"Please, Mama. She is Melissa."

For a heartbeat, the other woman's elegant composed features flickered, but she had herself back in hand so quickly Melissa did not believe she'd seen what she'd thought she saw.

"I do hope you will call me Elizabeth."

"And you may call me David," the marquess said, giving Melissa a smile that looked a bit strained.

They all laughed, even though it wasn't funny, and stood staring rather awkwardly at each other.

Magnus took the initiative and leaned down to kiss his mother's cheek. "Perhaps we might take a half hour and meet you downstairs?"

"Yes," the marchioness said, "That is perfect. Dinner isn't until nine but we knew you'd be famished so we'll have something to ease your hunger. We'll be in the Rose Salon, it is so much cozier than any other room at this time of year."

Once they'd gone, Melissa turned to the man who thought he was her husband.

Magnus held her by the shoulders for a moment before pulling her into a crushing embrace. He'd not touched her since the day before and the feeling of his body was almost her undoing. She was teetering on the edge of sinking to her knees and telling him the entire truth and begging his forgiveness—pledging her word to marry him for real this time and embrace their future in earnest. Before she could speak, he did, his words bringing her hurtling back to the reality of their situation.

"I'm sorry about this, old thing. I know they look frighteningly conservative, but they'll get over your past and love you just as much as I do. I promise you."

Melissa laughed, and it wasn't untinged with hysteria. Could he really be this naïve? But she didn't ask him that. Instead she said, with mock severity, "What did I tell you about calling me that, Magnus?"

She asked the question because she knew he expected it and because it was easier to jest than to talk about how misguided he was about what his parents, his family, the *ton*, or *anyone* would think once they found out about her past.

"I'm sorry darling, you can punish me later," he promised.

"You know I will."

They chuckled softly together. Never had she felt less like jesting in her entire life but she felt some of the tension ease from her husband's body, so it was worth the effort.

When he put her at arm's length he leaned down and kissed her forehead. "All will be well, Melissa. I know it will."

Thankfully the urge to throw herself at his feet had fled. Instead, her attention now focused on the gravity and urgency of her situation.

Melissa and The Vicar

She needed time—at least a day—to make plans. She couldn't stay in London. She knew Magnus would leave no stone unturned to find her. No, she would need to be gone when he finally learned the truth.

"Darling?" he asked, a notch of concern between his beautiful blue eyes. "Are you not feeling well? Would you like to simply go to bed and perhaps have this conversation in the morning, when you are—"

Melissa did what she always did when she wanted to manipulate a man.

"Unbutton yourself, Magnus."

His eyes widened. "Now?" he asked, a visible struggle taking place inside his head: propriety versus desire.

She opened the catches and began unbuttoning him.

"But what about tea? My parents?"

"This won't take long, unless you dither."

He stared at her and she could almost see his resolve melting away.

Melissa sank to her knees and brought his pantaloons down with her. "I'm tired of talking, Magnus. Aren't you?" She lowered her mouth over the tented muslin of his drawers, sucking him hard through the fabric and making him shudder and groan before pulling the tape and yanking them down. "I want you to take me. Hard."

She swallowed him deep and then deeper still, opening herself to him until the hot hardness of his cock bumped the back of her throat.

He gave a low, guttural grunt of pleasure and then thrust his fingers into her hair.

There was no more talking

***

Magnus owed his wife the biggest and most heartfelt apology of his life.

"What have you *done?*" his mother repeated for the third time.

His father, on the other hand, hadn't said a word. He'd also not stopped staring at Melissa as if she were a poisonous insect that had somehow found its way into his sitting room

Beside him, Melissa sat with her hands folded in her lap, her eyes fixed on the flames dancing and crackling in the hearth.

He reached for her hand and she let him take it. It was limp and cold, a contrast to his own hands which were hot and sweaty—as was his entire body as the enormity of the situation crashed down on him.

"You will have to leave the Church." His father's expression was no longer aghast. Instead, he appeared detached—just as he looked when dealing with a tradesman or servant. It was not an expression his father had ever directed at Magnus before, and it was like glass in his stomach.

He nodded. He couldn't bear to tell them of the debacle in New Bickford. Not now.

"What will you do?"

"We shall live at Briar House."

The marquess nodded, his eyes distant, as if his attention was somewhere else, anywhere else.

"But you can't think to *live* here?" his mother demanded in a voice dripping with horror. "Surely you should go to the Continent?"

Magnus bristled at her tone. "Yes, in fact we do plan to live here."

"But you—"

"Elizabeth."

Magnus had never heard his father speak to his mother in that tone of voice. In fact, he couldn't recall his father using such a coldly commanding tone *ever*.

It seemed to send a shockwave through his mother's slender body—like a bolt of lightning—and when it was over, his mother had the identical expression to his father: cool, aloof, like someone other than his beloved mother inhabited her body.

Before she could open her mouth, the door opened and tea arrived.

"Thank you, Dawks," his mother said in a voice so normal Magnus could only stare. "Would you mind serving, er, Melissa?" she asked, the slight flush on her cheeks the only sign of what it took for her to force the word between her lips.

"Of course," Melissa said, her own expression as cool as his parents. Magnus felt like he was in a dream.

The feeling heightened after Dawks and the maid left and his mother chattered on about inconsequential gossip while his wife prepared their tea.

His father demurred when she asked his preference, going to the sideboard and pouring a half glass of whiskey, which he consumed while standing, and then poured another.

Nobody drank tea or consumed any of the delicacies on the tray. His mother continued to fill the silence although she was beginning to sound a bit harried.

She lunged to her feet at a soft knock on the door and was halfway across the room when it opened. "Yes, Dawks? What is it?" she asked in a breathy, high-pitched tone.

Melissa and The Vicar

Before the butler could answer a man appeared behind him.

"Hallo, Lizzy, David." His eyes lighted on Magnus and his face broke into a grin. "Why Magnus, I didn't know you were in town."

"Oh, John!" his mother wailed before Magnus could answer. Everyone watched in shock as the Marchioness of Darlington flew across the room and launched herself into his Uncle John's arms and commenced to sob.

Magnus briefly closed his eyes and turned to Melissa, who was staring down at her hands, which were clasped in her lap, the knuckles so white they looked like snow.

"Melissa?"

She didn't answer, nor would she look up.

"Mel, is—"

"You'll have to excuse Lady Darlington," his father's cool voice cut through the sound of his mother's crying. "She's not seen her brother for quite some time."

Mel's head whipped up. "Brother?" The word was barely a whisper.

The marquess nodded, his eyes the color of crushed ice. "Yes, her elder brother—the Earl of Vanstone."

Chapter Twenty-One

Melissa shook her head at the footman who hovered beside her with yet another bottle of wine. She was, she saw, the only one refusing him. Indeed, the wine was flowing rather freely all around this evening. She was the only one abstaining. It was all she could do to even put a morsel of food in her mouth and swallow it without vomiting.

Luckily nobody was paying her too much attention. Even Magnus had only asked her once if aught was amiss before leaving her to her own devices. He, like the other three, was too busy behaving as if everything were normal.

After the marchioness had told her brother that she was just feeling rather emotional about the upcoming wedding they'd all sat down around the tea tray and discussed the latest town gossip. If such an activity appeared more than a little ironic to Magnus's family, they were too well-bred to let on.

For her part, Melissa had not been able to look away from Lord Vanstone's face long enough to know what her other three dinner companions were thinking. Although she could certainly guess given the tense silences that fell every few moments.

Lord Vanstone, after his initial moment of stunned surprise, behaved with all the ease of a man assured of his place in the world—at this table, in this household, with these *people*.

He was her husband's uncle.

That thought was primarily what circled her brain, around and around like a raven circling carrion.

If there had been even a scintilla of doubt about her decision to leave Magnus it was now gone, eradicated by the very man who'd put her on this road in life to begin with.

Melissa took morbid pleasure in watching John Mixon, the Earl of Vanstone, interacting in an environment other than the one they'd shared for over three years. Looking at him from this perspective she had to admit that he was a handsome man—his dark hair had gone

Melissa and The Vicar

silver at his temples in the almost thirteen years since she'd last seen him. There were more lines on his narrow, handsome face and around his pale gray eyes.

"Isn't that true, Melissa? *Melissa?*"

She wrenched her eyes away from the object of her fascination, who'd turned to meet her gaze for only the second time in the last few hours, his thin lips flexed into a smile but his gray eyes like daggers.

Everyone had stopped to stare at her, which made her realize her husband had asked her a question.

She turned to find Magnus's concerned gaze on her.

"I beg your pardon, Magnus. I'm afraid my mind was wandering."

Melissa would have sworn the entire table heaved a collective sigh of relief at her words. Magnus, his parents, and his uncle all spoke at once, each declaiming they'd not realized how late it was, how tired Melissa must be, what beasts they'd been to keep her up. Dinner broke up with such haste that the men did not even indulge in an after-dinner drink. Instead, his uncle begged off, claiming he'd ridden most of the day.

"You needn't show me out, Lizzy." He kissed his sister's temple, his gaze on Melissa. "No need to stand on ceremony with your big brother." His lips curved into a smug smile as he embraced Magnus, the two men thumping each other on the back and insisting they would ride together soon.

He took Melissa's hand in a grasp so light it was almost not there and bowed over it. "It has been a pleasure, er, Melissa."

Not to be outdone, she reached deep inside herself and found something beneath the anger and fear: her battered pride, which this man had done everything in his not inconsiderable power to eradicate.

"The pleasure is all mine—" She hesitated and forced herself to smile. "Should I call you Uncle John?"

The silence was so sharp you could have cut a diamond with it.

Magnus was the first to break it. He laughed, giving her a genuine smile, clearly pleased that she'd taken to his uncle, of whom he was so obviously fond. "You should, darling. Uncle John has always been a favorite in this house." He slid a hand around her waist and pulled her to his side, apparently not caring how the action brought horror to his parents' faces: their perfect son, embracing a whore.

Once Vanstone had gone, Lord and Lady Darlington made haste to retire to their own chambers. No doubt to discuss the horrific turn of events until dawn.

Mel could see the same idea was on Magnus's mind as he opened the door to her chambers.

The moment he closed the door she turned to him. "I'm terribly sorry, but I have a horrid headache. I know you wish to discuss—"

"No, of course not, darling."

Because she was weak, she allowed him to pull her into his arms and hold her. Why not? It might be the last time.

"I'm sorry about this evening, Melissa," he murmured into the top of her head. "But now that we've told my mother and father, the worst is over."

She closed her eyes, having to bite her lip to keep from laughing hysterically. Instead she nodded, kissed his neck, and then pulled away.

"I hope you don't mind if I sleep alone tonight," she said, dying a little inside when she saw the quickly covered up hurt in his eyes.

"Of course not. I understand. Is there anything I can get for you?"

She shook her head and he hesitated. After a long, painful moment he nodded, accepting his dismissal, and walked toward the connecting door. "I shall see you in the morning. Good night."

Once the door closed behind him she headed directly to her writing table.

As she scribbled the first of a series of letters she thought not about tomorrow or all the gray days after that, but wondered how long she'd need to wait before Magnus would go to sleep and she could summon a footman to run her messages.

***

Magnus had known it was a mistake to go to Brooks, but he must have been spoiling for a fight. Hell, he knew he was. Especially after Melissa had all but tossed him out of her bed tonight.

He was bloody furious. Oh, not at her—at his parents. How could they behave this way? He knew he was naïve when it came to such matters but it wasn't as if members of the aristocracy hadn't married women with scandalous backgrounds before. Everyone knew of Sir John Lade and the Gunning sisters before them. Hell, the Gunnings had married three bloody dukes all told. Magnus was not the heir; he was a son who hated society and would never come to London again as long as he lived.

He pulsed with fury—and violence. It seemed that violence, once you embraced it, became addictive.

Melissa and The Vicar

So that was the real reason he'd gone to Brooks. After all, he could have merely walked his anger out. But that wasn't good enough.

He'd known when he'd walked in—it was half-full, but deadly quiet—that something was out of the ordinary. He went to a table, waved over a waiter, and ordered a drink before picking up a paper and pretending to read.

They must have drawn straws over who would come ask him. It took them a while, three-quarters of an hour, by his reckoning. Not surprisingly, it was their ringleader Royce—the bastard from his last visit to Brooks—who came over

"How are you this evening, Stanwyck?" He glanced behind Magnus almost theatrically. "I hear you have a companion at your parents' house this week." The others lurking behind him chuckled.

Magnus had already had two brandies more than he was accustomed to drinking. That, plus numerous glasses of wine at dinner, had erased what little restraint he had left.

He tossed the unread paper aside. "Oh, and who told you that?"

He shrugged. "You know how servants are—they talk."

Magnus knew the man spoke the truth. On their last visit there'd only been a few trusted retainers. This time, the servant quarters were full to bursting for the upcoming wedding.

Royce leaned toward him when Magnus did not speak. "Where's your little companion now—I daresay you had to turf her out before the mater and pater showed up? You should have brought her round here." He laughed in a way that made Magnus feel as though he'd been buried in burning coals. The men behind him were an ugly chorus that egged him on.

Magnus cocked his head and forced himself to smile. "Do you bring your little *companions* to a gentleman's club, Royce?"

The viscount's pudgy, red face darkened at Magnus's sarcasm and tone of loathing. "I say, I'm not sure why you are taking that tone with me. I'd just come over to congratulate you on landing the elusive Ice Madam. No need to get in a twist about it. I daresay you're not accustomed to such conversations—being a man of the cloth as you are. But you'd better accustom yourself damned quick because your name is already in the betting book."

The muscles of Magnus's face did not seem to be under his control. He stood, towering a good half-a-head over the smaller, but heavier, man. "The Ice Maiden? To whom are you referring, you *puling* worm?"

Royce's face was genuinely amusing: shock, anger, and grave insult were just a few of the emotions. "Just what the devil are you getting so bent out of shape about? So, what if you brought your wh—"

Things became confused after that. Fists flew and Magnus's next clear recollection was when three others pulled him off Royce—thankfully before his face looked like Barclay's had. It occurred to Magnus—belatedly—that for a man who'd not engaged in physical violence all his life he'd certainly taken to it like a fish to water.

"Do you wish for satisfaction?" he asked Royce, horrified by how much he wanted the man to say yes. But Royce was not a Corinthian, neither did he know Magnus well enough to be aware that both his pistol and sword skills were laughable.

"Just leave me be," Royce said through a split lip. "I'll not challenge a man who is obviously cupshot.

Before he could argue, somebody put the flat of their hand on Magnus's back and propelled him toward the door.

"Good God, Magnus! What the bloody hell is wrong with you?" It was Taylor, the same friend of his brother's he'd seen the last time he'd made the mistake of coming to the club. Did the man not have a bloody home?

Magnus ignored him, but Taylor fell into step beside him. "Where are you staying?"

"Darlington House."

They walked in silence for a few moments. "You must be here for Michael's leg-shackling, although that's still a week off, isn't it?"

"Yes," he answered rudely, wishing Taylor would leave him alone.

"Look, Magnus, it's no odds to me, but if you're seen consorting with a woman like Melissa Griffin and decide to come the ugly whenever a bloke comments on it, well—"

"She's my wife."

Taylor stumbled beside him. "Uh, come again? I thought you said—"

"She. Is. My. Wife."

"Melissa Griffin? The Ice Ma—"

Magnus stopped and shoved Taylor up against a lamppost, the sound of his body making a dull clanging noise when it hit the cast iron. "Don't say it."

Taylor pushed him away, and Magnus let him—even though the man was a good two stones lighter. He shoved his hands into his greatcoat pockets and resumed his walk, the sound of Taylor's boots behind him making him grimace.

"Look. Don't thrash me, Magnus, but am I to believe that you—the son of one of the most well-respected peers in England—have married a—a—well, a woman who operated a brothel for almost a decade?"

"Yes, Taylor. That about sums it up."

"Good God! Does your father know?"

"Why? Are you thinking you might like to tell him?"

"Give over, Magnus. Why are you treating me like I'm the bloody enemy? I'm just trying to figure out who knows about it."

Magnus had no intention of answering questions about his wife.

Taylor trotted beside him, not turning to him again until they passed Hay Hill.

"Look," he finally said, when it was clear Magnus was going to walk all the way home without saying another word "I shan't say anything, all right? But you might want to avoid going out." When Magnus didn't respond, he sighed. "You might not know this—the fam doesn't like to talk about it—but my second eldest brother ran off with a married woman. This was back in '91, and they still live somewhere in Italy, apparently. Anyhow, I know how this—"

Magnus stopped and turned and Taylor flinched away. "I am not running off with some other man's wife. She is *my* wife."

Taylor raised both hands, palm out. "Yes, yes, old man. I got that bit. I just wanted you to know you can count on my discretion."

"I never asked for your discretion. She's my wife and I'm not ashamed of it nor am I planning to keep it a secret. Tell whomever you bloody well choose."

Taylor was shocked into silence by the heat in Magnus's tone. But not for long. "Well, I'm *not* telling anyone."

Magnus grunted and turned onto Berkeley Square.

"I'll see you when Michael gets to town, all right? I'm one of his groomsman."

Magnus didn't turn or say anything when the man stopped following. He was angry. And ashamed at how he'd treated Taylor, who'd just wanted to help. But he couldn't help it. He suspected all the drink he'd poured down his throat wasn't entirely responsible for his vile humor, either.

He let himself in as there was no footman in the chair in the foyer. Magnus guessed the man was off kipping somewhere and he could hardly blame him. At least the he'd left a candle waiting on the table.

He found Peel—the young footman Dawks had assigned to valet him—waiting in his chambers.

"You don't need to wait up, Peel. I 'spose I should have told you that before I left." He started to shed clothing and Peel came to the rescue—at least of his garments.

"Er, you're bleeding, my lord," he said while removing the stickpin from Magnus's cravat—something he must have put there earlier without him even realizing it. Magnus didn't even know that he *owned* a stickpin.

"Hmm?"

"Your lip, sir. And your eye—it's a bit swollen. As if you may have struck it on, er, somebody."

Magnus gave a bark of laughter. "Yes, I think I struck it on somebody's fist."

"I see, sir. I could go and get a beefsteak."

Magnus blinked. "What the devil would I want a beefsteak for at this time of night?"

"It's the customary remedy to stop an eye from blackening. Or swelling."

"Oh." Magnus supposed he would learn information of this type if he continued to brawl at the drop of a hat. He turned to the waiting servant. "Thank you for the offer, Peel, but it sounds revolting. Just give me my robe and take yourself off to bed."

Peel was gone within moments and Magnus saw there was a decanter on the writing desk in his sitting room. He opened it and sniffed: brandy. He poured himself a generous portion even though he didn't need it and went to lie on his bed.

He must have nodded off because he woke up when something cold slithered down his chest. He sat bolt upright and realized the brandy had spilled. He fumbled with the glass to put it on the nightstand but it tumbled with a soft thud to the carpet.

He stank, and he was wet. When he tried to squirm out of the sodden robe, he only managed to knock the nightstand itself over. That made an almighty crashing noise and dislodged a half-dozen items that went skittering across the floor.

"Damn and blast."

"Magnus?"

Melissa and The Vicar

His head whipped up so fast it left him dizzy.

"Melissa?" he said rather stupidly. She was standing in the dressing room doorway, her brow creased as she surveyed the room and then looked at his face.

Her hand flew to her mouth and her eyes widened. "What happened?" She came toward him before he could answer, her eyes gazing down into his.

Which is when Magnus realized he was still lolling on his back while a lady—*his* lady—was in the room.

"I'm sorry, Mel," he slurred, and then bit his lip. When the hell had that happened? He lurched to his feet and tugged on both ends of the sash to tighten it around his naked, bruised body. But the silken cord seemed to have become knotted.

"Oh, bother," he muttered with an irritated huff.

Her hand was cool and gentle on his jaw and he jerked away. "I'm sorry, did I hurt you?" Before he could answer she sniffed the air. "You've been drinking."

Magnus grunted.

"And you've been *fighting*." It was not a question. "About me." Neither was that, but he answered it, anyhow.

"Yes, I have."

"Why?"

He gave an ugly laugh. "Why the devil do you think?" He looked away from her stunned expression down at the sash, which he'd worried into such a tight knot it might never come loose.

He shrugged the wet robe off his shoulders and then shoved it down his body, where it puddled on the floor. When he looked up, it was to find her eyes on his naked body. Predictably, he hardened.

He watched her throat move as she swallowed, her eyes roaming over him without shame or embarrassment.

"You're so beautiful." There was wonder in her voice, as though she'd never seen him before. But she had, hadn't she? She'd seen a whole bloody lot of men. His vision went red at the thought.

"Well, I guess you're the expert."

The slap was more a surprise than anything else—to both of them. She stared at her hand and then his cheek. Magnus raised his eyebrows and then moved his jaw side to side, as if to check if it still worked. It hadn't been hard—but it appeared to have cleared the fog from his head. And a lot of his anger, with it. He also felt completely sober.

"I'm sorry," she said, still staring at her hand. "I have never struck another person."

"It seems to be in the air," he muttered. He took a step toward her but didn't touch her. "I deserved it. It is I who should apologize. I *am* sorry. Deeply." His face twisted. "I don't want to be angry with you, but I can't seem to stop it. I haven't yet worked out a way to manage this tumult of emotions. It is not your fault—not even a little. Even so, you should probably leave because I cannot promise you that I will not say more hateful things." He turned away but she caught his arm.

"I don't want to leave, Magnus. I want to talk—I know you fought with Barclay but I don't know what you said. I want to know."

"Why didn't you tell me about him threatening you? Why must we have so many lies between us?" His tongue felt thick and wooly and it was hard to force out the words he wanted to say. He desperately wished he was not so bosky, but he could hardly do anything about that now. All he could do now was not insult her again.

"I'm sorry I didn't tell you. But you must know I never would have gone to meet him, Magnus. And I've never had anything to do with him before—at least not personally. He was a customer at The White House at one time but he was banned for life after hurting one of the women. That's part of why he hates me so much—I thwarted his will and he is not a man to forgive or forget."

"What about what he said to me—was he lying?"

"I don't know exactly what he said to you, but I am going to take a guess he was not lying."

He closed his eyes and sat down on the side of his bed, covering his face with his hands. He felt the mattress move beside him, and then her arm slide around him, the silk of her dressing gown cool against the bare skin of his back.

He sat up and looked at her, and her arm slid away. "I thought you told me everything that night, Melissa. I asked you and you said you had."

"I know. I know I did. I thought I was protecting you, Magnus."

"But I'm not a child, Melissa—I am your husband. It is *my* job to protect *you*." He cringed at his drunken, whiney tone. Good Lord. Why couldn't he just shut up?

"You cannot protect me from my past, Magnus."

"Well, it doesn't look like I can protect you from the present or future. I'm terribly sorry about my parents. I was dead wrong. So very,

very wrong. And I'm a fool. I suppose I can't blame you from keeping things from me."

She leaned her head against his shoulder, looking away. "I wanted to tell you everything—

He grabbed her and turned her to face him. "Please," he said, all the misery he felt in that one word. "Please trust me enough to share your past." She hesitated and he said. "I want there to be no secrets between us. I love you and do not want to live this way—angry and distant from you."

She shook her head, her beautiful auburn hair, which glowed a rich red in the low light, dancing around her pale, pained face. "Are you certain? Because once you've heard it you cannot *un*hear it."

"I love you, Melissa. I need to know the entirety of what I'm facing."

She stared at him, suddenly intent. "You regret marrying me, don't you?"

Magnus opened his mouth to deny it and then remembered he'd just asked for the truth from her, no matter how painful.

"I won't lie to you, Melissa, I've had my doubts since the incident with Barclay. I don't doubt that I love you, but I *do* wonder if we can ever deal honestly with each other. If we cannot, we will be picked apart by all those people trying to drive a wedge between us."

Rather than look offended, as he'd feared, he would have sworn she looked relieved. Perhaps she, too, simply wanted there to only be truth between them.

He squeezed her body against his and tilted her chin up with his free hand. Her beautiful green eyes were glistening and he leaned down and kissed the corner of one. "I'm sorry, my love, I never meant to make you cry."

"You didn't, Magnus, I'm crying for my own stupidity. And also for what I have to tell you."

"Is it so bad?"

A tear slid down her cheek. "It is bad. Very bad."

Magnus looked into her eyes and felt a chill.

"Will you take me to bed, Magnus? Perhaps if we love each other first—"

"You don't need to give me your body to make me love you. Nor do you need to bribe me with—"

"I know that. I just want to be close to you before I have to say what I need to say."

He leaned down to kiss her and his cock, which had begun to harden at the word "bed," stiffened the rest of the way. Oh, men were such sad creatures. And he was as sad as all the rest. Sadder, maybe, because he'd believed—

"Magnus?"

He realized he'd been self-flagellating while she'd been waiting.

"I've missed you," he whispered against her soft, wicked lips.

"Not as much as I've missed you."

He chuckled, his hands going to the fastenings of her dressing gown. "It is not a *contest,* Melissa."

"I want you a different way tonight," she whispered against his throat, licking and biting and sucking as their hands clumsily shoved off her gown, until they were both naked.

"Any way you want me," he said, claiming one of her breasts and sucking her to instant hardness.

Melissa pulled away and he made a noise of frustration. She turned and crawled onto the bed on her hands and knees, positioning herself in the middle before spreading her knees and looking over her shoulder, slowly inching her way down until her forearms rested on the bed and her bottom was canted up at an angle that left her wide open.

***

Magnus looked at her for what felt like forever—until she was soaking and quivering for him.

His blue eyes were black with desire, his lips parted as he stared at her sex, the heat in his gaze making her clench and swell. His mouth curved into a smile that was all the more appealing for being so rare— a hungry, lustful expression tinged with possession.

"Perhaps we should have disagreements more often—just to make it up to each other." He chuckled at her scandalized expression. "I'm toying with you, love." His jaw hardened as his eyes slid from her face back to her sex. "But not as hard as I will be toying with you shortly."

She was about to beg him to come to her when his gaze shifted, and his lips began to curve ever so slowly.

"I think I will like this; it is very primal—earthy—and there is an element of physical domination that is—perhaps—unseemly, but also exquisitely . . . carnal."

Melissa gave a breathy laugh at his obvious excitement and very Magnus-like observations. But he also needed to get on with it before she exploded. She shifted her weight from knee to knee, opening herself a wider. "Please, Magnus."

His eyes narrowed until his expression was almost cruel, as if he were enjoying tormenting her. He moved toward her without haste, not getting up on his knees to mount her, but leaning on his elbows and bringing his face close enough that she could feel his hot rapid breaths against her sensitive skin.

"You are so wet and pink. I could look at you for hours. Perhaps I might."

"Please."

But he just laughed, the puffs of air making her shudder.

"I find that I enjoy hearing you beg, darling."

She growled.

"Hush, my love. Let me remind you it is your wifely duty to obey your lord and master in all things. Now would be a good time to begin."

Who *was* this man? Surely not her proper, godly husband? How was it—

"Don't worry, my love," he said, the laughter in his voice obvious for all that he suppressed it. "I want to taste you too much to make you suffer. At least not this time."

He took her cheeks and spread her.

"Very pretty," he said, his voice shakier, far less amused. And then his tongue was there, cradling her taut bud with a few massaging flicks before he sucked her into his mouth.

"Ah, God, Magnus."

He shoved her thighs wider and then pulled her toward his open mouth, tonguing her in firm strokes from her entrance to her stiff clitoris, holding her open with his thumbs, plunging his tongue into her.

Her shivers grew increasingly violent as he rhythmically sucked and invaded. He used his teeth, tongue, chin, and even his nose against her, until she was moaning shamelessly, grinding against him. Only then did he insert two fingers into her, rising up onto his knees as he did so, pumping her with deep, slow strokes.

"I want you so much," she panted, her hips straining to push higher and open wider.

He manipulated her toward climax not once, but three times, bringing her to the edge and then letting her slide back down; it was a naughty trick he'd learned from her. Her lover was a quick learner in every way.

By the time he shoved his long hard thickness into her, she was ready to explode.

He held her still and full, pressing his chest to her back, wrapping his arms around her and forcing her to bear his weight while he stroked her stomach and breasts with one hand and reached between her lower lips with the other, flicking and circling the aching bundle of nerves until she gave in to sensation.

He groaned as she flexed and contracted around him. "I love being inside you while you have an orgasm," he whispered, leaving her throbbing bud alone while she shuddered with release.

Instead he teased and pinched her nipples to painful hardness—just as she'd taught him to do—and then pulled out of her body until his flared head was all that was inside. And then he plunged back in while the last contractions gripped her body.

He held her covered, his hips stilling. "Too sensitive?" he murmured, his lips smiling against her temple while he flexed his erection inside her, making it dance against the taut, sensitive flesh.

She gave a weak laugh. "You're a cruel man, Magnus."

"Mmm hmm." He began pulsing his hips. "But I think you love it."

Melissa tightened around him.

"I think you're ready for more," he said.

She clenched hard enough to elicit a hiss of surprise.

"Again, Magnus. Please."

Her words prodded him like the lash of a whip and he grabbed her hips in a punishing hold and rode her, his pounding savage.

"Yes," she grated, wanting him to know he should take whatever he wanted, however he wanted. "I want all of you."

He shuddered and slammed into her so fiercely it drove them both face down onto the bed. He kept her trapped beneath his body, his hips, chest, and stomach muscles tensing like hot steel over and over again as he filled her with jets of heat.

Chapter Twenty-Two

They fell asleep, neither of them waking until gray light peeked through the gap in the curtains.

Magnus's arm and leg were flung over her body, his breathing deep and steady. Melissa did not move; she was not in any hurry to wake him. Part of her thought they could just get up, pack their things, and get in a carriage. They could go anywhere; Magnus was very wealthy. Even if his property was occupied, they could live in Brighton or Bath. Or, if those places were too filled with people who might recognize her, they could go to somewhere farther afield—perhaps Manchester? Leeds? Scotland, Land's End? Or, God forbid, even the wilds of America?

"Are you awake?"

Well, so much for her dreams. "Yes."

His arm tightened and drew her closer. "Want to stay in bed? Perhaps for the rest of our lives."

"You must be reading my mind."

"Tell me, Melissa." His voice was weary and she realized perhaps he hadn't been sleeping at all, but thinking, as she had been.

She inhaled deeply and then exhaled. "Before I tell you everything, I want a promise."

It was his turn to breathe deeply. "That is not fair, Melissa."

"No, but then life is not fair."

He snorted softly. "Very well, what do you want me to promise?"

"Give me your word you'll not search for the man's identity or challenge him if you do learn his identity or goad him into challenging you."

"That is not—well, I am not sure I can promise you that," he admitted.

"Then I cannot tell you the rest of my pitiful tale."

She could almost hear his teeth grating against each other. "Fine. I *won't* actively search for him. But if I find were to inadvertently find out . . ." He groaned. "Lord, just tell me, Melissa—tell me the worst of it all so that men like Barclay can never use the unknown against us again."

"Surely you do not expect me to tell you about each and every time I've been with a man?"

"You are fencing with me, Melissa. I'm asking you to tell me the extent of your activities with . . . John—" he shoved the word through clenched teeth. "As for the rest—your tenure at The White House, well, I've already heard a good deal about that."

His words sickened, but did not surprise, her. "Where?"

"At my club. Well, my erstwhile club. I shan't be keeping a membership there, or anywhere else like it. Before you start worrying about that—it's not a hardship for me. I've always found going there vapid and annoying. Now I merely find it vapid and enraging."

"Oh, Magnus."

"Oh, Melissa," he teased. His tone once again became serious. "It's all I can promise you—not to seek him out."

She supposed it was as good as she would get. Besides, she would be gone by tomorrow night—what did it matter?

"Fine."

He moved away, as if to sit up.

"No, don't go. I want you to hold me. Perhaps if we are touching when I tell you—" she sounded like a fool.

He settled back behind her without a word, but she could feel the anxiety and tension in his coiled body.

"You recall that I told you John changed toward me as I approached my seventeenth birthday?"

"Yes."

"That is where I diverged from the truth. First, it had actually started earlier than that. The day I turned seventeen was actually the day I was free. But before then, for some months, he'd come to me less and less."

His arm tightened and she could tell it was not what he expected.

"You see, I'd become too old for him. He liked his mistresses younger. Or at least he liked their bodies to *look* younger. I, as you may have noticed, have a womanly figure. I went from sylvan and flat to voluptuous rather quickly. I think he would have cast me off then—before I was seventeen—if he'd not put so much money into . . . well, into my training."

He shivered at the word and then said, "Go on."

Melissa and The Vicar

"The other men in his small group did not share his attitudes. In fact, the more womanly I became, the more these men pressured him to, er, share me."

"Who are these men, Melissa? Who? You can tell me about them, at least?"

"I can't. Not after you hear the rest."

"Oh God." It was so soft she almost didn't hear it.

"Frequently the men shared their mistresses. John didn't like sharing—not because of any attachment he bore me, but rather because he had a terror of contracting disease. But one night he was put in a position where to have refused to share me would have been viewed as unusual and unacceptable. Others had brought their mistresses and—" She stopped, surely that was honest enough? Wasn't it?

She was in agony and just about to speak when he did. "The rest, if you please."

"He allowed things to happen that night as long as, er, sheaths were used."

This time the silence was all but unbearable. Again, it was Magnus who spoke.

"I've heard of such things and, quite frankly, applaud their use." His rather cold tone turned wry. "Unlike many others—both in the clergy and out—I don't believe the open availability of sheathes would encourage sexual behavior and I can understand how they would stop the spread of disease. Go on."

She closed her eyes. "After that first time he began to attend these parties more and more often."

"You are speaking of orgies." He breathed in deeply and exhaled a shaky breath, his heart beating hard against hers.

"Yes." Now that she had begun this confession, she found she did not wish to stop. "Do you remember the woman I told you about—Dorothy?"

"Yes, the one who helped them do this to you."

She could not deny it. "Dorothy came to me three months before my seventeenth birthday. The original duration of my contract was until I turned eighteen, but she told me I could escape my contract early, and with all the money I was promised. The price was that I would have to attend certain . . . parties. These were the functions I'd only occasionally attended in the past—always leaving early, before—" She struggled to find the words.

"Melissa—"

"No. Let me finish. This was a small club of elite aristocrats that sometimes brought their mistress, sometimes not. They played cards, drank, what have you. I'd sensed a growing pressure among them. I knew they shared their mistresses at these gatherings—yes, they had orgies—but John had never stayed for those occasions. Dorothy told me I'd only have to endure three months to gain a year of freedom. You might not think much about Dorothy, but she warned me of the nights ahead, going so far as to give me laudanum to get through them."

His arm was so tight it almost cut off her breathing.

"Dorothy had tears in her eyes." Mel still recalled her words: *"I'm dreadfully sorry I became ensnared in this. A mistress is one thing—but . . . this? He is desperate for money and wishes to settle some debts by using you. He has—well, he's already begun with another girl.'"*

"Good God, Melissa."

She barely heard him. "Dorothy told me that night that she'd renegotiated the agreement on my behalf. I should have been angry, but I knew she was far savvier than I."

"I've done the only thing I can for you, Melissa. I've had it written into the agreement that you would leave early—voluntarily—so that he will not bear the expense of your upkeep. You will give him the months until your next birthday in exchange for a year. He will forfeit the house and contents to you if he allows anything to occur without protection. I'm sorry, I know it is nothing, but it's the best I can do."

"It wasn't nothing," Melissa said, as if Magnus had argued. "Only later did I understand that Dorothy had probably saved my life—not to mention the lives of a few of those men—by insisting on that requirement. Given the way they lived, it was probable that more than one of them was diseased. I refused opium and even alcohol."

Melissa turned until she faced him. "Why should I turn myself into a dead-eyed addict after enduring everything? No, I would not do it. I'd done nothing wrong. It was *him* and it was *these men*."

A tear leaked out of one eye but Magnus didn't stop her.

"I had nothing to be ashamed of and vowed I would face all of them head on, not bowing my head or escaping. I especially kept my gaze on *him*. Because instead of just whoring me out and leaving, he stayed. He didn't engage in the debauchery—he was too fastidious for orgies—but he *enjoyed* watching the show with a glass of brandy in his hand."

Melissa and The Vicar

Melissa's vision clouded over with nightmare visions of the past.

"He was so pleased with himself! What a prize he was offering them. He looked on, chatting with the other men. I knew he never cared for me—not even after three years—but I never imagined he would just sit back, preening when they complimented him on my abilities, my obedience, my resilience. All the while smiling—as if he were witnessing nothing more than the breeding of one of his horses. Allowing all those men to—"

Magnus pulled her close. "Stop," he said. "Please, my love. Stop. I know, I know."

Melissa hadn't realized until that moment that she'd been crying so hard her eyes burned. She gave a watery laugh at the irony; she'd never shed a tear back then.

But now she was crying as if her life were ending.

Because it was.

***

Thankfully, after the horror of her story, Melissa had fallen asleep, exhausted by the harrowing revisiting of her past.

Magnus sorely wished he'd not accepted his uncle's invitation to go riding. He would have stayed with her, even though he felt as though his body had been struck by lightning.

Still, she slept so soundly that she didn't even move when he got up. It was likely he could come back before she woke—she'd never even know he'd gone.

While he didn't want company, he *did* need to ride, hard. He would ride with his uncle to the park and then beg off, claiming he needed to return home. And then he'd go off alone for a bruising gallop on Friar. It would be just the thing to work this nerve-wracking energy from him body.

He covered Melissa with blankets and then rang for the maid who'd been assigned to her, telling her not to disturb her mistress.

After he threw on his clothing it was still not light so he went down to the library, only to find the charwoman still setting the fire. After she'd gone, he threw himself into his father's favorite chair, a ratty old thing his mother always threatened to throw away, and stared into the blaze, re-playing what Melissa had told him.

He'd been beyond horrified by the whole sordid tale of this man named only John.

Had it been wise to hear everything? Probably not. Magnus knew himself; it would be a daily struggle not to hunt and kill the man.

Melissa had been wise—as usual—to not give hm a name. Magnus would likely be in Newgate right now if he knew the truth.

But that didn't stop him from wanting to know.

He was still trying to figure out ways of learning the man's identity without breaking promises to his wife when he realized pale yellow light was spilling through the gap in the drapes. He pulled the bell.

"Have Kelvin bring Friar around," he told the footman.

While the man went off to carry out his orders, Magnus went back up to his chambers to check on Melissa: she was still sleeping soundly in the exact same position. He scribbled a quick note at the desk, telling her he'd be back shortly, tiptoed to the bed, and left it propped up on the nightstand in front of the clock, where she couldn't fail to see it.

Booted and coated, he headed out the front door. Movement across the street drew his gaze and he smiled to himself before turning to the footman.

"Tell Riley to bring Friar across the street to me, I'm going to talk with my uncle." He strode across the green and put a little distance between him and the house before shouting. "Uncle John."

His uncle, who'd been speaking to his groom, looked up. "Ah, Magnus—I didn't really expect you to make it this morning."

They embraced warmly. His uncle had always been as affectionate as Magnus's own parents. Although they rarely saw each other now—Magnus's parents rarely coming to London during the Season—Magnus often saw Lord Vanstone when he came up to Yorkshire to visit. His mother and her elder brother were very close, which meant his uncle visited often.

His lordship looked over Magnus's shoulder. "I see Kelvin is bring Friar over—still have that old nag, do you?"

Good-natured insults were traded back and forth as his lordship's groom adjusted the earl's saddle.

"Town is still very thin," the earl said after they'd mounted and were headed through the brisk, cold winter morning toward the park. "Perhaps we can have a decent run without tripping over park saunterers." He cut Magnus a sideways smile, "That is if that old bag of bones can manage it."

Well, so much for a solitary ride. Still, it was better than no ride at all.

"Your wife seems an interesting woman. Do I know her family?"

Melissa and The Vicar

Magnus shuddered. Lord, he hoped not. "I don't think so," he said. "She is not one of our crowd, although she was born and raised in London."

Even though he was certain his uncle wouldn't frequent a place like The White House Magnus had decided—as he'd lain sleepless in bed last night—that he didn't want to give the earl Melissa's infamous name. Not yet.

It had been his plan not to tell anyone—not even his beloved uncle—anything until after he'd talked to his parents again today. No matter how close he was to Lord Vanstone, his mother and father hadn't seen fit to share the information with him last night. Magnus had wanted to give them one last chance today to accept the situation and provide a united front.

But being in the comforting company of his Uncle John made him reconsider that decision. Magnus had gone to him for advice in the past on important occasions—like when he'd decided to take orders—and the earl had been a source of encouragement and wisdom. Perhaps he might be so again? After all, it wasn't as if Magnus could—or wanted to—keep his wife's identity a secret.

He gave his uncle a surreptitious glance; although the Earl of Vanstone was deeply religious, Magnus knew he did not judge and was a fair man. Just looking at his uncle's familiar, patrician profile gave him comfort. Magnus would wait to see how he felt about confiding in the earl until after he'd ridden hard enough to clear the anxiety from his taut body and tense mind.

"I didn't think you would ever marry," the earl said as he steered his mount around a deep, half-frozen puddle. "I didn't think you even had time for women."

"I didn't have time for them—at least not until Melissa." Magnus deliberately changed the subject. "Do you usually come to town so early, Uncle?"

"No, but I was coming for Michael's wedding and decided to arrive a bit early and take care of some business before the session starts."

"And will Aunt Letitia be joining you?"

"She'll come for the wedding, as will Jonathan—who is finished at Oxford. But neither will stay—they've got some house-party planned." The earl's tone had chilled considerably when he discussed his wife and son. Magnus had never understood how a man who was so warm and loving with his sister's family could be so distant from his own wife and son.

Magnus did not know either his cousin or his aunt well—neither did anyone else in his family. Lady Vanstone had always been remote and standoffish with Magnus's parents. He knew Lord Vanstone's wife was not of their class and supposed the sudden elevation in status had been more than the woman had been able to manage. Unlike Melissa, who spoke and behaved like a lady, Lady Vanstone still smelled of the shop, even after all these years.

While neither of his parents particularly liked her, they'd made repeated efforts toward her—for John's sake more than anything. But not only had she remained distant, she seemed to have poisoned their son against his own father.

Magnus had often heard his mother complain bitterly about John marrying such a low-bred woman. "She should be eternally grateful that a man as well-respected, powerful, and gentlemanly as my brother lowered himself to marry her," the marchioness had said of her sister-in-law after Lady Vanstone had once again refused to accompany her husband to Lady Darlington's Christmas festivities last year.

Magnus had been stunned by his mother's vehemence and uncharitable words, but he'd excused her unkindness because he'd also felt the absence of his favorite uncle quite keenly.

"By the by, Magnus—I'm afraid I made rather a mull of it last night when your mother asked me to come by to breakfast today. It turns out I have a business matter I had completely forgotten about and need to take care of early."

"I'll tell her," Magnus said, ignoring the slight pang of regret at the news. After all, it was probably better if his uncle stayed away for the time being. He did not deserve to be exposed to the uncomfortable, charged atmosphere.

"Perhaps we might meet this evening—go to the theater?"

Good God. Magnus hoped not. "I'll have to check with Melissa to see if we are engaged elsewhere already." His face heated at his lie, but his uncle merely nodded as they guided their horses through the gates into the park.

"Now," the earl said, before glancing off to the side, his brow furrowing. "What the devil is that?" He pointed his crop just behind Magnus. When Magnus turned to look, the earl spurred his magnificent horse forward.

Melissa and The Vicar

Magnus laughed and set off after him. "Such dirty tricks are beneath you, my lord," he called out, but the older man could not have heard him, his lead was already so great.

Magnus leaned over Friar's neck and gave him his head. "Let's show him how it's done, old chap."

***

Melissa watched the two men greet each other from the window in her sitting room. She'd heard Magnus return and leave her the note—she'd already been awake—but had wanted to have some time to herself. Their conversation had left her wrung out like a rag.

It made her shiver to see Vanstone put his arms around Magnus and watch the two men embrace with so much affection.

Vanstone had kept himself fit and his bone-thin body was still straight-backed. He had always been vain about his person and she knew he went to pains to keep his appearance as youthful as possible. No doubt the gray in his hair annoyed him.

They released each other and he patted the younger man on the shoulder. She was too far away to see his hands, but she could remember them all too clearly. Fine, long-boned hands which had always been soft, pale, and untouched by work. But for all that they'd looked so elegant they'd been powerful and adept at dealing out pain. Melissa probably knew better than his horse that the crop he held in one hand with such apparent negligence could be used to hurt, but not scar. In that one way he was different than Sir Thomas. He did not train his pets by drawing blood. His means were far more subtle.

The men chatted with the ease of old friends as Vanstone's man prepared his mount. As ever, Vanstone had superlative cattle. He looked as stately as a king as he rode, he and his magnificent gray moving together with effortless grace. But Magnus, she could see, even with her untrained eye, was a cut above him. He and Friar moved as one being, as they had that day on the beach.

She watched them ride away and stood in the window even after she couldn't see them any longer.

She didn't turn away until the maid knocked on the door.

"You rang, my lady?"

She smiled at the young girl. "Did you speak to Lord Magnus this morning?"

"Yes, my lady. He said he was going for a ride but would be back in no more than two hours." She gave a shy smile, her soft cheeks turning red. "He said to let you sleep, m'lady."

"Thank you. But I believe I'm ready for my bath, now."

The girl bobbed a curtsy and was gone.

Melissa turned back to the window. The street was quiet—it was early and not even many servants were moving about. She let her gaze linger on the majestic gray house across the street: *his* house.

Last night she'd sent messages using a footman whose discretion she'd purchased for a great deal of money. She'd arranged for a post chaise and sent word to book passage from Dover. She'd also written three other letters, which would be mailed today.

The only bag she would take with her would be the small cloth suitcase she'd brought to Darlington House. The footman had already taken the bag to the posting inn, where it would be waiting for her.

All she needed to do was bathe, lie to her husband, and then pay one last visit to the Earl of Vanstone.

Chapter Twenty-Three

Melissa felt like a fool, but better to feel like a fool than to get caught going into the Earl of Vanstone's house through the servant entrance in the middle of the day.

The hackney cab was one of the cleanest of its sort; Mel had to give the young footman credit for that. She'd been stuck inside of it for the past hour and a half while Magnus—unexpectedly—paid a visit to his uncle after she'd told him she needed to visit her solicitor and did not want him in attendance.

After she'd hurt him, yet again.

He'd stiffly agreed with her request, insisting she bring her maid with her.

Melissa had dropped the girl at her mother's house after informing her that she could take the day as a holiday.

Once freed of her maid's presence, Melissa had the carriage take her back to Darlington House, which they passed again and again until the footman finally popped out, saw the carriage, and nodded. So, Magnus had left Lord Vanstone's. It was time.

She flipped down her veil and pulled her rough gray cloak around her before hopping down from the carriage, unassisted. The driver had already received his instructions and only waited until she opened the unlocked door before driving away. He would wait for her where the mews met Hays Street.

Once inside she followed the directions Vanstone had sent in response to her message. True to his word, there were no servants lingering in the back hallways and stairwells.

On the second floor she opened the fifth door on her right.

Inside was a library to rival that at Darlington House. The room was warm—a fire raging in the five-foot tall fireplace. As badly as Barclay said he was hurting for money, he didn't appear to be stinting his comforts. But then, he never had.

The room appeared empty and she stood in the open doorway, hesitating.

"Come inside and close the door before someone sees you."

The command came from her right, and she saw he was seated at a massive desk.

The drapes were closed yet he'd only lighted two candles. Melissa knew instinctively he'd done so out of vanity: he'd not wanted even a whore to see how he'd aged.

The notion made her strong and she strode toward him with renewed confidence, staring at him boldly as she tugged off her gloves.

"Hello, John."

He smiled, the smoke from his cigar curling around his face. "Please, have a seat." He gestured to the two seats in front of his desk. He did not, however, stand.

If he meant the gesture to be insulting, he'd mistaken her. His obvious derision only fed her confidence.

She sat in one of the chairs and tucked her gloves into her reticule.

Mel turned to him and caught his true expression—the one he wore beneath the urbane suit and handsome face. If she'd ever wanted revenge against him—which she had—his gut-wrenching hatred and fear went a long way to sating her hunger.

The expression was gone in an instant, but she'd seen it. And he knew she had.

"I'm sure you can imagine my surprise when I entered my sister's drawing room to find you sitting there as if you belonged." His jaw ticked and his smile faltered. "I always suspected you were a shrewd little tart but I never imagined you would have the gall to entrap and marry my own nephew to get your revenge."

Melissa couldn't help it. She burst out laughing. And when she started, it seemed impossible to stop.

Tears streamed down her face before she could get her mirth under control. By that time, he was no longer bothering to hide his hatred, although he kept his fear tucked away.

Mel wiped a tear from her cheek and shook her head. "I apologize. That was—"

"Obnoxious? Ill-bred?" he suggested.

She shrugged. "Why not?"

"What do you want?" he ground out.

"Nothing you can give me."

His confusion was like the famed nectar of the gods to her. "Then *why?*"

Melissa and The Vicar

"I don't suppose it ever occurred to you that I was just as surprised as you when you walked into that room last night?"

His mouth twisted. "Just how stupid do you think I am?"

"I think you are impressively stupid."

His jaw dropped and the prominent vein in his right temple began to pulse. That sight, more than anything since entering this room, recalled the monster who sat before her.

When she'd belonged to him, that vein was always accompanied by a crop. For a moment she wondered if he would lunge across the desk and strike her.

But then he surprised her. He chuckled. But unlike her laughter, his was not born of genuine mirth. No, his was born of a loathing so weighty it was like a third presence in the room.

"Your *husband* came to me after our ride today."

"I know."

"Can you guess what he wanted to talk about with his favorite uncle?"

She smiled.

"What do you think I told him when he confessed that he'd married one of England's most notorious whores?"

"I don't care."

She could see that was not the answer he'd been expecting and he sat back as if she'd struck him. But as genteel as he appeared, he had the resilience of a weed and sprang back.

"You should care about what I *didn't* tell him, my dear. Your real name, for instance. I quickly surmised that the name on the marriage license is not the real one. What do you think he will do when he learns you're not really married?" He laughed. "Magnus has always been loyal, his standards higher for himself than anyone else. But even so I could see the doubt that is already blooming inside him—he is not yet regretting this marriage, but he will be soon. And when—somehow—he learns you are not really married? Well, he will toss you out like the rubbish you are." His laughter was ugly.

She looked into his cruel, expectant eyes and smiled. "I don't recall you being this amusing when I knew you, John."

His jaw muscles spasmed with words he prudently caught before they escaped. "What do you want, *Hannah*?"

She shivered at the familiar sound of her name on his tongue and he gave her a venomous smile. Melissa hadn't expected this encounter to be so entertaining. Regardless, she did not have all day—she had less than an hour to indulge herself before she was scheduled to climb into her chaise at the Swan With Two Necks.

"Here is what I'm going to do, John. I am going to offer you a proposition that is far better than you deserve. I will leave here today and disappear from Magnus's life. I will not tell him or his family about the monster you really are. In return, I want you to release the girl you have now and I want you to compensate her with twice as much as you promised her."

He stared, his nostrils flaring, as if he were struggling for breath.

"But that is not all I want."

His thin-lipped mouth twisted into a hateful sneer. "Oh, here it comes—the demand for money."

She snorted. "You really *are* stupid, John. I know you are below the hatches. I know you are taking loans—loans you have no chance of repaying."

His expression of horror was most gratifying. "How—who—"

"That doesn't matter. What matters is this: I don't need your money, even if you *had* any. I have plenty of my own—far more than you, *Lord Vanstone*."

His breathing was audible. "Then *what?*"

"After you release the girl from her *servitude* you will never take another. I've written down enough gory details of our years together to tarnish even *your* name. And I've given the letter to my solicitor to hold if you do not abide by my demands."

"You're *mad*," he said, but the accusation lacked heat. Instead, it reeked of fear.

"And then there are the names of the men you invited to use me. Just how do you think they'll be received when it is known they were involved in repeatedly raping a sixteen-year-old while you watched?" She allowed all the hatred she felt for him to come to the surface. "What do you think your darling sister would say then?" She sat back, indulging in another chuckle. "And when the truth is known, how will you appease your creditors—men like Sir Thomas Barclay?"

"That bloody bastard," he hissed.

"Ah, but he is a rich bastard. I daresay he's not the type of man to look kindly on men who cannot pay their debts. He is no tailor—he will not extend you endless credit. He will want to be paid, and he will take the money out of you somehow. There will be no—"

He was like a blur, diving across the surface of his huge desk and landing right on top of her, his hands unerringly finding her throat.

Melissa and The Vicar

"You *bitch*!" He squeezed her neck so hard her eyes bulged. "You fucking, grasping bitch," he repeated, shaking her. "If you would have just left—just tucked your tail between your whore thighs and taken yourself off to some hole I would have left you alone. But you had to—"

A fist struck the side of Vanstone's face and knocked him to the floor, his head bouncing against the leg of the nearby chair.

Melissa knew who the fist belonged to even before Magnus crouched down beside her. "Can you breathe, darling?"

His anxious blue eyes flickered over her, fear and love flowing from them.

She nodded, unable to speak.

"Thank God," he gasped.

"Magnus . . ."

Magnus's expression hardened at the sound of his uncle's voice. But before he turned, he took her hand and squeezed it. "Are you certain you are all right?"

She smiled and squeezed back. Hard.

He released her hand and turned to face Lord Vanstone.

***

Magnus's stared down at his uncle's prone figure through a maelstrom of emotions so thick he could hardly see.

His hands wrapped themselves around the neck of a man he'd loved like a father until mere moments earlier. Fueled by rage, Magnus easily lifted the older man and slammed him against a bookcase.

"You bloody monster!" He shook him hard enough that he could actually hear his teeth rattle. "You're a rabid animal that needs to be put down. Death is the only way to stop you. I will be doing the world a favor." His hands began to tighten around his throat

"Please," the earl whispered in between head-bashings. "Mercy."

"Mercy?" Magnus repeated in a voice three octaves higher than normal. He turned to look at Melissa, who was watching them with eyes that burned. He knew she would not stop him; did he want to stop? He didn't think so.

He swung around and stared at Vanstone's red face. "Did you show mercy to Melissa? Or the other girls you purchased and repeatedly raped and abused?" A grating sound filled his head as he thought of this man defiling the only woman he'd ever loved.

Death was too quick—too good for him. Even eternal damnation for his shriveled, evil-ridden soul was not enough. He deserved to live on and suffer under the condemning eyes of those who'd once loved and respected him.

Magnus looked the other man in the eyes and then flung him away, feeling as if he'd been clutching something so unclean that he might never wash away the stench.

"Killing you would be too kind. You'll have to live with what you've done. You may not be put in jail—where you belong—but your life will be worth nothing between the scandal and the debt. I will ensure you never hurt another girl again."

He turned to his wife, expecting to see disappointment that he'd let the other man live. Instead, she smiled up at him, her eyes glassy with unshed tears.

"How did you know I was here?" she asked.

He snorted. "I didn't. I left my bloody hat here—it's the only one I have left since I abandoned my other hat at the vicarage—and came back to fetch it. On a whim I decided to pop up and ask the bastard to ride with me again tomorrow." He shook his head. "What a bloody fool I've been. I'm so sorry, Melissa. So very sorry."

"It's not your fault, Magnus. You didn't know."

"I didn't know because I've been naïve. Far too naïve for far too long."

Melissa's body shook and the tears began to fall.

"Oh, darling," he said, catching her up in his arms and hugging her so close neither of them could breath. "Don't cry, Melissa, we shall see each other through this."

She began to squirm in his arms, gasping into his chest.

He released her, realizing suddenly that he might have hurt her. "Lord, I'm sorry, dar—"

"Magnus," she wheezed, pushing against his chest, her horrified gaze on something behind him. "Stop him! Magnus—"

The terror in her eyes told him what was happening and he wrapped his arms around her and threw her to the floor, covering her with his body. Just as he heard the gunshot behind him.

Chapter Twenty-Four

Magnus was exhausted; the mess at his uncle's house had taken hours to clean up and was far from over. Although the constable's curiosity had been quelled by the presence of a marquess on the scene, there was still the matter of the Earl of Vanstone's suicide to be dealt with in the days ahead, but for the moment everything that could be done, had been. Magnus had stayed with his father until his uncle's body had been removed and messages had been sent to his wife and son.

They climbed the steps to Darlington House in silence.

Peel met them at the door. Magnus handed him his hat and began to strip off his gloves. "Did Lady Magnus return from her solicitor's?" he asked, his need to see her sweet face almost overwhelming.

"Lady Magnus is not here, my lord."

Magnus frowned. "What?" he barked in a sharp voice that was not his own. "Where is she?"

"I don't know, sir."

"Summon her maid."

Peel looked as though he wanted to sink between the cracks in the wood floor. "Lady Magnus's maid is not here. Nobody knows where they've gone, my lord."

The fury Magnus felt was solely directed at himself. He should have *known*. He should have *known* she'd left his uncle's house far too easily and quietly. He should have *known* she would run. Isn't that what she did?

"Er, I did find this for you, my lord." Peel was holding out a letter, the handwriting Melissa's.

He snatched it out of the other man's hand and tore it open, quickly reading the brief contents. It contained nothing that he'd not already learned while listening to his uncle earlier: he and Melissa were not truly married. Magnus was free to return to his life.

The butler winced at the stream of curse words Magnus released into the air between them—most of the words were ones he'd never before said aloud.

He crumpled the sheet of paper and flung it away. So, at least this time she left him a letter—such as it was—to tell him she'd gone.

Magnus jabbed a finger at the waiting servant. "I want you to assemble every bloody servant in the house. Tell them they'll all get the bloody sack unless I get answers immediately—*somebody* will have helped her. And I also want you to find out where her maid lives."

"Right away, my lord."

As the man scuttled from the room Magnus's father stepped up beside him, setting a hand on his shoulder. "Perhaps this is for the best, Magnus."

Magnus whipped around, all the worry he felt turning to rage. "What did you say?"

The marquess took a step back, his forehead furrowing. "Get control of yourself, son. She is gone and it was the wise thing to do. And you know it, even though you refuse to accept it. You're angry right now, but it won't be long before you're—"

"Don't you bloody *dare* say I'll be glad about it," Magnus snarled.

"How dare you speak to your father that way!" His mother had appeared at the top of the stairs. It was the first time Magnus had seen the marchioness looking less than perfect. Her hair was loose, her face tear-streaked and pale. She stumbled down the stairs, her eyes wild. "It's hardly your father's fault if the woman wishes to run off. You should expect such—"

"Elizabeth."

Her teeth snapped shut at her husband's tone and, once again, Magnus marveled at his father's ability to control his wife. He probably could have lived with Melissa for a hundred years and not been able to stop her from saying what she wanted. Nor would he have wished to.

Lady Darlington's face crumpled and she grabbed Magnus's forearm. He looked down into her eyes, red-rimmed from crying over a beloved brother and now forced to deal with a son who appeared to have gone mad. His heart ached for her—for the pain she was feeling for a man who wasn't worth a single tear.

"That woman leaving here is the best thing that could ever happen to you."

His pity evaporated like water on a red-hot stove. "What?" Magnus took a step toward her, holding up his hand at his father when the marquess stepped toward him. "No, Father, I want to hear what she has to say," Magnus said, never taking his eyes from his mother, a woman he'd adored, respected, and worshipped all his life. Until yesterday.

She glared up at him. "I was going to say you should expect behavior like that from such a woman."

"Such a woman," he repeated in a tone of wonder.

"Yes, Magnus—such a woman. As much as you might want to deny it, she is not like us. She is a low, moral-less creature of the street and her kind do not understand the rules that govern decent society. You made a dreadful mistake marrying her but at least she had the decency not to use her real name."

"How the devil do you know that?"

She recoiled at his venomous tone.

His father put an arm around his wife and drew her back. "She knows because the woman—whatever her name is—left us a letter, son."

A choked sob escaped Lady Darlington and she began to cry. "It is the only kind thing she did for you, Magnus. You are free. Don't you understand? We've told nobody. I thank God that we never told my poor brother John that his favorite nephew had married a who—"

"Don't. You. Dare." Magnus closed the distance between them, looming over her, their eyes—almost identical in color—locked on one another. The vile truth about her beloved brother John teetered on the end of his tongue.

Why should his parents be allowed to live in blissful ignorance of the monster they'd embraced all these years?

Magnus opened his mouth to let all the bile pour out, but he couldn't. Melissa had bound him with her promise as they'd stood looking down at the body of the man who'd ruined her life.

And now she'd left him.

The sound of a throat being cleared came from the direction of the corridor and all three of them turned.

"Excuse me, my lords, my lady." Peel looked nervously from face to face. "But one of the footmen has confessed to knowing Lady Magnus's whereabouts and—"

"Where?" Magnus demanded.

"Er, he delivered her bag to The Swan With Two Necks earlier today, sir."

Magnus snatched up his hat.

A hand landed on his shoulder as he turned toward the door and he spun on his heel.

"Unhand me, madam." Magnus glared down into his mother's angry, weeping eyes and realized Melissa had been wrong about one important fact. His parents didn't deserve to be protected against the truth. But neither did they *deserve* to know Melissa's story.

His father laid a hand on his shoulder. "Son, you're making a mistake. Please, your mother is right. She is not our kind and never will be. Just wait and think—"

Magnus threw off his father's hands and strode toward the door.

"Magnus! Where are you going?" his mother called, her voice breaking.

"Away from here—away from *our kind* of people."

***

The post chaise was gone by the time Melissa managed to escape the chaos that erupted after Lord Vanstone shot himself.

The best thing to come out of his death—other than his actual death—was that he'd given his servants the morning off in anticipation of her visit.

That meant Melissa and Magnus had time to formulate an explanation for Magnus's parents. But first they had to argue about whether to tell them the truth about a man the marquess and marchioness had loved and admired.

"Are you *mad*?" he demanded when she told him that his parents must never know.

Melissa laughed.

"I fail to see the humor in this, Melissa." He shook his head and ran a hand through his already furrowed hair.

She stood on tiptoes and kissed him. "Shh, I'm only laughing because it is what I've asked you a time or two. But as to the other thing—telling your parents? No, it is my story, Magnus—my secret—and I forbid you to tell it to another soul."

His jaw sagged. "But *why*? Why shouldn't they know that a man they respected—a man they were proud to call family and friend—was worse than even the most depraved criminal? You must—"

She laid a finger over his lips and he stopped. "I must be allowed to keep my secret, Magnus. It is mine."

They went around and around in this vein a few more times before she pointed out Lord Vanstone was growing colder by the moment.

Then they decided on their plan. Magnus had come over to give his uncle the name of a man who might want to buy his uncle's matched chestnuts and had discovered his uncle already dead. He'd tell his parents how his uncle had confessed the level of his debt to him earlier in the day, during their ride. He would also tell them that he'd comforted the earl and convinced him that all was not lost, but apparently he'd been wrong.

"Meanwhile, I should go to my solicitor's office—which is what the servants heard me say," Melissa insisted.

"But are you sure, darling? Are you not too—" He cut a look at the cooling corpse behind them and threw up his hands. "I don't know—upset?"

"No," she said, finally telling her husband something that was true. "I am not upset."

So, she'd left and they'd agreed he would deal with telling his parents and come to her later—after she returned from her supposed errand.

They'd shared one last passionate kiss, and she'd again left him believing she would see him in a few hours instead of never again.

And then she'd arrived at the posting inn to find they had no carriage for her.

"Sorry, ma'am, but we've had a run of turrible luck today," the harried innkeeper said, his red face and bloodshot eyes attesting to his mental condition. "The soonest I can get you out will be tomorrow morning. But I can put ye up for no charge tonight."

Melissa had given in, realizing the man hardly wished to be in this predicament. Besides, it hardly mattered whether she left tonight or tomorrow. By the time Magnus learned she wasn't either at The White House or with Daisy or any of her other friends she would be long gone.

So, she'd taken a room and ordered a meal. And then she'd pushed around some food before sending her dinner back.

She'd washed and was lying in bed pretending to read when the sound of breaking glass made her sit up. Even before she heard his voice, she knew who it was.

She closed her eyes and sank back into the pillow. Oh, no. Not again.

But inside, her heart was singing.

Epilogue

Eight Months Later
A half-day's journey outside Paris

Melissa watched her husband from their terrace as he ran from the screaming, laughing horde of children who chased him across their lawn.

As usual, he let them capture him and wrestle him to the ground. His laughter drifted across the yard, accompanied by the sound of his voice.

"Please, I surrender," he said in French, the language of the thirteen orphans who crawled over him like so many exuberant puppies.

He struggled to his feet, his clothing somewhat the worse for wear, and the three nurses who'd been enjoying a brief reprieve from their boisterous charges came toward him and shuttled the children back to the small, gray, stone building where they took their daily lessons.

Magnus strode toward her with a grin, bits of grass in his hair and green smears on the knees of his buckskins.

He saw her staring pointedly at his knees and stopped to look, grimacing. "I guess buckskin is a mistake. I should probably switch back to black."

Although he smiled as he said it, she knew he always felt a pang when he remembered his divorce from the Church.

He sank down beside her, peering at the basket that sat on the table between them, pulling back the blanket with one finger. "I just need a peek."

"Shh," Mel said automatically, "Be careful not to wake her." She put aside the sock she was attempting—badly—to knit. The children ran through socks like geese ran through grass so Melissa had decided that knitting might be an excellent way to occupy her hands while she spent afternoons watching various children—either their own newborn or the thirteen they'd taken in since moving to the rambling and somewhat dilapidated chateau.

Melissa and The Vicar

Magnus chuckled softly. "If young Cornelius could sleep through our extremely noisy and inaccurate reenactment of the Battle of Austerlitz she can sleep through a bit of fatherly admiration."

Melissa knew he was correct—she didn't have much experience with babies, but all the nurses told her she was lucky with her first born, who slept often and fussed remarkably little.

"You know, Melissa," he said, "we'll need to agree on a name sooner rather than later. The baptism is in less than a week."

"I refuse to name our firstborn child Cornelius."

"It is my great-grandfather's name and it is splendid."

"Yes, well, it is perfect name for a great-grandfather or even a great-grandson. But not for our daughter, Magnus."

"Your mama is a tyrant," he told their month-old baby girl.

Their nameless daughter merely sighed heavily.

"You know, when I was a lad my parents would let me name all the barn kittens," Magnus told her.

Melissa had heard this story almost daily since telling her husband she was going to have their baby.

He needed no reply to go on. "They once let me name some hound pups, but Cecil made them stop because he has no sense of humor."

That was her cue to argue—which he appeared to love. "I can't believe you want to give our child the same names you gave to your barn cats."

"Why not?" he demanded in mock outrage. "What is wrong with Mouser Stanwyck? Or Catkins or Whiskers, for that matter? They are fine, noble names."

She laughed even though she'd heard the argument times beyond counting; she laughed because she loved him.

He reached for her hand and squeezed it, sprawling out in his chair and tipping back his head, lazing in the sun like the barn cats he so admired.

Living in a foreign country was both easier and harder than Melissa had expected. It was easier because her husband spoke French and could smooth their way in hundreds of little transactions. She was quickly picking up the language—which she discovered she had an unexpected knack for—but he handled most of their affairs even after half a year.

One of the messages Melissa had sent out that night so long ago on Berkeley Square had been to Joss, who'd recently moved to France to escape his own scandal. Her message had warned him she would be visiting.

He'd been more than a little surprised when Melissa arrived on his doorstep with Magnus in tow, but—fortunately—it had been pleased surprise.

Melissa had only met his wife, Lady Selwood, once before—and she'd been manipulating and untruthful on that occasion. Luckily the beautiful countess appreciated how Melissa's manipulation had brought her together with the man she loved—even though Joss still bore a grudge. Melissa suspect he was only still sulking because she'd shown him, once again, how much smarter women were than men.

They'd stayed with Joss and Alicia for a month before finding the perfect place. It had been Joss who'd suggested taking in orphans once he'd seen how unhappy Magnus was as a man of leisure.

"Europe is full of children needing homes," Joss said. It was the same night he told them about the orphanage he and his wealthy wife sponsored. "A new orphanage would fill up quickly," he predicted. And he'd been correct.

The rambling house they'd taken had room for fifteen children but Magnus had just placed two with families, which meant they were down to only thirteen.

They could have put children with families more often, but Magnus insisted—and Melissa agreed—that they do a thorough investigation of each couple or employer who came to them.

Children over twelve they would apprentice, but only if the master possessed a sterling reputation. That meant they did not place as many children as other orphanages, but it also meant they slept easier at night.

Although they were over fifty miles from Joss and Alicia they still visited as often as their two infants would allow. Melissa and Lady Selwood had given birth only a few weeks apart; the Gormleys had a son rather than a daughter.

Melissa and Magnus didn't have many other visitors, although the number seemed to have increased in recent months.

First it was Lady and Lord Darlington, who'd shown up after Lady Darlington had written Melissa a humble, pleading letter, asking if they might visit their only grandchild.

Magnus had left the decision to her, but she'd seen how he yearned for his family. The tenor of the letter was significantly

Melissa and The Vicar

different than their last exchange. Melissa believed it had something to do with their oldest son's marriage.

Cecil wrote to Magnus—apparently a first for the outdoorsman whom Magnus hadn't believed actually knew what a letter *was*. Emboldened by his little brother's scandalous marriage, Cecil had procured a special license of his own and married his long-time mistress, a widow almost a decade older than him. Not only was the woman of the merchant class, but she was beyond her child-bearing years.

"My brother loves Stanwyck," Magnus said after reading the letter. "But it has never bothered him to think of Henry or James inheriting rather than his son. He's been with his mistress—or Lady Sydell I suppose I should say—for years. I am glad he's chosen with his heart rather than his head."

And so the marquess and marchioness had come.

They'd been shadows of their former selves and Melissa had felt for them. Their heir had married a farmer's widow and was destined to remain childless; their favorite had married a whore.

They'd stayed only two weeks although she knew Magnus's mother would have stayed indefinitely with their granddaughter if her husband had not put his foot down.

Melissa knew that neither of Magnus's parents could ever love her. Indeed, it was questionable whether they would even like her. But they fiercely loved their favorite son's child. Melissa was satisfied with their civility, although she knew it pained Magnus that they couldn't accept her with open arms.

Perhaps the most unexpected visitors were Daisy and her husband, Joe.

Daisy, Joe, and Sarah had purchased an inn not far from Calais on the advice of Daisy's friend Julia, another woman who'd once worked at The White House, but now lived in France with her husband.

Daisy sent regular letters and Melissa often read them aloud, bringing Magnus to tears with stories of three *very* English people in a country where they had no knowledge of the language. It was good luck for all of them that Sarah fell in love with the inn's cook, who stepped in and saved the business from failure before it was too late.

Joe's parents still operated the inn in New Bickford and were a constant source of information. It was through them that they learned a new vicar had come. Mr. Heeley, it seemed, had suffered from a weak heart. When he died from a sudden attack Mrs. Heeley had been fortunate enough to have a younger sister she could live with.

It was also through them that they learned about Sir Thomas.

"Burned to death 'e was—in Mr. Felix's barn," Daisy told them during a visit Mel suspected she'd made especially to relay that information.

"How?" Melissa had asked, Magnus too shocked to speak.

Daisy shrugged. "I dunno. Neither does anyone else. It seems there was a lantern found in the wreckage."

"Do they suspect Mr. Felix?"

"Oh no, 'e was up in Lincolnshire." She cut a look at Magnus. "It appears 'e's got a piece of land up there that'll take care of that family of his."

Melissa had gaped at Magnus. "Do you have something to do with this, Lord Magnus?"

He'd shrugged. "Perhaps." But the slight smile on his face told her it *was* him. Her husband was no longer their curate, but he was still helping the parishioners of New Bickford.

"So if it wasn't Mr. Felix . . ." Melissa began.

"Folks reckon Sir Thomas had a few too many and knocked the lantern over himself," Daisy said. "Anyhow, that's what the magistrate decided and most people seem keen to accept it and get on with things—especially Lady Barclay. He won't be missed."

No, that was certainly true, Melissa thought, turning the small sock to inspect a mysterious hole in the heel.

"Darling?"

Melissa looked up from her disastrous knitting to find her husband watching her, a gentle smile on his face. "I thought you'd fallen asleep," she said.

"I was, but then I had a dream." His eyes shifted to their daughter and back to Melissa. "An angel came to me and told me what we should name her."

Melissa choked back a laugh. "Go ahead, then—let's hear it, my lord. Tiger? Boots?"

He shook his head, his expression serious but gentle. "We should call her Hannah."

As if she had been cued to do so, their newborn opened her magnificent blue-green eyes.

"Hannah," Melissa said contemplatively.

Melissa and The Vicar

Magnus nodded, tracing the sweet curve of the baby's cheek with one big finger. "This Hannah will have a wonderful childhood, surrounded by people who love her."

"Yes," she whispered, her eyes on their beautiful little girl. "Hannah."

Melissa didn't realize she was crying until he looked up and said. "Oh, darling—what's wrong?"

She smiled through her tears—happy tears this time—at the man she loved with all her heart. "Nothing is wrong, Magnus. Not one single thing."

Thanks so much for reading MELISSA AND THE VICAR! If you enjoyed the book, here's a sneak peek at Book 1 in The Masqueraders, THE FOOTMAN ...

Chapter One

London
1802

Iain Vale was examining a marble statue of some poor armless bloke when the door beside it flew open and a whirlwind in skirts burst into the hall.

"I *will not!*" the whirlwind yelled before slamming the door, spinning around, and careening into Iain. "Ooof." She bounced off him and stumbled backward, catching her foot in the hem of her dress in the process.

Iain sprang forward, reached out one long arm, and caught her slim waist, halting her fall. He looked down at his armful of warm female and found surprised gray eyes glaring back at him. Her mouth, which had been open in shock, snapped shut. Iain hastily righted his bundle and took a step back.

"Who the devil are *you?*" the girl demanded, brushing at her dress as though his gloved hands might have soiled it.

"I'm the new footman, Miss."

The gray eyes turned steely. "Are you stupid?" She didn't wait for an answer. "I'm not a *Miss*. I am Lady Elinor, your employer's *daughter.*"

Iain's face heated under her contemptuous eyes. He'd been spoken down to many times, but never quite so . . . effectively.

"You are welcome, *Lady Elinor.*"

"What?" she demanded. "*What* did you say?" Her eyes were so wide they looked to be in danger of popping out of their sockets.

"*I said,* 'you are welcome, my lady.'"

She planted her fists on her slim hips. "I'm welcome for what?"

"For saving you from a very nasty fall," he retorted, unable to keep his tongue behind his teeth even though he was breaking every rule in the footman's handbook. If such a thing existed.

The unladylike noise that slipped from her mouth told Iain she was thinking the same thing. "You are an intolerably insolent *boy*. Not to mention the most ignorant footman I've ever known."

Iain couldn't argue with her on that second point.

"Besides," she added, looking him up and down, "I wouldn't have needed your clumsy rescuing if you'd not been listening at keyholes."

Listening at keyholes? *Why the obnoxious little—*

Iain had just opened his mouth to say something foolish and most likely job-ending when the door Lady Elinor had exited so violently opened and Lady Yarmouth stood on the threshold. Her gray eyes, much like her daughter's, moved from Lady Elinor to her newest footman and back again.

"What is going out here, Elinor?"

The girl scowled. "I have just asked our new footman to run away with me, Mama."

Iain's jaw dropped.

Lady Yarmouth's lips thinned until they were pale pink lines. She raked the younger woman with a look designed to leave her quaking in her slippers. Her daughter glared back, un-quaked.

"Come back inside this instant, Elinor." The older woman turned and retreated into the room without waiting to see if her daughter obeyed.

Lady Elinor gave an exaggerated sigh and rolled her eyes at her mother's back before limping toward the open doorway. She stopped and turned back to Iain before entering the room.

"You'll catch flies if you don't close your mouth." She slammed the door in his face.

Bloody hell.

***

Iain yawned. It was almost three in the morning and the festivities showed no sign of abating. Other than his encounter with Lady Elinor earlier, the evening had been quiet. Disappointingly quiet not only for his first ball, but also his first day as footman.

The only other entertainment had been watching an overdressed dandy cast up his accounts on his dancing slippers while trying, and failing, to make it to the men's necessary.

The Footman

Iain adjusted the lacy cuffs of his fancy new shirt and examined the stranger who looked back at him in the ornate mirror. The black livery made him appear taller than his six feet and the well-tailored coat spanned his shoulders in a way that made him look lean and dangerous rather than scrawny and puppyish. His wiry red hair had been cropped to barely a stubble and was now concealed by a white powdered wig that gave him dignity. Of course his freckles were still there, but there was nothing he could do to hide them—unlike his age.

"You don't look five-and-ten, Iain," his Uncle Lonnie had said upon seeing Iain in his new clothes earlier today. He'd then grinned and squeezed Iain's shoulder. "Go ahead and give us yer story one last time, lad."

The story was one his uncle had concocted when Iain first came to work in Viscount Yarmouth's household three months ago: Iain was nineteen and had spent six years in Mr. Ewan Kennedy's household, two as a scrub boy, two as a boot boy, and two as a footman, even though he was unusually young for that last position. Uncle Lonnie also told Lord Yarmouth that Iain had come to London seeking employment after Mr. Kennedy died and there weren't any other suitable positions in the tiny town of Dannen, Scotland.

That last part was the only *true* part of the whole story. Dannen was more a collection of shacks than a real village and there'd never been any Mr. Kennedy, nor any work as scrub boy or footman. Iain had written the letter from "Mr. Kennedy" himself, under his uncle's direction.

"Admiring your pretty face?"

Iain yelped and jumped a good six inches. Female laughter echoed down the mahogany-paneled corridor. He turned to find Lady Elinor behind him, her small, almost boyish, frame propped against the wall in a very unladylike manner. Her white gown looked limp and tired, as if it were ready to go to bed. Her hair, a nondescript brown, had come loose from its moorings and fine tendrils wafted about her thin, pale face. Only her large gray eyes held any animation.

Iain drew himself up to his full height and glared over her shoulder at nothing. "How may I be of service, my lady?"

"Oh, stuff! You're angry with me, aren't you?" She didn't wait for an answer. "I'm sorry for being beastly earlier. I was wrong. Pax?" She held out her hand and limped forward. Iain stared, not because of her limp—he already knew she was lame—but because of the gesture. Surely a footman wasn't permitted to shake a lady's hand?

Besides, he hadn't forgiven her. His mother and uncle both accused him of being too grudging and slow to forgive. He looked down at her little hand and chewed his lip. Maybe they were right; perhaps it might be advisable to *appear* to forgive her. He'd just decided to say 'pax' when Lady Elinor grabbed his hand.

"Don't be angry with me. I apologized."

"I'm not angry," he lied, tugging not so subtly on his hand to free it from her grasp. He suspected it would not do to get caught holding the hand of the daughter of the house at three in the morning, or at any other time of the day or night, for that matter.

"Why aren't you in there," he gestured with his chin toward the ballroom, "dancing? Er, my lady," he added a trifle belatedly.

She snorted and hiked up her dress, exhibiting a shocking amount of leg. "With this?"

Iain gawked. He'd seen girl's legs, of course, but never a *lady's* leg. Her stockings were embroidered with flowers—daisies, perhaps. His groin gave an appreciative thump as he studied the gentle swell of her calf. She had shapely legs for such a tiny thing.

She dropped her skirts. "Are you ogling my limb?"

"What do you expect if you go around hiking up your skirt like that?" The words were out of his mouth before he could stop them. Iain squeezed his eyes shut and waited for her to start screeching. But the sound of giggling made him open them again.

She eyed him skeptically. "You're not like the other footmen."

What was Iain supposed to say to that?

"You look *very* young. How long have you been a footman?"

"Today is my first day."

"You shan't keep your job very long if you argue with any other members of my family. Or ogle their limbs."

His face heated and he pursed his lips.

She looked delighted by whatever she saw on his face. "How old are you?"

"Nineteen, my lady."

"What a bouncer!"

"How old are *you*?" Iain bit out, and then wanted to howl. At this rate, he would be jobless before breakfast.

The Footman

"Sixteen." She stopped smiling and her eyes went dull, like a vivid sunset losing its color. "But I might as well be forty. I shan't even have a Season."

"I thought all young ladies had at least one Season." What drivel. What the devil did *he* know about aristocrats, Seasons, or any of it? It was as if some evil imp had taken over his body: some pixie or spirit determined to get him sacked. Or jailed. He clamped his mouth shut, vowing not to open it again until it was time to put food in it.

Luckily his employer's daughter was too distracted to find his behavior odd.

"Tonight was my betrothal ball." Her shapely, shell-pink lips turned down at the corners. "Why should my father go to the expense of a Season when he can dispose of me so cheaply without one?"

It seemed like an odd way to talk about a betrothal but Iain kept that observation behind his teeth.

"The Earl of Trentham is my betrothed," she added, not in need of any responses from him to hold a conversation. "He is madly in love."

The silence became uncomfortable. Iain cleared his throat. "You must be very happy, then," he said when he could bear it no longer.

Her eyes, which had been vague and distant, sharpened and narrowed. "He's not in love with *me*, you dunce. He is in love with a property that is part of my dowry. Some piece of land that is critical to a business venture he and my father have planned."

Iain's flare of anger at being called *dunce* quickly died when he saw the misery and self-loathing on her face.

"Lord Trentham will have his land, my father will get to take part in the earl's investment, and I? Well, I will have—" She stopped, as if suddenly aware of what she was saying and to whom she was saying it. She glared up at him, her gray eyes suddenly molten silver. "Why am I telling *you* any of this? How could you ever know what it is like to be an ugly *cripple*? You will never be forced to marry someone who is twice your age. A man who views you with less pleasure than he does a piece of dirt." Her mouth twisted. "I am no more than a broodmare to him."

Her expression shifted from agonized into a sneering mask. Iain hadn't thought her ugly before—plain, perhaps—but, at that moment, she became ugly. Fury boiled off her person like steam from a kettle and Iain recoiled, not wanting to get burned.

She noticed his reaction and laughed, the sound as nasty as the gleam in her eyes. "What? Do I scare you, *boy*?"

Iain felt as if she'd prodded him with a red-hot iron and he took two strides and closed the distance between them, seething at the undeserved insults and bile. He stared down at her, no idea as to what he planned to do. Not that it mattered. The second he came within reach, her hands slid up the lapels of his jacket like two pale snakes. He froze at her touch but she pushed closer. Small, firm mounds pressed hard against his chest.

Breasts! Breasts! a distant, but euphoric, part of his mind shrieked.

His breeding organ had already figured that out.

Iain looked down into eyes that had become soft and imploring.

"What is your name?" she asked, her voice husky.

"I—" He coughed and cleared his throat. "Iain, my lady."

"Would you like to kiss me, Iain?" It was barely a whisper and Iain wondered if he'd heard her correctly. He cocked his head and was about to ask her to repeat herself, when she stood on tiptoes and pressed her lips against his.

Iain had kissed girls before. Just last week he'd done a whole lot more than kiss with one of the housemaids in the stables. But this kiss was different. It was a gentle, tentative offering, rather than a taking. To refuse it was somehow unthinkable. He leaned lower and slid his hands around her waist, pulling her closer. She was so slim his hands almost spanned her body. She made a small noise in her throat and touched the side of his face with caressing fingers, her pliant body melting against his.

"You bloody *bastard!*"

The girl jumped back and screamed just as Iain's head exploded. He staggered, his vision clouding with multi-colored spangles and roaring agony. When he reached out to steady himself on the wall, he encountered air. A foot kicked his legs out from under him and he slammed onto his back, his skull cracking against the wood floor.

"Lord Trentham, *no!*" Lady Elinor's voice was barely audible above the agonizing pounding filling Iain's head.

A body—Lord Trentham's?—dropped onto Iain's chest with crushing force. Soft but powerful hands circled his neck and squeezed.

"You rutting pig, how dare you touch *my* betrothed?" The choking eased on his throat just before a fist buffeted the right side of his

The Footman

head. "How *dare* you put your filthy hands on your betters?" Another blow slammed into his left temple.

"*Stop it! Stop this instant, he did nothing wrong. It was me!*"

"I'll deal with you next, you little whore," the earl said, his tone even harsher than his words as his fists cracked against Iain's head over and over again. Iain's mouth filled with blood and he struggled to spit it out before he choked on it. And then a knee jammed between his thighs and he screamed, the world going black.

"*You're going to kill him!*"

Iain retched and Trentham scrambled off him, clearly wishing to avoid becoming drenched in blood and vomit. Iain rolled to his side and cupped his hands protectively over his aching groin, his stomach convulsing until there was nothing left to expel.

He wanted to die.

"What the devil is going on here?"

Iain distantly recognized Lord Yarmouth's voice.

"Make him stop, Papa, he will kill him!"

"I will certainly make him *wish* he were dead," Trentham snarled just before a foot made contact with Iain's side.

"*Ooof!*" Iain groaned and rolled away, unwilling to take his hands from his groin and risk more gut-churning abuse.

"Trentham, what is going on?" Yarmouth asked again.

"This lout was in the process of mounting your bloody daughter when I caught them."

"That's not—" Lady Elinor began.

"Silence!" her father roared.

"Is this the kind of household you run, Yarmouth? Has this happened before? Is she even *intact*?"

"I assure you, Trentham, this is the first time such a thing has happened. Look at her. Do you think she poses much of a temptation to any man?" The viscount continued without waiting for an answer. "Besides, this is a mere boy. I told Lady Yarmouth he was too young to be fit for the position. We shall discharge him immediately and forget this ever happened."

"I won't forget it, Yarmouth. And I won't marry this lout's castoffs—not unless my doctor examines her and swears she is intact. And I want *him*—" a kick glanced off Iain's shoulder—"put where he belongs."

"We did nothing wrong, Papa. It was just—"

"Another word from you, Elinor, and you will regret it most severely." The viscount's normally soft voice was thick with disgust and rage. A pregnant pause followed his words before he spoke again. "Very well, Trentham."

"*Papa, no.* It was only a kiss. He didn't even want to, I begged him—"

"*Enough!*" The word was followed by a loud crack and a muffled cry.

"I want him taken in for attempted rape," Trentham said, his voice suddenly cool and collected.

"Very well," the viscount said. "Thomas, Gerald, take him. You can put him down in the cellar while one of you fetches the constable."

Four hands closed around Iain's arms and began to lift. He struggled weakly against their efforts, squirming and thrashing his way across the plush carpet.

"You incompetent fools." The Earl of Trentham's voice came from behind. "Let me ensure this piece of rubbish gives you no trouble." Something hard slammed into Iain's head and the world faded to black.

About the Author

SM LaViolette has been a criminal prosecutor, college history teacher, B&B operator, dock worker, ice cream manufacturer, reader for the blind, motel maid, and bounty hunter.
Okay, so the part about being a bounty hunter is a lie.
SM does, however, know how to hypnotize a Dungeness crab, sew her own Regency Era clothing, knit a frog hat, juggle, rebuild a 1959 American Rambler, and gain control of Asia (and hold on to it) in the game of RISK.

S.M. also writes under the name Minerva Spencer and historical mystery under S.M. Goodwin

Read more about SM at: www.MinervaSpencer.com

Made in the USA
Monee, IL
06 January 2023